AMICUS CURIAE

AMICUS CURIAE

BRIAN CLARY

AMICUS CURIAE

iUniverse books may be ordered through booksellers or by contacting:

iUniverse
1663 Liberty Drive
Bloomington, IN 47403
www.iuniverse.com
1-800-Authors (1-800-288-4677)

ISBN: 978-1-4917-8318-4 (sc)
ISBN: 978-1-4917-8320-7 (hc)
ISBN: 978-1-4917-8319-1 (e)

Library of Congress Control Number: 2015920845

Print information available on the last page.

iUniverse rev. date: 12/17/2015

Amicus curiae—Lat. A friend of the court. A bystander (usually a counselor) who interposes and volunteers information upon some matter of law in regard to which the judge is doubtful or mistaken. A person who has no right to appear in a suit but is allowed to introduce argument to protect his interests (*Black's Law Dictionary*, West Publishing, revised fourth edition, 1968).

Dedication

The most anguishing and unnatural act that any parent can do is to bury their own child. My mother, Bernice Delight Clary, did it twice. Phyllis Diane Clary (age two and a half) and Douglas Phillip Clary Jr. (age thirty-seven). My mother's strength taught me how to cope with adversity and to persevere through life's challenges. Diane and Doug have silently motivated me to live my adult life as if for three and not for just one. This book is dedicated to the three of them.

Acknowledgements

Special thanks goes to David Livingston for taking the time to read the manuscript and to Frank Deloache for lending his editorial expertise.

PROLOGUE

Winter brought an ominous wind to the plains of the Texas Panhandle. Recent events had rendered the phrase "that will never happen here" a meaningless cliché, and the people there longed for solutions. It would take a combination of fortitude and fate to determine from whence the wind blew.

CHAPTER 1

DECIPIMUR SPECIE RECTIE

(We Are Deceived by the Semblance of What Is Right)

Delano, Texas
December 10

The area around Delano Texas was flat except for the occasional mesa, or cap rocks, as the locals referred to them. The Abram family lived in a good, upper-middle-class neighborhood of mostly one-story, ranch-style homes situated on large lots. Out of necessity, the Abrams and most homeowners in the Texas Panhandle, planted a series of tall, slender cedar trees within inches of their home, strategically placed on the south and west sides to protect the wood veneer and trim boards from the ravages of the occasional blistering red-sand wind storm. Delano was large enough to support two movie theaters; two shopping malls, one older than the other by two decades; and several chain restaurants. The town of just over fifteen thousand residents was also home to some industrial concerns, most of which were associated with oil extraction, but Delano's agrarian roots were well established. Commencing at Delano's city limit and continuing in all directions sat medium and large family farms, with most growing cotton, the crop most conducive to the native red-clay soils. The summers there were often oppressive, with relentless dry heat, and the winters could be frigid, with each year delivering a fair amount of snowfall.

The Abrams were older than most couples raising a teenage

daughter, and theirs was named Taylor. Each in their mid-fifties, Bess Abram was a retired school teacher, and Ted was a geologist who had spent most of his career in the oil patch. Now partially retired, Ted, solely at his own choosing, continued to serve as a consultant on several projects per year. Taylor was fourteen and, by all measures, an excellent student, and Bess would have it no other way. Taylor was well behaved, disciplined, and the pride of the Abrams in every respect. To the Abrams and the community as a whole, news of abductions of teenage girls in the neighboring town of Brinkman had spawned much conversation since the first of such crimes hit the news a month earlier. Despite the reports, Delano residents had gone about their daily affairs largely undaunted, as most viewed Brinkman, with population over 86,000, as the "big city." That fact, coupled with a geographic separation from Brinkman of over twenty miles and the recent crisp winter weather, had the folks around Delano eagerly focused on the approaching holidays.

The day prior, reports of another winter storm that threatened to deliver a treacherous layer of ice on the community, compelled the local school district to preemptively cancel classes for this day. Despite the forecasts, the front stalled overnight, weakened and delivered only a dusting of snow. Taylor sprang from her bed that morning and immediately looked sleepy-eyed out her bedroom window. She confirmed what she had hoped for, that the storm had fallen well short of the predictions, and the roads were clear.

She found her mom in the kitchen starting breakfast and sought permission to use the fortuitous day off from classes to shop, and Bess agreed. Taylor called two of her girlfriends, and recruited them for the trip. They all agreed to meet in the mall parking lot at 9:00 that morning, a time that coincided with the opening of the major stores. Months of babysitting and a semester-ending, straight-A report card had earned Taylor Abram a tidy sum of money. She was proud that for the first time she had the wherewithal to buy Christmas gifts for her family and select friends. There would be no five-and-dimes this year, as Taylor had set her sights on the mall. In recognition of Taylor's benevolent intentions and her steadfast devotion to her studies, the Abram's had agreed to match, dollar for dollar, the funds Taylor earmarked for gifts to others and for any donations made to their church. For days, Taylor had researched the presents she would buy and from where she would buy them, employing no less than three catalogs, each sporting dog-eared and paper-clipped pages.

Taylor took a long, warm shower before donning blue jeans, a white blouse, a pink vest, and her new pair of pink tennis shoes. She stared into her dresser mirror, brushing her long blonde hair, before pulling it back into a ponytail, and securing it with a pink rubber band. Taylor had a pleasant slim face with flawless alabaster skin and a few fading freckles showed on each cheek. The thin lips of her narrow mouth had upturned ends that made her look at all times as if she was about to laugh. She put her fleece-lined winter coat on and reached deep into the folded clothes of her top dresser drawer to remove a well-worn pink leather change purse, given to her by her grandmother. The pouch was stuffed with bills and coins to the point that it strained the silver clasp needed to snap it closed. She shoved her change purse in her hip pocket and the folded catalog pages in the pocket of her coat and walked from her bed room and into the kitchen.

"Bye, Mom. Bye, Daddy," she said, giving each a kiss as they sat at the breakfast table.

"Your mom says your off to the mall," Ted Abram said.

"Yes, Daddy! The weather's been so bad that I haven't been able to Christmas shop. I've planned for this for days and, I'm very excited."

"We were just talking, and though we didn't get the ice they predicted, it's still pretty cold and windy. Why don't you hold off until your Christmas break starts?"

"Well,—the weather could be worse then," Taylor said. "Plus, Bond's is having a good sale on some of the items I want and I need to get them before they run out. That's why I'm leaving now meet Chris and Janet."

"Aren't you going to eat breakfast, dear?" Bess asked, pointing to a platter on the table.

"Thanks, Mom, but I'm not really hungry."

"Taylor Lynn, I'm not letting you out of this house with an empty stomach," Mrs. Abram said.

"Okay. I'll take a breakfast bar to eat on the way."

Bess glanced at her husband then back to Taylor and said, "I wish you'd eat a hot breakfast."

"It looks great, but the girls are already heading there," Taylor explained.

"Fine, you can go. But only if you promise to eat the breakfast bar."

"Thanks, Mom. Save the pancakes and bacon, and I'll eat them tonight."

"You won't be home for lunch either?" Bess asked

"Part of my plan was treating Chris and Janet to lunch as their present."

"That's nice, dear," Bess said.

Ted lowered the business page. "Do you want me to drop you off over there, honey?

"Thanks, Daddy, but I can walk."

"But if you buy gifts, how are you going to get them home?" he asked

"I'll be fine, Dad, and if I need help, my friends can carry a bag or two."

"Okay, but call if you change your mind," Mr. Abram said. "You do have your phone, right?"

"The battery is out and it's charging, but any of the stores will let me call if I need to."

"Just be careful, you hear?" Bess said as Taylor nodded and headed for the door.

The Abrams lived near the newer of the two local shopping centers, and Taylor had walked or ridden her bicycle there many times. Though small by big-city standards, this mall represented the largest concentration of shopping options in Delano. It featured two large department stores on each end and several specialty shops, a food court, and game arcade in between. Taylor often met one or both of the girls there, usually to hang out at the arcade or snack bar and to talk to or about boys. But this trip was different since shopping claimed Taylor's undivided attention.

The most direct way to the mall from the Abrams' house was to walk north on their street, which terminated at the entrance to a neighborhood park. A tall, black wrought-iron fence bordered the perimeter of the rectangular-shaped city park, which had matching gates on each end that the city employees unlocked daily at sunup. A sidewalk meandered through the park that led to a street on the other side, which bordered the mall's southern parking lot. As Taylor walked toward the park, the bright morning sun aided her fleece lined jacket in protecting her from a brisk northerly breeze. She marveled at the sight of the light snow that had fallen overnight, dusting the trees and housetops and sticking to the shaded portions of the neighborhood lawns. As she entered through the gate and into the park, Taylor initially veered off the sidewalk opting for the grass. She delighted at the crunch that the lightly frozen grass made under the soles of her tennis shoes, and she took time to glance back to see the footprints she had left in the frost. She returned to the sidewalk and as she walked, she opened the breakfast bar wrapper and took a bite. As she chewed, she passed the neighborhood swimming pool, which was now covered with a large blue tarp, sagging in the center from the partially frozen rainwater atop it.

The middle of the park featured benches and picnic tables, and on this morning there was a gathering of pigeons scavenging about the tables and the partially full garbage cans. Taylor stopped to watch the pigeons and patted her pockets to confirm the presence of both her leather pouch and the catalog pages. The pigeons now eased toward her, attempting to judge her intentions and to assess the contents of her hand. Taylor threw small pieces of her breakfast bar to the ground and immediately empathized with the pigeons not large or fast enough to get a share. She broke up the rest of her breakfast, tossing the pieces in directions that favored the more disenfranchised birds. Taylor reached the gates on the other end of the park, carefully crossed the street, and entered the outer edge of the mall parking lot. It was then that she saw her two friends standing next to one of the tall parking lot light poles, hands in their pockets, struggling to stay warm.

"It's freezing out here," Janet complained as Taylor neared.

"Janet, you wore a windbreaker, and it's in the low thirties. Duh!" Christine teased.

"Yeah, what were you thinking?" Taylor chided.

"Come on. Let's go to the arcade and warm up," Janet said, turning toward the entrance to the mall.

"Wait, guys. Today I'm buying presents and stuff, so I want to do some *real* shopping for a change."

"All right," Janet said. "So where do you want to shop?"

"I've got three stores in mind but mostly Bond's," Taylor said as Christine pulled a cigarette from her purse. She flicked a butane lighter, cupped her left hand to her mouth and the dancing blue flame fought the breeze until the cigarette was lit. In a futile attempt to be grown, she inhaled—and immediately began coughing and gasping. Her face turned red as she leaned forward and smoke belched from her mouth.

"Oh, that's real cool!" mocked Janet as Christine offered her the cigarette, her attempt was likewise far from glamorous.

"No thanks," was Taylor's response when Janet offered her a drag. "Now, about the shopping, I really—"

"I don't mind shopping for a while," Janet interrupted. "I'd actually like to get my brother something."

"You don't understand. I want to shop—you know—by myself," Taylor explained.

"Oh, I got it. Taylor's got all that money this year, and she's too stuck up for her friends," Christine mocked.

Taylor rolled her eyes and explained, "It's not that. It's just that I've prepared for this day for a while and want a little time to myself to get it all done."

"What do you mean by 'a little while'?" Janet asked as Christine suffered another puff.

"Just an hour or so, and then we'll meet up at the arcade. We'll hang there for a while, and later we'll have lunch at Mighty Burger, on me. Okay?"

"Fine. We'll go to the game room and meet you there in an hour," Janet said as she and Christine turned and walked quickly toward the mall entrance. Taylor remained, and reached for her change purse and when she freed it from her pocket the bulging pouch opened. Two of the bills on top took flight in the brisk wind, each landing a few yards from her and picking up speed as they tumbled away.

"Crud!" she said as she chased after them. The bills tumbled away from her until the wind abated and the bills settled, and she picked up the pace before another gust took them farther. One of the bills lodged next to a parking curb, and she managed to step on the other. Taylor knelt to grab the first bill, and as she did she turned and watched her friends, who were now at the mall's main entrance. Taylor shook her head as Christine appeared to choke, yet again, on the cigarette smoke. Taylor walked to the other bill by the parking curb, and as she squatted, she saw a quick flash of light in her peripheral vision. She turned her head to the left and saw a small car in the parking lot just as it flashed its lights a second time, before driving away. Taylor rose and returned both bills safely to her pouch which she now held tightly in her right hand. With the wind remaining calm, she thumbed through the catalog pages, arranging the ones from Bond's department store on top as she walked. Though it was the Christmas season, it was a weekday where bad weather was predicted, and the parking lot was far from full. This was especially true in the outer area of the lot where she now stood. Suddenly, a man's voice interrupted Taylor's concentration.

"Excuse me, young lady," the man said in a soft, polite tone.

Turning, Taylor saw a man sitting in the driver's seat of an older model, brown van that he had backed into a parking space at the fringe of the parking lot.

"Are you talking to me, mister?"

"Yes, can you help me, please? I'm really in a bad spot here," the man said through the open driver's side window. By nature a friendly, outgoing girl, Taylor was always willing to help people in need, but her parents and other adults had schooled her from an early age to be wary of strangers. She eased laterally to her right so she could get a better view of the driver and saw that he was a young man with bushy brown hair and a light beard. She was captured by the distressed look on his face and moved closer.

She looked in all directions and then asked, "What do you need, sir?"

"It's my dog, Tippy. He got out of the fence *again* and ran off to play. He's a yellow Lab, and someone said they saw him on Milam Street, which is supposed to be near this mall. I've looked and looked but can't find that street or Tippy. Have you seen him by chance?" Taylor shook her head but immediately empathized with his predicament. She too had lost her dog once and knew well the anguish of searching the neighborhood and stapling notices with pictures on sign posts and telephone poles. As she moved closer to the van, the man continued, "He's my best friend, and I'm really worried about him. Do you think you could help me?"

"My school's on Milam, and it is very close to here," Taylor explained as the man perked up, and as Taylor began giving him directions, until a loud clattering sound startled both of them. The man in the van leaned his head out the window and looked past Taylor, joining her in assessing the source of the noise. They saw a uniformed mall employee standing next to his car, staring at them while lifting his metal lunch box from the hood of the car. He was a large man with very dark skin and neatly trimmed, graying hair. He was dressed in a khaki shirt and pants, with black boots, and he had a black leather belt with pouches and loops for tools. His lunch box had slid from the top of his car to the hood, creating the noise, and the man got in his car with the lunch box. As he started the engine, he paused briefly to stare at the two of them, as if assessing the situation before driving away.

Taylor turned back toward the van and explained, "Mister, once you go out of the parking lot here and back down that street," she pointed to the road adjacent to the mall, "all you need to do is go to the very first stop sign and—"

"Look, miss," the man interrupted. "I appreciate this, but someone already gave me directions. I'm confused and still haven't found the street and was wondering if you could show me exactly where Milam is. I'm scared to death that Tippy is gonna get picked up by someone or, worse, run over." Taylor took notice of the fast-moving traffic on the nearest road as the man urged, "Please show me the way? I can have you back here in no time."

Taylor took two paces backward, asking, "You want me to go with you?"

"I'll bet you know the area well enough to find my dog. Please help me before something bad happens." She thought of walking away but considered how awful she would feel if she were to later learn that Tippy somehow was injured, or worse killed because she delayed. The man smiled as she walked to the passenger side of the van and waited for him to unlock the door. The man leaned over and pulled on the inside handle to unlock the door. Taylor struggled with the door, and its hinges screeched as it swung open enough for her to climb in. Taylor took a seat on the torn and stained fabric of the passenger side captain's chair and buckled her seatbelt.

"What does Tippy look like? I'll watch for him," Taylor said as they drove out of the mall parking lot.

"Oh, he's … uh … well, a large dog and has a dark, furry coat," the man stammered.

"Dark? I thought you said he's a yellow Lab."

"Oh … he is, but … well, he's you know … he's dark yellow, you see."

They drove down the tree-lined avenues of the quiet neighborhood until they reached a stop sign. Taylor pointed to the left, but the man suddenly turned the steering wheel to the right and sped in the opposite direction, and Taylor Abram screamed.

CHAPTER 2

⚖

QUI AUDET A DIPISCITUR

(She Who Dares Wins)

Taylor County Courthouse
Brinkman, Texas
Friday, December 11

"Ladies and gentlemen, trials are a search for the truth," declared Michelle "Mickey" Grant as members of the jury leaned forward to hear her closing argument. Years of training and hard work were on display at a trial that represented Mickey's first real opportunity to shine in defending one of her law firm's largest clients. "The plaintiffs took on an awfully heavy load in filing this lawsuit, including the burden of proof. The mere filing of this suit and showing up for this trial is proof of nothing. They were obliged to bring credible evidence in this search for the truth and to prove each and every one of the serious allegations they've made against my client. Before you consider awarding the millions and millions of dollars they've requested, you must be convinced they've brought you the truth *and* met that serious burden."

In addition to the judge and jurors, several of Mickey's friends and colleagues claimed seats in the public section of the courtroom to see this defining moment in her brief but upstart legal career. Mickey was a promising talent at the Brewer, Baylor, and Becker law firm, known among the locals as "Triple B." It was the oldest law firm in Brinkman,

Texas, the seat of Taylor County. This was her first significant solo trial and an important one on several levels, considering that the allegations involved the death of a young child and the suffering of a devoted mother. Her client, Accel Manufacturing Company, stood to lose a considerable sum of money and suffer a tarnished reputation if the jury delivered a staggering verdict, a result that would have implications far beyond this one case. Adding to the equation was her opponent. Unlike many of the lawyers Mickey had faced previously, the grieving mother's attorney was neither fresh out of law school nor an aging practitioner whose prime was a distant memory. To the contrary, George Cameron brought an impeccable reputation, keen advocacy skills, and a dominant courtroom presence to the trial.

Each side had spent hundreds of hours over many months preparing their respective cases. That effort, and tens of thousands of dollars in expense, had resulted in a mountain of exhibits, stacks of deposition transcripts, and intricate briefs arguing the facts and the law. This stately Texas district courtroom had become a judicial battlefield strewn with yards of electrical wires taped down on the floors, computers atop the tables, and numerous demonstrative exhibits, including several sizable rigid boards displaying enlarged photographs.

The suit stemmed from an accident involving the Sportiva, one of Accel's subcompact automobiles. The Accel legal department had handpicked Mickey for this trial, due in part to their growing faith in her abilities, but also because of the profile of the plaintiff they were facing. At the time of her accident, Linda Monroe, a single mother, was only slightly injured in the crash. However, she lost her seven-year-old son, Todd, in the one-car collision. Though Mrs. Monroe was admittedly at fault in the accident, she was nevertheless suing Accel for designing a car that their experts claimed to be defective. The suit focused on the passenger-side air bag that nearly decapitated young Todd when it deployed in what was otherwise a minor collision. Mrs. Monroe had given heartrending testimony describing how she watched on helplessly as life slipped away from her only child. This so-called crash-worthiness theory of liability had been successfully argued in the past to bring automobile manufacturers to task over perceived improper safety designs. Accel felt Mickey would give a human, humane, and sympathetic appearance to the otherwise faceless corporation. Using a young woman who herself was a single mother was calculated to allow the defense to appear less callous to the plaintiff's loss while presenting a meticulously planned tactful defense.

At the last hour, Accel's legal department abandoned their plan to use subtlety and tact in favor of going aggressive. Mickey embraced the change in strategy and had dutifully rehearsed her argument countless times in her mind and aloud in front of a mirror. While addressing the jury, though, she fired off her comments as if they were spontaneous and direct from the heart, and she seemed to have captured the attention of all twelve. But the risky approach came as a shock to some present that morning, not the least of which was Ford Becker, one of the Bs in the Triple-B law firm, and Mickey's supervising partner.

Mickey was just shy of six feet and had a trim but shapely figure. For her closing argument, she had pulled her dye-aided jet-black hair into a tight bun in the back and applied a modest amount of face makeup to complement her smooth, olive skin tone and her engaging dark eyes. Mickey dressed for the finale in a tailored, dark gray business suit and a white, semi sheer blouse, and on this day, her skirt was shorter, the heels a little higher, and the neckline lower. She sought to accentuate the femininity of her fit and trim frame, revealing only enough to capture the attention of those inclined to notice, but not so much to offend the others.

"I listened to Mr. Cameron's eloquent closing argument very carefully and know each of you did too," Mickey said, looking back at her opponent. "He too discussed the burden of proof and made assertions about how he met it, and I actually found myself wondering if he was talking about the same trial," she said smiling, drawing snickers from a couple of jurors. "Even though this case is a search for the truth, truth is not what was sought by the plaintiffs, because the truth is not their ally. This case is and always has been about money, and a whole lot of it, and, I say they deserve nothing, and I intend on explaining why," she said, making eye contact with the jurors.

"One way they tried to convince you that their case has merit was to present experts. You see, these guys that they hired to testify confessed on that witness stand that were paid consultants. During the day, while you and I are at work or home tending to family, they're traveling from town to town rendering opinions for those writing them checks. It's kind of a 'have opinion, will travel' thing, you see. Hired guns whose objective is to convince you to favor their side over the other. We've proven that Ms. Monroe's car, the Sportiva, was built to exacting industry and governmental standards, including the passive restraint system that we all call air bags. You've heard what Accel goes through in designing their cars with all of the testing, engineering, and regulatory compliance. We think they got it right, even though the hired Monday-morning quarterbacks disagree. You're going to have to reconcile these competing views, and I know that when you consider the whole picture and not the out-of-context sound bites and images, like those on these display boards, you'll arrive at the truth." Mickey returned to the podium for a sip of water to soothe the dryness in her mouth and throat.

"I know y'all feel remorse for Mrs. Monroe, and I truly feel for her, as well. You see, I too have a young child, a teenage girl, and can't imagine how I would go on if she was taken from me like little Todd was taken from her. What person with a heart would not feel for Ms. Monroe and the agony that this tragedy must represent to her? But the judge will instruct that you each must make your decision free of the sympathy we all feel as human beings. I know it's tough to do that, especially with all of these bloody and horrific blown-up images on my opponent's sign boards. Speaking of that, have any of you asked yourselves why they made them? Have you wondered why they then choose to show us all, including, Ms. Monroe these horrific photos? Do they prove anything about the design of the car? Of course not. These photos were shown to Ms. Monroe on that witness stand, knowing to a moral certainty that when she saw them, it would make her breakdown and cry, and she did … but why? You each swore on day one to set aside sympathy, passion, and prejudice to make your decision. When you deliberate, you have a right to consider if these images represent an attempt to urge you to violate that oath.

Mickey returned the water glass, left the podium, and moved to the rail separating her from the jurors. "You all are the sole judges of the facts of this case and the credibility of every witness. You, and you alone, will sit in judgment of Accel, which, despite the arguments of my esteemed opposing counsel, is not a 'heartless, soulless corporation' but rather an assemblage of conscientious, devoted, well-trained individuals dedicated to their craft. It's these professionals you sit in judgment of today and not just some symbol on the Stock Exchange ticker."

"But while you're required to set aside sympathy and bias, the judge will not ask you to check your common sense at that door!" Mickey said in a flourish while pointing toward the jury room and walking toward the judge's bench. She stopped and glanced over her left shoulder, noting for the first time the presence of Ford Becker in the audience. She subtlety nodded and then turned back to the jury. "Look at the scales of justice up here," Mickey said, pointing to the large bronze statue of Lady Justice, blindfolded and holding the shiny brass scales. "Those scales represent an idea, the notion that justice should be blind, but though her face has shielded eyes that doesn't mean to ignore what has happened during the course of this trial, but rather it serves as a reminder that you are to judge this case *only* on the facts and evidence. When you do that, these scales represent a measuring device for justice. In theory, you put the evidence presented by each side on the scales, and you weigh them to see which has the greater weight. But I submit that you're not required to put *all* of what you've seen and heard on the scales. As the judge will instruct, you need only consider the *credible* evidence. Consequently, any evidence or testimony that you don't believe, or that your common sense dictates to you is not truthful, or evidence only intended to appeal to your sympathy weigh *nothing* on those scales! If you do this, I'm confident that you will find that the plaintiffs have failed to sustain the required burden of proof, and you will return a verdict that vindicates the hardworking men and women of Accel Manufacturing."

Mickey returned to her seat next to Calvin Webster, general counsel for Accel, knowing she had given her best. She put her head in her hands and drew a deep breath as Webster patted her gently on the back. She then leaned back in her chair as the judge began directing the jurors. The bailiff then ushered them toward the jury room, and two law clerks from Mickey's firm entered and began loading a flatbed cart with boxes of documents and exhibits. Mickey began packing her briefcase, then exchanged cordial pleasantries with George Cameron, each congratulating the other for their performance. Ms. Monroe, on the other hand, sat silent, exchanging a less-than-friendly expression with her. Mickey then glanced to the gallery and noticed Ford Becker was no longer in the room, and she anxiously walked out of the courtroom and into the corridor. Mickey searched for Ford and then looked out the window at the end of the hall. She caught sight of him on the sidewalk, talking on his cell phone. She rushed down the stairs and out the front door, and as she drew near, Becker hung up.

"So what did you think?"

"You'll either pour 'em out, or the jury is going to wax the courthouse floor with you."

"Was I too tough?"

"Directly attacking the lawyer on the other side and the greed of the mother of the dead kid? This is dangerous, Mickey, and I thought we all agreed to soften all of this up."

"We did, Ford, but Accel felt that the case had been tried well enough to cut through all the crap and tell it like it is," Mickey explained.

"So Calvin and the legal department signed off on this?" Ford asked.

"Yes," she replied firmly, and Ford sighed with relief. "It was literally a last-minute deal. You see, I had this worked up two ways—Ms. Nicey Nice and bitch—and at the last moment they picked bitch."

"I see. What changed?"

"Webster sensed that the jury wasn't buying their crap, especially the 'whores,' his term not mine, that they hired as experts. He believed that if we gave an inch to the plaintiffs, it would add legitimacy to their claims, and we would be just trying to just mitigate the damage award. Based on that, we elected in the end to go for broke."

"I wish you wouldn't have said broke," Becker said with a nervous grin. "Did Webster think the trial went well?"

"I think so … I mean, he was very complimentary," Mickey explained. "Where is he?"

"He had to call the headquarters and report in," Mickey explained. She reached into her purse and pulled a cigarette from a crumpled pack.

"You should stop that, you know," Ford chided as she struck a match and lit it.

"I know," she conceded, blowing a stream of smoke upward and away from Becker.

"Did you buy a pack?"

"No. I've been bumming 'em off the bailiff."

"Really?"

"Yeah, I've been trading advice on his divorce for cigarettes, and he gave me an empty pack to keep those he rations from getting crushed."

"Smoking OPs is just as bad for your health, Mickey."

"You sound like Reagan and Tyler," she said, referring to her daughter and ex-husband. "But you know I only smoke when I'm nervous or having drinks. How was my closing argument?"

"You executed it perfectly, but you dumped all the experts in the grease, including ours."

"I know, Ford, but ours were more believable and had less baggage. Plus, I felt that with them having the burden of proof, if the jury cancels out the experts, it's like trading a queen for a queen in a chess match, where a tie goes to us."

"I guess you're right, but—"

"Well, Ford, what do you make of our rising star?" Calvin Webster said in his deep Georgia accent as he approached the two with a cheerful grin. Webster was a large, rotund man with a round, washed-out, ashy face and had thick, wavy, graying hair.

"I thought she did great," Ford said.

"I did too and just reported that observation to Atlanta. I tried to envision how this strategy would look, and Michelle's execution of it exceeded my expectations in every way."

"Thank you, Mr. Webster. I appreciate that more than you know," Mickey said as she dropped the cigarette to the pavement and stomped it out.

"Well, you deserve it, girl. I don't know how this will turn out, but I know in my heart that you gave us our best shot."

Emboldened by the praise, Mickey returned to the courtroom to wait out the deliberations. For the first time since the case began, Mickey had no way to influence its outcome and now could only wait and wonder. Ford returned to the courthouse midafternoon with a newspaper, a sack lunch, and a growing concern about the length of the deliberations. "Here, I brought you a turkey sandwich and some chips," he said, extending a brown paper bag to Mickey.

"Thanks. I'm not hungry right now, but I'll put it in my briefcase for later, since it looks like I'm in for the long haul here," she said nodding toward the jury room. "They haven't sent out a single question and have only taken one break."

"A lunch break?"

"No, it was just a twenty-minute coffee break. Do you think that's a bad sign?"

"The rule of thumb is the longer they take, the less likely it is for a defense verdict."

"Sorry I asked," Mickey said.

"But listen, it's a complex case with a lot of technical exhibits, and the fact that they're deliberating so hard signals to me they want to get done before the weekend."

"That's good. Because if they don't decide today, it's going to ruin my time with Reagan."

"Oh, that's right. You have her this weekend?"

"Yeah, and I truly hope we'll have something to celebrate."

"Speaking of her visit, there was another mall abduction yesterday," Ford said.

"I haven't really seen any news since this trial started. Was it another young girl?"

"Yes, a fourteen-year-old named Taylor."

"Jesus. Did it happen here?"

"No but close enough; it was in Delano," he replied, displaying the front-page article. "I know you're preoccupied right now, but this is really serious stuff."

"Thanks for looking out for us, Ford."

"Say, where's Calvin?"

"He's back downstairs, making more phone calls. He stays on that cell phone, you know?"

"Yes, I know. Is he worried about the deliberations?"

"If he is, he's cool as a cucumber about it."

"Look—I think I'll get back to the office to tie up loose ends before the weekend. If anything happens, you'll let me know, right?"

"Of course."

Another hour elapsed, and Mickey retreated to the hallway, with waning hopes for a verdict before the weekend. Standing at the window at the end of the hall, Mickey looked down at the majestic oak trees that stood among the rolling knolls of grass in front of the old granite courthouse. Her concentration was broken when she saw a reflection in the window of an approaching figure from behind her. She turned to see the bailiff, and by his gait and expression, she knew it was important. When he gained her attention, he stopped and motioned for her to follow, and she headed back toward the courtroom. As Mickey trailed him, she saw to her left Webster coming up the stairs, and she motioned him to follow her. As the three reached the courtroom door, the bailiff held the door for them and said, "They've got a verdict!"

Mickey and Webster entered and took their seats at the counsel table. "All rise!" yelled the breathless bailiff as the judge entered and motioned for him to retrieve the jury. When the bailiff returned with them, they slowly filed in and then stood in front of their assigned chairs. Mickey looked for some glimpse of their decision in their expressions, but saw little more than diverted eyes and blank faces.

"You may be seated," the judge told all present. He then asked if the jury had reached a verdict, and a woman seated on the front row rose announced they had. Mickey was intrigued that the jurors had chosen a female to lead them and pondered the importance of the choice. The bailiff accepted the papers from the woman and walked them to the judge, who read the verdict silently. The judge paused and removed his reading glasses as Mickey began tapping the tabletop with the painted nail of her right index finger.

"Question number one: do you find from a preponderance of the evidence that the Accel Sportiva automobile in question was defective?" The judge read and looked over at Mickey, whose involuntary tapping increased in rapidity. "The answer to question number one is 'We do not.'"

The tapping ceased, and Mickey exhaled, knowing that Accel had won, and the remaining questions on the form were meaningless. She sat back in her chair to soak in the moment as she struggled to contain her joy. She was determined to remain dignified in her triumph, but suddenly heard a steady, soft sobbing from the adjacent table. Turning slightly, she could see from her peripheral vision Ms. Monroe venting her emotions on Cameron's shoulder. Separating Mickey from her moment of empathy, Webster congratulated her, whispering, "You pulled it off, Michelle. Great job!"

With feigned bravado, she whispered back, "I knew this one was in the bag all along!"

"You can't bullshit an old bullshitter. You were as nervous as a long-tailed cat in a room full of rocking chairs."

"You're right," she conceded with a grin.

After the judge dismissed the jury and the attendees were disbursing, Webster offered to buy Mickey a celebratory drink before heading to the airport. She politely declined, explaining that she hoped to report the verdict to her colleagues before they departed the office for the weekend. She drove the short distance to her law firm in the fading sunlight, and when she arrived, she punched the code to the gated entry of the ground-level garage. Above the garage were two stories of the firm's office space. As the gate slid open and Mickey drove into the garage, she took a mental inventory of the vehicles present before coming to a stop in her assigned parking space. She was pleased that Becker's vehicle was among those still in the garage, but was doubtful that any other partners were present. There was an elevator in the center of the garage and two sets of stairs on each end that provided access to the front and rear portions of the building.

With briefcase in hand, Mickey took the elevator to the first floor of the office, which opened to a sizable reception area. The centerpiece of this space was a large, horseshoe-shaped oak reception desk. Beyond the desk, on the opposite side of the elevator, sat elongated space with frosted floor-to-ceiling glass panes that served as a conference room for firm meetings and the taking of depositions. On all of the reception area walls hung large paintings in custom-made wooden frames, each depicting battle scenes from the fight for Texas independence, including the Alamo, Goliad and San Jacinto. On each side of the reception area, doors led to hallways, each with attorney offices on one side, and opposite each sat padded cubicles for the secretary or legal assistant supporting each lawyer. Between the reception desk and the conference room was a spiral staircase that connected the two floors.

On the second floor, directly above the reception area where the spiral staircase terminated, was the firm's law library. It had a large mahogany conference table and high-backed leather chairs. Surrounding the table stood matching floor-to-ceiling bookshelves lining the walls, each filled with leather-bound codes, statutes, case reporters, and legal research volumes. This area also had doors on each side leading to hallways. One hall led to an area with rows of file cabinets containing the firm's active case files. Other rooms housed equipment for copying, mail handling, production of trial exhibits, and the firm's computer network. Down the other hall sat an area of smaller offices used by bookkeeping and accounts receivable staff, law clerks and paralegals. The second floor was the longtime domain of Woodrow "Woody" Perkins. Related in some way to the firm's patriarch, Harrison Baylor, Woody had mental challenges but ran the area with an exacting precision that assured that at all times all resources were in the right place and up to date. Regarded as some sort of document savant, Woody was harmless and dutiful but derived his greatest joy from finding violations of his meticulously enumerated polices.

Mickey paused at the reception desk where the firm receptionist, Wanda Walker, sat engrossed in a paperback romance novel. Mickey cleared her throat, startling the young woman, and reached into a slotted plastic carousel to retrieve her paper messages.

"Who all's still here?" Mickey asked.

"Mostly associates," Wanda confided.

"Any partners besides Becker?"

"I think all the others have left for the weekend."

Becker stuck his head into the reception area and said, "I thought I saw your car pull up. Great job!"

"Oh, thanks," Mickey said with a wide smile. "How'd you find out?"

"I called the court reporter for an update, and she gave me the good news. Come on back to my office," he said, motioning her toward the hallway.

"Okay," Mickey said as she pulled two books from her briefcase. "Just let me put these rule books back in the library before Woody pitches a fit."

"He's gone home," Becker said motioning for her.

"Well, I still better get them up there so he doesn't have a coronary on Monday."

"I'll take them up for you, Ms. Grant," Wanda offered.

"Thanks, Wanda, but I got it."

With the books in hand, Mickey ascended the spiral staircase to the second floor and, just as she had hoped, she found three fellow associates in the library, sitting around the conference table. All had heard of her victory, and each congratulated her, though Mickey detected some subtle insincerities. She described some of the high points of the trial and answered some questions, including what it was like facing George Cameron. Having milked the moment to her satisfaction, she placed the books in the designated spot on Woody's desk before descending the stairway to the first floor of the office and heading to Becker's office.

"Let me pour you a drink," Becker offered, removing a crystal decanter of bourbon and two matching glasses from a dark wooden cabinet on his credenza.

"I'll gladly accept that!"

Ford poured a generous portion in each glass and handed Mickey hers, while taking a seat on the client chair adjacent to her. "Accel's going to be thrilled with this outcome."

"I hope so, Ford. Do you think Cameron will appeal?"

"Maybe, but from what I've heard, it was a clean trial, so I wouldn't worry too much about it."

"I hope you're right. I enjoyed the experience but wouldn't want to try the case a second time."

"Here's to victory!" he toasted. They clinked glasses, and each took a sip. The slight burn of the whiskey on her tongue and throat warmed her, and she took a deep breath and laid her head back, awaiting its soothing delivery.

"Mickey, you've done a lot for your career today—and mine too for that matter."

"Thanks, but how did it help you?"

"First of all, this was a great win for Accel, a very important client. Plus, you're on my team, you know. We partners go out on a limb for those on our team, and you delivered big time for me."

"I'm glad to hear that, but I guess I never thought about it from that angle."

"You see, the associates aren't the *only* ones here who are competitive."

"Associates? Competitive?" Mickey asked, feigning ignorance.

"Come on, Mickey. I noted your victory lap through the library," Ford said.

Mickey lowered her head, chuckled under her breath, and said, "Guilty."

"I don't blame you though. This was a tremendous result."

"Thanks, Ford," she said, enjoying another sip of bourbon. "You know that making partner here is my highest aspiration."

"I know that, and this trial is a big leap forward. I can't tell you how concerned I was about Webster, but I could tell he thought you did great job, and the outcome validates that."

"Have you spoken to him since the verdict?" Mickey asked.

"Yes, I hung up with him just before I saw you drive up. He's headin' back to the airport and was very delighted, and gave you great kudos too."

"I really liked working with him. He's a good guy and really knows what he's doing."

"I'd say so. After all, he was wise enough to pick you for the trial."

"Oh, quit it. You would've gotten the same result."

"Perhaps, but that doesn't diminish your performance. Just don't steal my client, will you?"

"I think you're safe. Webster's a big fan of yours, Ford. He said some really nice things about you during the trial."

"That's good to know. Have time for another drink?"

Mickey declined, saying, "Thanks, but I have to go. Tyler's dropping off Reagan this evening, and I …" She froze and glanced at her watch. "Oh shit, it's late! Sorry, Ford, but I need to get going or Tyler's gonna be pissed!"

"Enjoy your time with Reagan and keep the peace with Tyler," Becker said as Mickey grabbed her purse and jacket and trotted away down the hallway.

CHAPTER 3

BELLUM DOMESTICUM

(Strife among Family Members)

Mickey's domestic troubles were well known to the Triple B partners from the beginning of her tenure with the firm. Becker had served as her confidant as her marriage deteriorated and knew all too well the history of the couple's contentious relationship. He had lent his ear many times and for many hours during the period leading up to the separation and split, and Ford came to know Mickey's life history and her struggles. Born Michelle Alicia Alsup, she was an only child. Her mother died of breast cancer when she was a teenager, and her father, himself a lawyer, balanced career and fatherhood and raised her well. A baseball historian and lifelong fan of the New York Yankees, her dad early on began calling her Mickey after his childhood idol, Mickey Mantle.

During her sophomore year at Texas Tech University, Mickey fell in love with Tyler Grant. They married a short six months after they met and a year and a half later celebrated the birth of their only child, Reagan. After graduation, Tyler went to work full-time, trying to build his accounting practice, and financial constraints and the care for their newborn daughter required Mickey to suspend her educational pursuits and stay home. Mickey placed education and career on hold for two years, focusing all of her energy on the household. Love and the joys and challenges of motherhood carried her for a while, but she slowly felt thwarted as her contemporaries passed her on the path to graduation. She aimed to follow in her father's footsteps in the pursuit of the law, and frustration grew to resentment as she calculated that she would be approaching her thirties before she could enter law school. Though she loved Reagan and was a good and nurturing mother, Mickey finally decided that full-time motherhood was not enough. During this time, her father died suddenly of a heart attack, just shy of his sixtieth birthday, leaving Mickey with a greater sense of her own mortality and a heightened urgency to chase her career goals.

Tyler's objections notwithstanding, she decided to resume her full-time studies, ceding Reagan's daytime care to Tyler, a series of babysitters, and later an on-campus day care. Mickey thrived as a more disciplined and mature student and graduated with honors two and a half years later. When Texas Tech School of Law accepted her, Tyler was less than overjoyed. His discontent only grew as the academic demands on Mickey's time dominated, and consequently the couple spent very little quality time together during the three years needed to complete her law degree. Mickey sat for the bar exam, and while awaiting the results, she accepted Triple B's offer of an internship. That November, she learned she had passed the bar, and the firm elevated Mickey to junior associate, and her time for family constricted further. Though her salary boosted the household finances, the continued devotion to career and the resulting loss of personal time marked the death knell of their marriage. By then Tyler was succeeding in his accounting practice, operating mostly out of their home, allowing him the flexibility to act as Reagan's primary caretaker.

Though he never questioned Mickey's love for them, Tyler concluded that they had become secondary in her life, and he saw little hope of that changing. Though Tyler filed for the divorce, the decision was mutual, but Reagan, ten years old at the time, had a tough time coping with the split. Because of Tyler's work flexibility, Mickey ceded custody of Reagan and their suburban home to him. Mickey spent the first post marriage year in a rented condo close to her office and later bought her own house a few miles away from Tyler and Reagan. Tyler excelled in nurturing Reagan, who now approached age sixteen, and was maturing into a poised and capable young lady. She was an attractive girl, sharing Mickey's flawless olive skin, dark hair, and large, endearing, dark eyes. Reagan was popular in school, successful in her classes, and involved in many extracurricular activities, including orchestra and cheerleading.

Due to preparation for the Monroe case, this visit with Reagan marked the first in a month, and in advance of it, Mickey had brought her Christmas decorations down from the attic and assembled a realistic artificial Christmas tree that she had ordered months earlier from a television infomercial. She had visited a grocery store and purchased the ingredients needed to bake sugar cookies, Reagan's favorite holiday treat. As Mickey turned the corner and onto her street, and spotted Tyler's car parked in front of her house, and glanced at her dashboard clock, and realized that she was near thirty minutes late. As she parked in her driveway and exited, Reagan was already dashing up the driveway to greet her, and they embraced.

"Mom!"

"What, honey?"

"You smell like cigarette smoke. You said you quit!"

Mickey continued her embrace and said, "I have quit, but I just … it's well … kinda complicated, dear." When Mickey opened her eyes, she could see Tyler approaching over Reagan's shoulder with a less than charitable expression.

"Well, better late than never," Tyler said, repeating a phrase often used against him for episodes of tardiness. Tyler was a goodhearted and patient man but on rare instances could be pushed into a contentiousness, especially when it came to their post-divorce relations. Tyler had thick, wavy, blond hair, blue eyes and a remarkable naturally brown skin, a tone that most in the area could only sustain in the summer or by frequenting tanning booths in the winter. He had handsome, chiseled facial features, including deep, pleasant dimples on each cheek. An all-state fullback in high school, Tyler remained very athletic and physically fit.

Mickey looked at him with exasperation as she opened her defense. "I'm sorry, Tyler, but time got away from me. You see, I was in court today, and I had to go back to the office and …" She stopped midsentence, realizing that the career-demands excuse was not persuading this one-person jury. Tyler had her on the ropes, but when he looked at Reagan's pained expression, he relented.

"Sometime things happen. Right, Mick?"

"Yes, Tyler, sometimes they do," she conceded.

"And these things can happen to *me* sometimes too, right?" Mickey nodded with a conciliatory smile as the relieved Reagan realized her parents had averted a greater confrontation. Reagan had long since given up the notion of her parents reconciling but remained a steadfast ambassador for their peaceful coexistence.

Tyler stepped back and looked at Mickey as she locked her car. "You look good, Mick. Have you lost some weight?"

"Why? Did I need to?"

"No, silly. It's just that you look—you know—really fit."

"Thank you! There's no diet like the trial preparation regimen."

"How did your case go?"

"It went well … I screwed around and won the damn thing."

He congratulated her, and appreciating the gesture, Mickey invited him to dinner.

"That's nice of you, but I have some errands to run."

"Dad's gonna to look for a car for me, Mom!" Reagan said with elation.

Tyler saw Mickey's expression change and said, "You don't know that, and—"

"Is that the errand you need to run?" Mickey asked with agitation. "I mean, isn't this something you and I ought to discuss?"

"Under the terms of the divorce decree, I get to—"

"Don't give me that decree crap! I'm fully aware of what it says, but I just think we should talk about things like this."

"You're right, Mick," he said, raising his hands in surrender. "We'll discuss it."

"Fine … sorry I snapped at you."

"So where are y'all going to eat?" he asked.

"I've made dinner," Mickey responded.

"Oh, my God, your mom's cooking? Now, there's a Christmas miracle!" Tyler said, perpetuating a longstanding joke that Mickey rarely cooked for them while they were married.

"Dad, she cooks sometimes, and I think those frozen dinners are actually pretty good," Reagan added, giggling.

"Oh, ganging up on me, eh?" Mickey said popping Reagan on her bottom. They all laughed, and she and Reagan began walking arm-in-arm toward the front porch.

Before getting into his car, Tyler shouted for Mickey and waited for her to walk halfway back across the yard. "I guess you heard about the latest abduction?" he asked out of earshot of Reagan. Mickey nodded, and he added, "Let's be real careful, okay?"

"I will. Believe me, this abduction crap is very scary," she said. She waved good-bye, walked into her house, and turned her full attention to Reagan.

They had a pleasant dinner, made sugar cookies, and discussed Reagan's upcoming week-long Christmas visitation, which Mickey enjoyed with Reagan on even-numbered years.

Mickey returned to the office on Monday morning and with the thrill of her win now behind her, Mickey found her feet once again planted firmly on the ground and under her desk. With a deadline looming for an important motion on one of Ford Becker's cases, she was asked to do a draft of the motion and buried herself for days performing the legal research that would serve as its foundation.

On the Wednesday before Reagan's arrival for the Christmas visit, Mickey was summoned into Harrison Baylor's open door as she passed. She eagerly entered and saw Ford Becker sitting across the desk from Baylor, each enjoying a cup of coffee. She was greeted by the pleasant smell of Baylor's pipe burning the Middleton's cherry-blend tobacco he favored. Though office policy forbade smoking in the office, all gladly granted an exemption to the senior partner. A distinguished-looking, silver-haired man, Baylor always wore a pressed suit with a perfectly knotted tie and starched shirts with monogrammed French cuffs, and his idea of casual Friday was taking his suit coat off—after hours. The walls of his office were adorned with certificates, mementos, and awards from nearly fifty years in the practice of law. Baylor had assumed the firm's leadership mantle three years earlier when cancer claimed the life of his longtime friend and law partner, Jimmy Brewer.

"What do you think of Accel's new hero, Harrison?" Becker asked as Mickey took the seat next to him.

"I think she has confirmed what we always knew, that she is one fine trial lawyer," Baylor said as Mickey smiled her appreciation. "And you defeated George Cameron. That's no small feat, Michelle. He's very good and doesn't take cases that he doesn't expect to win—and win big."

"Thank you, but, I did have a little help," she said, glancing at Becker.

"I know you did, but you don't get results like this without talent and a lot of hard work."

"Thanks, Mr. B."

"Are you still getting Reagan for a whole week?" Ford inquired.

"Yes, starting Friday, and I can't tell you how excited I am to have her. But just know that I'm working on the Trans-Con motion and hope to have a draft to you in the next few days."

"That works out well. I want to be able to work on it over the holidays, considering it has to be filed in the second week of January."

"I'll make sure that happens."

"That son-of-a-gun's at it again," Ford said, pointing at the front page of the newspaper.

"Another abduction?" Mickey asked.

"Yes, it's a girl from Delano of all places," Baylor informed.

"Yep, a fifteen-year-old," Becker confirmed. "But she's the second from over there, Harrison. A fourteen-year-old went missing from there while you were in Wisconsin."

"Lord, I hope they catch this menace soon," Baylor said.

"When did this happen?" Mickey asked.

"Yesterday. Same type of thing as the others—snatched in broad daylight at a shopping center parking lot."

"This makes six now, doesn't it?" Baylor asked.

"Seven," Ford corrected. "There was one over in Avondale too, and this article says that the cops fear he may pick up the pace as the holidays approach."

"But with the larger crowds for the holidays and the stepped-up security, wouldn't the threat be less?" Mickey asked.

"Ask him," Ford said, pointing at Baylor, who had devoted much of his practice as a criminal defense lawyer.

"You can't presuppose that these characters think like you and I, because they don't," Baylor explained. "One of the first things that police detectives are taught in training is to disregard what you believe someone like you would do under any given circumstance. The criminal mind doesn't always operate that way. More often than not, they gravitate to the higher-risk challenges. Committing crimes in public brings the threat of getting caught, adds to the thrill and makes these types unpredictable and, may I say, very dangerous."

"Thrill?"

"Yes."

"That's creepy. So what do you think he's doing with them?" Mickey asked.

"Who knows, but it doesn't look good," Baylor said.

"You think they're dead?" she asked.

"Probably," Ford said as Baylor nodded. "But I pray they catch this guy and find them all alive and well."

"I do too," Mickey said. "This is just so tragic."

"Yes, and I've been warning everybody in the firm to be especially careful this year," Becker added.

Baylor excused himself for a board meeting, and as Ford walked Mickey down the hall, she asked, "I need to do some more shopping, do you think that's all right?"

"Sure, go about your normal routine. Just be smart about it. It'd be better if you went with someone, but whatever you do or wherever you go, just be very aware of what's going on around you. Sorry for being such a worry wart. My wife's about to kick me out of the house from nagging her and our girls about all of this."

"I think it's very nice of you."

"Thanks, so what's the game plan for Reagan's visit?"

She stopped and turned to him and said, "Oh, Ford, she's really excited about Christmas this year—more so than in many years. She was thrilled on her last visit that the tree was decorated. I'm going to try to complete my shopping today and plan to have everything else decorated and the presents wrapped and under the tree for Reagan's arrival."

"That makes me very happy."

Mickey awoke the next morning with shopping on her mind. The moderated temperatures and full sunshine made for a perfect atmosphere to wrap up her shopping. She worked until midafternoon on research and made extensive handwritten changes to the draft of the motion. She ceded the edits to her secretary, Marlene Kennedy, to prepare yet another draft for her to review. With nothing more she could do on the motion that day, she left the office and spent the afternoon roaming from store to store. She bought gifts for Reagan and the office staff, until the sun was rapidly fading, and the temperature was dropping. She decided on one final stop to purchase Christmas cards and gift wrapping.

Darkness had arrived by the time she reached the substantially full parking lot of a strip center located close to her house. She selected a parking space as close as possible to the greeting-card store, but she nevertheless found herself a good forty yards away from the store's entrance. When she turned off her headlights and killed the engine, it got very dark. She realized that the space she occupied was not near any of the several security light poles, and for a moment, she considered moving to a better-lit parking spot. But, surveying the area, she saw nothing suspicious and chided herself for worrying.

She removed the keys from the ignition, exited the car and locked it. After donning her coat, she commenced walking toward the store, but seeing movement out of the corner of her eye, she turned her head slightly to the right and caught a glimpse of a figure two aisles over walking in the same general direction. The figure appeared to be a tall, thin man dressed in very dark clothing. Mickey was unable to make out any facial features, and she continued on deliberately. A moment later, she heard a noise and turned to see the silhouette of the same man now in the aisle closest to the one she occupied, and sensed he was cutting across it to get even closer.

With the man now essentially between her and her car, returning to it was no longer an option. She continued walking briskly toward the store, and as her breathing became labored, she picked up her pace, focusing on lights and safety afforded by the store front. As she neared it and started to feel relief, until she heard the increasing pace of hard-sole shoes behind her, drawing rapidly closer. She stepped up onto the sidewalk, and as she reached the entry door, the dark sleeve of an arm extended from behind and grabbed the door handle. She wheeled around and stared directly at the white collar protruding from the neck of a dark suit, and with great relief she realized her would-be pursuer was a Catholic priest.

"Merry Christmas, sister," he said as he held the door open for her.

"Merry Christmas, Father," Mickey uttered.

Once inside the store, she caught her breath and let her heart ebb to a normal pace. She was simultaneously amused and irritated for allowing herself to be so influenced by news accounts and admonitions of others, and for succumbing to such uncharacteristic fear. She made her purchases and headed home.

Later that evening, while relaxing on her bed, she switched on the local news. The lead story promised breaking news on the abductions, and she used the remote control to increase the volume. The news anchor recounted that police had disclosed no clues or suspects in the first seven abductions. Then, stopping in midsentence, the anchor pitched the broadcast to reporter for an on-the-scene report directly from the Delano Police Station.

"We just attended a very brief press conference with Chief Franklin Hopkins of the Delano Police Department. He informed that investigators have interviewed a witness who claims to have seen a suspect in the abduction of Taylor Abram that occurred here in Delano on the tenth. This is the first potential breakthrough on these troubling cases. This unidentified witness came forward today after seeing reports of the abduction here on News 13. Details are sketchy, but the chief indicated that the witness saw a girl fitting the description of Taylor Abram next to a van in the mall parking lot. Back to you, Rich."

Mickey turned off the TV, hoping this news might signal an imminent end to these tragedies, and turned attention to wrapping gifts and preparing another batch of Reagan's favorite cookies.

On the Friday before Christmas, Mickey left the office at five thirty to assure that she would be home in plenty of time for Reagan's planned arrival at six thirty. Her house was now decorated with lights, wreaths, stockings, and wrapped gifts were piled beneath her expertly trimmed Christmas tree. She was anxious for Reagan to see all her preparations, and to her delight, Tyler arrived early. Reagan, dressed in jeans and a sweater, rushed through the door and embraced Mickey, who signified her appreciation for Tyler's promptness with a smile and a thumbs-up.

While Tyler carried Reagan's backpack and overnight bag into her house, Reagan stepped into the living room and gasped. "Oh, Mom! Everything looks fantastic!"

"It does look nice if I do say so myself," Mickey said, nodding.

"The tree's lovely, Mick," Tyler said. "You always had a knack for it."

"Why thank you, sir," she replied.

"Three stockings?" Tyler asked with raised eyebrows as he stared at the fireplace mantle.

"It's not what you think. I'm taking a chance that you've been good enough this year to get something," Mickey explained as she straightened the third stocking to reveal his name.

"Whose is this, Mom?" Reagan asked, now on the floor surveying the wrapped gifts.

"Hey, hey, hey! Get your mitts off of those, or I'll take them all back!"

"Boy, I haven't seen her this excited in a long time," Tyler whispered, and Mickey nodded.

"Wanna cookie, Reagan?" Mickey asked as she displayed a tray piled with them and Reagan eagerly abandoned the gift surveying to partake.

"Hey! What about me?" Tyler protested.

"Sure, take all you want. I certainly don't need 'em," Mickey said, patting her stomach.

"What are you talking about? I haven't seen you this fit since before Reagan was born."

"Why, thanks again. Hell, I'd like to bottle this moment."

This civil exchange between her parents added greatly to Reagan's delight as she hugged her dad good-bye.

"See you in a week," Tyler said. "I wish you both an early Merry Christmas!"

"Merry Christmas, Daddy!"

As Mickey walked Tyler to the door, he asked, "You will have her call me, right?"

"Of course, every day. And look—I know this is my week and all, but you're more than welcome here for Christmas Eve dinner or lunch on Christmas day or both."

Moved by her offer, Tyler replied, "I don't have much planned and might just take you up on that."

"It'll be no trouble if you decide to. All I have to do is set another place," she said. Tyler thanked her and walked to his car.

"I sure wish you and Daddy could always get along, Mom," Reagan said as Mickey joined her in having a cookie.

"I understand, dear, but sometimes I believe your dad goes out of his way to test my patience."

"He says you do that to him."

Mickey patted her cheek and said, "I know, Reagan. I guess it takes two to tango."

"Do you mean two to *tangle*?" Reagan said as they chuckled. "The cookies are yummy. Can I have another?"

"I wish you wouldn't. I'm cooking supper," Mickey said.

"What are we having?"

"Lasagna."

"Yum! I thought I smelled garlic," Reagan said. Then, giving Mickey her most soulful look, she asked, "Mom, can we go shopping tonight?"

"No, Reagan. We'll start that this weekend."

"But, Mom, it's still early, and I need to get some gifts, including for you and dad."

"Listen, Reagan, I've got to get dinner finished, then we have to eat and clean up, and by that time, it'll be late," Mickey explained.

"You won't have the food ready for a while, and I'm not even hungry right now. Why can't I ride my bike over to the mall, shop for a while, and come back for dinner?"

"No way, Reagan! I can't let you go over there by yourself, especially at night," Mickey argued.

"Is it because of that guy in the news?"

"That's part of it, but it's just not a wise thing to do any time."

"You've let me go before."

"Stop it, will ya?" Mickey said, taking a playful swat at her with a dishrag. "We'll have plenty of time before Christmas to do all of the shopping you want."

"Then what about tomorrow?"

"I was actually thinking we could go to the gun range tomorrow. You haven't shot the pistol in a while, and I could sure use the practice."

"I'd really like to do that, Mom, but just not tomorrow."

"That's fine. I've got to go into the office tomorrow morning, but only for a little—"

"Office! You said you wouldn't be working during my week!"

"No—I said I'd keep my work to a minimum."

"Tomorrow's Saturday. So why would you have to work at all?"

"I'm working on a very important motion for Mr. Becker that's due right after the holidays. Ms. Marlene left the latest draft on my desk, and I have to finish the final edits and leave it so she can get on it first thing Monday morning." Sensing the escalating disappointment, she added, "Look—I promise it won't be too long, sweetie. Once I do this, I'm through with *all* work until after Christmas, and we'll have plenty of time to go to all of the stores you want!"

Reagan reluctantly accepted Mickey's plan and resumed her custom of picking up and shaking each gift, trying to divine the contents. The two shared an enjoyable dinner, caught up on everything from her grades to boys, and settled in for the night.

Reagan awoke the next morning just before sunup, and though she was excited about the planned shopping excursion, she wondered how she would pass the time until her mom returned. She yawned sleepily at the kitchen table while Mickey cooked her favorites, waffles and hickory smoked bacon, and Mickey nibbled as she cooked.

"So what time are you coming home?" Reagan asked.

"That depends on my progress, but I promise no later than noon."

"There's nothing for me to do here while you're gone, you know. I have no homework, and there's nothing but cartoons on TV."

"You used to like cartoons."

"Yeah, when I was in kindergarten."

"Sorry, dear, but I'm sure you can make do for a couple of hours."

"It's over four hours, Mom. What if I go on to the mall this morning, and you could meet me at the food court for lunch when you're done?"

"I don't think so, honey," Mickey said as she poured the batter on the waffle iron. "You'll find something to keep you busy, and I'll be back here before you know it."

"Sitting around here alone wasn't exactly what I looked forward to for the visit."

"You could come with me to the office," Mickey offered.

"That's worse than being here," Reagan lamented. "I am growing up, Mom, and you know I've gone to that mall a hundred times."

"I think a hundred is a little exaggerated."

"You know what I mean, mom. I've been there a bunch of times."

"I know, but I just can't let you go there alone."

"Fine. I'll go with Carol."

Carol James was Reagan's friend in the neighborhood, and the two often spent time together when Reagan visited. Desperate for Reagan to have an enjoyable time and feeling guilty about working even a half day, Mickey relented. "All right, you can go, if Carol can. Understand?"

"Thank you, Mom!"

"So you'll get ahold of Carol and ask her, right?"

"Yes!" Reagan said excitedly as she reached for the phone.

"Hang on now! It's too early to call. Not everyone gets up at the crack of dawn on Saturdays. Plus, we haven't worked out the details," Mickey said, placing Reagan's orange juice in front of her.

"Here's the deal, Mom. Later on, I'll call Carol, and if she can go, we'll ride our bikes to the mall together. We'll shop, and when you're done at work, we'll meet you at the mall for lunch. After that, we'll shop more. Deal?" Reagan asked, extending her right hand to shake on it.

"Hold on. If I didn't know better, I'd think you were the lawyer in the family!" Mickey said, grinning. "Okay, we'll do it that way but *only* if Carol goes with you, you hear? Reagan nodded eagerly. "I aired up your bicycle tires earlier this week, so you should be good to go. Wait until nine o'clock to call Carol, and if she can't go, just call me at the office, and I'll pick you up here after I'm done. But if she can go, I'll meet you there."

"Got it, Mom."

"Is your cell phone charged?"

"About half, but I'll let it charge until I leave."

"Good, and it's straight there and only there, and remember to be aware of what's going on around you at all times. Stay on the main road too, and don't use the bike trail. If I don't hear from you differently, I'll meet you and Carol at Pablo's Pizza in the mall food court at twelve thirty, deal?

"Deal!"

"What time are we meeting?" Mickey tested her.

"Twelve thirty!" Reagan confirmed.

"Right. Be sure and lock the front door on the way out."

Feeling that they were on the same page, Mickey kissed her good bye and left as Reagan finished her breakfast. Mickey labored on her brief in the quiet of the empty office building, until a voice interrupted.

"What in the world are you doing here?"

"Jesus, Ford! You scared the crap out of me."

"Sorry, I should have knocked. But really, what are you doing here?"

"The Trans-Con motion. I've got a final draft almost done, and Marlene should have it on your desk Monday afternoon."

"How's it coming?"

"I don't mean to brag, but I found some really good cases to cite and think the thing's gonna be great."

"That's good news. Where's Reagan?"

"She's at the house, but I'm meeting her at the mall later," Mickey replied as she returned her concentration to the motion, but Becker's silence signaled that more questions were coming.

"She's not going alone, is she?" he asked.

"Of course not. She's going with a girlfriend of hers," Mickey said, but his expression did not change. Mickey dropped her pen on the desk and went on the offensive. "Ford, this whole thing's been blown way out of proportion. We're letting some scumbag creep dominate our lives."

"How so?"

"I'll give you a prime example. You know that evening when I wanted to do a little shopping?"

"Yeah, I remember."

"Well, I went over to that strip center over on Fannin close to the roller rink. It was pretty dark by then, and as I walked across the parking lot toward the store, I saw something out of the corner of my eye. Any other time, I'd have thought nothing of it, but because of all of this news, I had the creeps. I truly felt like this guy was following me. He was dressed in dark clothing and crossed two aisles to fall in behind me as walked. I know we all have to be cautious, but damn it, Ford, the sheer panic I felt was awful."

"You thought it was the abductor?"

"Yes, and it turned out to be a Catholic priest who just wanted to open the door for me and wish me Merry Christmas. It's seven girls, Ford! Seven out of tens of thousands of girls just in this part of Texas. The chances of meeting up with this guy in broad daylight at the mall are less than getting hit by a bus driving to it."

Ford sighed. "Perhaps you're right. These local news people are so starved for ratings that they take something like this and whip everyone into a frenzy."

"Yes, they do. We all need to be on the lookout at all times. I get it that we live in that kind of world, but we just have to use a little common sense too."

"You're right," Ford conceded. "So, about that evening at the shopping center. You really thought that the abductor was after you?"

"Yes, I was convinced of it."

"Why?"

"What?" Mickey asked curiously.

"Why were *you* scared? After all, this guy only goes after young victims!" Ford said, sprinting out the door and ducking the ballpoint pen that hurled by Mickey.

Mickey worked diligently, and when she edited the last page of the motion, she placed the stack of papers on Marlene's chair. She felt a sense of liberation knowing that her last task for the year was done and done well, and she said good-bye to Becker and headed to the parking garage. She checked her watch and saw she was actually running ahead of time. She made the short fifteen-minute drive to the mall and parked as close as she could to the entrance nearest the food court. Though the mercury hovered in the mid-fifties, the overcast sky and a steady, easterly breeze chilled her. She entered the mall, welcomed the warmth, and removed her jacket as she walked directly to the food court. She perused the tables and chairs and scanned the area for Reagan and Carol. As she neared Pablo's Pizza, she paid particular attention to each of those waiting in the lengthy line but saw no familiar faces.

Considering the girls might have opted for something other than pizza, Mickey walked from one end of the string of eateries to the other, tiptoeing to see over those standing in each line, but there were no sign of the girls. Checking her watch, she noted that she was still a couple of minutes early, so she decided to walk down the mall and peek into a couple of stores where she felt they might shop. She slowed and peered into a costume jewelry shop and then a store specializing in embroidered jeans. Reaching the east end of the mall without sighting them, she started back toward the middle. She arrived back at the food court and again scanned the crowd, including those seated and those in line.

She then paced toward the west end of the mall, glancing into the arcade and a teen shoe store, to no avail. It was now 12:39, and she decided to station herself amid the bustling food court crowd, and as she stood, she watched each approaching figure. But as the minutes ticked by, the lines were getting shorter, and Mickey decided to take a seat at one of the several empty tables. She selected one close to Pablo's Pizza, but one that likewise provided a clear view of the passing mall traffic. She cleared crumbs and wrappers from the tabletop, took a seat, and straightened condiments to occupy her mind. She checked her watch again, and it was 12:58, and she began suppressing unpleasant notions with thoughts of plausible explanations. Soon it was past one o'clock, and the dining area crowd was thinning out. She checked her cell phone and saw a message from her home number from earlier that morning. *Hell, I had it on mute. This could explain everything.*

She pressed the button on the phone to retrieve the message and heard Reagan's soft voice. "Hi, Mom, it's me. I think you left with my hairbrush in your purse. Can you bring it with you to the mall? The waffles were great and thanks *so* much for letting me go shop. Love ya!" Mickey walked to a quieter corner of the food court and immediately called her home number.

The phone rang until she heard her own greeting and the beep. "Reagan, dear, I'm up at the mall and waiting for you and Carol. Call me right away if you get this, okay?" She dialed Reagan's cell number and it went direct to voice mail, but she left a similar message.

Soon, more than an hour had elapsed since the agreed-to meeting time, and with each additional minute, she found herself less capable of calming herself. She was sweating heavily, so she removed her coat as she sat and waited. At 2:02, Mickey heard a commotion coming from the mall's atrium. This was an area toward the east end of the mall that at this time of year was decorated as a winter wonderland, the centerpiece of which was a towering Christmas tree made entirely of bright red poinsettias. The tree was surrounded by life-size toy soldiers and tall red and white striped candy canes and layers of fluffy cotton mimicking snow.

A crowd was gathering there, but Mickey could not tell the nature of the disturbance. Whatever was happening, it seemed to be drawing more and more onlookers, and she hastily headed in that direction, straining for a better view as she walked. As she neared the atrium, she noticed uniformed security guards among the throng, and she weaved her way around slower patrons toward the middle of the gathering. Her breaths became short gasps, and her brisk walk became a trot. Desperate to get to the center, she elbowed through the onlookers, drawing stares and intemperate remarks. As she breached the last line of resistance, she stumbled into the center of the crowd, and all eyes turned to her and away from the grade-school glee club on risers preparing to sing Christmas carols.

Embarrassed, Mickey turned and moved away from the atrium as the sweet-but-tone-challenged voices commenced "Joy to the World." Starting back toward the food court, Mickey remained vigilant, and as she glanced through a set of glass entry doors on her right, she saw an electric golf cart with "Mall Security" written on it passing through the parking lot. Racing through the doors, she pursued the cart, yelling, "Sir! Excuse me, sir!"

The cart stopped, and the man turned his head back to her, saying, "Yes?"

"I need help. I was supposed to meet my daughter and her friend here over an hour and a half ago. They never showed, and I can't find them anywhere."

"Okay," he said dismissively. "What can I help with?"

"Have you seen anything wrong? Has there been any ..."

"Abductions?"

"Well ... yes."

"Ma'am, I ain't seen nothing like that."

"No crimes at all?" she asked.

"Oh, now that's a whole 'nother question. There ain't a day goes by that we don't get somethin' like a car break-in, a purse snatcher, or shoplifter or something."

"Anything like that happen here today?"

"Don't know. All I can say is ain't nothin' like that's happened out here on the lot, and that's all I care about, since the inside ain't my deal."

"Whose *deal* is it then?"

"You'd need to go to the security office, down toward Sears. It's in a hall between the ice-cream shop and where that greeting card store used to be. But listen, we've had many parents think they have a victim of this guy, and it's turned out every time to be a false alarm."

Mickey nodded and rushed back inside the mall, and when she found the hallway the man described, she wondered how she had never noticed it during her countless previous trips there. She walked down the hall and through a glass door also marked "Security" and stood at an unattended counter. She looked around for signs of who, if anyone, was attending the desk and noticed what she felt sure was a two-way mirror behind the counter. She strained to peer through the reflective glass for any activity on the other side, until she heard movement from behind the door to the back office. She moved around the counter for a closer vantage point, and when the door swung open, a uniformed officer and a woman walked out with a scruffy young man in handcuffs. Startled, Mickey quickly backed out of the way as they led the man in custody past her. He had long, unkempt hair and wore a red-and-black flannel shirt and dirty blue jeans. All three walked out a door leading to the back of the mall, they proceeded toward an idling squad car, and Mickey wondered the nature of the crime.

Mickey cast a quick glance into the back room and saw a woman wearing a dark blue windbreaker, with Mall Security written on it in yellow on the back, who sat dividing her time between watching a wall of video monitors flitting from one camera angle to another and a stack of paperwork in front of her. Mickey cleared her throat to get her attention, and wheeling around in the rolling metal chair, the woman rose, saying, "You can't be in here!"

"I'm sorry, ma'am, but I waited out—"

"Doesn't matter," she insisted as she ushered Mickey by the arm back around the counter to the waiting area. "Now, can I help you?"

"Yes, I was supposed to meet my teenage daughter and her girlfriend here at twelve thirty, and neither showed. I've looked everywhere and can't find them," Mickey explained.

"Someone will be with you in a minute, lady. Until then, have a seat and stay on this side of the counter." The woman instructed and returned to the back room and her paperwork. Though incensed by the apathy, Mickey was reluctant to sever her only link with mall authorities.

Though frustrated and scared, she obeyed by taking a seat on a plastic chair and waiting silently, as one of the office phones began ringing. Soon an obese man wearing the same type of blue windbreaker entered. When he passed Mickey, without acknowledging her and grabbed a clipboard off the counter. He reviewed papers attached to it as the phone continued to ring. The man turned and walked back past Mickey, and she rose and grabbed his arm.

"What do you want, lady?" the man asked.

"I want to know about my daughter, goddamn it! Isn't there a person here in one of those blue jackets that gives a shit?"

"What about your daughter?"

"She's gone. I can't find her, and no one here will help me!" Mickey said as tears appeared on her cheeks and the phone continued to ring.

"Look, ma'am—I'm sorry, but we don't have any information on anyone being missing."

"I just gave you information about someone being missing, and you all—"

"I understand. All I'm saying is there's been no unusual activity reported today," he said as the ringing phone continued.

"No unusual activity? Y'all just take a man out of here in handcuffs, and can someone please answer that goddamn phone!"

"Jackie, can you get that?" the man yelled to the woman in the office, and the ringing stopped.

"Sir, my daughter and her friend are well over an hour and a half late in meeting me here. Maybe that guy y'all hauled out of here is the reason why!"

"Calm down, ma'am. That guy was just a thief. He tried to snatch a purse, and unfortunately for him, it was an undercover cop," the officer explained.

Mickey collapsed onto a chair. "Just a thief? Couldn't someone who would snatch a purse snatch a girl?"

"Maybe, but he didn't have no girl. The problem you got here ain't unusual for us," he explained as Mickey looked up at him. "You see, teenagers come to the mall not to just shop but also for socializing and sometimes for mischief. Now with these abductions in the news, everyone's all of a sudden worried about 'em, and every time a girl's a few minutes late, their parents dial 911 or come flooding in here, and, might I add, every time it's turned out to be a big bunch of nothing."

"But, my daughter is missing," Mickey pleaded.

She could be out in the parking lot with a boy or smoking a cigarette or something.

"My daughter doesn't do cigarettes or boys!"

"Teens do a lot of things up here they don't do at home. I know you believe that yours is somehow different, but I've placed many a handcuff on such little angels."

"Please help me," she sobbed.

"Take this paper and write down your contact information and a description of both girls, and I'll send out a bulletin to all on patrol. If something comes up, I'll let you know." Mickey thanked him and wrote two paragraphs describing Reagan and what she remembered about Carol. She then walked back to the food court as the faint melodic tones of "Silent Night" echoed from the atrium. She saw only a few patrons in line, and that half of the food-court chairs were now stacked on the tables, and a man was mopping the floor floors beneath them. She decided to return home.

CHAPTER 4

⚖

CAUSA LATET, VIS ESTNOTISSIMA
(The Cause Is Uncertain, but the Result Is Known)

When Mickey walked through the front door of her home, she found Reagan's syrupy breakfast plate and a near-empty glass of milk on the kitchen counter. Her open overnight case and her clothes from the day before were still on the floor by her bed, and there were no messages and no note. She thumbed through her address book finding the James family number, but she stopped in the middle of dialing it, realizing she had to settle on what to say and how to say it.

If the girls are there, then fine. But what if they aren't? And if the James aren't there, do I leave a message? What do I say if I do? If they say Carol's at the mall, how do I respond? Wouldn't I be bringing them into their own nightmare?

Setting indecision aside, she dialed and hoped desperately for something positive as the phone rang, until the James's voice mail greeting began. Following the beep, Mickey froze momentarily and then mustered, "This is Michelle Grant, Reagan's mother. Could you please call me at 555-1210? Thanks."

That's done, but what about the police? Should I involve them at this point? Will they blame me for this? Oh hell, it's gotta be wrong to consider myself in this, but God if I make the call and the girls are fine, this will get all blown out of proportion. Tyler might find out—and shit, it could get back to Ford and the whole the firm. Just a while longer— after all, until I hear from the James, do I really know the situation? Hell, for all I know, they're over there having a great time outside and just didn't hear the phone. But what if my delay in calling the police could have made a difference? How would I live with that? Oh God! What have I done? I tried to tell her, I truly did, but will anyone believe me? Shit, it won't matter what I told her. I was well warned—it's all on me!

She sat on a barstool at her kitchen counter, opened a drawer, and took a cigarette from a crumpled pack of Virginia Slims. She struck a match, and as she raised it to the tip of the cigarette, she noticed her hand was trembling. She managed to light the cigarette and took a deep draw, exhaling a stream of smoke toward the ceiling. She considered driving to the James' home when another thought jolted her—she had not looked for Reagan's bicycle. Rushing through her laundry room to a door that led into her garage, she confirmed that the bike was gone.

It was now almost three hours beyond the meeting time, and she decided to trace the most likely route Reagan would have taken from their neighborhood to the mall. As she drove, Mickey searched every yard, each open garage, and all empty lots for clues. When she reached the oval-shaped road that circled the outer perimeter of the mall parking lot, she began scanning in all directions. She focused on the parking spaces, bike racks, and landscaped areas, including several elevated knolls that served as a scenic sound barrier between the mall property and adjacent, busy thoroughfares. Passing one such ivy-covered mound, Mickey caught sight of something peculiar. Braking quickly, she focused on what appeared to be a rubber tire protruding from the ground cover and shrubs atop the knoll. With a gnawing dread, Mickey exited her car, opting for a closer look.

On this particular knoll, grass started at the edge of the parking lot and transitioned to a thick covering of Asian jasmine as it sloped steeply upward toward a collection of prickly holly bushes. Climbing the hill toward the gnarled vines and shrubs, Mickey confirmed that what drew her attention was indeed a tire, complete with a rim and spokes. Still in heeled shoes, Mickey crept unsteadily upward and closer until she could kneel down and grasp the wheel. As prickly leafs from holly bushes assaulted her knees, she braced herself with her left hand and tugged hard on the tire with her right. Her effort moved the tire but only slightly, and it remained ensnared in the thick shrubbery. With both hands, she reached into the prickly leaves for a better grip and jerked it enough to bring the rear of a bicycle into view. She immediately noted the frame was the same color and type as Reagan's bike. When she tugged hard again, she lost her balance and fell backward down the knoll, while grasping the tire. The force of her fall and her tight grip had wrenched the bike free of the shrubbery, delivering it atop Mickey's lower body, on the slope. With the front wheel spinning and squealing, she used her hand to stop the tire and moved the frame off her legs to a point where she could sit upright. She saw a leather loop on the handlebars imprinted with the word "Reagan." A boy had given Reagan the bracelet months earlier, and Mickey stood up, unsnapped the bracelet, and hugged it to her breast before placing it in her jacket pocket.

She set the bicycle on its wheels and rolled it to the back of her car, then leaned on the bumper and used her hands to brush the dirt and mulch from her pants and shoes. She then noticed the palm of her left hand and knees were bleeding from holly pricks. She pulled napkins from her purse and dabbed at the cuts as she again scanned the knoll for another bike or signs of a body. Finding neither, she struggled to put Reagan's bike in the trunk, and once in, she did not care that the trunk lid would not close. She drove home with the trunk lid bumping the bike with each start and stop and more so as she traversed the mall speed humps on her way to the exit. Once home, she returned the bike to her garage and went inside, noting a call from the James house on caller ID. Now well past four o'clock, Mickey marshaled her thoughts and dialed the number. On the third ring, she heard the voice of Mrs. James.

"Hi, this is Michelle Grant. Thanks for returning my call."

"No problem. How are you?"

"Fine, thank you. Is Carol there?"

"Yes, she's here," Mrs. James replied.

"How about Reagan?"

"No. Is she supposed to be?"

Mickey, desperately trying to control the fear in her voice, said, "It's kinda complicated. Have you all heard from Reagan at all?"

"No, I haven't. Why do you ask?"

"Reagan and Carol were supposed to go to the mall today, and they were to meet me there at twelve thirty."

"I don't understand. Carol had a dental appointment this morning, and I've been with her all day. Just a minute. Let me get her on the phone." Mickey heard a muffled conversation before Mrs. James said, "Pick up the extension, dear."

"I'm here," Carol said.

"Carol, Reagan's mom's on the phone. Have you heard from Reagan today?"

"Yes, Mom. She called this morning when you were in the shower and asked if I could go to the mall. I told her I couldn't because of my appointment with Dr. Abraham."

"Is that all y'all discussed?" Mickey asked.

"Basically. She did offer to have lunch, but I explained that I was getting my braces tightened, and I didn't think I'd be eating so soon after that."

"Thank you both," Mickey said. "Listen, if either of you by chance hear from Reagan, would you please let me know right away?"

"Of course. I have your number right here," Mrs. James confirmed.

Mickey was now out of excuses and reluctantly dialed 911.

"Dispatch. What's your emergency?" answered a male voice.

"Emergency? I don't think that—I mean it's probably just …" Mickey stammered.

"Ma'am, just tell me the nature of your call."

"All right, sir. I'm Michelle Grant, and I need some help finding my daughter," Mickey said, trying to sound composed but serious. "She was to meet me at the Town East Mall several hours ago but never showed." The detailed discussion that followed only heightened her fear. Then the officer asked Mickey to stay on the line to speaking with Detective Adams. Mickey recognized the name from the news as the officer taking the lead in the investigation of the missing girls from Brinkman.

She held for a couple of minutes until she heard, "Homicide, Adams speaking." Taken aback by his greeting, Mickey was momentarily speechless. "Hello … anyone there?"

"Yes, sir—I'm here."

"I see from my dispatcher's form that you have a missing teenage girl, and she was supposed to meet you at the mall."

"Yes, at Town East at twelve thirty, but she never showed. I still haven't heard from her."

"Mrs. Grant, I also see that that your daughter's in her mid-teens," said the detective.

"Yes. She's fifteen, about to turn sixteen."

"Is she slim and attractive?"

"Yes, yes. She's a very pretty girl. Does this make any difference?" Mickey asked, puzzled.

"It does. You see, I'm just trying to establish whether or not your daughter fits a certain profile. To assist you, we have to ask specific questions, some of which may not make a lot of sense to you, but there're very important to us. You see, this guy's consistently targeted a particular type, and I'm just trying to see if your daughter fits it."

"When you say 'guy,' you mean the mall abductor?"

"Yes, ma'am."

"Oh God! What's he doing with these girls?" Mickey cried.

"I'm not saying your daughter's a victim. She probably isn't."

"But if she is, what's he—"

"I'm sorry, but we don't know what's happened to any of the girls at this stage. That's why this type of information is crucial."

"I see," Mickey said.

"What was your daughter wearing today?"

"She was in pajamas when I left this morning, so I really can't tell you."

"Ma'am, this is very important for us to know. Can you go through her closet and try to determine what's missing?"

"I'm sure she had on a light blue coat, but for the rest, I'd have to talk to her father."

"Does he know what she wore?"

"He might. You see, she was spending Christmas week at my house," Mickey explained.

"Oh, so you're divorced?"

Not pleased with the implication, she responded, "What do you mean by that?"

"Nothing, it's just that in a disappearance investigation, this could be a factor."

"I don't understand. Are you suggesting that her father kidnapped her?"

"It's a common occurrence, ma'am." Adams explained.

"She lives with him."

"So you lost custody in the divorce?"

Mickey had gone from despair to agitation. "Look. I didn't *lose* custody. I gave—"

"Mrs. Grant, I'm not trying to point fingers, but a missing child's domestic history can be a major part of the profile."

"Again with the profile thing. Look—I desperately need to find my daughter, and you're focusing on me?"

"No, ma'am. It's just that we've found that young girls and boys from broken homes tend to be—shall we say—a little more flighty."

"She's not a runaway if that's what you're getting at."

"How can you be so sure?" Adams asked.

"First off, she'd never do such a thing. Plus, I found her bicycle!"

"You did?"

"Yes!"

"Where?"

"It was in the outer part of the mall parking lot buried in some shrubs."

"Are you certain it's hers?"

"Positive."

"And you brought it back to your house?"

"I did. It's back in my garage," she confirmed.

"Good, but don't touch it anymore. We'll need to lift fingerprints from it and check for blood evidence."

"Blood evidence? Shit!"

"Try to calm down, Ms. Grant. Do whatever you can to determine anything your daughter might have had on, from her shoes up to anything in her hair. I need your address and your ex-husband's full name and contact information so we can interview him," Adams said and Mickey complied. "Thank you. I'll send my field detective over to take down a full report."

"Great. Another interrogation. Can't y'all do something *now*?"

"Mrs. Grant, if I could snap my fingers and bring your daughter back to you, I would. But I can't, and we'll need a lot of help to investigate this. After you meet with the officer, be sure and give him the exact location where you found the bike. He'll go there and look for more evidence. It'll be easier if you just wait at home, and the detective will be in touch."

"Jesus! I'm just supposed to sit here while God only knows what's happening to my little girl?"

"I empathize, but there's really nothing for you to do. Try to get some family or friends to come over. In the meantime, let us do our job, and I assure you that we get calls every week about missing youngsters, and fortunately, nearly all—"

"Turn out to be nothing. I've heard that all day."

Wanting him to hear it from her, and not the police, Mickey dialed the person she dreaded calling most, and as the phone began to ring, she closed her eyes and focused on her delivery.

"What's up, Mick?" Tyler asked.

"I don't know how best to say this except direct. Reagan's missing."

"Missing? What do you mean?"

"Just that. I was supposed to meet her at twelve thirty at Town East, and she didn't show."

"Town East Mall? She went there alone?"

"Please don't start in on me!"

"I'm sorry, but—"

"Look, Tyler—she was supposed to go with her friend Carol James, and I was to meet them at the food court for lunch, but they never showed."

"Carol James?"

"Yes. She's the girl from the neighborhood. You met her at the cheerleading camp."

"The one with the braces?" he asked.

"Right."

"I see. Have you called the police?"

"I've spoken to them and be prepared for a call from them too. They're working on this, and a detective is supposed to come here soon."

"Mickey, if you were supposed to meet them for lunch, this happened hours ago. What took you so long to call me?"

"I've kinda had my hands full, you know. Besides, until an hour or so ago, I thought she was going to turn up. I spent a couple of hours searching for her and making calls. Then it took me a while to get hold of the James family, and when I did, that's when I found out Carol couldn't go to the mall this morning."

"So Reagan *did* go there alone!"

"Apparently, Tyler, but I swear to God that's not at all what I instructed her to do!"

"And where were you, Mickey? At your office?"

"Goddamn it, Tyler! Don't start this finger-pointing bullshit! I can't take it right now!"

"Sorry, Mick, but I ..."

"I can't blame you for being upset, but I'm so scared and confused."

"I'm sure she's okay, Mick. Perhaps she didn't go to the mall at all."

"She must have. I found her bike in some shrubs on the mall parking lot."

"Oh, God ... Are you sure it's hers?"

"Positive. Same brand and color, and it had the leather band on the handlebars with her name on it."

"Oh, Jesus, this is terrible! Have you tried her cell phone?"

"Yes, several times, but it just goes to voice mail.

Do you want me to come over?" Tyler offered.

"Thanks, but that's not necessary. I'll let you know as soon as I hear something. By the way, do you know what clothes she packed to come over here? The police really need to know what she might have worn today."

"She packed it herself, but she likes to wear that softball T-shirt on weekends."

"I know that shirt, and it's in her bag," she said. "Can you think of anything else?"

Tyler thought for a moment and said, "No. I can't believe we're having to talk about this."

"I know ... I'll let you know what I here."

She hung up and walked to her refrigerator, pulled an uncorked bottle of chardonnay, and poured a full glass. Her first sip told her the wine was stale, but undeterred, she took a gulp. Her doorbell rang, and when she walked to the front window and saw the police van parked in front of her house, she opened her front door and invited the young uniformed officer inside. They took seats in her living room and next few minutes were spent answering questions from a list attached to a clipboard. The inquiries that didn't alarm her irritated her, but she did her best to remain calm and cooperative. She then described Reagan's physical appearance and provided recent school photos. The officer donned plastic gloves, and walked with Mickey out to her garage. There, he collected evidence from Reagan's bike before placing it in his police van. The officer returned to Mickey's living room and said, "I'm done for now. Do you have any questions?"

"Do you believe my daughter's case involves the mall abductor?" Mickey asked directly.

The young man winced, and his reaction delivered the answer, but he cleared his throat and mustered, "You know, it's really hard to say for sure since—"

"Thank you for that, but I can tell you believe it to be true."

"Why do you say that?" he asked defensively.

"Your expression said it all," she explained.

The officer was now embarrassed and said, "We've been ordered not to say what we think if asked and now I've ..."

"Don't worry," she said.

"I guess I have to work on that."

"It only means you have a heart," Mickey consoled. "Just don't take up poker, okay?"

"He nodded and said, "But look, I've done a lot of these missing child interviews, and most of the time, they aren't missing at all."

"So I've been told."

Mickey walked him to her front door and watched as the officer drove away. After updating Tyler, she realized that, for the first time in hours, she had nothing to do. There was no one to call, nothing to search for, and no questions to answer or ask. She had not eaten anything since breakfast, and though not hungry, she felt she should get something in her stomach. She saw nothing truly appealing in the refrigerator but settled on a carton of cottage cheese she had opened two days earlier. She used a spoon to eat a couple of bites and then poured another glass of the chardonnay. She took a drink of the stale wine and another spoonful of cottage cheese. The tastes clashed horribly, so she put the lid back on the cottage cheese and tossed it into the garbage. The wine on her near empty stomach had a mild calming effect. Mickey then sat in an easy chair in the dead-still quiet for the better part of an hour as she drank the balance of the wine. At sundown, she went to her bathroom and took two over-the-counter sleep aids. She stripped down to her underwear, slipped on a calf-length T-shirt, and kicked her pile of clothes to the corner. She switched on the ceiling fan above her bed, turned off her bedroom lights, and slipped between the cool sheets. She stared at the glow that her bathroom night light cast on the whirling fan blades— until the pills and the wine carried her to a restless sleep.

CHAPTER 5

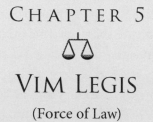

VIM LEGIS

(Force of Law)

Brinkman Police Department
December 21, 9:30 p.m.

That night, Brinkman Chief of Police Randall "Bud" Buchanan assembled a group of officers to prepare for a raid on the home of the suspect in the mall abductions. The team was comprised of personnel ranging from rookie beat officers to veteran detectives, and all were seated around a long conference table in what they referred to as the "war room." The mood was serious but upbeat, considering that they were pursuing their first real lead since the first of the abductions in November. The entire department had felt the public pressure to solve the cases, and each dared to hope that a conclusion was imminent.

As a thirty-year veteran of the force, Buchanan had long since abandoned the standard issue uniform in favor of a solid-black suit, bolo tie, and a vest that bulged under the strain from his sizable belly. He wore freshly shined black dress shoes, a small-brimmed beige Stetson, and a silver badge with a Texas star stood out on his lapel. He had a nearly perfectly round face with dark, serious eyes partially obscured by thin, pale eyelids. In recent years, Buchanan rarely briefed officers or accompanied them on raids, but he had inserted himself into this high-profile investigation from the beginning, and it was no coincidence that the election primaries were just over three months away.

He closed his leather dossier and said, "As your assignment sheet shows, our suspect is William a.k.a. 'Willie' Lee Flynn. Robert Jackson, an eye witness in the Abram girl's abduction, provided the license plate number for an older model, brown van, and we traced the van to the address on your sheet. Jackson's a janitor at the mall and as such was required to park his car on the perimeter of the parking lot during the holidays. He was pulling a five in the morning to two in the afternoon shift and left the Delano mall that morning on his lunch break. He was walking to his car when saw what is believed to be the prelude to the Abram girl's abduction. His full statement is included in your packet, and according to Jackson, the man driving the van appeared to be in his mid-twenties to early thirties and had semi long, bushy, dark hair and a light beard. Y'all also have a sketch as well. Questions?"

One of the rookie officers raised his hand and asked, "If this happened in Delano, why are we acting on this?"

"Cold feet?" Buchanan asked.

Flushing red, the young beat officer said, "No, it's just that—"

"Look—we have a proper warrant, and since Flynn's a Brinkman resident, we're executing on it. Delano PD tried to horn in, but I told 'em politely, 'We got this,'" Buchanan said to the amusement of the other officers, knowing Buchanan was no shrinking violet when it came to publicity. This characteristic had aided in his election to twelve consecutive two year terms as chief, more than half of which were unopposed.

"This Flynn guy's a low life," Buchanan continued. "He has a record and served some time, but for nothing violent. We've had his mother's house under surveillance, and as you see on your maps, the address is 506 Roosevelt in the The Heights. Y'all are familiar with that area … we've all been there. Surveillance has spotted two young men at the residence, and we're positive the taller of the two is Willie Flynn. Don't let the fact that this guy has no history of violent felonies mislead you. He has a long drug history, and you must approach him with the assumption that he's armed. Extreme caution is warranted, and full body armor is required—*even* for detectives."

"What about body armor for you, Chief?" veteran officer Ronnie Phelps asked.

"Never!" Buchanan retorted, patting his belly. "I aim to be on TV tonight, boys, and don't want to add two inches to this fabulous figure. Bottom line is all of this ends tonight, you hear? Though you have authority to use deadly force, let's focus on an arrest. I want this guy taken in alive if at all possible."

A caravan of six police vehicles proceeded to a seedy side of Brinkman, originally called the Upper Heights. This area was once a prestigious area of town, but members of the department now knew it as the "Lower Heights" or just "The Heights," and it had become synonymous with squalor and crime. Most all of the original families had abandoned the area many years earlier, and the succeeding decades of decline had left many dilapidated structures, some uninhabited, and in others, migrant workers, hired seasonally by the local cotton farmers,. As the cars with Buchanan, three detectives, and six uniformed officers converged on the street, they paused a block away to survey the surroundings. From that vantage point, they could see the front of the subject house and the driveway running up the right side of it to a detached garage. The rundown, single-story home had a covered front porch spanning the length of the front elevation. There were windows on all sides, and most were covered by bed sheets or towels tacked up from inside, except those on the west side, which featured a covering of aluminum foil, likely to repel the heat of the west sun in the summer. At the end of the driveway, they could see the rear of an older-model, brown Dodge van matching the description given by Robert Jackson.

Buchanan gave the signal, and each squad car, with all lights off, crept slowly forward, stopping in front of the home and blocking the driveway. Phelps used a flashlight to confirm the match to the license plate number provided by Jackson to that on the brown van. To prevent anyone inside the house from escaping, officers were assigned to cover all four sides of the house, including three officers that were sent to scale the wooden fence running from the detached garage to the back of the house. The rickety, five-foot structure featured rotted and splitting cedar slats. Two of the three officers managed to get over the fence without incident. But as the third got one foot over the top, each heard a cracking sound and a section of the fence collapsed into a pile in the backyard, and all three momentarily froze. Buchanan and other officers in the front heard the crash and moved with pistols drawn up the driveway as one of the officers from the rear of the house leapt over the fence debris and made his way toward the others.

"What the hell was that?" Buchanan whispered.

"That piece-of-shit fence collapsed, Chief. No one's hurt, but it made a hell of a racket."

Buchanan nodded and shooed the officer back to the rear as everyone looked for signs of activity on the inside. After a few moments with no detectable movement, each returned to their positions, preparing to execute the warrant. Buchanan and Adams eased onto the porch, with each step on the wooden slats making a creaking sound that pierced the crisp night air. Trailing behind, was the muscular Phelps, heaving a battering ram. Buchanan peered through the gap in the bed sheet in the front window and got a view into the dimly lit living room. There was an old, heavily stained, orange couch and matching chair and a coffee table in the middle of the room. Several empty soda cans stood on the table, along with a stack of hardbound and paperback books. A bearded young man slouched in the chair, seemingly asleep. A small, black-and-white television was on but showing only snow on the screen.

"Flynn's in there," Buchanan whispered to Adams. "He's asleep on the couch in this front room."

"Is there anyone else in there?"

"Not that I see, but we have to assume that other guy's in there somewhere."

"Then we should split up when we go in, right?" Adams suggested.

"Good point," Buchanan said. "I want to get Flynn myself. So when we go in, you and Jenkins clear the other rooms, and me and Phelps will take Flynn. The others need stay out here and make sure no one gets out of this yard, until Flynn's secured."

"Got it. Did you see any weapons?"

"No, and all the more reason to take him in," Buchanan said. "Radio all to be on standby and when we do go, signal everyone that we're moving." Adams whispered the plan to the others via the microphone clipped to his shoulder and waited on the front porch for Buchanan's signal. The chief peered back through the window and, seeing that the scene remained the same, gave Adams the nod. Adams positioned himself in front of the door and rapped sharply on it and yelled, "Police! Open the door!"

Buchanan watched through the window and saw the man in the chair stir, open his eyes, and sit up. Buchanan motioned to Phelps and Adams moved away from the door and radioed all officers that they were entering. Phelps thrusted the battering ram, and with one surge of it, he forced open the hollow entry door. They rushed into the now unoccupied living room, then ran through the house and into the back bedroom. They found Flynn straddling the windowsill, half-in and half-out. With officers on each side of the window now training their guns on him, Flynn raised his hands and silently surrendered by sliding back inside and onto the bedroom floor. The officers put him face-down, and Phelps put his knee on Flynn's neck until he secured his wrists with handcuffs.

Buchanan motioned Phelps out of the way and knelt on the prisoner's back, asking, "Are you Willie Lee Flynn?"

"You know damn well who I am!"

"Chief, we found this one under a bed," Jenkins said, shoving a thin, sleepy eyed young man, wearing ill-fitting soiled clothes, into the room.

"Are you his brother?" Adams asked, and the visibly frightened boy nodded.

"Let him go! He ain't a part of this!" Flynn demanded.

"Hush your damned mouth," Buchanan barked.

"What do you want to do with him Chief?" Jenkins asked.

"Cuff him and put him in one of the squad cars till we wrap up here. Anyone else in in the house?"

"No, Chief," Jenkins confirmed.

"You know why we're here, don't you?" Buchanan prodded as he returned his attention Flynn.

"If you're looking for the girl, you won't find her here," Flynn said through gritted teeth. Buchanan continued to kneel on Flynn's back while leaning over to view his face, which was contorted by the pressure.

"You're talking about the Abram girl, right, Willie?" Buchanan pressed.

"I didn't know her name!" Flynn said.

"What about the Baines girl, Kristen Hayes, or the Quincy girl?" Buchanan asked.

"I took all of them, right? Is that what you want?"

"Wait a second, Chief!" Phelps interrupted. "He needs to be Mirandized."

"Shit! You do it," Buchanan instructed.

Phelps informed Flynn of his rights, and Buchanan resumed, "What'd you do with 'em, Willie?" Beginning to appreciate his predicament, Flynn decided to heed the right to remain silent and offered no further response. The others present remained inside to get Flynn up and to search him as Adams and Buchanan walked to the front yard, lit only by a yellow porch light.

"Well, kiss my ass. Did they put that filthy-assed brother in my car?" Buchanan carped, pointing to his cruiser.

"Looks that way, Chief. Want me to move him?" Adams offered.

"Hell yeah! I want Flynn's ass in my car, and when that's done, contact those leaches over at the newspaper and the TV stations and tell 'em what we have here. I'd like some cameras at the department when I get back there. Understand?"

"Got it, Chief. Are we going to take the brother down to the station?"

"We've got nothin' on him, but we can't leave him here at a crime scene investigation," Buchanan reasoned. "Take him in and hold him until we're done here and find out what he knows."

"That means holding him for a day or two."

"That's true," Buchanan said, pondering. "Here's the deal, get him downtown and book him on suspicion of something—you know, like conspiracy or aiding and abetting. We should be done here by Monday, and we'll drop the charges and cut him loose."

"That means jailing him."

"So what! Are you his social worker or something?" Buchanan fired back. "Put his ass in a cell for a couple of days. Hell, it can't be any worse there than this rat trap that they live in here."

The next morning, Brinkman detectives, led by Adams, continued their extensive inspection of the Flynn house. Inside they found old newspapers, empty fast-food packages, more aluminum cans, and other debris but no clues. A makeshift front door replaced the shattered original, allowing ingress and egress and the ability to secure the house when necessary.

"I wonder if he robbed a bookstore too," Phelps said, looking at the stack of books beside the living room couch.

Adams picked up the first few off of the top. "Wow. Faulkner, Steinbeck, F. Scott Fitzgerald …"

"Yeah, and here's *The Old Man and the Sea*," Phelps said as he handed Adams the worn, hardback edition.

"Huh, they're from the library," Adams remarked, displaying the slot for the library card with the name and address of the branch on the inside-cover.

"A kidnapper with a library card. Go figure. I guess if the kidnapping charges don't stick, we'll get him on overdue book fines!"

Adams shook his head. "Not so fast. These are all current."

The phone was disconnected, but Adams found an address book next to it and, with his gloved hand, placed it in an evidence bag. The two men walked out on the porch, and Adams noticed three houses down, on the opposite side of the street, a man in his yard feeding chickens.

"Has anyone talked to him?" Adams asked, pointing.

"Uh huh. No one answered when we knocked earlier," Phelps replied.

In addition to the chickens, the man's fenced yard also featured several plywood A-frame brooders and one tethered goat, but it nevertheless represented one of the better maintained properties in the neighborhood. Adams crossed the pothole-laden street toward the house, and the man didn't notice him approaching as Adams reached the chicken-wire fence perimeter.

"Excuse me," Adams said, startling the man, who took two steps back at the sight of Adams and his uniform. "Sorry to bother you, but could I ask you a couple of questions?" The man's frown prompted the detective to add, "There's no trouble with you, sir. I just have a couple of questions about your neighbor over there," Adams said nodding toward Flynn's house. The man was a tall and stocky and had wiry blonde hair, a thick beard, and a large, red face with interspersed white-splotches. His bloodshot eyes accentuated his piercing stare, and he had a chaw of tobacco in his left cheek and wore faded overalls. His shirt was a threadbare button-up, with the cut-off sleeves exposing his large, leathery, tattooed arms. Setting the feed bag on the ground, the man wiped his hands on his pant legs as he walked closer to the fence.

"I'm Detective Garland Adams. And your name, sir?"

"George Merit," the man said as he spat and stared.

"So, George, I guess you've noticed all the hoopla going on across the street."

"I ain't paid no mind to it—ain't none of my affair."

"Do you know the fella who lives over there?"

"Not really. He came around a couple of times, askin' if he could do chores, like mow grass or do handiwork for cash, but that's about it."

"Did you ever hire him for anything?"

"Naw. He didn't have no tools or equipment. Plus, I can do everything myself."

"So you mow your own grass."

"Most of it. She takes care of the rest," he said, pointing to the goat and flashing a grin that revealed his gapped, yellowing teeth.

"Is doing odd jobs how he made a living?"

"I thought he had a real job, seein' how he was gone a lot during the day."

"Anyone else live or visit over there?"

"Until lately, an older woman did. I think she owns the place, but I ain't seen her in a while. Now, there's some younger skinny cat that's over there a lot too," he said as he spat a long, dark stream of tobacco juice that coagulated with the dirt as it hit.

"Did you ever see anything unusual going on over there?"

"Not really. I mean, don't get me wrong, the guy's kinda weird, but I ain't seen nothin' that I could put my finger on."

"Does he drive that van over there?"

The man looked across the street and nodded. "Yeah, it's his, all right."

"Thanks for the info, mister," Adams said, handing the man his business card. "If you think of anything else, you can call me directly, all right?"

Adams started back across the street until the man said, "Hey, wait a minute." Adams stopped and returned to the fence. "There was somethin' a week or two ago. I was up on the roof back there, patchin' a leak around a vent pipe. I stood up to go back down to the ladder, and I seen that dude across the street in that field over yonder." The man pointed toward two side-by-side empty lots directly across from his house and three lots from the Flynn property. Each lot was overrun with high weeds and littered with debris, except for cement slabs, upon which homes once sat. Though the underbrush hindered his sight, Adams could see a dry creek bed that ran parallel to the back property line of each lot. "That's when I seen him over there next to the creek bed chunkin' somethin'. But hell, I've seen people flingin' trash and junk back there for years, so I didn't think nothin' of it."

"Any idea what it was?"

"Naw, except whatever it was wasn't very big, since he chunked it with one hand. I only mention it 'cause that guy kept lookin' around like he was nervous or somethin'." Adams thanked the man again and returned to the Flynn house, where the officers were now scouring Flynn's van. Adams looked through the open, passenger-side door and saw the ashtray overflowing with cigarette butts and trash littering the floorboards.

"Anything of value in here?" Adams asked.

"No, not unless you recycle aluminum," Phelps said. "I've searched dumpsters cleaner than this."

"Say Ronnie, come with me for a minute. I want to check something out." As they walked on to the vacant lots, Adams relayed the neighbor's observations. Then high-stepping through the brush and tall weeds, they worked their way to the creek bed, split up and looked closely for signs of anything that Flynn might have discarded. Present in that area were several abandoned appliances, discarded furniture, scores of beer cans, whiskey and wine bottles, and the bed of one rusted-out Ford pickup truck. On the ground next to an old washing machine, Phelps spotted a shoe. After looking unsuccessfully for its mate, he picked it up with a stick and examined it closely.

"I've got something over here. It's a tennis shoe," Phelps said, holding up the stick.

Adams poked his head up from behind a discarded love seat and said, "Big deal. An old shoe in this field of shit."

"That's the point. It looks pretty new, and it's pink with sequins, so it's a girl's shoe, and there's a couple of dark spots on it too."

"Blood?" Adams asked as he rose to his feet.

"Maybe," Phelps said, placing the shoe in an evidence bag and handing it to Adams.

"Hey, I think you're right. Any sign of its mate?"

"No, I checked," Phelps.

When Adams arrived at the station, Buchanan was pleased with the find and informed Adams that Robert Jackson had driven from Delano to the Brinkman and positively identified Flynn's mug shot from a photo array. In less than forty-eight hours, they had their man behind bars, identified by an eye witness, and they had captured potential physical evidence.

CHAPTER 6

⚖

AGUSTIA ET FIDEM

(Anguish and Faith)

Brinkman Police Department
Christmas Eve

At 10:45 a.m., a Brinkman 911 dispatcher received a call from a man who said he had found a human body while walking a rural roadside. The man spoke with a heavy Spanish accent and was demonstrably anxious and upset. He refused to give his name and the dispatcher transferred the call to Adams.

"I understand you found a body?" Adams asked.

"Si, si. She's layin'—you know—right there in weeds, man!"

"Try to calm down, sir. Let's start from the beginning. What's your name?"

"Can't say, man. Just can't."

"Look. If you have an immigration issue, we won't—"

"It's no that. I have green card, you know. I just can't get into all of this dead-body shit."

"I can't do anything unless I know who I'm—"

"Look, man. I hang up if you—"

"Don't hang up!" Adams urged. "Just take your time and tell me what you saw."

"I park my truck on side of road, and as I—I—I was, you know, I walk by the ditch, I saw—you know ... a leg with ... with ... sock sticking out on the leg."

"Wait, slow down. What were you doing out there, sir?" asked Adams as he scribbled notes.

"Pickin' up cans. I sell cans, for—you know, re–recy–"

"Recycling?" Adams said.

"Si … yes … that's what I do. I saw her there, man—I saw her!"

"So it's definitely a female?"

"Yes."

"Listen, please don't touch anything, and we'll—"

"Oh no, man! I no touch nothin'. You see, I gone from there. I have a pay phone here."

"It's important that I know exactly where you found the body. All right, sir?"

"Okay, I–I–I will tell you," the caller stammered. "I was, you know … I was on—how do you say, fa–fa–farm, you know?"

"Farm to market?" Adams asked.

"Si, si. It was Farm Market two-nine-two-oh. You know where that is?"

"Yes, sir, but where on FM 2920? It's a very long road."

"Yes. She's about two miles oeste. You know oeste?" the caller asked.

"East?"

"Si, si. It was east … east of eight-four."

"Two miles east of highway 84?" Adams confirmed.

"Uh huh … two miles or so. It's by old windmill that don't work! She was there in the weeds, you know, just on the ground by the fence."

"Did you say a windmill?"

"Yes. It's old and no work. Find it, and you find her!"

The man abruptly hung up, and Adams wasted no time summoning Phelps and two other officers. They took two cars and drove directly toward the described location. When they arrived and parked on the shoulder of the highway, they began walking both sides of it. Adams and Phelps were walking on the right side parallel to a barbed-wire fence when they spotted a rusty, old windmill. "I think this is it," Adams said and beckoned the other two officers. All four focused their attention on that portion of the roadside by walking the strip of high grass and weeds between the highway and the fence, while scanning the overgrowth beyond the fence. They searched dutifully until one of the younger officers shouted and pointed. They raced to his side and each could clearly see a body clad in a blood-stained white blouse, with blue jeans and a pink sock on the one foot that was visible. Each officer took turns prying the strands of barbed wire apart until all had crawled through to the other side. The officers then slogged through the brush toward the decomposing corpse.

Though the wind was blowing across the road, through the fence and toward the body, the smell of the decay was still enough that all had to resist gagging by placing an arm or part of a shirt over nose and mouth as they moved closer. Though Adams had seen photographs of all of the missing girls, this body was too swollen, discolored, and muddy to discern the identity. The skin on the face was bluish gray, and there were crusted bloodstains on her face and in her hair. Though the identity could not be discerned from the facial features, the detective knew that the clothing matched the description given by the Abrams and recognized that her shoed foot seemed to have the mate to the shoe already in their evidence room. The wind shifted, delivering the full force of the stench, sending Phelps and another officer into dry heaves. At Adam's direction, an officer eased back through the fence and returned to the patrol car to retrieve a camera and to radio the station to send someone from the coroner's office. Adams snapped photographs before they all returned to the squad cars. The two field officers stayed at the scene to wait for the coroner, and Adams and Phelps drove back to the station.

"That was God awful to see," Phelps said, shaking his head.

"Yes, and such a damn tragedy."

"And that smell! Hell, you've done this for twenty years. Do you ever get used to it?"

"No! And I hope I never do. I think if you ever get used to that, you're lost."

Christmas day arrived, and not wanting to spend the holy day alone, Mickey invited Tyler to her house. He was conflicted and felt awkward by the offer, and his first instinct was to decline. But Christmas without Reagan was going to be challenging enough, and facing it alone seemed more dreadful than any uneasy feelings he harbored. He accepted, and when he arrived that morning, Mickey greeted him with a tight and prolonged hug. They entered her living room, and scenes of colorful floats from a parade filled the television screen.

"Reagan loved these parades, didn't she?" Mickey said.

"She *loves* these parades," Tyler corrected.

"Yes of course," Mickey said.

"Is that in Manhattan?" he asked.

Mickey nodded. "I promised that I would take her there someday."

"She will love that, Mick. I can picture you two now, traipsing around the Big Apple, hitting all of those overpriced stores on Fifth Avenue."

"I'd give anything to …," she started, until she began to cry.

"Now, look—we'll have none of that," Tyler said, patting her thigh. "We need to stay strong and positive, especially on this day."

"I'm sorry," Mickey said, drying her eyes. "Just as I begin to think I've cried my last teardrop, the water works start up again. How are you holding up?"

"Better than I expected. But I pray a lot and try to stay hopeful. I was actually thinking of going to a late Mass, if you're interested," Tyler offered.

"I went this morning, but I'd certainly be willing to go again. I'm really glad you decided to come over. I know this isn't any way we ever envisioned spending a Christmas day, but I just couldn't imagine staying here alone and staring at that tree."

Tyler looked at her and then to her to the Christmas tree and said, "It's a beauty though, and Reagan sure lit up when she saw it. But it looks to be getting a little brown. Do you want me to pour some water in the base?"

"You can if you want, but it's artificial," she said as Tyler blushed.

"Perhaps it's the misery loves company thing, but I'm glad you invited me here," he said.

"I hope you'll find a way to forgive me for all of this," Mickey said somberly.

"Mickey, there's nothing to forgive," he said, reaching to tilt her chin up. "I've had plenty of time to think this all through, and I've concluded that if roles were reversed and Reagan was pestering me to go and said she'd go with a friend, I'd have done the same thing."

"Thank you for that, but you wouldn't have gone to work and put yourself in that spot."

"That's not fair, Mick. I'm self-employed and have the privilege to work at home. You have to work in an office, and you're accountable to others, so you can't compare the two. There's only one person to blame for this, and thankfully he's sitting in jail."

She had no way to gauge Tyler's sincerity, but just hearing the words brought her great consolation. "I appreciate that more than I can say. I don't know if the roles were reversed that I could be so charitable with you."

"Mick, I believe in forgiveness and redemption. We can dwell on this and let it consume us, or we can be forward thinking and hope for a positive outcome. I look forward to Reagan's return, but if it never comes, we need to live our lives in a way that Reagan would want us to, right?"

"Are you running for pope or something?" Mickey joked, and Tyler laughed. "Of course, you're right though. It's just not easy, but it's certainly the healthy thing to do."

Tyler looked toward the kitchen, sniffed twice, and said, "I thought I'd be smelling some nice aromas coming from the kitchen, by now."

"Well, I had an idea about that. Since there's nothing at all conventional about this Christmas, I thought that we would go all-out unconventional and go to a restaurant."

"Dine out? What do you think will be open on Christmas day?" Tyler asked.

"Chinese, of course!"

"Mick, I think that's a grand plan! Do you think Ling's will make Kung pao turkey?"

"Maybe, so you'll do it?"

"Why not!"

"Great. Say, how's your mom taking all of this?"

"Better than I would have imagined. She's heartbroken of course, but has been very positive and has amassed a large prayer group to pray daily for us."

"That's so nice, and she's such a sweetheart. Please send her my best when y'all speak again."

"I will."

"By the way, that gift over there is yours," Mickey said, pointing to a red-and-green package by the tree."

"For me?" he asked.

"Yes."

"But I didn't get you any—"

"It's not from me," she informed as Tyler walked to the tree, stooped, and looked at the flat box. "Go ahead and open it. Reagan picked it out herself."

Tyler brought the box back to the couch, and after tearing away the wrapping paper, he lifted the top off the box and pushed aside the tissue paper. He held up an orange-and-purple striped sweater.

"What do you think?" Mickey asked.

Tyler looked at it, glanced to Mickey and back to the sweater, and asked, "Truthfully?"

"Of course."

"This is one of the ugliest things I've ever seen!"

Mickey laughed. "Isn't that the truth? Reagan selected it out of a catalog, and I ordered it. I tried to gently dissuade her, not wanting to hurt her feelings, you know. But she would have none of it. So merry Christmas!"

"Thank you," he said, pulling the sweater over his head.

"What are you doing?"

"I can't think of anything better to wear to a Chinese restaurant on Christmas day!"

CHAPTER 7

⚖

CORPUS DELICTI

(Body of the Crime)

Brinkman Police Department
December 26

Chief Buchanan placed a call to Taylor County District Attorney, Lyndon Tucker, to discuss the discovery of the body. Though murder cases had been tried successfully without the proverbial corpus delicti, the lack of a body gave the defense an advantage that prosecutors did not welcome.

"What's up, Chief?"

"I didn't expect to catch *you* there the day after Christmas," Buchanan said sarcastically.

"Why'd you call then?"

"Never mind. Listen, did you hear we recovered the Abram girl's body?"

"I heard y'all recovered *a* body. Do y'all really think it's really her?"

"We're sure it is. She had the same clothes as described by the mother and wore the mate to the shoe found near Flynn's house."

"That's good work, but that poor couple. Did you notify 'em?"

"Shit no! I'm known around here as a heartless son-of-a-bitch around here, but even I'm not going to call parents on Christmas Eve and tell 'em their teenage daughter's in the morgue."

"Getting soft in your old age, Bud?"

"Not on your life. So look. Flynn's fingerprints are on the shoe we found by the house, and we sent some of his and the Abram girl's DNA to the lab to compare it to the blood we found on the shoe. We fully expect a match to one or both of them."

"Good. Are y'all going to have the Abrams down to identify the body?" Tucker asked.

"That's why I'm calling. If the DNA matches, do we really need to do that? I mean this body is in gruesome condition, and—"

"Bud, we have to. I hate like hell to say that, but if you don't do it, some defense lawyer will be on that like stink on shit.

"I figured as much," Buchanan said.

"But if they do identify her, I think we have plenty to indict Flynn," Tucker said.

"When can the grand jury hear this one?"

"They're adjourned until uh," Tucker paused, looking at his calendar, "I believe the second week of January, but their docket's light."

"Good. Any chance they'll no-bill?"

"No. So the Abrams aren't aware of the body or the shoe?"

"No. We've kept a lid on it up to now."

"Damn. Their whole world's about to come unwound. Are you going to do it?"

"No way. This is a good job for Adams."

"I really do think you're getting soft."

"You know better than that. Now, since we have to do this anyway, I'm going to have Adams get them in as soon as possible. Do you want to be present?"

"Hell, no! I leave this gory shit to you gum shoes."

Adams phoned the couple and asked them to come down to the department that afternoon. He deftly dodged their questions as to the nature of the visit, but they agreed. When they arrived, officers escorted them into a conference room. The apprehensive couple took seats, side-by-side, in two low-back, rolling leather chairs at the long table, the top of which was clear except for a full box of tissues. Adams sat across from the couple and noted that Bess Abram's heavy makeup could not conceal the dark, puffy bags under her eyes.

"Thank you both for coming down on short notice. How are you two getting along?" Adams asked, prompting Bess to shake her head and sob. "Here you go," Adams said, sliding the box of tissues closer to her.

"Thanks, but I came prepared," Bess said as she pulled a clear plastic packet of tissues from her purse and dabbed her mascara-streaked cheeks. "This is such a strain on us, you know. We're truly glad y'all caught the guy, but we won't rest until we have our Taylor back."

Adams swallowed hard. "I fully understand … I do have some news for y'all, some potentially very bad news." Husband and wife looked at each other and braced themselves. "First, the eyewitness that was there at the mall parking lot in Delano has positively identified Willie Flynn as the guy in the van that Taylor was talking to. Here's the photo he identified," Adams said, sliding a copy of Flynn's mug shot toward them.

Bess looked at it. "Oh my good Lord!"

"Sorry, ma'am, but you're going to be seeing him sooner or later. I figured a picture now would be better than seeing him for the first time in court."

She raised the photo and turned it toward to Ted. "Why, oh why would Taylor deal with this … animal?"

"That's the way Taylor was," Ted said, squeezing her hand. "She was always trying to help people."

"Right, but look at this creep. Lord God, she had to know better," Bess said, sliding the picture back to Adams.

"With this identification, we'll soon be sending this to the grand jury, and we're confident they'll indict Flynn. But I know there's is no antidote for what I'm about to show you," Adams said, placing the clear plastic evidence bag with the pink shoes on the table. Reaching his gloved hand into the bag, he removed each and displayed them, and Bess whimpered. "I'm sorry, Mrs. Abram, but are they hers?"

"They're hers, all right. I bought them for her," she confirmed.

"This shoe here was found near Flynn's house, and his fingerprint and perhaps his blood DNA was on it. The other … we found on a body on the twenty-fourth."

"No!" Bess Abram wailed and placed her face on her folded arms on the table, moaning and trembling. Ted silently rubbed her back as tears trickled from his eyes. Adams waited compassionately for several minutes until Bess composed herself.

"While the shoes go a long way toward linking all of this up, it's important that we get the body identified by one of you."

"I'll do it. Where is she?" Ted asked.

"Thank you, Mr. Abram. The body's at the county morgue, which is close to here. Before we go there, I want to discuss the case a little. If the grand jury does return an indictment, this goes to the DA's office for trial."

"Good. We want this guy punished!" Ted said as Bess nodded and blew her nose.

"That's what I needed to hear. To win, though the DA will have to put on proof on every aspect of the case. The shoes and the Jackson identification help a lot, but we'll need some testimony from you two as well. We need you both to attend the trial and testify with this guy staring right at you. Can you do that?"

"I certainly can," Ted Abram said, turning to his wife.

Bess Abram looked at Ted and then to Adams. "I will do whatever it takes to put him away for good."

"Thank you, ma'am. I know this won't be easy. I also want you to know up front that we're not going to seek to just 'put him away,' as you put it. We'll be working with the prosecution to charge Flynn with capital murder."

"Death penalty?" Ted Abram asked.

"Yes, sir. This case qualifies for it, and our district attorney, Lyndon Tucker, has never lost one. Does that fact change your mind?" The couple shook their heads. "That's good," Adams said, and asked Ted, "Are you ready to go over to there?"

"I don't know about ready, but I'm willing."

"Mrs. Abram, why don't you wait here? We have a lounge around the corner with water, soft drinks, and snacks. Would you mind relaxing in … I mean—"

"Yes, I will wait in the lounge," Bess said, and then she rose, hugged Ted, and whispered, "You know that I would be better able to identify her clothes, so why don't I …"

"No!" Ted said emphatically. "I'm doing this, and recall most of what she had on. If there's some problem, we'll go to plan B." Ted put on his full-length overcoat and followed Adams out of the police station into the cool winter air. They walked three blocks and entered the morgue, and Adams signed in with a desk clerk. He was given a card with a number on it, and he motioned for Ted to follow him. They walked down a short hallway to a large stainless-steel door. Adams looked back to see Mr. Abram removing his overcoat.

"You might want to keep that on, Ted. It's quite chilly in there," Adams advised as he turned the handle on the door and pushed it open. Mr. Abram felt a rush of frigid air and noticed a long wall of numbered stainless-steel vaults, each with handles. Holding a card with a vault number on it, Adams walked slowly along the wall, scanning the vaults for the matching number. He stopped just beyond the midway point and turned to Abram, who stood, hands in his pockets, with faint wisps of his breath emanating from his mouth. "Ready?" Adams asked gently, and Ted nodded and walked toward him, stopping immediately behind the detective.

Adams pulled on the handle, and a metal drawer slowly slid open to reveal a sheet covering what had to be a small body. The fully retracted vault reached chest high to the two men. Ted watched from over the detective's right shoulder as Adams grasped the top edge of the sheet. Adams looked back at Abram, as if to seek his consent, and got the nod. Not wanting to reveal any more of the body than necessary for the identification, Adams eased the top of the sheet up and over in a way that revealed the body's hair. The blonde strands were tangled and matted with clumps of coagulated blood. Adams noticed that Mr. Abram's misted breath increased in strength and frequency, with each puff now passing over his shoulder and traveling several inches before dissipating. Adams removed more of the sheet, revealing the swollen bluish-gray skin of the forehead, and the puffs surged harder. He peeled the sheet away enough to reveal the girl's open eyes. Ted gasped a blast of breath and used his left hand to clutch Adams's arm, and with his right hand he instinctively reached to Taylor's face and closed her eyes, for good. Then he turned away and hung his head.

"Mr. Abram?" Adams said softly.

"It's Taylor."

Upon learning of Reagan's disappearance, Ford Becker had left Mickey a sympathetic message and demanded that she take the first few weeks after Christmas off. This was always a slow time for the firm, and with her work on the motion completed, he saw no need for her to come in. But Mickey grew weary of waiting for news at home and wanted desperately to return to work, for if nothing else a connection to something normal. She arrived at the office early on New Year's Eve knowing that fewer than normal office personnel would be there. While she dreaded the inevitable uncomfortable expressions, and comments of sympathy she was sure to receive, she knew she had to face them at some point. Walking into the reception area, Mickey checked in with Wanda, who nodded and smiled awkwardly. Mickey retrieved her message slips and thought, *one down and a whole hell of a lot to go.*

She walked the short distance down the hallway toward Becker's office and noticed a light shining from beneath the closed door. Though she wanted to avoid most of the others in the firm, that sentiment didn't apply to her mentor and confidant. Tapping softly, she eased the door open and stuck her head in. Becker, who was leaning back in his chair reading the bar journal, lowered it. Seeing Mickey's face, he sprang to his feet and eagerly motioned her inside. "What are you doing here, Mickey? Didn't you get my message?" he chastised as he walked around his desk and hugged her.

"Yes, and thank you for that. But I can't spend my days just sitting around the house any longer. There's only so many silly talk shows and lawyer commercials a person can stand."

"I can appreciate that, but we don't expect you to—."

Mickey smiled and said, "I want to be here."

"We've all been so concerned for you and Tyler. Have you learned anything more about Reagan?"

"Not a word," she responded sadly, turning her head to hide the tears forming.

"How's Tyler holding up?"

"I'm sure he's taking it hard. But, Ford, he's been *very* strong and amazingly supportive."

"It's good to hear that y'all aren't at war over this. What have the police told you about their suspect?"

"Just that he's not talkin', but I'm hopeful that will change."

"Maybe this will all work out, and you'll have Reagan back home soon."

"God, I hope so."

"Are you following the news coverage on this?" he asked.

"Not really. It's so hard on me, and they get so much so wrong that I try to get updates directly from the police."

"You have to maintain hope," Becker encouraged.

"Oh, I still believe, and I'm wearing out my knees praying. But let's be real—even you and Mr. Baylor said that the girls were likely, well ... gone."

"Well that didn't mean—you know, that's just ..."

Mickey appreciated his awkwardness. "Don't worry, I don't know what words to say most of the time either. I just pray all of the girls will be found safe and sound and home soon."

"Except for that poor Abram girl of course."

"What about her?" Mickey asked with alarm.

"You haven't heard, have you?" She shook her head. "Hell, you're going to find out anyway ... Mickey, they found the body of that Abram girl."

"Dead?"

"I'm afraid so."

"Oh no! When?"

"Christmas Eve, but it just broke in the news late yesterday." Mickey began to cry, her shoulders slumped and her whole body trembled. "I'm sorry, Mickey."

"Don't be. I needed to know. God, I hope that creep gets what he deserves."

"I'm sure he will. That same article indicated that the case against him is very strong."

"That's good. I heard they're going to arraign him on Tuesday," she said, drying her eyes. "I want to attend, but what exactly will they do?"

"It's pretty routine. He'll just appear and plead not guilty and—"

"Not guilty? Ford, the police say he essentially confessed to doing these things!"

"Well, that was before he had counsel. Undoubtedly, his lawyer will advise him to plead not guilty and will vigorously attack any confession at trial," Becker explained.

"I hate lawyers," Mickey said, and they both chuckled.

"This part's not completely on the lawyers. A capital murder defendant is not allowed to plead guilty unless the death penalty is off the table, and that ain't gonna happen."

"The judge will set a real high bail, right?"

"No, since it is a capital case, Flynn wouldn't be entitled to bail."

"Thank God for that."

CHAPTER 8

PACIS ET JUSTITIAE

(Peace and Justice)

Mickey awoke Tuesday morning, anxious about witnessing Flynn's first court appearance, but thankful that Tyler would attend with her. As they drove, each shared their apprehension with an awkward silence, and the tension grew when they neared the old district courthouse. She found it ironic that the same building where she had wielded her skills like a sword would now bring such visceral angst. She empathized with Tyler, who had no experience there beyond two tours of jury duty. As they arrived, the courthouse square was bustling, and the normally plentiful, angled parking spaces around the courthouse were occupied. Among the many vehicles present were television satellite trucks from as far away as Dallas and Oklahoma City. Tyler found a parking space a block and a half away, and they walked arm in arm down the sidewalk. With the sun out and no ground-level wind amongst the multistory buildings, the cold morning walk proved tolerable.

"Do you know what court to go to?" he asked.

"Yeah. It's in the criminal district court on the third floor."

"Are you familiar with the judge?" Tyler asked as they neared the entrance.

"I've never appeared in front of him, but I know his reputation. According to Mr. Baylor, he can be real strict."

"Strict—I like that," Tyler said.

Mickey guided Tyler through security and up an elevator to the third floor. As they entered the courtroom, Tyler was struck by its majesty. The judge's bench was elevated and faced with rich, hand-crafted, stained-oak carvings. Square bronze panels adorned the high ceiling, each stamped with the same design. From the ceiling hung large, tarnished, brass chandeliers extending downward several feet, each having no less than a dozen, tulip-shaped, opaque glass shrouds with small bulbs, which collectively managed only enough light to cast a dreary atmosphere on the gathering crowd. A heavy wooden banister with a swinging gate spanned the middle of the courtroom, marking the line of demarcation, known as "the bar," that separated the litigants and court personnel from the gallery of onlookers and the media. The floor was made of square vinyl tiles and, except where worn away in the higher-traffic areas, they were alternating colors of black with white speckles and white with black speckles.

An empty balcony extended from the rear of the courtroom and reminded Tyler of scenes from old black-and-white courtroom movies. This balcony was accessible only from the fourth floor, and on this day and on most all other days, its doors were locked. Ten-foot-tall, heavy, wooden double doors, with clear glass panels at the top of each, guarded the entrance to the courtroom from both floors. The doors leading to the judge's chambers, the jury room door, and the one to a hall leading to the prisoner holding cells were equal in height but narrower and had no windows. The main-floor gallery featured twelve rows of long, pew-like wooden benches, each bolted to the floor. Two aisles divided the rows, creating three sections. Facing forward from the vantage point of the gallery, the right side of the courtroom had four large windows protected by old blinds with wide, thick, darkly stained, wooden slats, and below them sat the jury box. The courthouse's antiquated heat and air system offered ineffective circulation and humidity control, and when coupled with the crowded room, it rendered the ambient air warm, and as thick as the mounting tension.

The presiding judge was Thomas Sullivan, and he had occupied this bench for more than two decades. Members of the bar regarded him as stern but fair. Some saw Sullivan as a pro-prosecution "hangin' judge," but when the local bar association polled lawyers annually to rate the local judiciary, Sullivan consistently ranked nearly as well with defense attorneys as prosecutors. One personality trait all lawyers agreed on was that he had little patience for nonsense and demanded decorum in his courtroom.

"I think that's Detective Adams," Mickey said, pointing to a uniformed officer talking with an older woman at the back of the room. "I recognize him from the news."

"Yeah, I've seen him as well."

Mickey pulled Tyler along toward the two. "Excuse me, detective" Mickey said, as the officer turned to her. "I'm Michelle Grant, one of the victim's—"

"Yes, of course. I'm glad to meet you, but sorry it's under these circumstances," Adams said.

"Me too. I'm sorry I was so abrupt on the phone the other day."

"You had a right to be," Adams said. "And you must be Mr. Grant?"

"Yes, we spoke that day too," Tyler said shaking his hand. "Any news on the girls?"

"I'm sorry, but other than the tragic developments on the Abram case, there's been nothing."

"Flynn's still refusing to talk?" Tyler asked.

"I'm afraid so."

"Thanks for all the work on this," Mickey said as she noticed the woman next to him wiping tears. She was short, with gray hair pulled up to a bun on top of her head. She had a full face, with pale skin and soft lines around her forehead, cheeks, and mouth. Her light blue eyes stood out, and her expression gushed sincerity. "This here's Evelyn Howard."

"It's nice to meet you," Mrs. Howard said. "I'm so sorry about your Reagan."

"Oh, you know about our daughter?" Tyler asked.

"She knows about 'em all," Adams said. "You see, she heads up a local crime victims' support group for cases just like this. She's done it for years, but this one's really keeping her hopping."

"Oh, I thought your name sounded familiar. This is a great thing you do," Tyler said, and she smiled.

"Mrs. Howard, your group's involved in these cases too?" Mickey asked.

"Oh, yes. While I have no loved one involved like you do, several people now attending our meetings are parents of missing girls."

"I think that's great. Don't you, Tyler?" Mickey said.

"Absolutely."

"It's been fulfilling working with these families over the years. If there's anything we can do for you two, just say the word," she said offering Mickey a card with her name and phone number.

Adams interjected, "Not only does she run the group's meetings, but she's also a great source for information. She keeps in touch with us and distributes the information to the members. It streamlines things for the department and gets information out to the families that they might not get as timely or as accurately from the news. Now, if you'll excuse me, I need to speak with the prosecutors," Adams said, walking through the gate of the bar.

"So you're like a conduit for information from the police to the group, huh?" Tyler asked.

"Yes, and unfortunately that includes bad news, like the details on our little Taylor."

"Do you know the Abrams?" Tyler asked.

"Oh, yes, I've known Bess Abram for many years from the PTA. We're both retired teachers, you see. They joined the group as soon as all this began with Taylor."

"You knew Taylor too?" Mickey asked.

"Oh yes. Sweet, sweet little Taylor. I was very fond of her and with both her grandmothers being deceased, she referred to me as her Nana," Mrs. Howard lamented, removing her glasses again, dabbing her eyes with a tissue.

"I'm so sorry. I'm sure this is very hard on them and they're fortunate to have you and the group," Mickey said retrieving a business card of her own from her purse and handed it to Mrs. Howard. "Please take this, it has my contact information."

"Thanks, Michelle. I'm sure we'll talk soon."

"All rise!" the bailiff's voice suddenly echoed throughout the courtroom, silencing all conversation and urging those standing toward their seats. The door to the judge's chambers opened, and the court clerk entered, followed by Judge Sullivan.

"Please be seated," the judge said as he reached the bench. Sullivan was a distinguished-looking man on his seventies, with a head of thinning, silver hair, a ruddy complexion, and a stern-serious face, which included a prominent chiseled lantern jaw. He had large, elongated ears and a bulbous, reddened nose, which might be associated with a longtime, unsuccessful prize fighter or a chronic drinker. The judge opened his file while the prosecution team was busy arranging materials at their table. At the adjacent table a man sat, still and quiet, except for the tapping of a pencil on the thin manila folder on the table in front of him. It was Chester Hill, and all would soon learn that he was Flynn's court-appointed lawyer. Hill had dishwater-brown hair and moustache, was of medium build, and was dressed this day in a light brown, western-cut jacket, dark brown slacks, and brown cowboy boots.

"Where's Flynn?" Tyler whispered to Mickey.

"I don't know. Maybe he doesn't have to be at this part."

The judge signaled Carl Johnson, his bailiff, who walked to a door on the left of the room, leading to the hall with prisoner holding cells. When Johnson unlocked and opened the door, those in the gallery with the proper angle could see the three cells down the dim narrow hallway. The defendant emerged from the first of three small cells, and followed the bailiff into the courtroom. Flynn was dressed in orange coveralls and a pair of county-issued rubber sandals. His feet and hands were shackled, and each connected to a chain around his waist. Flynn entered slowly, struggling with the leg irons, and had a noticeable limp. Flynn's beard was gone, but his hair was bushy, unkempt, and matted in spots. Flynn glanced around the courtroom, seemingly intrigued by the number of people present, then took a seat beside his counsel, who commenced whispering to him. When Flynn turned his head to respond to Hill, Mickey noticed bruises and swelling on that side of Flynn's face. The exchange, though not audible to those in the gallery, appeared to grow contentious until Judge Sullivan said, "Let's get started gentlemen."

Hill rose to his feet, and tried to pull his client up by his arm. Flynn rose, but did so slowly and awkwardly, and when he stood erect, he winced in pain. Sullivan nodded toward Maggie Carter, his court reporter, and said, "All right, we're on the record in case number

TX-150374, *State of Texas versus William Lee Flynn*. Are the parties ready to proceed with the arraignment?"

"Yes, Judge," Chester Hill said.

"The state's ready," Lyndon Tucker added.

"Mr. Flynn, you know that this court has appointed Mr. Hill here as your lawyer, correct?" Sullivan asked Flynn, who simply nodded. "Listen, when I ask you a question, you'll need to answer me aloud. The court reporter can't take down a nod. Do you understand?"

"Yes. And I also understand that he's my lawyer."

"Good," Sullivan responded. "Now the—"

"But I don't need him!" Flynn spoke over the judge, and his attorney's expression showed exasperation.

"What'd you say?" the judge asked, leaning forward.

"He's not necessary, you're not necessary, and neither is a trial," Flynn stated defiantly.

"Considering the crime you're charged with, by law you don't have a choice but to be represented by counsel. Now, unless you have some objection to Mr. Hill's representation, we're going to move forward with this arraignment. Understand?" Flynn stood erect but did not respond. "Do you understand?" Sullivan repeated loudly as his face flushed redder.

The bailiff moved toward Flynn, prompting him to say, "I understand."

"Do you know what we're here for today?" Sullivan continued.

Hill, intervened, saying, "He knows, Your Honor. I've spoken with him and he—"

"Chester, you know good and well I'm asking your client and not you!" Sullivan snapped. "Mr. Flynn, you're here to enter a plea, got it?"

"Yes."

"Are you ready to proceed?"

"I can hardly wait," Flynn retorted mockingly. The judge shook his head in disgust as Hill again whispered to Flynn.

Sullivan opened the indictment and recited, "William Flynn, you've been indicted by a duly seated grand jury, and the state of Texas has charged you with the crime of capital murder, alleging you willfully and intentionally kidnapped Taylor Lynn Abram, a minor child, and, then and there, willfully and intentionally inflicted serious bodily injury to her, resulting in her death, against the peace and dignity of this state. Now, how do you plead, Mr. Flynn?"

"I wouldn't be here if I didn't do it, right?" Flynn sneered. Hill grabbed Flynn by the arm, and they both paused and looked up at the judge, who had now expended all patience.

"I'm going to ask you once more. How do you plead?"

"I plead that I be placed in isolation so that I don't continue to look like this," Flynn said, turning his head to reveal his swollen and bruised face. The judge signaled Bailiff Johnson, who responded by standing within arm's length of Flynn.

"Mr. Flynn, the only purpose of this hearing is for you to enter a plea of guilty or not guilty. And if you don't give one, I'll enter one for you."

"I certainly hope you choose the right one," Flynn said, drawing gasps from many in the gallery.

"That's it! I enter a plea of not guilty on your behalf," Sullivan said, shaking his head. "Since you're charged with capital murder, you're not entitled to a bond. As such, you'll be remanded to the county jail, where you will remain until the conclusion of this case."

"Thanks, Judge," Hill said.

"Anything from the prosecution?" Sullivan asked.

Tucker rose. "No, Your Honor."

"Good. Now, get him out of here, Carl," Sullivan said.

"Hey, what about this, Judge?" Flynn yelled as he attempted to point toward his bruised face. Johnson took control and led him out of the courtroom and back toward the holding cells.

"May I approach, Your Honor? I have a matter to discuss," Hill asked.

"Does it involve this case?" Sullivan asked.

"I'm afraid so, Judge."

"Okay. Y'all come up," the judge said, motioning to Hill and Tucker to the bench.

"Judge, as Mr. Flynn mentioned, he would request a cell to himself," Hill explained. "As you can see, he's already been the subject of some violence in the general population. For his own safety, he needs to be isolated."

"Well Chester, perhaps we should just put him in a suite over at the Hilton," the judge responded sarcastically as Tucker chuckled under his breath.

"Judge, I apologize for his behavior. He's one screwed-up dude, but he really does need isolation pending trial. If this keeps up, I'm afraid that—"

"Look, Chester—I'm not trying to take this out on you. I know you didn't want this case, so I appreciate you taking it, I really do. But it's not my job to order isolation. The county will decide what's suitable for him, not me."

As Sullivan closed his file and rose, the bailiff bellowed, "All rise!" And the judge disappeared into his chambers.

Mickey was outraged by Flynn's defiant display, but she was likewise taken aback at the notion that Flynn's case seemed to be based solely on Taylor Abram's murder. She asked Tyler to wait, as she rose and walked through the bar and over to one of the assistant district attorneys. "Excuse me, sir," she said to an assistant DA, who glanced up from packing his briefcase. "I want to know why Flynn's being charged with only this case."

"Excuse me?"

"The trial. Why is it only about Taylor Abram? What about the other victims?"

"Can I ask what difference this makes to you?" the prosecutor asked.

Taken aback by the tone and tenor of the question she shot back, "My daughter's one of the missing girls, if you must know"

He stopped his packing. "I'm sorry for your loss, ma'am … I didn't know. As it stands now, we don't have enough evidence to go to the grand jury with the others, but don't you worry, ma'am. You can only execute a man one time, and we fully intend to do just that for *all* of y'all."

That Friday, Chester Hill arranged for a conference with Flynn and arrived at the jail that morning in the pouring rain. As he trotted toward the entrance, his umbrella offered little protection from the cold, wind-driven drops. Once under the awning above the entrance to the jail, the bedraggled counselor attempted to wipe the water from his clothes with a handkerchief but finally gave up. He wadded the handkerchief and returned it to the pocket of his overcoat.

"Good morning, Chester," said a grinning Sergeant Patrick McKinley as Hill entered.

"Good morning, my ass. You should see it out there!"

"Looks like you really got it."

"That's solid police work, Mac."

McKinley belly-laughed. "So where to today, Chester?"

"I'm going all the way to the penthouse," Hill replied, referring to the top floor of the five-story jail, which was reserved for more violent inmates.

"Wow, you must have a dangerous one."

"Ever heard of the presumption of innocence?"

"We let you lawyers worry about that stuff. Plus, ain't you heard from the papers, we shoot first and ask questions later here?"

"I bet you don't get many answers that way."

"So what did this one do—allegedly?" McKinley asked.

"Haven't *you* read the papers?"

McKinley raised his eyebrows. "Oh yeah! So you got the kid-killer huh?"

"How about using *accused*, Mac?"

"Oh hell, Chester. Save that for the jurors and reporters. So how'd you draw the black bean to get this one?"

"Just lucky, I guess."

"All right. You know the drill, Chester," McKinley said.

Hill signed the visitor's sheet and handed over his driver's license and a state bar card that through years of use barely displayed his name and bar number. Though Hill had been visiting the jail for decades, McKinley perused the credentials as if Hill was a first-timer.

"Everything in order?" Hill asked facetiously.

"Sure, Chester. Millard will take you up," McKinley said, pointing to the deputy.

"I don't recognize him. Is he new?" Hill whispered.

"Very. So did your client do it?"

"You ask me that every time, and I give the same answer. No!"

Hill followed the young deputy to the elevator, and on the way up, Hill asked, "So Millard, you're new here, huh?"

"No."

"Oh?"

"I'll have been here a full month next Thursday," Millard responded as Hill just stared at him in silence.

When the elevator doors opened, Millard took Hill to the visitation area. Adjacent to this space was a small room surrounded by bulletproof glass where guards could monitor the visitor's area and all four cell blocks as well as the adjacent inmate recreation room. Friends and family members met with inmates in a more public common area, but due to the law's protection of attorney-client conversations, lawyers met their clients in a more private area. Counsel for the accused were assigned one of four small meeting rooms, each with a metal table and two metal chairs. Protocol allowed guards to monitor the meetings, but only from behind a Plexiglas window, and were not allowed to listen in on the actual conversations.

After speaking with the other officers, Millard signaled for Hill to go to room number three. Another deputy emerged from the monitoring center and unlocked the door, and Hill entered and took a seat on one of the metal chairs. He opened his thin manila file folder, which contained the charging documents and other information provided by prosecutors, along with two newspaper clippings covering the case. Hill heard the sound of the inmate door being unlocked and watched as Flynn shambled in. Dressed and shackled as he had been in court, Flynn now sported a scab from a cut on his cheek and a scraped and bruised forehead. He winced in pain as he eased onto his chair and shifted gingerly, trying to sit in a way that hurt the least. Millard chained Flynn to the bolted-down table leg and took up vigil on the guards' side of the glass.

"What happened to you Willie?" Hill asked.

"What do you think?"

"The other inmates again?" Flynn nodded. "How many?"

"Seven total, but three don't fight."

"You couldn't whup the other four?" Hill asked, trying for humor.

"This ain't no joke, man! These guys are gonna to kill me in here."

"Sorry, Willie. What's their beef?"

"They really haven't consulted with me on that."

"Is it that they know about what you're charged with?" Hill asked.

"No, at least I don't think so."

"You're bleeding," Hill said, seeing a trickle emerging from one of the scrapes at his hairline, and pitched Flynn his rain-soaked handkerchief from his overcoat.

Flynn spread out the wadded handkerchief, saw the embroidered C.H., and said, "This has got your initials on it."

"Don't worry about it. I got a drawer full of 'em."

Flynn struggled with the shackles and lowered his head in order to raise it to his forehead but lacked the slack to get the cloth to the wound.

Hill stood and said, "Here, let me have it back." Careful not let his client's blood contact anything but his handkerchief, Hill dabbed Flynn's cut and then applied pressure to it. His motion caught Millard's attention, and he emerged from behind the glass.

"What do you have there?"

"Sorry. It's just my handkerchief," Hill said, continuing to ply it to Flynn's wound.

"Open it up," Millard demanded.

Hill opened it and held it carefully by the corners, showing him both sides. "See? No file!"

"Fine. But he can't take it back to his cell," Millard said.

"What? You mean he can't keep a rain-soaked handkerchief, bloody from injuries caused in a cell that your colleagues are supposed to be guarding?" Hill fired back, drawing a smile and a nod from Flynn. Millard smirked and returned to his space. Hill kept the pressure for a couple of minutes and then checked it, assuring that the flow had stopped. He then fished a used sandwich bag from his coat pocket and carefully placed the handkerchief in it. He sealed it and tossed it in the metal garbage can in the corner.

"Willie, let's get a couple of things straight up front. Like it or not, it's my job to defend you. As I told you at the courthouse, I can't do it if you confess things to me. Understand?"

"Yes."

"I really don't give a damn what you've done or how you did it. It doesn't affect what I have to do in the courtroom, so just don't volunteer any information on that subject."

"Fine," Flynn said.

"I'm sorry about this abuse. I'll keep working on the isolation thing."

"You gotta do something, man."

"Look, Willie—this is complicated. Your case is in the public eye, and we have elected officials in charge that can't be seen as going soft on you."

"Is keeping me from being killed in here considered going soft?"

"I see what's happening and wanna to help, but I'm just your lawyer and not your guardian angel."

"Did you ask the judge?

"Yeah, but you didn't help the cause."

"I know, but what did he say?"

"Honestly, I thought he was going to hold me in contempt for even asking."

"Shit!" Flynn said, hanging his head as Hill opened his folder.

"Just so you know, the judge said it wasn't his job to order isolation."

"Is that true?' Flynn asked.

"Technically, but he could influence it if he had a mind to," Hill informed. "But Willie, things like this just can't happen," Hill scolded, holding up a newspaper article with the headline *Murder Suspect Jousts with Judge*

"I know, I was just real frustrated and in pain."

"I understand, but none of your interests will be served by pissing off Sullivan. You really need to behave every minute you're in that courtroom."

"This is really a big deal for you, ain't it?" Flynn said.

"What do you mean?"

"You know, with the news stories and publicity and all."

Hill laughed. "Most of the good citizens of the community already hate my ass just for defending you, and if somehow I am able to win the case, I might never get to work in this county again."

"You volunteered for it, didn't you?"

"No. Judge Sullivan called me himself and asked me to take it."

"Why'd he call you?"

"He knew no one local would want it, and he didn't want to go outside of Taylor County to find a taker. So he figured if he asked me to do it as a personal favor, I would."

"Well, with a big case like this, the money must be good."

"I don't think you know how this works. Once I put in the number of hours necessary to prepare and try this case, I doubt the pay will add up to minimum wage."

"I'll make this one easy for you, Counselor. I don't want to win. I don't care what you have to do, but I want you to lose and lose big, if you know what I mean."

Hill glanced to the guards and back to Flynn. "I don't get you. Are you saying you want to be found guilty?"

"That's exactly what I'm saying."

"Look—this DA won't negotiate this down to a lesser charge."

"I'm not lookin' for a plea deal. In fact, I'm willing to plead guilty as charged."

"Willie, you won't be allowed to plead guilty to capital murder either. It's against the rules."

"You're kidding, right?"

"No. Don't ask me why, but it's in the penal code," Hill advised.

"Then why did I have to do that thing in court?"

"It's a constitutional formality, that's all."

"Fine. Then let 'em win."

"The state of Texas is trying to execute you. Don't you understand that?"

"You're the one that don't understand!" Flynn interrupted, leaning forward in his chair and pointing the index finger of his shackled right hand. "I can't spend any more time in jail and ending up like this. I've been down this road, you see, and I just *can't* do it!"

"Keep it down," Hill urged and glancing to the guards. "Now, come on, Willie. What's this all about? An insanity plea?"

"No! You see what's already happened to me in just a few days in here. Just think what my life will be like in state pen for years on end," Flynn urged. "Don't you see? I'm a dead man either way. It's either death by state or death by inmate, and I pick the state."

"I can't believe my ears. If you're sentenced to death, you'll be confined for years too."

"Yes but in isolation!"

Knowing his client was right, Hill leaned back in his chair and said, "You've really thought this through, haven't you?"

"Yes."

"You know, Willie, they've made a lot of changes in the penal system since you were last incarcerated," Hill said.

"Don't bullshit me, man. I know a lot of people who've come in and out of the joint, and it ain't no different. The papers and politicians may say it's changed, but it ain't so. Oh, you can update the prisons and create more rules and laws, but you can't change the people in 'em! And you know well that guys charged with this type a crime don't fare well in the pen."

"Willie, don't you think that the prejudice against child-related crimes is a thing pf the past?"

"Even you don't believe that, and that's why you asked if those animals in my cell knew about my charges."

"There's an old saying, 'That which seeks to kill you only serves to make you stronger.'"

"Counsel, I doubt Nietzsche was ever in a state penitentiary, and plus I think he went nuts in the end."

"So you're familiar with Nietzsche?"

"Yeah. I've read some of that philosophy stuff. Some of it's interesting, but one thing I've learned about it is that it don't mean shit behind bars."

"So you like to read, huh?" Hill asked.

"Yes, and I'd love to have a couple of books in here."

"I'm an avid reader, and have a good library at home. I'll see what they'll let me bring you."

"I appreciate that, but don't do it until I get isolation. Those animals in my cell will destroy them."

"Okay, Willie. Now back to the trial. What if we can win it?"

"They'll just tag me for one of the other cases, and I'll be back here in this hellhole, fending for my life each day."

"Why not try to win and see what happens from there?"

"No offense Counselor, but I'm not pinning my hopes on a court-appointed lawyer who's representing me at minimum wage, as a favor for a judge that hates me. The best I figure you can do is get me hit with manslaughter or something like that, and that means nothing to me other than a long, miserable, dangerous general confinement."

Try as he might, Hill couldn't muster a good counterargument. "I hear you, Willie. Let's just see how things go. I'll keep working on the isolated cell thing, and you focus on behaving in court." Hill removed a business card from his jacket pocket and, after showing both sides to Millard through the glass, he handed it to Flynn. "You'll be given access to a phone if you request it. Call my office if you need anything."

"Okay, but can I make other calls here?"

"Non-lawyer calls are a little more—let's say—discretionary, but you can try." Hill said as he motioned to Millard and picked up his file.

"Can I have another card and borrow your pen?" Flynn asked. Hill complied and showed each to Millard before handing it over. Flynn scribbled on the back of the card and gave it and the pen back to Hill, who flipped it over to see that Flynn had written a phone number and a request: *Call my mother and tell her I'm doing okay* As Flynn shuffled out of the room, he cast one last look back at Hill, who held up the card and nodded.

As the days passed, Mickey found herself no closer to knowing Regan's fate as she did the day she disappeared. Mounting frustration urged her to reach out to Evelyn Howard's support group. The notion of joining a victims' support group was antithetical to her independent nature, but she was drawn to Mrs. Howard's kindness and her unique access to the police department. After finishing a sandwich and cup of fruit at her desk for lunch, she retrieved Mrs. Howard's phone number from her purse and dialed.

"Good afternoon, Mrs. Howard. This is Michelle Grant. We met at—"

"Oh yes. I've actually been meaning to call you about our upcoming meeting."

"Well that's good since I'm interested in attending."

"That's wonderful, dear. We would be thrilled to have you."

"That's very kind of you, but I was curious about what I have to do to join."

"We're an open group, and you're welcome to come to any of our meetings."

"No membership application or nomination and vote or—"

"None of that and no secret handshake either," Mrs. Howard said, to Mickey's amusement. "You and your husband need only to show up."

"Tyler, my *ex*-husband, seems to be handling things his own way, so I don't know if he'll care to participate or not. But either way, I'd like to come to the next meeting."

"I'm sorry. I didn't know you and Tyler are divorced. But you're welcome with or without him, dear."

"No need to apologize, Mrs. Howard. Even I sometimes forget that we aren't married."

"Is there any news on your Reagan?"

"No, not a word. I was kind of hoping you had an update."

"I'm sorry, Michelle. I continue to ask Detective Adams, and he just says that they're working on the other cases."

"I see. So where do we go from here?"

"I have your card with your contact information, and will add you to our distribution list and will send you some details right away. Just so you know, we're meeting at the Browns' house a week from Friday, and we would love to have you there. I'll include their address and directions in the packet of information I'm sending you."

"Thanks," Mickey said. "Say, if you don't mind me asking, I was curious as to how you came to create the support group."

"As you might expect, it was borne out of tragedy. Our granddaughter and her girlfriend were killed by a drunk driver six years ago. Another boy in their car was partially paralyzed."

"Oh no, that's terrible!"

"Yes indeed. And when it happened, we felt the need to do something. So, in the aftermath, my daughter I started this group to help ourselves and the parents of those other kids. Our initial purpose was simply to assure that the man that caused all of this paid a heavy price. We united and made it well known to the prosecution that a light sentence wasn't going to cut it."

"So the drunk survived the crash?" Mickey asked.

"Walked away without a scratch."

"Isn't that always the case?"

"It seems so. But we kept meeting, and soon others got involved, each with their own circumstances, and the group was formed. My daughter and son-in-law eventually moved off to Kansas, but I decided to keep it going, and we've grown from there."

"I'm so sorry for your loss," Mickey said. "What was her name?"

"Helen. And she was a lovely, smart, and charming sixteen-year-old, and my husband and I were very close to her."

"What'd you do to get over it?"

"Oh, dear, you never get over it. All you can do is cope with it and live with it and try to make something good come from it."

"Well, you've certainly done that. Does your husband participate in the group?"

"Harry's very supportive, and he helps a lot, but he finds it too painful to actually participate in the meetings. Some people take great relief sharing such things, and others don't."

"I don't know if Tyler is a Harry or not, but one way or another, I'll be at the next meeting, and I look forward to seeing you there."

Mickey ending the call with a positive feeling, and wasted no time in phoning Tyler, and to her delight, he agreed to attend. He took encouragement from her decision and wanted to foster it.

When the day of the meeting arrived, Mickey left the office early and waited anxiously at her front door. Tyler reached her driveway ahead of time, and once in his passenger seat, Mickey kissed him lightly on the cheek.

"I appreciate you doing this," she said as they drove out of her neighborhood.

"No problem. I'm proud you reached out to them."

"Proud or surprised?"

"Yes," he responded, smiling.

"I'm a little surprised too, to tell you the truth, but I sense from Mrs. Howard that this is a good group of compassionate folks with a common cause."

"Mrs. Howard sure seems like a nice lady."

"Oh, Tyler, she's a gem. You know, this all started when a drunk driver killed her granddaughter and another girl in a car wreck."

"Goodness. I can't think of anything worse than that."

"You say that, but in a sense I think we've got it worse," Mickey replied.

"How do you figure?"

"At least she knows where her granddaughter is and what happened to her. They got a viewing, a service, a burial and ..."

"Closure?" Tyler finished.

"Yes. I used to recoil at the use of that term, but I see what people mean by it now. I think it's what we don't know that haunts me more than what we do know."

They arrived at the Browns' home with a growing sense of apprehension, and walked silently hand in hand toward the front door. Anticipating Mickey's arrival, Mrs. Howard had kept a watch out of the Brown's bay window while other members mingled. She knew that first time attendees typically found the initial meeting an intimidating experience and wanted to make theirs as comfortable as she could. Seeing the couple ambling up the sidewalk, she opened the front door just as Tyler was reaching for the doorbell.

"You scared me!" Mickey said, grabbing Tyler's arm.

"I'm sorry, dear," Mrs. Howard said. "I saw you coming up the walk and wanted to welcome you."

"That was very kind," Mickey said.

"And I'm glad you're here too," she told Tyler and shook his hand.

"My pleasure, ma'am."

Once inside, they took note of the elegantly decorated, two-story brick home. Rugs, antiques, and artwork lent character to the Browns' home, and the sunken living area was tailor-made for entertaining, with three sofas and several small accent tables, each bearing trays of hors d'oeuvres and finger sandwiches.

"Good evening, folks. I want to introduce to you Mr. and Mrs.—I mean—" Mrs. Howard stammered, sensing her miscue

Mickey stepped in. "I'm Michelle Grant, and this is my ex-husband, Tyler."

"Their little girl, Reagan, is feared to be a victim of Willie Flynn," Mrs. Howard informed, eliciting a collective murmur and sympathetic expressions. "Since I see at least three other families here that share that unfortunate circumstance, I know that you all will want to talk at some point. So why don't you welcome them as we continue the social portion of our meeting. We'll convene shortly, but before I forget, we owe special thanks to the Browns for inviting us to their lovely home and preparing such delicious food."

Mickey and Tyler accepted condolences and welcoming comments from several members, each with their own history of misfortune. Mrs. Brown, playing the hostess role, circulated with a tray of glasses of champagne. Mickey eagerly took two, handing one to Tyler, completing hers in two gulps and grabbed a second on Mrs. Brown's next pass. They spoke to two of the couples with missing daughters, and Mickey immediately felt a common bond.

"Welcome to both of you," came a voice from behind them, and they turned to see a tall man. "I'm Ted Abram, and this is my wife, Bess."

Mickey shook hands with the couple. "You're the parents of …"

"Yes," Mr. Abram said, dropping his head slightly.

Sensing Tyler had not made the connection, Mickey informed, "These are the parents of Taylor Abram."

"Oh, I see. We're terribly sorry."

"We're sorry for *your* situation too. We just hope you have a more … well—favorable outcome," Bess Abram said. "We're glad you came though. This is a good group, and we've drawn great strength from the support of these folks," Bess continued, as Mickey found herself staring into Bess's eyes. Mickey detected the ravages of heartbreak and the long, desolate road that she felt she somehow shared with her.

"All right, everyone," Mrs. Howard said, returning the room to silence. "Let's get down to business. Michelle, since this is your first meeting with us, why don't you start by telling us a little bit about your daughter, Reagan?"

Mickey was taken aback by the request, and though accustomed to speaking in front of people in court, this represented a much different challenge. *I should have grabbed a third*, Mickey thought to herself, referring to the champagne as she moved toward the center of the room and gathered her thoughts. "Oh God, where do I begin? Reagan was a beautiful girl and a …" Mickey caught herself in midsentence, realizing she had referred to Reagan in the past tense. She paused for a few seconds, with tears filling her eyes, and Tyler placed his arm on her shoulder. "Reagan *is* a beautiful girl. She's very bright, and she makes good grades. She's the best daughter I could have ever hoped for. She's so kind and considerate and would never hurt anyone. She was abducted at the Town East Mall the week before Christmas, and we haven't seen her since," she concluded as many in the room dabbed their own tears.

"I'd like to add something," Bess Abram said. "I, myself, have only two goals at this point. The first is to see that you all are reunited with your children, and the second is to see that this creep never walks the streets again. It's true that it's too late for our Taylor, but it may not be too late for some of you. Michelle, dear, you were right to correct yourself a moment ago. Don't you dare give up! Refer to your precious young girl in present tense until someone proves that you shouldn't!" Mickey flashed a tearful smile and nodded.

"Thank you for sharing that with us, Michelle," Mrs. Howard said. She then delivered a treasurer's report and opened the meeting for general discussion.

"When will the Flynn trial be?" asked Toni Hayes, a mother of an abducted girl.

"Detective Adams told me the DA's office will place this case on priority status and will seek a quick trial setting," Mrs. Howard explained. "But even with that, he warned that it will likely be several weeks. As we discussed last time, when the trial *does* start, we should have a good presence at the courthouse to support the prosecution and, of course, the Abrams."

"That's right! The crimes of Willie Flynn are crimes against all of us!" Barry Brown declared.

"So you all show up at the trials?" Mickey asked with interest.

"Oh, we most certainly do," Mrs. Howard replied. "Our purpose is to be a voice for all victims and keep the lawyers honest."

"Is that possible?" Mr. Brown said, drawing laughter.

"You know what I mean, Barry. We don't want criminals getting a simple slap on the wrist," Mrs. Howard explained.

"Hell, Lyndon Tucker's askin' for the death penalty," Brown responded. "There won't be no sweetheart deals on this one, and the only slap on Flynn's wrist will be when they put his butt on a gurney and slap the strap on his arm to inject the bye-bye juice!"

Happy to see this was no mere "wet handkerchief crowd," Mickey found herself drawn to the group's activist stance. She gravitated to the sense of solidarity and the thought of participating in the upcoming trial. "Being in the courtroom is great, but I would suggest taking that a step further," Mickey said, and everyone turned toward her. "I went to Flynn's arraignment, and there were a lot of media there. I say some of us get there early on trial days and let them all know what this group and its purpose is all about!"

"What are you envisioning?" Mrs. Howard asked.

"Taking advantage of the media. We can be vocal and explain the objectives of the group and to speak for Flynn's other victims."

"I like it!" Mrs. Hayes said.

"Yeah, I like the thought of it too, but is it legal?" Mr. Brown asked. "I don't want to end up in a cell with Flynn for trying."

"Good question Barry," Mrs. Hayes said, as all present turned to Mrs. Howard.

"My heavens, don't look at me," she said as she backed up a step. "Since Michelle's a lawyer, let's ask her."

"Uh oh, sorry for the lawyer wisecrack," Barry Brown said.

"I'm used to it, Mr. Brown. Look, guys—the courthouse is the people's house. The First Amendment says we all have a right to be there, both inside and outside, as long as we don't incite violence or break some other law."

"I thought the First Amendment was about freedom of press and religion and stuff," Toni Hayes said.

"It's that too, but it also protects our freedom of speech and the right to peaceably assemble, and after all, that's what we'll be doing, right?" All nodded and seemed receptive to the concept.

As they drove away that evening, Tyler sensed Mickey's contentment and said, "You were great in there."

"You think?"

"Sure! They seemed to really perk up when they heard you're a lawyer."

"I sensed that too," she said.

"So you liked the meeting?" he asked.

"Not at first. Hell, it began like an AA meeting—you know, with me having to engage in the confessions of sorrow and all, but they have a good and proactive attitude about things … I like that."

CHAPTER 9

⚖

SINE MIXTURA DEMENTIAE FUIT

(There Has Been No Great Wisdom without an Element of Madness)

Law Offices of Chester Hill
February 16

With the trial date set, Chester Hill was in his office, struggling with Flynn's implacable directives to purposely fail at trial. Intentionally losing a case—even at the request of the client—presented him with a serious dilemma. Flynn's desire to lose—and lose in the biggest way allowed under Texas jurisprudence—directly conflicted with his sworn duty to provide him a vigorous defense. But not performing as Flynn directed would likewise violate his duty to act at the client's direction. Hill worked late into the evening and poured himself a gin and tonic as he pondered the conundrum. He took a long taste of the drink, leaned back in his chair, and stared at the ceiling. *He's not asking me to do anything illegal, but what if he's nuts? He doesn't seem to be, but do I have a duty to at least explore an insanity defense? After all, if death row's acceptable to him, a mental hospital should be too ...*

Though he thought Flynn to be competent, Hill decided at a minimum that he needed to know more about him and to at least test the waters for an insanity defense. He knew Flynn was originally from Ohio and had served time there, and pondered how to find resources to illuminate Flynn's early life history. He began by returning to the materials that the prosecutors were required to give to him. He focused on records from Flynn's prior incarcerations, but the documents proved far from enlightening. Hill knew from experience that state agencies, such as the Ohio Department of Corrections, kept more detailed records for inmates than what was represented by the state's document production. But he likewise knew Ohio officials would not voluntarily produce such records. Hill had a law school classmate, Zachary Coveleski that had moved with his wife and children to Ohio and now held a prominent position in the Ohio attorney general's office. They had remained friends, exchanging occasional e-mails and sending gifts at Christmas. Hill located Coveleski's office number in his rolodex and decided to give him a call.

After three rings, a voice emerged. "This is Zach."

"Yes, sir. This here's Bob Johnson with the Internal Revenue Service, and I'd like to discuss our upcoming audit of your tax returns," Hill said in as low and serious a voice as he could muster.

"I know a goddamn Texas accent when I hear one, and this must be my old chicken—shit ex-friend, Chester!"

"What do you mean ex-friend?"

"I note that you didn't refute the chicken –shit part," Coveleski said.

"That part's a given, but do you not love me anymore?"

"Well, shit, man! You haven't called in ages, leaving me stranded me up here in Yankee land with no contact with the Lone Star State!"

Chuckling, Hill said, "I'm sure you're doing just fine up there."

"Oh, yeah? I'm looking out my window at three feet of snow and growing."

"Well, I'm not. But it did look like rain when I finished the eighteenth hole a while ago," Hill lied.

"Sure, go ahead and rub it in, you old prick!"

"Hell, Zach, I expected to get your voice mail this time of day. What's a bigwig like you doing there this late?"

"You wouldn't believe the caseloads we have up here in the Cuyahoga County division. Look—if you ever wanna take the Ohio bar exam, I'll—"

"Not a chance, my friend. You lost me with the three feet of snow." They laughed and exchanged some stories and caught up on careers and family before Hill got down to business.

"Zach, I need a favor."

"Oh shit, I should have known," Coveleski responded sarcastically.

"I thought you'd say that, jackass."

"What can I do for you, buddy?"

"I've been appointed to represent a defendant in a capital murder case. It might become necessary to get him shrunk."

"Thinking insanity?"

"Perhaps. I don't have much else on this one, and I need some records from up there. It seems that my hero served some time in Ohio, two stints, and I'd like to get the skinny on it."

"Are you trying to get me fired?" Coveleski said.

"Look, Zach—if you can't get these records without jeopardizing your cushy, overpaid, civil-service-protected government job, I understand."

Coveleski chuckled. "Give me the guy's name and social security number, and I'll see what I can do."

"I'll send that and an inmate number too. Do you need me to send it in a letter?"

"Shit no. I don't want a paper trail for this," Coveleski chided.

"Hey, Zach, joking aside, I don't want you to—"

"I'm just kidding, Chester. This isn't a big deal. Just send me a signed authorization from the client to cover my ass."

"That might be a problem. I don't really want him knowing I'm requesting these records."

"I see. Hmmm ... I'll tell you what, send a simple Open Records Act request directly to me, and I'll expedite it."

"Deal! I owe you one, pal."

"You damn sure do! Why don't you and the wife come up here sometime? We'll catch an Indians game and do the town."

"Do the town? In Cleveland?" Hill remarked. "Isn't that the same town where the river caught on fire a few years ago?"

"A few years? That was decades ago!"

"Well, I'm just saying ... you know a town that—"

"Do you want these records or not?" Coveleski pressed.

"Sorry, sorry," Hill responded. "Let those bitter, lake-effect snows subside, and we'll do just that."

"I'll get on this for you ASAP, but it still may take me a while. When's your trial date?"

"Next month, but I've got a psychiatrist designated, so as long as I get the records before trial, I'm fine," Hill explained.

"Sounds like you got a real doozy."

"You don't know the half of it, brother."

The Friday prior to the commencement of Flynn's trial, Chester Hill sat at his desk. Having done all he thought he could to ready himself for his case, he turned his attention to the mail that had accumulated during the days of near-nonstop trial preparation. Aided by the light of a small lamp on the corner of his desk, he culled the pile of open envelopes, putting the contents of some in his outbox with notes for his secretary, while most ended up in the trash can that he straddled between his feet. Toward the bottom of the stack, Hill uncovered a brown envelope bearing the seal of the Ohio attorney general's office. He slit it open and removed a half-inch-thick collection of rubber-banded papers with a handwritten note from Coveleski on top: *You owe me a thick steak and a cold beer or two or ten next time we're together!*

Hill grinned and began to read the materials. Most of the documents were routine administrative forms, until he reached a series of incident reports. Prison personnel had documented Flynn's history of fights and skirmishes with fellow cell inmates. These encounters included some that escalated to physical violence, resulting in Flynn sustaining varying levels of bodily harm and one attempted sodomy. Flynn had repeatedly pleaded for isolation, but those entreats were either ignored or allowed only on a temporary basis. The reports documented Flynn's injuries, a few requiring treatment from the prison medical staff and two resulting in brief hospital stays. One such report caught Hill's eye:

Discharge Summary

Inmate William Lee Flynn (OH0-60609-01) was treated for injuries sustained in an altercation in his cell with a fellow inmate. He had several abrasions and lacerations to his face and torso. Two abdominal lacerations required sutures, and the wounds were consistent with those made by a sharp instrument, such as a knife or handmade shank. Security has been notified. The patient was admitted for bed rest and a regimen of antibiotics. The patient will need to return in two weeks for the removal of the sutures. The patient complains of ongoing symptomologies unrelated to the altercation. Comparisons with early records reveal a clinical pattern consistent with a progressive motor neuron disease. A full pathological analysis was requested and performed by the Mayo Clinic, and this inmate suffers from ALS. The inmate has been advised of this diagnosis and the available inmate treatment programs. All of the patient's questions have been answered to his satisfaction. Mr. Flynn has been further informed that this disease is currently incurable, and this unfortunate young man is aware the gravity of this diagnosis and understands his life expectancy is greatly compromised.

"I'll be damned." Hill sighed, leaning back in his chair. "He's dying."

Mickey embraced her new role as a support-group activist and plotted her strategy for the trial. She wanted to capture the attention of public and more importantly the press. As outlandish as the notion seemed at first blush, she decided to create signs depicting provocative messages to display at the courthouse. She realized that some might view the tactic as extreme or weird, but she could not envision a better way to engage the group's members and insert their cause into the public eye. After a trip to a crafts store, Mickey set up shop in her garage, with several white flexible sign boards and cans of spray-paint in various colors. The air that evening was particularly crisp, but she nevertheless had parked car in the driveway and had the garage door open to disperse any paint fumes.

She stared at her first would-be canvas, searching for inspiration. Then, with red spray-paint can in hand, she dashed the vivid color on the white board, deriving primal satisfaction from that mere act itself. "Take that!" she exclaimed as she stepped back and gazed at her first feat of handy work. "Murderer" was written in large, blood-red letters, and for affect, she then stood the board upright, allowing the paint to run down the board. She crafted two more signs, let them dry, and placed them in the trunk of her car.

CHAPTER 10

⚖

JUSTITIAE OMNIBUS

(Justice for All)

March 28

Tyler had committed to attend at least the commencement of the trial, easing some of Mickey's mounting anxiety. He even offered to pick her up that morning, but after she explained her strategic plan, they agreed to meet inside the courthouse thirty minutes before the scheduled start time. Mickey reached the courthouse square early that morning, and noticed that the number cars present was much greater than the morning of the arraignment. She searched for available spaces and settled on one three blocks away. She parked and ambled, with signs in hand, toward the courthouse. She took a sidewalk that wound its way along the rolling knolls of in front courthouse, and focused on finding a spot that offered the best vantage point for maximum visibility to all arriving. It was then that Mickey realized that the trial had also drawn more news trucks, and their satellite antennas jutted high toward the cloudless blue skies. Despite that presence and to her dismay, she saw no reporters or cameramen. But when she heard her name called, she turned and was pleased to greet other members of the support group as they arrived.

"Good morning, guys, I guess today's the day," Mickey said as the others nodded.

"What should we do?" Toni Hayes asked.

Mickey pointed in the direction of the news trucks, saying, "For now, let's go to that corner of the lawn nearest the trucks. Here, take these signs if you want," she said, handing out two and keeping one.

"This is great," Mrs. Hayes said, hoisting hers.

"Mine says 'You're Going to Burn, Willie!'" Mr. Brown added.

Another arrived and asked, "Hey, do you have a sign for me?"

"I'm sorry I only made these three, but I'll make more for tomorrow. The objective is to get the attention of the media. I'm not sure where they are, but they've gotta come around here at some point since their vans are over there."

Mrs. Hayes asked, "Do you think they're inside the courthouse?"

"Maybe, but listen, there are plenty of people coming in and out. If anyone asks what you're doing here, just explain we are the faces and voices of *all* victims and that includes the other missing victims of Flynn."

They all agreed and took their places, and over the following forty-five minutes, some passersby stopped and looked at the signs, but none ventured as much as a question. The hour of the trial drew near, and they decided to disburse for this morning. Though disappointed that few people showed more than a passing interest, Mickey was happy with the attendance and thanked them all. As she gathered the signs, she instructed, "Listen guys. I don't know why, with all these news vans out here, we didn't draw some press attention, but let's do it again tomorrow! I'll make some more signs, and y'all feel free to bring your own." They eagerly agreed, and Mickey returned the signs to her car.

She then walked briskly back to the courthouse, up the steps and once inside, she headed to the bank of public elevators. As she waited, she noticed movement down a hallway leading to the rear exit of the building. She stared curiously through an open door and saw that it led out to an alley behind the courthouse. She had never paid attention to the exit, and when she walked toward it for a better view, she noticed several people waiting just outside the backdoor. As she eased closer, she was startled when two police officers in thick bulletproof vests marched in, with a shackled Willie Flynn in tow. After they passed and turned away from her, Mickey could now see through the door and into the back ally. Present there were more officers, along with a throng of people, including news reporters, on each side of a rope line and at three idling police cars. *That's where they were!*

She turned back to Flynn and his entourage and saw that they were stopped and waiting for a separate service elevator. She then realized just how Flynn's appearance had changed. He sported an ill-fitting but nevertheless nice gray business suit, white shirt, and tie. He was clean shaven, and his hair was still bushy, but trimmed. When the service elevator door opened, Flynn and two officers entered the padded elevator car and the remaining officers kept onlookers at a distance until the door fully closed.

Mickey turned and saw Tyler approaching, and they took one of the three public elevators to the third floor. When the elevator doors opened, they saw a boisterous throng of reporters and spectators mingling in the hall. As Mickey, Tyler, and others parted the crowd and eased into the courtroom, Bailiff Carl Johnson met them. "The courtroom's already reached capacity," he said firmly. "Y'all won't be able to stay." Johnson stood stoically as the others that had entered with them relented and turned to leave. The stunned Mickey glanced up at the balcony and saw that the fourth floor doors were unlocked and that it too was filling with spectators. She stepped forward toward Johnson, but before she could speak, Johnson turned to younger bailiff, instructing, "Jim! Hey, Jimmy!"

"Yeah, Carl."

"Make a sign to tape to the door explaining that we're full and stand out there and enforce it until we get started in here. I got a lot on my hands and can't be playin' gatekeeper all morning."

"Sure thing," he said as Carl turned to walk toward the bench, with Mickey trailing.

"Excuse me, sir," Mickey said, gaining Johnson's attention. "We must be here. You see we're—"

He turned back to her. "Didn't I just tell y'all to vacate!"

"You did, but we have to be here because—"

"Everyone wants to be here for one reason or another, lady," Johnson interrupted. "But we can't have spectators sitting on each other's laps, now can we? Now, move along to the hall, or the fire marshal's gonna shut this whole place down!"

Mrs. Howard, who had secured a prime front-row seat, witnessed the exchange and rose to intervene. "These aren't mere looky-loos, Carl. Their little girl's a victim of the defendant." The veteran bailiff's expression softened. He nodded and found space for them on a bench toward the rear of the courtroom.

Just prior to the top of the hour, the holding cell door opened, and officers escorted the now unshackled Flynn to the defense table.

"Wow, he looks a lot different," Tyler whispered to Mickey.

"Yeah. I saw him when they brought him in downstairs.

"Where are his shackles?" he asked.

"I'm not sure. I guess it's because they can't have him cuffed in front of the jury."

"Why? That doesn't seem fair or safe."

"Presumption of innocence, I guess," Mickey opined. "Did you notice the two extra bailiffs?"

"Yes. Is that unusual?"

"I've never seen it," Mickey said.

Chester Hill, dressed in a black western-cut suit, with ostrich-skin boots, took his seat beside Flynn while the buzz in the courtroom increased. Then the door to the left of the judge's bench opened, and the court clerk emerged from the, carrying a wire basket with the court's file. She was followed closely by Judge Sullivan, and when he reached his chair, Johnson called the court to order, and the chatter in the courtroom faded to silence. Once seated, Sullivan started by calling the prosecutors and Hill to the bench.

"Chester," Sullivan whispered, his hand covering his microphone. "Do I understand that you don't have any defense motions?"

"Right. You've already granted my motion at jury selection on them not mentioning the other missing girls."

"I recall that, but is that it?"

"Yes, Judge. We thought we had some competency issues, but we don't."

"Lyndon, does the state have any?"

"No, Judge."

Sullivan adjusted the microphone and spoke to the assembled crowd. "All right, we're on the record in TX-150374, *State of Texas versus William a.k.a. Willie Lee Flynn*. As you all can see, the room is at capacity, and that means it can get warm and noisy in here. I see some of you already fanning, and I'm sorry about that. But, while I can't help the temperature in here, I *can* control the noise, and I don't want any distractions when the jury comes in. If you feel at any point like you can't watch your mouth, that's the time to consider headin' for the hallway. Any questions?" No one so much as peeped, and Sullivan closed his file and signaled to Johnson to retrieve the jury. All present stood as the group of eight men and four women strolled single file into the jury box. As they took their assigned seats, Flynn slouched back in his chair, propping an elbow on each arm of it.

The judge asked for the prosecution's opening statement, and Tucker rose to the call. A man of average height, Tucker was moderately overweight and had a thick head of salt and pepper hair, parted neatly on the right side and kept securely in place with a generous application of hair spray. He wore a three-piece navy suit with a starched, white shirt and a red, green, and blue, diagonal-striped tie. Heavy-soled, black, wing-tipped shoes added dignity to his walk to the podium, and a prominent American-flag pin on his lapel added a calculated tinge of patriotism. He assumed the podium, with a yellow legal pad in hand, saying, "Good morning, ladies and gentlemen. As I told you last week in the voir dire examination, we, as the prosecution, have the burden to prove our case beyond a reasonable doubt. This is a tough standard, and it ought to be, and it's a standard we as the state of Texas gladly accept. The key to this this standard is the word 'reasonable,' for if it were to be beyond *all* possible doubt, there would be no way to ever convict anyone of a criminal offense. You'd have to have witnessed the crime yourself, and even then, you might doubt your own lying eyes," he said as he grinned, and the jurors chuckled.

"Let me give you an example. Let's say I told you that there was a country called China on the other side of this big blue marble we call Earth. Most of you, through your life experience, would know to a moral certainty it was true. There would be no reasonable doubt about that even though most of you, if not all of you, have never stepped foot on the continent of Asia, much less in the nation of China. To have some trivial doubt, having never traveled halfway around the world, is to be expected.

But would there be any level of 'reasonable doubt'? Certainly not. Now, none of us in this room witnessed the heinous crime committed on young Taylor Abram, save one, of course," Tucker said, glancing back at the defense table. "Only two people—for sure—were eyewitnesses to this crime in its entirety. We believe one is Willie Lee Flynn, and as the judge explained last week, he doesn't have to testify. The only other would be precious little Taylor Abram, but she can't testify, and tragically we all know why. Nevertheless, you will hear the voice of Taylor Abram, through her parents seated to my right and other witnesses and strong and ironclad physical evidence that we will present."

Tucker then provided the jury a meticulous rendition of the evidence they would present and the expected testimony of witnesses that they planned to call. He then placed his hands on the rail in front of the jury box. "Discarded in a vacant field two lots down from the house that Willie Flynn lived in was one of Taylor Abram's shoes. A neighbor will testify that he saw Flynn himself throwing something into that field shortly after Taylor turned up missing. We will present proof that Taylor's blood and the defendant's blood and fingerprints were found on that shoe, a shoe that Taylor Abram was missing when officers discovered her lifeless body, discarded and alone, in a ditch and wearing the mate to the shoe." Mr. Abram patted his weeping wife's shoulder, and the jurors were drawn to the couple's emotional angst. "Finally, ladies and gentlemen, you will hear testimony of an admission of guilt by the defendant when the police captured him, thus ending his reign of terror on our community."

"Objection, Judge!" Hill said, rising. "May we approach?" The judge nodded, and Hill and Tucker walked to the bench. "Judge, this case concerns *only* the death of Taylor Abram, and I think the 'reign of terror' comment violates your ruling from last week ordering them not to mention the other cases," Hill argued.

"I tend to agree," Sullivan said, turning to Tucker.

"For starters, I didn't mention the other girls. I simply—"

"Come on, Lyndon," the judge interceded. "What did you mean by it if it wasn't about the other victims?"

"I … well … I don't think use of word 'reign' connotes a series of crimes," Tucker struggled.

The judge shook his head and whispered, "Don't give me that, Lyn. You knew exactly what you were doing. And just so you know my connotation of it, if y'all bring up 'reign of terror' again in this trial, you better have Robespierre's ass on the witness stand!"

Walking back to the podium, Tucker cleared his throat and continued, "There are essential elements of a case, such as the DNA testing, admissions of guilt and eye-witness testimony—we have those. Then there are elements, like a murder weapon, or a motive. It's nice to have them, but they're largely non-essential. All crimes are a puzzle, and with the aid of Chief of Police 'Bud' Buchanan and the fine men and women of our police force, we have the *essential* pieces to this puzzle, every one of them. Each of these provable facts will clearly establish the guilt of Willie Lee Flynn, so much so that when we we're done, you will be as convinced of Flynn's guilt as you are that there exists a country called China."

Tucker walked slowly back to the prosecution's table, and Sullivan asked for Hill's opening remarks. The eyes of the jury that had been trained on Tucker now seemed distant and disinterested. Two folded their arms, and one stared at the floor as Hill fumbled with his notes at the podium and peered at the jurors over his half-glasses. "The case that was just described to you by Mr. Tucker is what's known in the law as a circumstantial evidence case. It's built entirely on speculative evidence and I predict it will be far from achieving the important beyond-a-reasonable-doubt standard. You will not—and I repeat—you will *not* hear from any witness who is able to say they saw my client, Willie Lee Flynn, lay a hand on this poor, unfortunate little girl. Unless someone comes forward to credibly describe those facts, you should not just have a moment's pause but rather a profound reluctance to send Willie Lee Flynn to the death chamber based on what the state calls 'puzzle pieces.' Perhaps that's good enough in countries like the one the prosecution seems interested in, China, but we don't do that here. Speculation and conjecture simply are not enough to make a man pay with his life."

Hill continued on by describing the constitutional rights and protections afforded to the criminally accused, including their historical importance. He emphasized the right of the accused to not testify in such cases. But the points seemed dry and academic and were delivered as if rehearsed.

"My client faces the most awesome machine in the law, and that's a prosecution by the government. All of the resources of the state of Texas stand in opposition to my client's freedom and, in this instance, poses a threat to his very existence. This requires the state to adhere to a strict and monumental standard. I couldn't help but think that as Mr. Tucker laid out his case, it seemed like an apology for the elements they don't have. He was conditioning you not to expect too much. But to build a capital murder case, it must be more than a house of cards built on shifting sand, and if they don't do better, then you have a sworn obligation to acquit my client." Hill returned to his chair, and after a break, Judge Sullivan asked for the prosecution's first witness.

They choose to lead off with their eye witness, and Carl retrieved a nervous Robert Jackson from the hall and escorted him to the witness stand. Jackson took a seat and his oath and then looked nervously around the packed room as Johnson adjusted the microphone in front of him. Walking to the podium was one of Tucker's assistant attorneys, Warren Smith. The young lawyer took Jackson through his background, his tenure at the mall, and then brought him to the day of Taylor Abram's disappearance.

"Where were you going when you left the mall that day?"

"I realized when I got up that I was out of my pills and needed to pick up a prescription from the drugstore."

"Was it your lunch break?"

"That's right."

"Is that why you had your lunch box with you?"

"Right. I was going to eat my sandwich and stuff on the way to the drug store."

"What time of morning was it?"

"A little after nine."

"Where were you parked?" Smith asked.

"Way out yonder in the parking lot where we're supposed to park at Christmastime."

"The paying customers get the good spots?" Smith queried.

"You got that right," Jackson said grinning.

"What'd you see when you reached your car, Mr. Jackson?"

"I saw this young girl, you know. She was talking to some dude in an old brown van."

Smith showed Jackson a school photograph of Taylor Abram and asked, "Is the girl you saw out there depicted in this picture?"

"Yes, sir. That's her, all right."

"Your Honor, the state would like the record to reflect that Mr. Jackson has identified Taylor Abram's school photo marked as state's exhibit six."

"Duly noted," Sullivan said.

"Did you get a good look at the man in the van?"

"Not at first. But when I accidently knocked my lunch box off the top of my car, it made a loud racket when it hit the hood, and that's when she looked back and he poked his head out of the van, and I got a look."

"So the lunch box hit hard enough that the driver looked over at you?"

"Yes. It hit hard enough to cause them to look and to have my thermos smash a perfectly good scrambled egg sandwich," Jackson replied, drawing smiles from jurors.

"Did you think anything was unusual about what you saw?"

"Yeah, you know, it was suspicious to me. You see, she was dressed—"

"Taylor Abram?"

"Yes. Well, I didn't know that then, but I know that now. She was dressed real nice, and it didn't seem right that she'd be talking to this guy."

"Why is that?" Smith asked, but Jackson seemed reticent. "Go ahead, it's okay."

"Well, he had real bushy hair, you know, and it looked kinda nasty, like it hadn't been washed in a spell. He also had a beard that was a little shaggy, and that van was all raggedy, and it just didn't make no sense that that girl should be speaking with him."

"So, shaggy and raggedy, huh?" Smith asked as Jackson nodded. "I don't guess he was all gussied up like he is today?" Smith said with a smirk.

"Objection, Your Honor," Hill said as he jumped to his feet. "The state hasn't—"

"Sustained!" Sullivan said sternly. "Mr. Smith, you don't refer to Mr. Flynn until you've establish the ID. Understood?"

"Yes, Your Honor," Smith said. "Mr. Jackson, do you see the man you witnessed in the van, in this courtroom?"

"It's hard to say. I mean, I think I know, but he don't look the same."

"I understand, "Smith said lifting another photograph from the prosecution's table. "Let me show you state exhibit twenty-one. Do you recognize the person depicted in this photo?"

Jackson looked at it and nodded. "Yes, it's the man I saw in that van that day."

"Judge, we would like the record to reflect that Mr. Jackson has positively identified state's exhibit twenty-one, which is the mug shot taken of Mr. Flynn."

"It's so noted."

"Mr. Jackson, if you were so suspicious, why didn't you say something?"

Jackson's head dropped. "Sir, there ain't a day that goes by that I don't think about that. If I had just said somethin', all of this might not have happened."

Tucker's team, feeling they had gotten everything they needed from Jackson, passed him to the defense. Hill's cross-examination began by taking Jackson through some additional background questions and then returned to the day of Taylor Abram's disappearance.

"You stated a moment ago, that all this occurred at shortly after nine o'clock in the morning, is that right?"

"Yes."

Hill stared at the jury asking, "Yet you've testified under oath that you were leaving for lunch?"

"That's right," Jackson confirmed.

"Which was it, Mr. Jackson, lunch time or nine o'clock?"

"For me, it was both."

"Why would you be going to lunch at nine?"

"It was mainly because I was hungry," Jackson said.

"At nine?"

"Sir, you ought to know that I came in at five o'clock that morning."

"I see. Mr. Jackson, what medicine did you *not* take that day because you were out of it?"

"For my blood pressure."

"Are you hypertensive?" Hill asked.

"My wife thinks so, but I just got the high blood pressure," Jackson said, creating some laughter.

Smith leaned toward Tucker and whispered, "The jury likes Jackson."

"They're eating this up," Tucker replied. "If nothing bad happens, don't redirect."

Hill continued. "It's true, is it not, that a moment ago you weren't able to identify Mr. Flynn as he sits here today, right?"

"That's right. He cleans up real nice," Jackson said to more chuckles.

"Objection, nonresponsive," Hill said to the judge.

"Overruled."

"Did you see Taylor Abram get in that van?"

"No, sir."

"See her sitting in the van at all?" Hill pressed.

"No, sir."

"Is it safe to say you never saw any harm occur to Taylor Abram?"

"That's true," Jackson conceded.

"And you can't tell this jury that Mr. Flynn ever laid a hand on Taylor Abram, right?"

"Right."

"Pass the witness," Hill said.

"Anything further, Mr. Smith?"

"No, Your Honor."

"Call your next witness," Sullivan instructed.

"The state calls Chief Randall 'Bud' Buchanan," Tucker said.

Johnson led Jackson back to the hall and summoned Buchanan, who entered the courtroom clad in his dark three piece suit. He marched proudly toward the witness stand, smiling and nodding at the jury as he passed. Once sworn in, Tucker led Buchanan to recount his impressive career, including his qualifications, training, and many awards and commendations he amassed on his assent to the top of the department. As a polished witness, Buchanan instinctively knew to direct his dark, intense eyes toward the jury to emphasize his more salient points. Tucker then took him chronologically from the beginning stages of the investigation and then to the evening of Flynn's capture.

"Were you present at the raid on Willie Lee Flynn's house the night he was arrested, Chief?" Tucker asked.

"Well, to be precise, this was his mother's house. But yes, I was not only present; I personally coordinated the full operation and even helped subdue the suspect at the scene."

"By suspect, you mean the defendant over there?" Tucker asked, pointing at Flynn.

"Correct. Willie Flynn."

"Did Mr. Flynn offer any comments upon his arrest?"

"Yes, he did."

"Please describe the exchange for the jury," Tucker said as Judge Sullivan glanced at the defense table, expecting an objection.

Buchanan turned to face the jurors. "The first thing I noticed was that he never questioned why he was being arrested."

"So he didn't ask, 'What's this all about?' or something like that?" Tucker asked.

"No, he did not. So I asked him if he knew why we were there, and he said, 'You won't find the girl here'."

"And y'all didn't find Taylor Abram there, because she was discarded out in that field, right?"

"Correct. So I asked him about the other girls, and he said, 'I took them all, right?'"

"Chief, what's your understanding of the cause of Taylor Abram's death?" Tucker asked.

"Blunt trauma to the head."

"You might be asked about a murder weapon. What do you say to not having one?"

"It doesn't matter. Most anything can cause blunt trauma, from a fist, to a frying pan, a chair leg or pool cue, even hurled brick."

"Is that list from experience?"

"Why yes. Every example I just gave were from actual cases."

"Nothing further," Tucker said, and the judge decided to recess the trial for the day. As everyone began to disperse, Judge Sullivan motioned for Hill to approach.

"Chester, are you all right?" the judge asked.

"Yes, Judge. I'm fine."

"I can't believe what you let happen today."

"Judge, this is a very complicated case. As you may suspect. I have some behind-the-scenes—shall we say—challenges. One day we'll have a beer, and I'll tell you all about it."

Sullivan shook his head. "I think it'll take more than one."

Mickey rose the next morning, optimistic and anxious to execute her new plan of attack. A late-season cold front had blown through West Texas, bringing a stiff, damp, northeasterly wind. Temperatures hovered around freezing, and she wondered if the conditions would discourage the attendance of the group members. Mickey arrived at the courthouse, and first noticed there were fewer vehicles present, but the same number of news trucks remained among them. She parked in one of the angled slots in front of the courthouse, opened the trunk of her car, and removed the signs from the day before along with the additional ones she had painted the evening prior. As she walked toward the courthouse, she saw other support-group members, including some with their own signs, and she motioned them toward her. She explained the vantage point she discovered the prior morning and asked them to follow her toward the rear of the courthouse. As they rounded the corner and into the alley, she stopped and gathered the group in huddle formation.

"Here's the deal, guys. I learned that the reason we didn't get any exposure yesterday is because all the press was gathered back here. As you can see over there, some are already setting up."

"Goodness, there are a bunch of 'em—and cameramen too," Mrs. Hayes observed.

"Yes, and that's why this is the perfect place to get us noticed and let Flynn know how we feel," Mickey added.

"Flynn?" Toni Hayes said, wide-eyed.

"Yes. If it goes like it did yesterday, police cars will deliver Flynn back here, and he'll enter the building between those yellow ropes."

Mr. Brown asked, "Are you sure we're allowed back here?"

"No, but there were others back here yesterday, and no one seemed to bother them, so let's do this!" Mickey responded confidently.

"But they may have had press passes or something and likely didn't have posters like these." A collective concern rose about the provocative nature of their signs. To be on the safe side, Mickey suggested that all holding one should roll it up and keep it obscured until Flynn's arrival. The apprehensive members followed her to the rope line and spread out on each side of it. Mickey assumed a prime spot close to where news reporters were standing. Cameramen continued setting up their video equipment while others just milled about, trying to stay warm. Mickey noticed two police officers smoking cigarettes and seemingly ignoring the entryway for the time being. One of the reporters made eye contact with Mickey and did a double take.

"Good morning!" the reporter said as he walked toward her.

"Hello," she replied with nonchalance, offering only fleeting eye contact.

"What do you have there?" he asked, looking down at her poster board.

"Oh, this? It's just a sign that I made to show Flynn when he arrives," she replied.

"I see. What's your interest in this case, if you don't mind me asking?"

She now made full eye contact and said, "My daughter's one of Willie Flynn's victims."

"Whoa! You mean you're one of the parents of missing girls?" the reporter asked, and Mickey nodded. "Hey, while we're waiting, can I tape an interview for the news?"

"Sure," Mickey agreed, and scanning the throng, she noticed that the other group members had heard the exchange and seemed thrilled by the prospect. The reporter motioned for his cameraman and explained the plan. The reporter pulled a small mirror from his pocket to check his hair and teeth, then he positioned himself next to Mickey and nodded. Mickey was startled when the bright lights atop the camera surged on as the reporter spoke. "We're here behind the courthouse anticipating the arrival of Willie Lee Flynn for day two of his capital-murder trial. Braving the elements with us on this frigid morning is a growing crowd. One such onlooker has a particular interest in this trial. Your name, ma'am?" he asked, holding his microphone to Mickey's face.

"I'm Michelle Grant."

"So what's your connection to the Willie Flynn case?"

Not pulling any punches, Mickey replied, "My teenage daughter's one of Willie Lee Flynn's victims. The same is true for some of these others here with me," Mickey said, as the cameraman panned back to capture some of the other group members before returning focus to her. "We're all here in solidarity to assure that justice is served and for all to know that there are other victims of this child killer, beyond the Abram case on trial."

"Very interesting. So how are you all connected?"

"Mrs. Evelyn Howard. She heads a group of families affected by crime."

"Our viewers should be very familiar with Mrs. Howard. She does great work," the reporter said, and Mickey nodded. "Say, I see you and some of the others have signs. Did you make yours?"

"Yes, as a matter of fact," Mickey confirmed.

"Are they to show Flynn when he arrives?"

"Yes."

"Mind if we get a sneak preview?"

"Not at all," Mickey said as she unrolled and displayed the board, which read in big black letters *Willie "Child Killer" Flynn*.

"That's powerful!" the reporter said. "Thank you, and best of luck on your daughter and the other girls too," the reporter said as the camera stopped and the lights dimmed.

Mickey was ecstatic, but her attention quickly returned to the mission at hand. Her own tension and the cold air had her shivering, and she rocked back and forth to stay warm. Mickey made eye contact with each group member, and they seemed edgy but resolute. Finally, she saw the convoy of three police cars turning into the alley, and as they approached, some in the crowd began to boo while others tiptoed for a better view. The crowd noise, bright TV-camera lights, and barrage of flashes from still photographers created an air of chaos. The officers in the alley stomped out their cigarettes and moved between the ropes to secure the pathway for the ingress of the entourage. Mickey nodded to the others and lifted her sign, and the other support-group members followed her lead. The noise and chants rose to a fever pitch as a shackled Flynn emerged from the car dressed in the same suit. He seemed undaunted by the lights and boisterous throng, even as the volume of boos and jeers rose and some began to chant, "Murderer! Murderer!"

"You're a child murderer, Willie Lee! Where's my daughter?" Mickey demanded as he neared. Hearing her comment, Flynn stopped and turned toward her. Despite his stare, Mickey didn't flinch, and though the officers attempted to move him forward, Flynn remained in front of her. "Where are the other girls, Willie? Tell us!" she demanded. The still-camera flashes erupted like fireworks, but Flynn just shrugged and walked with the escort through the courthouse door, and when the door closed, the crowd began to disburse.

"That was great!" Toni Hayes said. "We sure gave it to him, and you're going to be on TV!"

"We all may be, but don't count on it," Mickey said. "They tape a lot of things that don't make it to the broadcast."

"Who cares? It was exciting just the same," Mrs. Hayes added, and the others agreed.

With each member committed to doing the same each day, Mickey hurriedly stowed her signs in her car and walked into the courthouse. Once inside, she began shedding layers and saw Tyler waiting near the elevators. They rode up to the third floor, and when they entered the courtroom, they found seats nearer to the front.

Back in the holding cell, Hill met with his client.

"Looks pretty bad for me, doesn't it, Counselor?" Flynn jested with a sly grin.

"Yeah, I thought you'd be happy about yesterday."

"It was fine, but you did raise hell a couple of times."

"I can't turn it all off, Willie," Flynn said. "I don't have a different suit for you, but I brought you a different tie," Hill said, pulling a silk, striped tie from his briefcase. It was already knotted and ready to slip over Flynn's head. "I don't see any new marks on you. Are things better?" Hill asked, placing the replacement tie under Flynn's shirt collar.

"It's a little better," Flynn said. "The assholes have been threatened by the guards with loss of rec time, and that helps."

"It's show time, guys," Carl Johnson said, opening the cell door and unlocking Flynn's shackles.

"Thanks, Carl."

"No problem, Mr. Hill. Hang in there."

"Put your jacket on, Willie," Hill instructed as they rose to enter the courtroom. With the judge and jury seated and all participants present, Buchanan was retrieved from the hall and brought back to the witness stand for Hill's cross-examination.

"Chief, there's no eyewitness to this crime, is there?" Hill asked.

"Well, I'm of the belief that there is, but I don't think we'll hear from him," Buchanan said, nodding toward Flynn.

"Chief, focus like a laser. You can't point me to a single person the prosecution's going to call to say they saw Mr. Flynn harmed Taylor Abram."

"That's true. But we have proof that—"

"Objection, Your Honor!" Hill snapped.

"Sustained. Please confine your answers to the question posed," Sullivan instructed.

"Yes, Tommy—I mean, Your Honor," Buchanan said, drawing chuckles.

"You also admitted yesterday that there's no murder weapon, right?" Hill asked.

Buchanan smirked. "Yes, there's no *known* murder weapon."

"In fact, you all don't know what weapon, if any, was even used. True?"

"I think we covered that yesterday, but yes, that's true."

Hill looked at the jury. "Sounds like the state's case is a circumstantial one, right?"

"There's elements of this case that are direct, and some that are circumstantial."

"Much has been made of the alleged comments made by my client at the arrest, right?"

"I accurately described them, if that's what you're asking."

"Sir, Mr. Flynn said nothing about killing anyone, did he?" Hill asked.

"No. But he clearly—"

"That's not a confession, is it?"

"I interpreted it as such," Buchanan retorted. "He knew exactly why he was being arrested, then informed us that Taylor Abram wasn't at his house and stated, 'I did them all, right.' Now, I don't expect you to agree with me, Counselor, but I treat that as an admission of guilt!"

"Truth is, Chief, Mr. Flynn didn't say that he abducted anyone, much less killed anyone, right?"

"Not in so many words."

"Thank you. Now let's get back to what you don't have. You don't have a motive, do you?"

"Don't need one!" Buchanan fired back.

"Judge, I object to the responsiveness."

"Sustained! Please just answer the questions as posed, Chief. You know the drill."

"Yes I do, Judge, but it doesn't mean I have to like it," Buchanan said, grinning.

"So no motive, right?" Hill asked.

"No, we don't know the motive."

"That's an important element in a murder case, right?" Hill asked pointedly.

"Not necessarily, especially in a serial-killer case like this."

"Objection! Your Honor, may we approach?"

"Sure. Y'all come on up," Sullivan invited.

As Hill reached at the bench, he said, "Judge, I move for a mistrial. You ordered them to not to bring up the other cases, and the chief blurts out 'serial killer' for Pete's sake!"

Tucker defended. "He was just answering Chester's question, Judge."

"They say you kicked that hornet's nest over with your question, Chester," the judge said to Hill.

"They spring-loaded him to get that in at the first chance, and it's very prejudicial."

"That's offensive, Judge," Tucker responded.

"This is a close call, Lyndon, but I consider this as strike two on stomping my order, and strike three won't be pretty. Bottom line is I'm not granting a mistrial, so let's get back to it, but Lyn you better admonish your witnesses and assistants that the next violator will be bedding down in the Taylor County crossbar hotel."

"Yes, Your Honor," Tucker said.

"The defense passes the witness," Hill said, returning to his table.

"Redirect, Mr. Tucker?" Judge Sullivan asked.

"Yes, Judge," Tucker said rising to his feet. "Chief Buchanan, you were asked by Mr. Hill about circumstantial evidence. How important is this type of evidence to a case?"

"Circumstantial evidence can be very important and is often more reliable than direct evidence."

"How so?" Tucker asked, knowing well Buchanan's answer from previous trials.

"Well, let's say that you have a child—for argument sake, a little boy. And he's in your kitchen, and you have instructed him not to touch a brand-new, uncut chocolate cake that's sitting on the kitchen table. Then a sibling—let's say his little sister—leaves the kitchen and comes a running. She then tells you, the parent, that little brother ate a piece of that cake. That constitutes an eye-witness account, and that would be direct evidence," Buchanan explained.

"Is that reliable evidence?" asked Tucker.

"It can be, but it can also be very unreliable," responded Buchanan.

"Please explain" Tucker asked as the two were now working together like an ace pitcher and a gold-glove catcher.

"Anyone with kids can answer that," Buchanan said as three jurors nodded. "You see, anytime you rely on the statement of an eyewitness, you have to consider bias and the reliability. A witness's statement can be mistaken or downright false. As one example, there are plenty of instances where multiple witnesses to the same chaotic event can each have a different perception of what they saw. You've all seen or heard of this, where some psychology or criminology professor will have someone rush in the backdoor of the classroom and run past the students to the front, snatch something like a purse, and run out. Students are then asked to identify the perpetrator by height, sex, tattoos, color of skin and hair, facial features, and the like. It's amazing how disparate the descriptions are."

"So direct evidence can be unreliable?" Tucker said.

"Yes. You have to consider the motivations and frailties of any witness is all I'm saying."

"Why is the motivation of a witness important, Chief?" Tucker asked, continuing to play pitch and catch while Hill stood at the plate with the bat on his shoulder.

"Let's return to little sister and the baby brother. This won't surprise some of you, but children will sometimes say things about a playmate or a sibling for no other reason than to get them in trouble," Buchanan said as many in attendance nodded. "Adults are no different, meaning that you have to examine this type of evidence to see if it's influenced by a false motive."

"Now, how does this compare with circumstantial evidence?" Tucker asked.

"I must be hungry—but sticking with our cake example. Let's say the mother returned to the kitchen and saw little brother sitting at the table with crumbs on his shirt, chocolate icing on his mouth and nose, and a slice of the cake missing. That's circumstantial evidence, and even though Mom didn't actually see him eating the cake, you can be fairly certain he did it. So the circumstantial evidence can be as reliable as—and sometimes more reliable than—direct evidence."

"I pass the witness," Tucker proclaimed with confidence.

Hill sat in thought until the judge asked if he had anything further for Buchanan. Hill rose and walked slowly to the podium. "Just a few additional questions. Chief, you stated a moment ago that direct evidence can be unreliable, correct?"

"That's right."

"You know who Robert Jackson is and his connection to this case."

"Yes, he's an eyewitness in this case, and I actually interviewed him myself."

"You just told the jury how professors prove eyewitnesses could be unreliable, right?"

"Sure, like those encountering an emergency or surprise situation, as in the classroom example."

"Then the direct evidence testimony of Mr. Jackson should be looked at skeptically by the jury, true?"

"Not at all. He was under no stress or urgency that day, and I know of no reason or motivation for Mr. Jackson to say anything but precisely what he observed."

"No urgency?" Hill said, glancing toward the jury. "According to the state's case, he was watching the prelude to a murder."

"Indeed he was, but he didn't know that at the time. No, I think Mr. Jackson's a *very* credible witness."

"Let's turn to my client's alleged comments when you arrested him. You consider that direct evidence, don't you?"

"Of course, and you can keep saying 'alleged' comments if that makes you feel better, but he said them, and others on my team heard them"

"Fine, but there's nothing circumstantial about that?"

"No, not at all."

"Now, I would assume Mr. Flynn was in an 'urgent situation,' to use your terms, right?"

"He would know best, but I think it's safe to say that he found being arrested for murder with guns trained on him and my knee on his back to be urgent."

"So his alleged statements are suspect under your analysis, right?" Hill pressed.

"Not at all. It's what's known in the law as an 'excited utterance' and a 'statement against interest.' You see, Flynn said something that was damaging to him and did so without deliberation or thought. These are always treated as highly reliable, *especially* in an urgent situation."

"So urgency can make things reliable or suspect, depending on what helps your case. Right, Chief?"

"Objection, argumentative and harassing!" Tucker shouted.

"I'll withdraw the question and pass the witness," Hill said.

The state then called Flynn's neighbor George Merit to the stand and established that he witnessed Flynn throwing a small object in the vacant lot across from his house, and Judge Sullivan recessed the trial for lunch. As Johnson escorted the jurors out of the courtroom, Sullivan nodded to Tucker and Hill. "I'd like to see you two in the back." The men followed the judge into his chambers and stood while Sullivan hung his robe in an antique armoire and sat at his desk.

"Have a seat, guys," Sullivan said as the two men complied. "Chester, you're taking a beating in there."

"I know, Judge. It's always bad during the state's case."

"I know that, but they're laying down a pretty compelling case and, well, you're not—"

"We'll recover, Judge," Hill interrupted. "You have to pick your battles with a Taylor County jury."

"That's another thing, Chester. Why in the hell are we trying this case in Taylor County? Don't get me wrong, I'm thrilled to be bedding down at home each night and not in some motel in Pampa or Lampasas, but why not move it?"

"That's complicated, Judge."

The judge turned to Tucker. "Do you really have the Abram girl's and the defendant's blood on that shoe?"

"I sure do. The DNA matched up and we have Flynn's fingerprint too."

"Look, Lyndon—I think you could save the taxpayers a lot of money if you'd offer first-degree murder and get this case over with. Do that, and I'll insist on a sentence that this guy won't likely outlive."

"Judge, I've got my record to preserve."

"Don't give me the record crap, Lyn! This guy should take anything short of death, and we could let those good eligible voters go home in an election year if you get my drift."

"I can shortcut this, Judge," Hill interceded. "First off, I don't think Lyn would offer a lesser included offense in this case, and even if he did, my client wouldn't take it."

"Excuse me?"

"It's true, Judge," Hill confirmed.

"Chester, I'm trying to yank the needle out of Flynn's arm, and you're telling me he won't take it?" the judge said with frustration, but Hill's silence confirmed the position. "All right then, fine. Go get lunch, and I'll see you guys in forty-five minutes."

That afternoon, Tucker called other officers from the crime lab and capped off the day by calling Bess Abram to the stand. She was visibly shaken as she took the stand, and Tucker took her gently through their family history and a heartwarming description of Taylor's character and charm. Finally, Tucker turned to the day Taylor disappeared, and Bess described in detail Taylor's noble intentions for the trip to the mall and how she was dressed that day.

"Now the tough part, Mrs. Abram," Tucker said, and he handed her the bag with the pink tennis shoes inside. "I've handed you prosecution exhibit numbers thirty-three and thirty-four. I'm sorry, but can you identify these please?"

She took a deep breath. "They're hers."

"Taylor's?"

"Yes," Bess Abram confirmed.

"Do you recall buying these for her?"

"Yes, sir, I do. She had begged me to buy them, for weeks. They were a little pricey, and I thought they were—well … kind of ugly with all of these spangles and things on them," she confessed with a tearful chuckle. "But you know how kids are. Her friends had them, and she wanted them really bad and even offered to pay for them with her own money. So, I relented and bought them for her."

"What shoes did Taylor wear on the day she went missing?"

"These, I'm sure of it. She had worn them every place she went, on every day since I bought them, except for church, of course."

Tucker passed Mrs. Abram, to Hill, who wisely declined to ask any questions.

"That's it for today, ladies and gentlemen," Judge Sullivan said. "We'll resume to tomorrow at the same time, and as always, don't discuss this case with anyone—not with each other, not with your friends or family."

As Tyler walked Mickey to her car, he asked, "Looks like it's going well, right?"

"Real well. If it was a fight, they'd stop it."

CHAPTER 11

⚖

CANIS CANUM EDIT

(Dog Eats Dog—Each Man for Himself)

That evening, the detention officers returned Flynn to the county lockup, and he sat alone in his top-floor jail cell. As time passed with no other cellmates, he dared to believe that his request for isolation had at last been granted. He secured a spot on the top tier of one of the four sets of bunks, each featuring an upper and lower bed. The cell featured a stainless-steel toilet, paper dispenser and sink, and a piece of scratchy sheet metal riveted to the wall to serve as a mirror. The gray concrete floor and cinderblock walls made for a damp, musty environment, and the area generally reeked of urine and mold. His particular cell anchored of one of four long halls on the fifth floor, with cells lining only one side of each. A heavy-gauge steel door guarded the other end of the hall, adjacent to the small room where guards took shifts monitoring feeds from cameras throughout the floor. Also present was a recreation room, shared on a rotating basis by all inmates on the floor.

Flynn flinched when he heard the faint sounds of voices and footsteps emanating from the other end the corridor. The conversations grew louder and were interspersed with intemperate comments and bursts of laughter. Hopes of isolation evaporated when he heard the large entry door to his cell unlock and screech as it swung open. He turned his head only enough to confirm the return of his tormentors from the rec room. Flynn tensed as the door closed and the heavy locking mechanism engaged, and lay still and quiet, facing the wall. As the cellmates took their bunks, one grabbed Flynn by his pant leg and jerked him from his bunk, sending him tumbling down to the sticky floor. The fall knocked the breath out of him and that was the only thing that kept him from crying out in pain.

"This is my bed, you goddamn child killer!" the inmate said as he climbed atop it.

The others laughed as Flynn writhed in pain and struggled to breathe. Though hurt, he was most concerned by the "child killer" reference. Flynn lifted himself from the floor and recovered his breath, then took the remaining unoccupied lower bunk.

"Hey, do you think he got him a little from that girl he killed?" asked an inmate.

"I don't know, man. I swear that dude looks like the type that would like little boys," replied a thin man with long, stringy hair, albino skin, and sleeve tattoos up each arm. Flynn didn't react, hoping that any continuing assault would remain only verbal.

"You ain't just a child killer, man, you is a TV star," mocked a large man with muscular biceps extending from the rolled-up sleeves of his orange jumpsuit. "We all saw you on the tube, and that was one ugly-ass mug shot."

"Yeah, and that lady said this dude's done some other evil shit out there too," the pale-skinned man added. "But he don't look so tough in here with men, now does he?" Flynn turned his head and stared at the man assessing him. He looked hardened, and as if he could hold his own in a fight. Flynn rolled back on his side, with his back to the others.

"Hey, baby killer, maybe you'd like to take on a man for a change," the muscled prisoner said as he leaned down and punched Flynn hard in the back. "Do you feel like a tough guy now?" Flynn's experience told him he was facing another battering, and his only hope of discouraging diminishing future encounters was by aggressively lashing back.

"Go to hell, asshole!" Flynn yelled loudly enough for the guards to hear, while moving quickly off his bunk. He stood and delivered three sharp jabs to the muscled man's abdomen, and the man gasped. Flynn then tried to finish it with an upper cut, but missed, causing him to lose his balance and stagger backward. The large exposed arms of the man lunged toward Flynn, and he braced himself with eyes shut. Flynn felt that man's hands and at least two other sets grasping his shirt and returning him to the floor. He yelled loudly as the attackers pinned him to the floor, and all he could do was shout, kick, and try to cover his face as he absorbed a barrage of fists, feet, and spit. Although it couldn't have taken more than a minute before guards arrived, Flynn felt the time go by much slower.

"Break it up! Break it up!" yelled one of the two guards entering the cell as each pealed inmates away. As Flynn eased his arms from his face, all could see he was bleeding. One of the guards pulled paper towels from the stainless-steel dispenser by the toilet and threw them on the floor next to him. Flynn struggled to breathe as he sat up and used the towels to begin wiping blood. The guards each took an arm and lifted Flynn to his feet. He felt woozy and found it hard and painful to inhale and had an intense pain in his rib cage.

"We want you guys to settle down and stop this shit. You understand?" demanded one guard as he held a metal baton in his right hand and was slapping it into the palm of his left.

"Hey, man, they ain't gonna to stop! You guys need to get me the hell out of here," Flynn pleaded.

"What? You're already in our exclusive penthouse," sneered the larger of the two guards as the inmates laughed.

Now irate, Flynn advanced and pointed his finger toward the guard's face and said, "You gotta do more than joke about this. I'm—" In a flash, Flynn's arm with the pointing finger received a blow from the baton, and Flynn groaned and reeled backward, saying, "What the hell?"

"Don't ever pull that again, or you'll get it real bad."

Flynn leaned against the metal sink, gasping for air as the other guard advised the group, "Look, fellas—I'm gonna be checking on y'all periodically. If this shit happens again, by *any* of you, you all can kiss rec time good-bye for a whole week. Got it?"

Flynn sat on his lower bunk, and as the guards turned to leave, he pleaded, "I got a busted rib."

"You look fine to me," the large guard with the baton smirked.

The other guard squatted next to Flynn, whispering, "Listen. Get some sleep, and if it's not better in the morning, we'll get you to the dispensary before you go over for court."

Flynn lay on the bunk, facing the wall, and closed his eyes. When the cell went lights out he heard a low voice. "There's always tomorrow … baby killer."

The next morning, Mickey and her sign-carrying brigade convened behind the courthouse at the ropes. When Flynn's escort rolled to a stop, the taunts flew, and as Flynn passed by, Mickey noticed that Flynn was moving slowly, and unlike the other mornings, his head hung low, and made no eye contact. Glimpsing at the right side of his face, she noticed it was swollen and discolored and dark scabs appeared on his arms and face. Mickey and the others held their signs and delivered gibes nonetheless until entourage crossed the threshold and the door closed.

"Shit, Willie! What happened to you?" Hill asked as he entered the holding cell.

"I got it real bad last night."

"The inmates?"

"Yes. It seems there was some sort of story on me on the news. When the animals came back from the rec room, they were on a tear about it and even called me 'baby killer'."

"A story, huh? My secretary said she saw something like that on the news."

"Yeah. I didn't see it, but it apparently showed my mug shot and talked about those other girls and all," Flynn said as he changed positions in his chair and then winced.

"What caused you to do that?"

"Man, I'm so sore that I can't move without pain. I really think I got a broken rib, but they don't think so."

"A doctor said that?"

"Shit no! The guard said so."

"Did you get *any* medical attention?"

"Yes, if you call throwing some paper towels to me while I'm on the floor, medical attention," Flynn lamented. "One guard said I might get in to be seen this morning, but it didn't happen."

"Beside your ribs, where else do you hurt?" Hill asked.

"It might be easier to say where I don't hurt. Man, they hit and kicked the shit out of me last night. My legs and chest hurt, but mainly it's the ribs hurting the most. I had trouble breathing last night, but it's a little better this morning."

"Have you had any more luck getting help from the guards?"

"Not really. In fact, when it blew up last night, it seemed they took their sweet time getting to the cell."

"I was assured by command that they would be more protective."

"Well, they ain't got the message on the cell block. I got this one from one of them for complaining the wrong way," Flynn said, pointing to the bruise on his right arm.

"Willie, this is just plain wrong, and I'm sorry. I'll talk to them again when we're done today.

"Do you think you can do this today?" Hill asked, nodding toward the courtroom.

"I think so."

"No offense, Willie, but you look like hell. Have you seen yourself?"

"No, all we have for a mirror is a piece of sheet metal and it's too scratched to see much. I tried to get a peek in the rearview mirror in the squad car but couldn't. All I can say is that if I look half as bad as I feel I must look like shit."

"I'm sorry, but I can't let you go in there like this. I'm gonna ask for a postponement till this clears up."

The comment caused Flynn to sit up and turn to Hill, but the move alone caused him to exhale rapidly like one who had just been punched in the stomach. "No delays," Flynn managed with a groan.

"Willie, if you go out there like this, the jury will make assumptions and—"

"I don't give a shit what they think, remember?"

"Listen, if we're really gonna do this today, I have to do something about your face," Hill said as the bailiff entered the cell.

"Good morning, Chester."

"Mornin', Carl," Hill said as he placed the tie from the first day under Flynn's collar and cinched it.

"Is he doing better?" Carl asked.

"A little."

"Hell, when they brought him over this morning I thought we were gonna to need to call an ambulance."

Hill rose and turned to Carl. "I got to fix him up some before he goes back in there. Can you buy me fifteen minutes or so?"

"I think so. We're still waitin' on a juror anyway."

"Thanks, Carl. I'll be back soon, but don't let him escape while I'm gone, all right?"

Carl smiled and said, "I'll do my best."

When Hill returned from the nearby drugstore and reached the holding cell, Carl watched as Hill went to work. He began by placing beige bandages that closely mimicked Flynn's skin tone over the red and purple abrasions and scabs. Hill then removed a small bottle of face makeup and began dabbing the contents on the marked and bruised spots on his face and hands, knowing his suit jacket would cover the rest.

"Hey, I've been meaning to ask you. Did you get a chance to speak with my mother?" Flynn asked as Hill finished up with the cosmetics.

"I did, and I told her who I was and that you sent well wishes."

"How is she?"

"I didn't ask her directly, and I don't know what she normally sounds like, but she sounded really weak and confused, Willie."

"Shit," Flynn said as he shook his head. "Thanks for doing that. Maybe if you have time down the road, you could check in on her again."

"Sure thing, Willie."

"He looks lovely," Carl said as the two men rose to follow him out.

The trial continued several days, during which the prosecution wound down its case by presenting testimony from witnesses, including the coroner and the remaining officers who participated in the raid of Flynn's home and collected evidence. Tucker took evidence from technicians who preserved the DNA samples and maintained the necessary chain of custody of them. A forensic expert was called to present an overlay of Flynn's fingerprint from his jail booking on top of the one found on the shoe, which demonstrated an exact match. This same witness discussed the DNA analysis and his comparison of the samples collected by the police, to that taken from Taylor Abram's body and Flynn. He described the testing and how results established that Taylor's and Flynn's blood DNA existed on the shoe found in the field with a match confidence of over ten million to one. Tucker's finale was to question Ted Abram, who answered questions about Taylor and her disappearance and concluded with wrenching testimony of his identification of his only child's lifeless body. The state rested.

That evening, Hill discussed with Flynn his right to testify on his own behalf and, more importantly, to reinforce his constitutional right not to. Hill was concerned about broaching the topic for fear that his volatile client would demand to testify, only to confess on the stand. But after warning that such an episode could cause problems on appeal and risk another trial, Flynn agreed to waive his right but questioned, "What's the deal with the appeal?"

"If you're convicted, the case will be appealed to a higher court for review."

"Why?" Flynn asked with agitation.

"Perhaps no one appealed any of your other cases, but all capital murder convictions are appealed, whether you want it or not."

"Who represents me on that?"

"Typically, I'd get another lawyer appointed to do it, but under these circumstances, I'll stay on for it."

"Where will I be during all of this?"

"Assuming you're convicted of capital murder, you'll wait it out on death row."

"That's good, but this appeal shit's stupid."

"I understand, but while we're on procedures, keep another thing in mind. If you succeed in getting convicted, the trial isn't over, there'll be a separate punishment phase."

"Punishment phase?"

"Yes. The jury needs to sentence you, Willie."

"I thought the judge would do that."

"Not in a capital case."

"I see. So what happens at this punishment thing?"

"The state will use it to explain why you should die, and we're supposed to prove why you shouldn't. I can't just roll over on this, Willie. I have to put someone on the stand that can vouch for you, like a relative, longtime friend, a pastor, or a family member."

"No family. Understand?" Flynn demanded.

"Look, Willie—I already know about your mom. Also I've checked your pre-sentencing report, and I know that you've got a brother here. Maybe he can—"

"You ain't involving them in this mess!"

"Fine, first things first. Let's get through this trial phase, and we'll take this up as it comes. But just know that I won't have a lot of time between the end of the trial and the punishment phase, so think about it."

On Monday, Hill began his anemic defense by calling police personnel to the stand and questioned each on how the DNA evidence was handled. He established two technical breaches of protocol but little else. As his last witness, Hill called a forensic expert that he had hired with the money budgeted for the psychological evaluation. Hill used this witness to discuss chain-of-custody irregularities and the potential contamination of some of the prosecution's evidence. Hill rested his case, with no rebuttal from the prosecution, and the judge informed all that closing arguments would commence the following morning.

Anticipating a quick conviction and the ensuing punishment phase, Hill used that evening to contact several of his colleagues that had defended capital murder cases. He explained his need for a witness to challenge the death penalty itself and settled on a clergyman from Fort Worth who had testified in several death penalty cases.

The next morning, Tucker strode to the podium on shiny, black, pointy-toed boots and launched an unrelenting attack on Flynn. During his address to the jury, he referred to Flynn as a "predator" and compared him to a "rabid dog" while recounting the details of the state's evidence. He emphasized that when Flynn was arrested, he acknowledged involvement. He observed, without any objection from Hill, that since Flynn's arrest, no other girls had disappeared from the community. Tucker's final words urged that to assure the community would ever rest well in the future, justice demanded a conviction.

"Your turn, Mr. Hill," the Sullivan said.

"Thank you, Judge," Hill said as he rose, buttoned his suit jacket, and faced the jury. "Today a human life is in your hands, and this is likely the most serious decision that each of you will make for the rest of your lives. What you do will stay with you as long as you're on this earth, and as such, you deserved the best evidence to base this serious decision on. With all of the resources of the state of Texas, they brought you no evidence that Willie Lee Flynn did anything to Taylor Abram. No murder weapon, no motive, and after all of this, do we even really know how Taylor Abram died? It would be easy to just pick a villain and convict my client and simply walk away. After all, someone should pay for this dastardly act of violence, right? But it will take courage for you to hold the state to its burden of proof, and I strongly maintain they did not sustain that burden, and find Willie Lee Flynn not guilty."

The jurors retired to the jury room to begin their deliberations, and Judge Sullivan advised all in the gallery that since the length of the deliberation was unpredictable, he would advise the media and wait thirty minutes before reading the verdict in open court. This would afford many who had watched the trial closely the chance to witness the verdict firsthand without congregating in the courthouse for the indeterminable period of time.

Mickey and Tyler opted to have lunch at the courthouse cafeteria and then to wait it out on the courthouse lawn on a concrete bench. They spent over two hours talking and reminiscing losing track of time along the way, until each noticed several vehicles simultaneously converging on the courthouse square. They knew that this activity signaled a verdict, and they joined reporters, support-group members, and others scurrying inside.

The courtroom filled with anxious spectators, and the atmosphere was electric until the judge entered and Carl Johnson called for silence, and all waited silently as Carl guided the jury in. Once seated, the judge asked the jurors if they had reached a verdict, and an older man on the back row, rose and acknowledged they had. Judge Sullivan asked Flynn to rise to accept the verdict as both extra bailiffs stood behind him. Client and attorney rose, and Carl handed the decision to the judge. Sullivan stoically unfolded the paper and read it in silence, then said, "The jury has answered question number one of the court's charge on the count of capital murder: 'Guilty as charged.'" An outburst of emotion erupted from the crowded courtroom. The Abrams tearfully embraced, and Tyler pulled Mickey toward him for a heartfelt hug.

"Silence!" Judge Sullivan barked and rapped the bench with his wooden gavel, but the uproar subsided only slightly. "Silence or I will have this courtroom cleared!" This time the spectators obeyed, and Sullivan continued, "Mr. Flynn, you've been found guilty of the offense of capital murder. As such, you are not entitled to a bond. Therefore I remand you to the county jail until the jury reaches a verdict on your punishment." He dismissed the jurors for the day, and Flynn, now handcuffed and staid, walked toward his holding cell, flanked by the bailiffs.

The punishment phase began the next morning, and as Mickey entered the courtroom, an enlarged photograph of a young girl immediately claimed her attention. She was certain it was Taylor Abram's school photo and had been selected by the prosecutors as the best representation of her youthful innocence. Tucker decided to call only two witnesses in this phase, Bess and Ted Abram. The two were in many respects mirror images of each other, each devoted parents, shaken, nervous and exhausted. But each were likewise determined to tell all present about Taylor's life and loves, dreams and goals, and the unhealable wound her death represented to them. Bess testified first, and many jurors and spectators cried as Tucker prompted emotional details with his questions. Mr. Abram followed and glared at Flynn through most of the questioning. At the prosecutor's prompting, Ted ended his testimony proclaiming that the only way to avenge his daughter's murder was to sentence Flynn to his death.

When Mr. Abram returned to his seat, Hill called his only witness, the Reverend Dwight Sims, to the stand. As he entered the courtroom with Carl, the jury saw Sims who was dressed in a long black robe with a large wooden crucifix hanging on a silver chain at the middle of his chest. He took the stand and used his own Bible to lay his left hand on as he rose his right and took his oath. Hill began his examination with a rendition of the reverend's background and theological bona fides. He then directed the focus to statistics from the Department of Justice that Reverend Sims had provided Hill in advance.

"Who does get charged with the death penalty in this country?" Hill asked.

"An analysis of the data shows that when you compare similar crimes and fact patterns, perpetrators who are poor or minority or both are at a three-to-one higher likelihood of being charged with a capital crime."

"As opposed to lesser charges like murder or manslaughter?"

"That's correct."

"You can see that my client's Caucasian, so why's he sitting here facing the death penalty?"

Tucker jumped to his feet and said, "Objection, Judge! He's facing the death penalty because he kidnapped and killed a defenseless child!"

"I object to the prejudicial speaking objection!" said the red-faced Hill.

Sullivan shook his head and looked scornfully at the two advocates. "Sustained and sustained. Now let's get on with it."

Hill turned back to Sims, asking, "Can you please answer the question, Reverend?"

"Yes. As I understand it, Mr. Flynn has lived his entire life well under the nation's poverty level, and as such, that makes him a likely candidate to be sitting in this situation."

"As opposed to simply facing a trial that would be limited to just a long prison sentence, right?"

"Precisely."

Hill stood in front of Sims and asked, "Now to the second question. Who gets the death penalty in this country?"

Sims looked toward the jury and said, "It should come as no surprise to anyone that the death rows in this country are full of minorities and the poor."

Prompted by Hill's questions, Sims then testified about the sanctity of human life and portrayed Flynn as a "wayward sinner" but nevertheless one of "God's creations" who was deserving of mercy. He then offered the obvious, that nothing the jury could do would ever return Taylor to the Abrams and urged them not to place tragedy on top of tragedy by taking another human life. Hill passed the witness, and though Tucker felt Sims offered little to sway the jury, he refused to take that chance.

"Reverend, you seem to be up on the crime statistics, so let me ask you this. Isn't it true that the overwhelming percentage of crimes in America, including violent crimes, are committed by the poor and minorities?"

"Yes ... but—"

"Thank you. Reverend, what church are you affiliated with, sir?"

"If you're asking about my denomination, I'm nondenominational."

"That's good to know, but I mean what church?" Tucker repeated, drawing a puzzled look from Sims. "Your church? You know, if I ever wanted to see one your services, where would I go?"

"I see. I don't have a church in that regard, counselor. I consider myself a shepherd to all flocks and choose not to limit myself to a single congregation."

"A shepherd, huh? You're more than that, you're a consultant too, aren't you?"

"I'm not sure what you mean."

"Aren't most of your flocks comprised of twelve sheep at a time?" Tucker asked, nodding toward the jury box. "I mean, how many times have you been asked to give this every-life-counts spiel to a death-penalty jury?"

"I don't know the total."

"Too many to keep up with?"

"Objection, Your Honor. Badgering the witness."

"Sustained. Move along, Mr. Tucker."

"Reverend, I see you're carrying a Bible with you."

"Yes, I don't go anywhere without the good book."

"I see. There's nothing in that Bible that prohibits putting murderers to death, is there? I mean there's the eye-for-an-eye reference and many examples of evildoers deprived of their life as a consequence of their bad behavior, true?"

"Yes, that's true, but I haven't said it was against the Bible to do so. But what the Bible also discusses fairness, mercy, grace, and compassion, not to mention the instruction to turn the other cheek."

"Mr. Sims, I know you didn't see the testimony of the parents of this murdered child," Tucker said, pointing to Taylor's picture. "But trust me when I say they aren't turning the other cheek! Pass the witness."

The punishment phase was concluded, and the jurors returned to the jury room for the last time to decide Flynn's fate. They wasted no time making their decision, reaching a consensus in less than an hour. With the jury seated, Johnson brought the jury form to the judge, who again ordered Flynn to rise. The courtroom was silent as Judge Sullivan said, "Mr. Flynn, the jury has sentenced you to death by lethal injection for the murder of Taylor Abram. Therefore, you are hereby remanded to the state penitentiary in Huntsville, Texas, where you will remain until the date of your death. May God have mercy on your soul."

Though he knew his client was pleased, Hill hung his head at the gravity of the moment. Flynn leaned over to his dejected lawyer and whispered, "Don't worry, Counselor. This is for the best."

Following the trial, Mickey's refuge from solitude, isolation, and languishing at home, was her work. She returned to the diligent pursuit of her cases, thus creating a barrier from the recurring bad thoughts that thrived during idle time and restless lonely nights. Flynn's conviction offered her only fleeting satisfaction though, considering that the verdict did not close the cases for parents of seven other girls.

Mickey drove home from work one night, drew a hot bath, soaked in the tub, and with eyes closed weighed her options. *I have to know the truth, and one person knows it. Flynn's trial's over, so maybe he'll be willing to talk about all of this. After all, he's got nothing more to lose and who knows more about all of this than him. But cooperate ... with me? That's nuts, isn't it? Plus, how do I get access to someone on death row? I know some prisoners get visits, but death row?*

As absurd as the notion struck her at first, she nevertheless found herself at the office the following evening, researching how one would go about communicating with an inmate. This included reviewing the visitation rules for the Texas Department of Corrections, but she failed to find anything conclusive with her initial foray. The next morning she arrived at the office early and was pleased that among the vehicles present were those owned by both Baylor and Becker, and she decided to float the concept to them. She walked from the garage, up the stairs to the first floor, and when she reached Baylor's door, she knocked lightly and when invited in she was pleased that both men were present.

"Hey, fellas," Mickey said taking a seat on Baylor's couch.

"Good morning, Mickey," Becker said. "That was a great victory in the Flynn case."

"Indeed it was," she said smiling.

"Having the trial behind you must be a big relief, Michelle." Baylor said.

"Yes sir, Mr. B. But I gotta tell you, watching as a bystander was as stressful as any trial I've ever had."

"We saw the news," Becker said. "I think you brought Mr. Flynn a little stress of his own."

"You saw the interview, huh?"

"Sure did. I think Harrison did too."

"Oh?" Mickey said, turning to Baylor.

"Yes, I did, and at the risk of violating the firm's harassment policy, I would add that you were lovely, articulate and very telegenic."

"Thanks, Mr. B, and if that is a violation, I'll sign a full release," she said, smiling. "But that's all behind me now, and I thank you both for the time off to see it through."

"We're glad it worked out, Mickey," Becker said. "How are you getting along otherwise?"

Her expression turned dour. "I'm doing okay, I suppose. I was happy to see Flynn convicted and all, but the result still leaves a lot of unanswered questions. I really want to know what happened to Reagan. That truly eats at me, and I know it's hard to understand, but I want to find her, even if she's ... you know."

"I think we can understand how you must feel," Baylor said. "But how do you think you'll get to that level of finality?"

"Good question, huh? I don't expect the police will devote many resources to this now, and that leaves only one person who has what I need, and he's rotting away on death row. So, I've been considering trying to reach out to Flynn."

"Oh, that'll work. After all, y'all got along so great behind the courthouse," Ford said.

"I understand, Ford, but can you think of another way?" Mickey asked as she sat forward on the edge of the couch. "The only guy who knows Reagan's fate has been tried and is going to be executed someday, and his knowledge dies with him. So, with his conviction, perhaps he'll help."

"How do you propose to get through to him?" Baylor asked.

"I could write to him. I researched the procedures on death row, and while it's quite a process, inmates can get letters there. But I'm afraid there's no way to effectively do what I want to by mail. I think it has to be in person."

"You want to go to the prison?" Baylor asked.

"I think I do. I've been looking into it but was curious as to what you know about the process."

Baylor dumped pipe residue in the ashtray. "I've visited death-row inmates, but I know for a fact that the TDC rules for lawyer consultations are different. But I do know families and members of the press have gotten access, so there must be a way."

"I know it's kind of nutty, but I'm really going to explore it."

"Let us know what we can do to help, Mickey," Becker offered. Mickey thanked the men, as she left for her office, Ford closed the office door and sat down.

"What do you think, Harrison?"

"I can see letting that resource go untapped being unacceptable to her, but I think it's a bad idea. I believe she'll be manipulated, and in the end, it'll have more of a chance to inflict further harm than to bring peace."

Mickey continued to turn to the support group for inspiration and updates, and they now viewed Mickey as a co-leader with Evelyn Howard. Her guidance on the public protests, the highly regarded television interview, and her legal knowledge had her ensconced as a trusted figure among the members. The first meeting after the trial was a mixer hosted by a local restauranteur in honor of the support group. Mickey decided to use the occasion to pitch the concept of traveling her to Huntsville, and was eager to gauge members' reactions. As the now-familiar faces trickled in, some helped themselves to hot appetizers from two large stainless-steel warming bins, and others sipped cocktails.

Evelyn Howard brought the gathering to order. "Welcome to you all and especially our newest members, Mr. and Mrs. Blake Thomas. We also thank Mr. Fitzgerald for arranging this celebration for us in his lovely restaurant. Now I'm informed that Michelle Grant has some business to put before us, so the floor is yours, dear."

Mickey set her cocktail glass on the table, rose, and said, "Victory is sweet, isn't it!" she said to cheers and applause. "With Flynn now where he belongs on death row, we can all sleep a little easier at night. Thankfully, the Abrams have found justice, and while I know well that the verdict doesn't heal all of their deep wounds, I hope it brings some sense of peace," she said and nodded toward the couple. "We likewise have to be thankful for the contribution of the DA's office, the police, and—"

"And don't forget Mr. Hill!" Toni Hayes said drawing laughter.

"Yes, let's not overlook Mr. Hill's contribution," Mickey said. "Let's hope his lackluster performance is replicated on the appeal."

"What appeal?" Bess Abram asked.

"I'm no expert on criminal law, but a lot of criminal convictions get appealed, and if I'm not mistaken, *all* death penalty convictions do."

"We hear that term 'appeal' on the news a lot, but what does it mean exactly?" Mr. Brown asked.

"It goes to a higher court where the lawyers point out mistakes that the trial court made. If they find enough error, it can be sent back for a retrial."

"God no!" Bess Abram said. "Do you think that can happen, do you Michelle?"

"I wouldn't worry about that. The prosecution tried a really airtight case," Mickey said.

"When will this appeal part be over?" Ted Abram asked.

"It depends," Mickey said. "This could conceivably go all the way to the Supreme Court."

"Oh my. The Supreme Court!" Mrs. Howard said.

"Yes, ma'am. So the execution could still be as far off as a decade."

"That seems awfully unfair," Ted Abram said.

Mickey smiled and said, "I understand, but the system's set up that way. Try to see it from the state's angle. We've all seen those documentaries where new facts emerge, like DNA evidence or someone else is proven to be the perpetrator, and the state has to apologize and let someone out of prison after years or decades of confinement. I think the state's very leery about that happening in a death penalty case and having to apologize to a tombstone."

"I see your point, and thank you for it," Mr. Abram said.

"We're all thankful, Michelle," Mrs. Howard added. "We're very fortunate to have your legal perspective, and you deserve a lot of credit for kicking our group up a notch."

"I agree," Barry Brown said. "Giving Flynn hell behind the courthouse was great!"

"That's right," Toni Hayes agreed, "hell, I haven't carried a protest sign since college, and we owe it all to you, Michelle."

"Oh, I don't deserve any credit, I just—"

"Nonsense!" Mr. Brown interjected. "Until you came, we were good about consoling each other and making our presence known in the courtroom, but now we have a higher purpose."

"They're right," Mrs. Howard added. "I was going to mention this in the treasurer's report, but our donations are way up. We've also received several calls since our last meeting, and as many as six new people are joining because we were so proactive."

"That's good news," Mickey said. "But all of y'all had a role in this success, and we need to keep momentum and forge ahead, and that brings me to the business I want to discuss. While justice has been served for the Abrams, for others like me and for several of you here, very important questions remain unanswered. The undeniable fact is that little is being done by the police to find our missing girls, and someone has to try to further these cases. Consequently, I'm working on a strategy that I'd like to share. You see, I am making plans to go to Huntsville to meet with Flynn."

The group broke out in in murmurs and whispers until Mrs. Hayes said, "I think it is a great idea. With him now convicted, maybe he'll want to come clean with all of us."

"That's what I've been thinking, Toni," Mickey said.

Mr. Brown said, "I see your point, Michelle, but considering your antagonism with him, are you really the best candidate for this?"

"Why, Barry, are you volunteering to go?" Mickey joked as he took two steps back and shook his head. "Look—I hear what you're saying, but I don't think he'll know who I am until I get there, so I'll have the element of surprise. Also, I've learned by talking to knowledgeable people that you shouldn't think of the criminal mind in the same fashion as you would the guy next door. In fact, their thoughts and actions that are often the exact opposite of what you'd expect. It could be that, in some perverse sense, I'm the best person to go. But, this is all in the preliminary phases and will be very difficult to pull off, but I just wanted you all to know what I'm thinking."

For the first time since the trial concluded, Mickey invited Tyler to her house. It was a Friday night, and she had prepared dinner and purchased two bottles of his favorite wine.

"I'm glad you asked me over," Tyler said as he entered her house and she walked him into her living room. He kissed her on the cheek and said, "Sure smells good in here."

"Thanks. I believe you'll enjoy it," she said as Tyler noticed that her Christmas tree, still stood, fully decorated, and with the gifts underneath.

"Now that it's been a couple of weeks, how do you feel about the trial?" he asked following her to the kitchen.

"It's great," she responded with a shrug as she used an oven mitt to pull a broiled chicken from the oven.

"Somehow, you don't convince me."

"No, really, it's fine. I mean, what's not to be happy about? Flynn was convicted and is off the street. Are you satisfied?"

"With the legal stuff I am. But I still can't believe our little girl's gone," Tyler sighed. "It's tough, but I guess it's time just move on."

"Easier said than done, huh?" Mickey said, mashing potatoes in a ceramic bowl.

"Yes," he responded as he walked to the silver mixing bowl and used his index finger to take a swipe of the mashed potatoes. "But I think a start would be to—"

"I know what you're gonna to say. We need a funeral or something," Mickey said, and Tyler's expression told her she guessed right. "Tyler, I just can't do that right now."

"I know how you feel about this, but we've discussed closure and finality, and our friends, our family, need to grieve too—you know?"

"I know in my heart that you're right, but I must have some proof before committing to something like that."

"Mick, your parents are gone, but my mom's still alive, and so are two of her siblings. You don't see it, but I keep taking heat on this, and just keep making up excuses. Look—it doesn't have to be a funeral, okay? It can be more like—you know—like a memorial. It's been months, Mick, and as difficult as it is, wouldn't Reagan want us to move on?"

"I am moving on, Tyler," she lodged, but when Tyler glanced over to the Christmas tree, Mickey was defensive. "I just haven't had time to get to that, okay?"

Tyler let it go and Mickey walked him over to the dining table and served up a nice home-cooked meal. When they were done, Tyler helped clear the table, and they were enjoying an after-dinner drink when Mickey floated her idea. "You know, Tyler, I think the only way we're ever going to know what happened to Reagan is to get the answer directly from Flynn himself."

Assuming she was joking, he said flippantly, "Sure, Mickey. Let's run over to death row and ask him." Mickey simply looked down while running the tip of her finger around the rim of her wine glass. "You're serious, aren't you?"

"Who else can help with this? The police? The support group? I mean, is there a true down side in trying to get to the truth before he's executed, for God's sake?"

"Fine. Why don't you write him a letter and see if he responds?" Tyler suggested.

"I've already thought about that, but he'll never answer a letter, Tyler. Plus, he needs to answer very specific questions about all the girls, some of which will depend on responses to other questions. No, this can't be accomplished in a written exchange."

"Maybe a series of letters? Why not try that?"

"First off, I have to get the letters to him. I've researched that, and it's very complicated, to say the least, and outgoing mail's even worse. Plus, he has to worry about his appeal and can't have a paper trail admitting all of this stuff."

"What are you suggesting?"

"I have to talk to him face-to-face to have any chance of success and to regain my sanity."

"What about therapy for sanity?" Tyler asked.

Exasperated, Mickey snapped, "Tyler, what therapist can tell me these things? Should I contact a psychic too while I'm at it?"

"Is that next?" Tyler asked grinning, easing the tension.

"I know this all sounds crazy, Ty, believe me, I do. But can you honestly think of a reason not to try? Even if it's a one percent chance, don't I have to take it? I know you're worn out by all of this, but if I can get it set up, will you go with me?"

Tyler sat up straight in his chair. "Me? Go with you all the way to Huntsville?"

She reached over and caressed his arm. "Please?"

He pondered and said, "I'll think about it."

"Great. That's not a no, so that means yes! Want another drink?"

"Make it a double, please!" he said. "But look—I'm not committing to it … I just need to … you know … think about it."

"Don't make me beg," Mickey pleaded.

"Mickey, you know I'm against this, but if you're dead-set on going, I'll support you."

"So you *will* go with me!"

"I didn't say that!"

She groaned and asked, "What did you mean by supporting me? Giving me bus fair?"

Tyler laughed. "That's the least I could do."

"Well, that's not enough, damn it. Go with me! It'll be fun—kinda like a vacation."

"Oh boy! A trip halfway across Texas to go to a prison?"

"Sounds exotic, doesn't it? So will you do it?"

He looked into her hopeful eyes and said, "Sure, why not?"

The next morning, Mickey was in the firm library continuing her research of the Texas prison system and its visitation protocols. She learned some helpful tips, but felt most of the information was not applicable to death row. With special dispensation from Woody, she took two books from the library to her office to review and began to place phone calls. She first tried the Department of Corrections in Austin, but after being transferred to several desks, no one seemed to have the answers. She decided to dial directly to the Huntsville State Prison, home of Texas's Death Row, and was transferred to a person in charge of visitation.

"TDC administration. May I help you?" a woman answered.

"Ma'am, my name is Michelle Grant, and I have a question about visitation there. I want to visit inmate William Lee or Willie Lee Flynn."

"We have a lot of prisoners here, ma'am. Do you know his inmate number?"

"No, ma'am, but he's on death row."

"Oh, that narrows it down," the woman said, giggling. "Let me make sure you're on his visitation list. What's your name again?"

"Michelle Grant, but I'm not going to be on his list," Mickey advised.

"Well then, that would be square one. You'll need to submit a request directly to the inmate, fill out and sign a form, and agree to a background check."

"I'll prepare the request, and I'm fine with the background check. I'm a lawyer."

"Oh. Are you his lawyer?"

"No, ma'am."

"I see. So once the request is done and the background check is complete, we'll see if the inmate will add you to the list."

"He must consent, huh?"

"Yes."

"What if he refuses?"

"Then no visit. Let me send you the paperwork, and we'll go from there. Okay?"

Mickey gave the woman her contact information, and that evening she crafted her written request:

> Mr. Flynn:
>
> I am making this request for you to place me on your visitor list. I would like to spend some time speaking with you. Please promptly notify the correctional authorities of your consent to my visit, and I will notify the Department of Corrections of the precise date and time of my arrival. I look forward to seeing you.
>
> Sincerely,
> Michelle Grant

Two weeks passed with no response to her letter, and Mickey phoned the prison and asked for the same visitation extension. She reached the same woman from her prior call and inquired if they had received her letter and her completed form. The woman readily confirmed that they had her documents and that the background check was in order but then informed her that Flynn denied her request.

"He refused? What was his reason?" Mickey asked.

"Ma'am, all I got here is a list that logs in the requests and the prisoner's response, and it says here, 'rejected per inmate.' They're not required to say why."

Mickey thanked the woman for the information and hung up, feeling cheated and powerless, but not ready to give up. She penned a second letter:

Willie Lee Flynn:

I recently sent you a request that I be placed on your visitation list, and I have since learned that you denied it. I was not surprised. You see, I am the mother of one of your victims, and you apparently don't want to look me in the eye. But I must remind you that you already have. I was outside the courthouse every morning when you walked in. I gave the interview on TV about you on the morning of the second day of your trial, and you have read my signs too. Remember?

You killed my innocent teenage daughter, and I want to know the truth as to what you did, how you did it, and where she and the other girls are. Unlike you, I do want to look you in the eye and hear every despicable detail. Show some guts and put me on the list! My girl's name was Reagan. She disappeared on December 14th from Town East Mall in Brinkman, and her picture is enclosed.

/S/ Reagan's Mom, Michelle Grant

Eleven days after mailing the letter, Mickey was working at her desk when Marlene buzzed her on the intercom. "There's a Captain Madison from the Department of Corrections on the phone."

When the call transferred, Mickey answered it and heard a deep voice say, "Mrs. Grant?"

"Yes, sir."

"Ma'am, I'm calling to inform you that you have been placed on the visitor's list for inmate William Lee Flynn, and the approval's good for ninety days."

"Thank you, Captain! How do I go about setting up a meeting with him?"

"Visitation is available Tuesday through Friday but no holidays. You need to give at least forty-eight hours' notice by phone of your intent to visit. This is needed to allow for the enhanced security arrangements for a death-row visitation. We may have scheduling conflicts, so you should call and assure my office has cleared the date before making any travel plans."

"Understood. What do I do when I get to the prison?" Mickey asked.

"Follow the signs to visitation, and when you get there, you can ask for me personally."

Mickey was delighted and immediately phoned Tyler and relayed the news.

"So when do you want to go?" he asked.

"As soon as possible! Now that I know I'm approved, I've got to do it right away. I'm required to give a minimum of forty-eight hours' prior notice, so depending on your schedule, I'd like to give the prison notice that we'll visit this Friday."

"My schedule's pretty light. Have you checked the distance?"

"It's six hours or so each way. If the prison can accommodate, I say we leave on Thursday, and I'll plan to meet Flynn Friday morning."

"Six hours, huh? You know it's almost June, and it's going to be a long, hot trip."

"Ty, it's the second week of May, and we're not going by box car," she said, sensing an attempt to back out.

"I know, but it's just that ..."

"Ty, quit it, will ya?" she said playfully. "Let's do this thing! I'll even drive if you want."

"Okay, okay," he relented. "I don't mind driving, but since my car's business owned, let's take yours."

"That's fine, and we can take turns."

"Okay. Listen, are you sure that this is something you really want to do?

"Tyler, there's no question I have to do this, and I'll get it set up. My only hesitation is missing a couple more days of work. But I'll knuckle down between now and Thursday and make it right."

CHAPTER 12

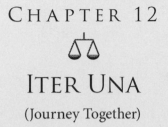

ITER UNA

(Journey Together)

The Trip to Huntsville
May 12

Thursday arrived, and Tyler met Mickey at her house. They loaded her car, and he drove the first leg of the trip, heading southeast across the plains of West Texas toward the Piney Woods of East Texas. They stopped only twice for fuel, snacks, and to switch drivers, and as they drew near to Huntsville, the largely flat expanses of mesquite trees gave way to thick pine forests and hilly terrain. They reached the Huntsville city limits and made their way down the town's major artery, Sam Houston Avenue. As they drove, each were struck by the quaint surroundings of the scenic college town. They spotted the sign for Sam Houston State University and looked left to see the rolling hills and stately buildings of the college campus. Mickey explained that she had discussed the trip with Becker, an alumnus of the university, and knew from his instructions that the motel, also bearing the name of the name of the Texas hero, would be nearby. She spotted the elevated sign with the image old Sam Houston prominently displayed on it. As they pulled into the parking lot, they assessed the older, two-story motel and noticed a separate building that served as a registration office, and Tyler parked in the courtyard near that building.

"So this is it," Mickey said, staring at the wooden sign with

"Registration" carved into it and suspended by a pair of chains above the entrance.

"It's certainly not the Waldorf," Tyler said as they walked toward the office.

"Oh, cut it out. It's a little dated, but I think it's cute."

"I'm sure it'll be fine, but is everything in this town named Sam Houston-something?"

"Becker says Huntsville was his final home," she explained as they entered the office.

"Looking at the age of this place, he might have died here," Tyler joked.

They placed their bags on the floor and stood at the counter, unnoticed. The elderly clerk sat at a desk licking stamps and applying them to a stack of envelopes. Tyler cleared his throat to gain his attention, but the attempt was in vain. Mickey turned her head to snicker as Tyler reached over and struck the top of a silver desk bell. The clerk jumped slightly, turned, and said, "Oh! Howdy, folks. How can I help you?"

"Good afternoon, sir. We need a room for one night," Tyler said.

"Do y'all have a reservation?" the elderly gentleman inquired. Neither had thought to make one, and a worried expression washed over Mickey's face, until the clerk laughed and pointed out the wide front window to the near empty parking lot.

"That's funny," Mickey said. "Things kinda slow right now?"

"Yeah, but it'll pick up for graduation or the next execution, whichever's first. So will you need one room or two?" he inquired as another attempt at humor, but the query called for an uncontemplated decision and creating an uncomfortable silence. The two looked at each other and simultaneously broke into laughter. "One room's fine, but we'll need double beds please," Mickey said to Tyler's relief. She paid cash for the room and received an oversized metal key attached to a large diamond-shaped piece of plastic embossed with their room number. They located the room, and Mickey opened the door as Tyler brought their bags inside. The room was small, but neat and clean, and it had a television and two nice beds. After they had put away their belongings, they realized that except for the snacks on the drive, neither had eaten. Tyler offered to buy dinner and she accepted.

"What are you in the mood for?" he asked.

"Well, since room service is out of the question and I'm starvin', I'd settle for just about anything."

"Why don't we drive around and see what we find?"

She agreed and they left the room for Mickey's car. Tyler drove north out of the parking lot, and they saw no shortage of student friendly choices such as diners, pizza parlors, and fast-food restaurants, but they wanted something more. They opted for a steakhouse that they spotted atop a hill and surrounded by tall pines. The sun light was waning, but from the road the two-story restaurant took on the appearance of an antebellum southern plantation, with a set of white steps leading up to large veranda in the front and stately white columns. The parking lot seemed full for a Thursday evening, so they felt safe in their choice.

Though dark inside, light from the tabletop candles softly illuminated the dining area's wood floors and wallpaper that mimicked sculptured red velvet. They were ushered to a corner table, and Tyler was pleased at the extensive list of quality wines. He selected a moderately priced cabernet, and as they savored the first glass, Tyler ordered a New York strip, and Mickey the petite filet. There was no agreement or understanding, but each instinctively refrained from discussing the purpose of their trip. Instead, their conversation drifted toward reminiscing. The soothing effect of the wine and the pleasing atmosphere allowed them to reflect on their past, and each helped the other recall events they had not thought of in years. Some remembrances evoked laughter while others brought tears. By the time they finished dinner and the better part of the second bottle of wine, they reflected on the time when they had first met as young college students and started dating. They didn't appreciate it then, but it was a simple, carefree time, and seeing the university campus earlier, enhanced the fondness of those revived memories. Then, urged by lowered inhibitions, they turned to their mutual theories on what went wrong with their marriage. Mickey was intrigued when Tyler insisted they had contributed jointly to the breakup.

"You're very kind to assume some of the responsibility, but it was my misplaced priorities at the root of everything that went wrong," Mickey confessed.

"Oh, come on, Mick. Our marriage didn't end just because of that. Bottom line is I was jealous of your aspirations."

"Jealous?" she asked with dismay.

"Yes, though I had my degree, I knew you were heading to career heights that I never would."

"Oh, you could have breezed through a graduate degree."

"Perhaps, but I didn't want to. I was done with school and ready to get on with my work and building a clientele. I wanted to make some money and for us eat more than ramen noodles, and I think that's why I was envious and resentful of your goals. As a couple, I should have set all that aside."

"But because of me, we weren't a couple. It was you and Reagan, and me off doing my own selfish things," Mickey confessed.

"It wasn't that bad, Mick. Things just get blown out of proportion, and the younger you are the worse it gets."

"Do you remember the goofy crap we fought about then?"

"Oh yeah, taking out the garbage, possession of the remote control, what side of the bed to sleep on, and—"

"Don't forget the toilet seat," Mickey added.

"Oh, how could I forget that? You know, it all seems so silly now, doesn't it?" Tyler said.

"It does now, but not then. We were two chickens trying to establish a pecking order." Tyler poured the remainder of the wine in her glass. "Trying to get me drunk?"

"Maybe," he said as he motioned to the waiter for the check. Tyler paid for the dinner and they finished their drinks, then walked arm in arm out of the restaurant and down the steps to the wide circle driveway in front of the restaurant.

"Mick, I know it's cliché to say, but we can't live in the past."

"I know," she conceded. "But you can't ignore it either."

"Sure, but let it be in your rearview mirror instead of it riding in the passenger seat with you."

"At this point, I'd like to kick the past out of the car and wait for it to cross the road and run over it," Mickey said with a sigh as he placed his arm around her shoulders.

They returned to the motel, and Tyler parked close to their room and killed the ignition. He left the radio on as they discussed their fourth date when they went to a drive-in theater to see a bad horror movie, the title of which neither could not recall, considering that they paid little attention to the screen. It was that evening that the two of them explored each other for the first time, with all of the sensations and awkwardness of young love. As the radio softly played, they moved closer to each other, and Tyler stared into her face, seeing the old familiar look that used to thrill him. It was obvious that they were deeply interested in each other, and they kissed. The wine and honest conversation had cleared the air between them in a way that a battery of therapy sessions could not have accomplished.

They left the car and started for the room to complete their reunion. Under the poor lighting of a dim yellow porch light, Tyler struggled to unlock the door, but once done, he flung it open for Mickey and waited for her to enter. He followed her into the darkness, then she turned rapidly and threw her hands over Tyler's shoulders and pull his lips firmly to hers. Without breaking the embrace, Tyler back-kicked the door, shutting it, and paused. With the glow from the motel's neon sign sending soft beams through the blinds, they stared into each other's eyes and separated for a moment, each assessing the other for hints of reluctance. Sensing none, they passionately embraced and tumbled atop the nearest bed.

Tyler grinned mischievously. "Should we be doing this?"

"Hell no," Mickey replied, locking her lips to his and delivering a deep, intense kiss. Then she pulled away and asked, "Will you still respect me in the morning?" Tyler kissed her harder and the two began to remove each other's clothes. The lovemaking was intense, each time, and then they lapsed into a deep, peaceful sleep on the sweat-dampened sheets.

The next morning, just before sunrise, the slamming of a car door just outside their motel window awakened Mickey. Her head ached from the wine, and her mind was foggy, but when she remembered the meeting with Flynn, she realized she had neglected to request a wake-up call. She looked hastily at the alarm clock on the nightstand, and seeing it was only 6:20 a.m. she relaxed and began to piece together the events of the previous evening. She readily recalled the dinner and most of the conversation, but when she rolled over, she was jolted when she felt Tyler's nude body next to her.

Shit, did we? ... Of course, we did, but what does this mean? Was it wrong? She searched her feelings and recalled a passage from Hemingway's *Death in the Afternoon*: "So far as morals, I know only that moral is what you feel good after and immoral is what you feel bad after." Mickey felt awkward and anxious, but she didn't feel anything that could be characterized as *bad*. But she also realized that moral did not necessarily equate to prudent or wise. *It was good though ... real good*, she thought as mental snippets of the evening returned to her. She closed her eyes and fondly savored the moments she could recall. *Was I good, though? And what will he think when he wakes up? Will he feel bad about it? I mean, I was drunk, but was he?*

She remained in thought, next to Tyler, as she had done so many times during their marriage, and in a strange way, it seemed as if they had never been apart. This was the first time, in a long time, that she felt truly good about something outside of a courtroom. As Tyler began to stir, she slid over to him and with feigned anger demanded, "What in the hell do you think you're doing in my bed?"

Confident that Tyler would encounter the same sense of fuzziness of mind, she wanted to add the pressure of her mock indignity. Tyler opened his eyes and, with a look of alarm, abruptly sat up in bed. He looked around, confused, and noticed the other bed was fully made up. As he struggled for words, he was relieved to see a wry smile on Mickey's face as she leaned over and kissed him gently.

"You were wonderful last night," she whispered as she laid her head on his chest.

He gently stroked her long black hair, saying, "You were terrific too, Mickey. I thoroughly enjoyed every aspect of it."

"Regrets?" she asked, and Tyler smiled and shook his head.

The pleasure of their evening quickly faded though, as the daunting task at hand assumed prominence. Mickey took a steamy shower, which cleansed her pores and evaporated some the lingering effects of the wine. As she soaped her body, the soreness in her low back and pelvic area was a discomfort she did not at all lament. For several minutes, she let the hot, pelting drops of water strike her face, neck, shoulders, and breasts and stream down her long, firm body. As she dried off and dressed, she quietly but methodically prepared for her encounter. She moved about the room as if she were alone, not unlike many of the mornings before the start of a trial.

She stood at the dresser mirror, buttoning her long blouse, as Tyler walked over and gripped her hand. "What are you going to tell this guy when you get there?"

"That's a good question, isn't it? I've been thinking about that a great deal."

"Really? I hadn't noticed," he joked.

She smiled. "I sacrificed the element of surprise, so I can't pretend I'm a disinterested party. He's going to know who I am and why I'm there. I feel I have to be firm, but at the same time, I can't be too aggressive or appear too desperate either. I think he would exploit either of those. I'm thinking calm and matter-of-fact as the approach."

"Business like?"

"Yeah."

"Have you written down any questions?" Tyler asked.

"No, only the other girls' names and dates and places where they disappeared. But I've memorized the questions I want to lead with and will go one at a time until we get down to the truth."

"Are you prepared for the truth?"

Mickey took a deep breath and said, "Yes."

"What if he won't cooperate?"

"If he turns out to be an ass about it, I'll have to rethink the strategy."

"Are you nervous?" he asked.

"You bet your butt I am!"

"Mickey, if anyone can crack this nut, it's you!" he assured her, squeezing her hand.

"With an emphasis on *nut*, right?" she said, smiling. "Thanks for being with me, Tyler. I don't mean just on this trip but all the way through this."

"I honestly don't know what's right or wrong about any of this, but just know that I'm with you every step of the way. Say, do you know how to get to the prison?"

"Sort of. Ford said if we find the university, which we have, the unit we need to go to is just north of the campus."

They returned the room key to the desk clerk and got in her car to leave. They drove north alongside the university campus, and a morning fog dominated the skies and hugged thickest toward the ground. Mickey noticed only early morning joggers on the sidewalks of the campus, until the fog suddenly gave way enough to reveal an imposing, dark-red brick façade. It was the Walls Unit, and each side towered fifty feet straight up with spirals of razor wire and elevated steel-and-brick guard towers atop each wall.

"Jesus! Is that it?" Tyler asked.

"I think so. Ford said the Walls Unit was close to the campus, but I couldn't imagine it being right next to it!" As they eased closer, Mickey spotted the fog-shrouded silhouette of a guard in one of the towers. The uniformed man stood with a rifle in one hand, a foot on the windowsill, and his other arm resting on his knee. He was smoking a cigarette and staring down into the interior of the prison, and Mickey could only imagine what he was witnessing inside the belly of this brick beast. As instructed, they pulled around to a separate building marked "Inmate Visitation" and parked.

"Ready?" Tyler asked, and Mickey nodded.

They walked silently, hand in hand across the parking lot and into the visitor's center, where they saw several uniformed officers working busily behind a counter. Mickey explained to a female guard that she had a scheduled visit and that was told to ask for Captain Madison. The guard had Mickey fill out a visitation form that included a release that Mickey signed and she instructed her to take a seat and wait. The room was painted a drab green, and the walls displayed old paintings and crafts representing the handiwork of past and present inmates. Mickey rehearsed her questions, and Tyler bided his time perusing stale issues of *Field and Stream.* More than twenty minutes elapsed when a deep baritone voice asked, "Are you here to see inmate Willie Flynn?"

Mickey rose to her feet. "Yes, sir. I'm Michelle Grant, and this is Tyler," Mickey said to the uniformed guard carrying a leather folio, her visitation form, and a large ring of keys.

"Good to meet you. I'm Captain Eugene Madison, and I'll be taking you inside."

"I thought so. I recognized your voice from our phone call."

"I see. People tell me I have a voice for radio and the face for it too."

Madison was a tall, broad-shouldered man with a dark skin and the presence and demeanor of a career military officer. He was dressed in a starched, light gray uniform, with a red stripe descending the side of each pant leg down to his pristinely shined, black, thick-soled shoes. He confirmed that Mickey was the only one of the two entering the prison and asked her to follow him. Madison escorted Mickey out the rear of the visitor's center, toward the entrance to the prison. Across an alley, Mickey noticed several men dressed in white prison uniforms sweeping a loading dock in the dissipating fog.

"Those *are* trustees, right?" Mickey asked.

"What'd you think? Escapees?"

"No, I just wanted to make sure. They're not from death row, are they?"

"Oh no. Those guys are from over at the Beto unit. They're just assigned over here for work detail. No, our condemned brothers don't see the light of day, except for an hour a day in the yard."

"Brothers?" Mickey asked as they walked.

"Yes, the university's not the only institution in this town with a fraternity. The condemned are a small fraternity but a fraternity just the same. The guards call this frat IGD."

Mickey looked at the grinning Madison, asking "Iota-Gamma-Delta?"

"No, Ima-Gonna-Die. Sorry, but that's our form of gallows humor." With one of the keys from his large collection in hand, Madison unlocked a heavy steel door, and when it swung open, Mickey got her first glimpse inside the Walls Unit. They walked down a short hall to a guard station and another large door. Mickey looked to her left, and was drawn to three guards sitting at a wide panel of illuminated buttons. Madison signaled to the woman, and when she punched the appropriate sequence, and the door clicked loudly and slid open automatically. Madison escorted Mickey down another hall and into a room with two tables with chairs, and a metal rolling cart with a television and video player on it.

"You indicated on your questionnaire that you have never been down here to visit an inmate before," the captain said as they took seats at the table.

"That's correct."

"Then you're required to have an orientation before we can go any further. Since we'll be going into a maximum-security area, I'll first show you a video on Department of Corrections rules and protocols. After that I'll give you some special instructions, before we go further." He started the video and explained, "This only lasts twelve minutes, I'll return after that."

Now in the prison, Mickey was glad to have some time to acclimate to the surroundings and gather her thoughts. She watched the screen and quickly realized the video was a series of rudimentary, common-sense instructions on proper conduct in the facility and the security measures that she would encounter. She found the instructions so pedestrian that her mind drifted to her meeting. The video ended, and moments later, Madison returned.

"Any questions?" Madison asked.

"No, sir."

"Good. Now, everything that you saw on the video is important, but I want to give you some other instructions about the area where we're going to that wasn't on it. There are no windows, and it's dark in that area, and it smells. You'll pass through metal detectors more sensitive than anything you've gone through at any airport, and you must submit to a body search." Seeing the look of concern on Mickey's face, he clarified, "Don't worry, it won't be a strip search or anything like that. There will just be a pat-down search by a female guard. You can't bring anything with you, except the clothes on your back, minus coins and accessories described in the video. Understand?" She nodded. "Here's a bag to put your purse and other things in, and there's a locker over there to stow the bag in," Madison said, pointing to five upright louvered metal lockers. "Once we're in the meeting area, the inmate will be separated from you by a thick, glass wall. You each will have to communicate by telephones on each side of the glass. The conversation will be monitored, so don't tell any deep, dark secrets. You can't hand him anything—physical contact is impossible."

"You don't have to worry about me wanting to touch him," Mickey said, grimacing.

"Are you not a friend or relative of the inmate?"

"No, sir! This man killed my daughter."

"Oh, I see … you're one of those," Madison said, shaking his head. "Now, listen carefully, ma'am. The TDC don't allow any trouble here. That means none from you and none from the inmate. Folks like you come down here from time to time, but if you're here to vent a bunch of anger at the inmate, you won't get very far. We leave that kind of confrontation stuff for the movies and daytime TV, and there'll be guards on each side of the glass to prevent such nonsense."

"Rest assured, Captain, I don't want any trouble. I simply want to speak to him."

"Speak to him, huh?"

"Yes, you see, he's the only person who can—"

"Oh, I got it," Madison interrupted. "You're not one of the yellers. You're a seeker."

"A what?"

"A seeker. You need to make the unthinkable make sense, right?" Madison asked, and Mickey stared down at the table. "Listen, ma'am. I'm very sorry about your loss, and he's agreed to see you, so you have every right to be here. But it's your type that concerns me most. The yellers just want to confront and vent anger, but seekers want the impossible."

"I'll be no trouble, sir," Mickey insisted.

"Oh, we'll make sure of that. But it's not trouble I'm worried about. I just don't think you understand what you're dealing with here. I've never seen a seeker walk out of here without some level of devastation," he explained.

"I'm already devastated," she said softly.

"Okay … That keeps it at 100 percent."

"Excuse me?"

"I've never dissuaded a seeker. A few yellers, yes. But never a seeker."

"I'm sorry, Captain, but I just need—"

"No apologies necessary. You came all the way here, and you're going to get your turn. So go ahead and place your bag in the locker. I'll lock it, and you'll get it when you return."

With her items stored, Madison led Mickey to two doors, one marked "General Confinement and the other marked "Condemned Zone—Max Security." Theirs was the latter and as they entered and walked, she noticed that the air was stale, and the brick walls lining each side were damp and musty-smelling, creating an atmosphere reminiscent of a cave. The sound of their footsteps echoed in the narrow passageway as they walked toward another checkpoint. Madison picked up a phone receiver and gave the person on the other end a code from a piece of paper. The locking mechanism in the door turned, and Madison shoved it open. They started down the next hall, and she flinched at the sound of the door slamming and locking behind them.

"Do you know this inmate?" Mickey asked as she followed Madison.

"Flynn? Yeah, I know him. He's newer and has been no real trouble since he got here. But he's an odd duck."

"Oh?"

"Yeah, the dude spends most all waking hours reading books."

"Books? Like what? Dime novels, comic books?"

"No, these are real books, and thick ones too. You see, each inmate's allowed three books at a time, and it's not unusual for him to turn in as many as three in a day and request replacements."

They reached the security checkpoint and Mickey noticed the large gray-and-black metal detector and two female guards. Mickey stood nervously as Madison whispered to one of the guards and then handed her some paperwork. He then nodded to the other guard, who stood waiting on the opposite side of the detector. This guard motioned for Mickey to proceed forward, and as she passed through the detector, a piercing alarm sounded, and she instinctively recoiled.

"Lift up your shirt," the woman next to Madison demanded.

Mickey's raised her thigh-length blue blouse.

"You didn't pay attention to the film, did you?" Madison asked, and Mickey froze. "You were supposed to leave all personal items behind."

"I did," she defended.

"What about your belt?" the female guard asked.

"My belt?"

"It was covered in the film," Madison said. Mickey, embarrassed, removed the black belt from her white pants and handed it to the guard, who again motioned her through the detector. This time, it did not beep.

"This is as far as I go, Mrs. Grant. I'll see you when you exit," Madison advised.

Mickey nodded and watched as Madison turned and walked back

down the dark hallway, and the second female guard instructed her to put her hands behind her neck and spread her legs. The guard then ran a metal-detecting wand over the front and back of her body and then between Mickey's legs. She started at her left shoe and ran the wand up to her crotch and then worked it back down to her right shoe. She then conducted a thorough upper torso pat-down including feeling around Mickey's bra strap. Next, the guard had Mickey turn around and hold her arms perpendicular to her sides. The guard then ran her a finger along the inside of her waistband all the way around, then felt the outside of her pant legs from her ankles up each leg.

"What's in your right pocket?"

"Oh, that. It's just a plastic pen and piece of paper and with names on it.

"Let's see 'em," the guard said, and Mickey complied. "She's good," the guard said to her counterpart. Mickey lowered her hands, and the guard with papers led her toward the visitation room.

"Nervous?" the woman asked as they walked.

"Yes, ma'am."

"Madison tells me you're a seeker. Is that right?"

"I wasn't aware of the term until a moment ago, but as I understand it I am."

"That's too bad. You seem like a nice lady."

They arrived at a small cubicles, with a chair, phone receiver and thick pane of Plexiglas separating her from the room on the other side. The pane showed scratches and wear, casting a vague opaque appearance to everything on the other side. Mickey was directed to take a seat, and was informed that Flynn would soon appear on the opposite side. The guard then took her post behind Mickey and pulled an emery board from her pocket and began applying it to the cuticle. Mickey tapped her finger on the Formica ledge in front of her and tried to breathe normally but jumped when she heard a clanging noise from beyond the glass. As the rusty steel door slowly swung open, she sat stiffly upright, her hands now clenched together in her lap. A guard emerged first, followed by Flynn and another guard trailing.

She first noticed that Flynn had gained some weight and had a shaved head, and in contrast to her, he seemed at ease. He took a seat opposite Mickey, and the guards on his side took seats behind Flynn, but within arm's reach. Flynn was dressed in the standard prison uniform of a white cotton shirt and white pants with a blue, lateral stripe from hip to ankle on each pant leg. He was chained and handcuffed but had enough slack to reach the phone receiver. He stared directly at Mickey as they simultaneously raised their phones to their ears. Mickey sat ready with her first rehearsed question on the tip of her tongue, but before she could speak, Flynn said, "What? No signs?"

Suddenly, her mind went blank, and she had cotton mouth. Clearing her throat, she improvised and in a subdued voice, "Thank you for meeting with me. As I put in my letter, I'm here to ask you about my daughter. Her name is Reagan Grant, and she is a beautiful—"

"Beg pardon, but I'm confused. You said 'is.'"

Flummoxed, Mickey said, "I don't understand."

"You said your daughter *is* Reagan, and 'is' means present tense. Your letter to me said I killed your daughter, so forgive me for my confusion."

"Well, didn't you?"

"No, no, no. It ain't fair to ask me about who I've killed if you're conflicted on whether someone's dead."

Trying to stay on track, she said, "The fact is Reagan's one of the seven missing girls, and I sent you her picture. She was taken from Town East Mall in Brinkman just before last Christmas, and I haven't seen her since, and I think you know why."

"Your letter said that you were on TV when I was on trial," Flynn said. "I didn't see it, but I was told that you all but tried and convicted me as a, let's see— 'child killer,' I believe was the term."

"Yes, I gave that interview, but I didn't—"

"Do you know what a brutal beating I took that night? My thug cellmates saw you on TV in the rec room, and when they returned, I was pulled from my bunk to the filthy floor and beaten."

Mickey then recalled how bad Flynn looked the morning after the interview and knew she was rapidly losing control of the conversation. "You can't possibly blame me for what those animals did."

"Now, ain't that an interestin' position. You say on TV that I'm a child killer, and the animals from my cell see it and that evening physically assault me while hollering 'child killer,' and *you* get to decide whether I can blame you or not!"

"Willie, let me get back to the point. I have to know—"

"You have a lot of balls to come here to ask me for help!"

"I can't change the past, Willie. All I want is to know the details about the missing girls, and please know I didn't come here to judge you."

"Oh, *now* you don't want to judge me!" he said, laughing and leaning back in his chair, prompting his guards to move closer to him. "Now, that's rich!"

"I just want information on the girls, like where to find them," Mickey pleaded, but despite her desire to remain stoic, her eyes were brimming with tears, and she noticed that her hands were trembling. Instinctively, she used her shoulder to hold the phone to her ear in order to keep her hands under the ledge and out of Flynn's sight.

Flynn shook his head. "I can't help with any of that, so why don't you just get your ass back to Brinkman, where you belong?"

"Come on, Willie, don't give me that. Listen, if you're pissed at me, fine, but please help the other grieving families. I have a list of the girls here with when and where each went missing," she said as she removed the piece of paper from her pocket with her trembling right hand, which only steadied when she pressed it to the glass.

In a flash, Flynn's face flushed red, and he yelled, "Lady, I don't have to tell you a goddamn thing! I'm gonna be right here, silent, until they rattle my cage and call me to meet my maker."

"Keep it civil, Willie," one of the guards on Flynn's side warned.

"I wanted to come here in good faith and for us to relate each other," Mickey said, hoping for de-escalation.

"Relate to each other? Are you shittin' me?"

"If you'd just—"

"You're wasting your time here, lady"

"Listen to me, Willie. I can be friendly and not so friendly. I can make your—."

"What are you going to do to me? Look around! If you haven't noticed, I'm on death row!" he yelled, waving his shackled hands, and the guards reacted.

"One more like that, Willie, and you're out of here," the guard said sternly.

"I don't blame you for being upset with me, but *please* help some of these families? You know it's the right thing to do, and after all, you just mentioned meeting your maker. If you believe in God, this would be a great way to redeem yourself, to—you know—to set things right."

"There's nothing I can do for you," Flynn said nodding to the guards and dropping his phone receiver which now dangled by its cord.

"Don't do this!" Mickey cried, as a guard hung up Flynn's phone and the other helped Flynn to his feet, but Mickey did not take her eyes off of him. Pent-up emotions surfaced as a boiling rage and she screamed loud enough that, though muffled, it resonated to Flynn, "You gutless, child-killing, son of a bitch! Meet your maker? Did you have some sort of a goddamn jailhouse conversion? You're going straight to hell, Willie!" The guard on Mickey's side took hold of her arm and pulled the phone from her hand and returned it to the wall. Flynn left the room, but Mickey sat and stared straight ahead, feeling as empty as the space on the other side of the glass.

"Don't feel bad, lady," the guard said, handing her belt to her. "It happens all the time."

Mickey rose to her feet, straightened her clothes, and walked with the guard back through the security section, retracing her steps all the way back to the classroom. Mickey stood by the lockers lacing her belt through the loops of her pants, and when Captain Madison entered and saw the devastation on her face. "It wasn't very useful, was it?"

She shook her head and whimpered. "Of course not. I feel like such a dope."

"Par for the course for a seeker," Madison said as he unlocked and opened her locker.

"To keep the stats in order, I went in a seeker but came out a yeller," Mickey informed.

Madison smiled and nodded. "There's no way to discourage someone in your position; they always have to see for themselves," he said and put his arm on her shoulder as she gathered her belongings. "Look on the bright side. At least now you know where you stand."

"Thank you, Captain Madison. You've been very kind to me."

When Madison ushered Mickey into the visitation area, Tyler glanced at her, dropped his magazine, and without a spoken word sensed he needed to get her to the car quickly. He embraced her and hustled her out of the visitor's center, with Mickey leaning her head against his shoulder as they walked, Mickey sobbed, and placed her hand over her mouth to muffle involuntary sounds she was making. Tyler unlocked the passenger side door, and she sat with a clenched fist over her mouth, gasping for air. As Tyler drove her car toward the exit, months of anxiety and tension flowed from her in a torrent of tears. Tyler remained silent, letting her weep and rubbing her back with his right hand as he headed toward Interstate 45. With Huntsville in the rearview mirror, Mickey placed her head in her hands and said, "What a dumb, dumb, dumb thing to do. Everyone, including you, knew better."

"I'm sorry, Mick. But you were right and brave to try."

"Thank you, Tyler, but this was stupid from the start, and what's worse, I actually humbled myself to him."

"I'm sorry for both of us that it didn't work out. But it wasn't a wasted trip."

"How can you say that?" she said, turning to him.

"There was last night," he said as she smiled and leaned over onto his right shoulder.

CHAPTER 13

⚖

POST TENEBRAS LUX, POST TENEBRAS SPERO LUCEM

(After darkness [I hope] for Light)

Mickey walked into her office that following Monday morning, sat at her desk, and stared uninspired at a stack of case files and an inbox overflowing with mail. She picked up an old newspaper off her credenza, from the day after Flynn's guilty verdict. She stared at the headline and the photo of Hill exiting the courthouse, and her mind began to work.

Who knows more about Flynn than Hill? No one, right? After all, he had full access to Flynn and to the case facts. Maybe he could help shed some light on things—or even better, perhaps he could intervene on our behalf and broker a dialogue. Flynn trusts him, but what about the appeal, and then there's attorney-client privilege? How much could he tell me without stepping over the line? But that's his call to make, isn't it?

Seeing no downside to reaching out to him, she took a chance and phoned Hill's office, and to her surprise he accepted her call. After explaining, who she was and the general nature of her inquiry, he agreed to meet with her that afternoon. After lunch, Mickey walked three blocks to Hill's small downtown office located in an old, three-story brick building. She entered Hill's cramped lobby, surveyed the room, and saw a sliding, frosted glass panel filling a cut-out space in the far wall. The counter below the window featured a silver bell and two signs: *Ring bell for service* and *Fees due at the time services are rendered*. Seeing movement behind the glass, Mickey rang the silver bell. A large woman sporting an amber beehive hairdo slid open the frosted glass and exclaimed, "Lordy, honey! I didn't hear anyone come in."

"I'm sorry if I startled you, ma'am. I'm Michelle Grant, and I have an appointment with Mr. Hill this afternoon."

Fumbling with a large desk calendar, the woman looked for Mickey's appointment. Shaking her head, she said, "I don't see you down for today, hon."

"You're looking at April," Mickey informed.

"Oh my goodness, you're right," she said, hurriedly flipping to the June page. "Oh, yes, here it is. Chester—I mean Mr. Hill—put it on here this morning. You're the lady who was down at the courthouse during Mr. Flynn's case, aren't you?"

"Yes, ma'am, that's me."

"I saw you on the TV too," the woman said as Mickey nodded. "Well, you have a seat over yonder. I think he's eating his lunch, but I'll let him know you're here."

Mickey thanked her and sat on a worn, lightly stained, tweed couch, and noticed several framed newspaper articles on the walls, most concerning noteworthy criminal trials Hill had won. She read the yellowed, fading news print of several of them, and one article featured a photograph of a much younger Hill, in a leisure suit, with a beard and a substantial head of thick brown hair, speaking to the local press after winning a racketeering case. Several minutes elapsed until the receptionist again slid the frosted glass panel aside and said, "Mr. Hill will see you now, but wait for me to unlock the door, hon." The woman opened the door for Mickey, adding, "We have to keep this door locked, as you don't know who's gonna wander in." She led Mickey through the door, down a narrow hallway lined on each side with dark wood paneling, and into Hill's office. Mickey stood on the other side of the desk, where Hill sat reared back in his chair with his cowboy-boot-clad feet perched atop it. He was eating the lesser half of a barbecue sandwich and had a paper napkin tucked in his shirt above his necktie. He motioned for her to take a seat.

"Baseball fan?" Mickey said, observing several framed, black-and-white photos autographed by greats of the game.

"No. I'm an old timer baseball fan. I couldn't care less about the modern-day millionaire crybabies."

"DiMaggio, Musial, Carl Hubbell," Mickey said as she pointed toward the pictures.

"Wow! I wouldn't have expected you to know that."

"My dad was a baseball historian and had lots of books on baseball, and I read 'em all."

"Really? I think that's fantastic," Hill said.

Mickey looked at one such piece to her left. "And there's my namesake, Mickey Mantle."

"I don't understand."

"It's a nick name. My friends call me what my dad did, Mickey."

"I see, I thought for a second that Mantle's nickname was Michelle," Hill said as Mickey chuckled. "Boy, he was a great one, though. If he'd had a better set of wheels, he could have been the best."

"Yep. That's exactly what my dad and Casey Stengel felt."

"Well, I must say I'm a little surprised to see you here," Hill said, dabbing barbecue sauce from his chin.

"I'm a little surprised myself, but I appreciate you fitting me in nonetheless. I know you're busy, so I'll get to the point. I'm here for some information about Flynn."

"I figured as much, and I think I know what you want to ask. But as a lawyer, you know that even if I had any knowledge, I couldn't tell you."

"How'd you know I'm a lawyer?"

"When you started doing all that sign-carrying stuff during the trial, I investigated you. I found out pretty quick that you work for Harrison Baylor."

"I do, and Mr. Baylor speaks highly of you, by the way."

"That's pleasing to the ear since I'm a big admirer of him. Truth be known, that's the reason I agreed to meet with you."

"So you investigated, huh?"

"Let me say upfront that I am sensitive to the attorney-client privilege. But I don't think what I want to know will violate it."

"If you want me to tell you if Flynn had anything to do with your daughter, I can't."

"You know that too, huh?"

"Yes, and I'm sorry for your situation, but I can't discuss my conversations with Flynn."

"I'm not looking for anything that direct. I just want to get a point in the right direction."

"Like what?"

"Help for any of the other girls. If I could just get some hint on where to find any of them, it would be a tremendous benefit to these poor families."

"Sorry, but I just don't discuss such things with my clients. I never ask details as to what they did or didn't do or how they did it, as it's largely irrelevant to my job. The prosecution makes their case and I poke holes in it, that simple. Plus, if clients reveal details, and then they elect to testify at trial and do so opposite to what I know to be true, I risk—"

"Suborning perjury?"

"Right," Hill said as Mickey nodded her understanding. "Ms. Grant, I've raised two girls of my own and have five grandchildren, three of which are also girls. I don't know what I would do if I were in your shoes, but I honestly don't know anything about any of the other cases."

"I thought that this was how it would go, but can I ask you a question about the trial?"

"You can ask whatever you want. The question becomes whether I can or will answer it or not."

"Fair enough," Mickey said as she paused in thought. "Forgive me in advance, but why didn't you challenge the prosecution's evidence? I know you had a tough case and all, but you're a very skilled lawyer."

"I'm not sure what you mean?"

"Come on, you just mentioned poking holes in the state's case. Granted, I'm not a criminal lawyer, but, pardon my French, it seemed like you gave it a half-assed effort. I've investigated you too, and read those articles out there in your lobby. You're much better than the performance you gave in that courtroom."

"Look, ma'am—with all of the forensic evidence, the eyewitness testimony of Robert Jackson and a Taylor County jury, we really were sunk. If we had tried to contest every possible issue, it would have likely inflamed the jury. So we had to pick our battles, you know—in hopes of avoiding the death sentence."

"Well, let's start with the Taylor County jury part. Why not ask for a change of venue? With all of the local publicity, you'd certainly have been entitled to it."

"Well ... uh ... You see, Sullivan personally asked me to take this case, and as such, I felt he should preside over it," Hill improvised.

She smiled. "Judge Sullivan *would* have presided over it, even if it was moved."

"Look. We did the best we could with what we had, okay?" he responded tersely, rising from his chair.

Feeling she had pushed too hard, she thanked him, picked up her purse and rose to leave until Hill asked her to wait. "Ms. Grant, I'm going to tell you something that I hope stays between us. As weird as it sounds, Flynn didn't mind being convicted. I know that's hard to comprehend, and I couldn't wrap my head around it at first, but it's true."

"If that's the case, why didn't y'all plead him to murder and spare his life? They probably offered that before trial."

"First off, Tucker never made such an offer. The prosecution made it clear from the get-go that they were going for the death penalty all the way. All I can say is Willie's been incarcerated a couple of times in the past and had bad real experiences with other inmates. Death row to him equates to solitary confinement."

"Solitude while he waits to be put him to death? That doesn't seem like much of a tradeoff."

"You believe that, I believe that, and most of the population would too, but not him. Adding to the equation, he has this disease, called ALS, and he knows that his life expectancy is limited. As a consequence he prefers to spend the time he has left in isolation."

Mickey did not fully comprehend what she had heard, but appreciating Hill's candor nonetheless, she again thanked him for the meeting. She left not feeling she like the beneficiary of any meaningful insight other than a vague glimpse at Flynn's twisted point of view. She returned to her office that afternoon, and seeing that Baylor was in his office, she hope a conference with him might help sort it out. She knocked on his open door and stuck her head inside.

"What's up, Michelle?" he asked, laying his pen on the desk.

"Sorry to interrupt, Mr. B, but I talked with Chester Hill today."

"Oh? About Flynn?"

"Yes, sir, and by the way, he spoke very highly of you."

"That's nice to hear. I hope he knows the feelings are mutual."

"He does, Mr. B. I made sure of that."

"Good. But I'm surprised he agreed to speak with you."

"Me too, but apparently me working for you helped. For the life of me, though, I don't understand what he told me," Mickey said as she recounted her conversation with Hill.

"Has this Flynn guy been in the pen before?" Baylor asked.

"Yes. According to Hill a couple of times."

"Well then, Flynn knows the score. Michelle, there are some lost souls who would rather die a death at the hands of the state than be committed ten minutes in regular confinement. This is particularly true for a man convicted of molesting or killing a child. Such a convict is doomed to constant abuse in the gen-pop."

"Gen-pop?" she asked.

"General population. He would be mixed in among everything from petty thieves and drug dealers to very violent felons. The abuse can be unrelenting and in many instances deadly."

"I don't understand the concept of accepting certain death in order to avoid potential confrontations," Mickey explained.

"You and I would never understand it, but we haven't walked in his shoes."

"Hill did say Flynn's got a bad disease. He called it ALS."

"That explains a lot too."

"You're familiar with the disease."

"Yes, and you are too. Its's Lou Gehrig's disease," Baylor said.

"Oh, that's right. That's a bad one, isn't it?"

"Very much so."

"But why take certain death in exchange for a cell to himself?"

"Don't forget, Michelle, even in today's pro-death-penalty environment, the appeals still go on for years."

"That's true. I told the support group that his execution could be a decade or more away."

"Right. I imagine that from Flynn's standpoint, he would much rather live several years in solitude than defending himself from fellow inmates."

"What if they don't give him his own cell?"

"All death row inmates are held in solitary by law."

"Now that I think about it, Flynn blamed my interview at the courthouse for getting him beat up in jail during the trial."

"You see, he got a dose of it here in our county lockup too."

"Is it that bad in our jail?"

"It can be. I've had clients seriously injured in there, and one that committed suicide."

"So you really think Hill tried the case to lose it?" Mickey asked.

"I personally find that hard to believe. He had a difficult case and knew the deck was stacked against him, but I can't fathom Chester just taking a dive on a death penalty case."

"But if he's anything like his reputation, he didn't do his best, and he basically admitted that the death penalty was Flynn's objective."

"I guess it's possible that Flynn wanted isolation so bad that he demanded that of Hill."

"I need to somehow play on that," Mickey said.

"Play on what?"

"Flynn's aversion to regular confinement."

"What are you getting at?" Baylor asked.

"I don't really know, but I'd love to have an angle to lean on him a little for information. Any ideas?"

"A couple, but I tell you what, I'm preparing for trial, so you take a stab at it, and let's reconvene."

"You'll do that?"

"Certainly. I'm be interested in what you come up with."

"Thank you, Mr. B. You're always so kind to take time to advise me on things."

"I'm not sure I did anything, but you're welcome just the same."

On Saturday morning, Mickey rose before sunup and put on a pot of coffee. She grabbed a packet of instant oatmeal but returned it to the cabinet. She had not eaten a hot breakfast in several days, and canvassing the refrigerator, she found a carton with two eggs and a package of bacon. Checking the expiration date on each and finding them close enough, soon the appetizing smell of the sizzling bacon and fresh-brewed coffee awakened her senses. She ate her breakfast eagerly and then sopped up the yellow remains of fried eggs with a piece of dry toast. She reflected on her meeting with Hill and Baylor's comments and tried to formulate a strategy around it. *The objective is to put pressure on Flynn. Since he's already suffered here in Taylor County, he would have to hate to come back. All I need is find a way to threaten a return for a hearing or some other proceeding, but how?*

With her breakfast plate and utensils in the dishwasher, she pulled a civil procedure book from her desk. She spent close to an hour perusing it for angles, but felt she was making little progress. Try as she might, she could not fathom a theory to lodge a credible threat. Nevertheless, she felt that she had formulated at least the foundation for a viable strategy to present it to Baylor, and was too anxious to wait until Monday to pitch it. Though it was still early Saturday morning, she knew where she was likely to find him. For as long as she had known him, Baylor spent a couple of mornings each week and most all Saturdays in downtown Brinkman. This historic section of town was no longer the bustling center of commerce it once represented, yielding that title to large shopping centers built out on the highway that now bypassed Brinkman proper. Despite a dwindling number of visitors to this area, a diehard core of mostly older residents clung to the past and patronized the downtown establishments. Baylor was included among those, and he and a group his contemporaries routinely gathered at a downtown drugstore there for morning coffee.

Mickey drove downtown, parked, and when she entered the drugstore, she could immediately hear laughter from the backroom. She had been there several times over the years, but it had been a while since her last visit. Little had changed, though and she knew exactly where to go. She sauntered down the aisles, past medicinal aids and a candy aisle, toward the back of the drugstore where the group of diehards were congregated. In this backroom there sat two round tables with chairs, surrounded by cabinets, a sink, and a Formica countertop that featured a heavily used coffee pot. She entered and saw Baylor and a couple other faces that she recognized among the men seating around the tables. These old-timers treated Baylor with reverence, and he was wrapping up a tale, and she joined the others in listening intently.

"So, the lawyer pulled up in front of his office in the red Porsche and opened the driver's side door. Then a speeding car came along and side swiped it, tearing the car door plumb off," Baylor said. "The lawyer was outraged and yelled to a beat officer on the corner, 'hey, did you see what that guy did to my car?' The officer walked over and said, 'You lawyers are all the same. You're so caught up with material things, like this sports car, that you failed to notice that that car also tore your left arm off at the shoulder! The lawyer look-up and said, 'Oh no, help me find my Rolex!"

All present, included Mickey, roared and when the laughter subsided, Mickey cleared her throat, and Baylor turned and smiled. "To what do we owe the pleasure of this most welcome visitor?" Baylor said as he and the other men rose to greet her.

"Good morning, fellas, and please keep your seats. Mr. B, after you're done here, could I have a moment of your time?"

"Now would be fine if—"

"No, no," Mickey interjected. "I don't want to infringe on time with your friends. I'm free all day, and whatever works for you is good with me."

"Now's fine, considering that according to the missus, I've exceeded my caffeine quota for today—and perhaps for tomorrow. Plus, I find myself fresh out of stories."

"Want us to leave, Harrison?" one gentleman offered.

"That's not necessary. We'll go over to the Dixie. Is that okay with you, Michelle?"

She agreed, and they started back out of the drugstore. "Sorry to bother you on a Saturday."

"Please, it's no bother," Baylor said. "Is this the Flynn thing again?"

"Sorry, but I'm afraid so. How'd your trial go?"

"It resolved. The DA had a witness go missing, and had to cut a deal."

They took the short walk to the Dixie café. Upon entering it, they saw only three tables occupied, and Baylor suggested an empty booth by the window.

"What'll it be?" asked the unusually chipper waitress, who stood vigorously chewed a piece of gum, with pen and pad in hand.

Baylor deferred to Mickey, who said, "I already ate, but how about a bran muffin and a coffee?"

"Yes, ma'am. And you, sir?"

"I'll have the exact the same—except decaf," Baylor replied with a wink.

The waitress brought the coffee, and between sips, Mickey began to lay out her theory. "I want to threaten Flynn with gen-pop—I like using that term now," she confessed with a smile. "Anyway, you were right, as usual, and there's no way to threaten him with that in Huntsville. Death row is 100 percent isolation, no exceptions."

"So what do you propose?"

"First comes the over-all premise. After talking to you and Mr. Hill, I realize that the only thing Flynn fears is a regular jail cell, and the idea is how to play on this. Since I can't credibly threaten to make that happen in Huntsville, I have to threaten it in some other venue, and the only logical place is right here in Taylor County. I spent some time looking at post judgment motions, but I couldn't find anything that I could facilitate, since the case is closed. So, I started thinking about the appeal and what Flynn would do if the conviction itself was threatened."

"I'm with you so far," Baylor said. "Mind if I smoke?"

"Not at all. So what if Flynn thought that the trial result could be reversed and that he'd be retried right back here in Brinkman?"

"Based on what you told me, he'd fear it. So what do you have in mind?" he asked while packing his pipe.

"I assume Hill's not going to try any harder on the appeal than he did during the trial. But perhaps the appeals court should know, from an outside source, just how justice was *not* done in Flynn's trial!"

"And that source would be you?"

"Yes!" Mickey confirmed as their muffins arrived.

"This is very dangerous territory, Michelle," Baylor warned.

"Oh, I fully understand that, but all I want to do is threaten to do this and use it as a bargaining chip."

"What do you propose?"

"There's the rub, Mr. B. I can't figure it out, and that's why I wanted to talk to you right away. What I need is a method that I can use to point out errors in the trial, but every appellate rule I have read contemplates me representing a party to the case."

"Let me get this straight. You want to convince this creep that you're going to intervene in the appeal and point out the trial errors?"

"Precisely."

"Very interesting," Baylor said.

"But how does a nonparticipant do it? That's the part I can't wrap my mind around."

"What you're describing is an amicus brief." Mickey had not heard that term since law school and recalled little about it. "It's amicus curiae in Latin, and the term literally means 'friend of the court.' Though it's rarely used, nonparties to a case sometimes file one to have their voice heard on a point of law at issue, with which they have an interest. They're usually seen in suits filed over the construction, intent, or legality of some law or regulation. Groups, often advocacy groups, that would be affected by the outcome file them to make their position known."

"I see. But can they be used at the appellate level?"

"Technically, yes. It's rare, and I don't know how much weight the court of appeals would give it, but that's the vehicle you're looking for."

"Then I'll threaten to create one, and if Flynn thinks that I have the power to even remotely cause a retrial, it should really grab his attention."

"It might, but I don't think a verbal threat will do it. As I see it, you'll need to actually draft the amicus brief for this plan to have any chance of it working. It'll also need to be good enough to get Hill's attention too, because if he doesn't buy it, Flynn won't either."

"You're right! I really want to pursue this, will you review a draft of it for me?"

"Certainly. I'd be glad to, and since my case resolved I have ample time for it," He confirmed taking small puffs from his pipe.

"Thanks, Mr. B. I'm going to put something together that'll scare the crud out of Hill and his evil client."

"To do this right, you'll need a copy of the trial transcript from the court of appeals."

"I'll do that right away."

"I'll warn you that it could be costly."

"I'm not going to let money stand in my way. After all, I'm *not* saving up for a red Porsche *or* a Rolex!" she said and Baylor smiled. "Just know, Mr. B, my work on this will be on my time and not firm time."

"Understood. I look forward to seeing what you come up with."

Early Monday morning, Mickey drove directly to the court of appeals to put her plan in motion. She walked up the courthouse steps just as a security guard unlocked the front door. She took an elevator to the third floor and followed the signs on the gray marble walls to the office of the court clerk.

"May I help you?" a clerk asked from behind a wooden counter.

"Yes, I want to get a copy of the reporter's record from this appeal," Mickey said, handing him a piece of notebook paper bearing the case number.

"I'll need to know the number of pages to calculate the cost," he explained and retreated to the file room. He returned pushing a cart with two stacks of bound booklets. Though the trial only lasted a few days, the transcript filled nine thick volumes.

"Wow!" Mickey reacted to the sight.

"Yeah, it's a lot. Do you want it all?" he asked, and Mickey nodded. He began calculating the estimated the cost, then said, "It'll be around six fifty, and I'll need a deposit of 50 percent upfront to get started on it." Though this was more than she anticipated, Mickey grabbed her checkbook, filled out a check, and handed it to him. The clerk promised to have her copy ready the following afternoon. Mickey used that day to catch up on her files and that evening to continue her research on the legal issues for the brief. The following afternoon, she returned to the court and true to his word, the clerk had the copies ready for her. She paid the balance, and took two trips to lug it all to her car.

That evening, she ensconced herself in Triple B's law library. Woody had consented to Mickey's use of it, and when she spread out all nine volumes of transcripts and the results of her research, she needed all of the extra space afforded by the conference table to work on the initial draft of the brief. Soon, she was marking the first transcript with dog-ears, asterisks, and sticky notes and emphasizing passages with highlighters of various colors. Though not trained in criminal law, she applied her civil law expertise in assessing errors in evidence introduced at trial. She referred to volumes of case reporters to research the legal issues and copied select rulings supporting her theories. Devoting two to three hours per evening on the project, by the end of the week, she believed she had amassed compelling arguments to include in the brief and was ready for a critique.

"Right this way, Mr. B," she said, as she escorted Baylor up the spiral staircase and into the library. "Voila! Behold my war room," she declared, pointing at a table with stacks of papers and the volumes of transcript.

"I see you've been quite busy on your homework."

"Yes, sir."

"Is Woody okay with all of this stuff in here?"

"Yes, but I've brought him kolaches or do-nuts each morning. It's like a form of rent for the table."

"Sounds like a fair bargain. Forgive the pun, but what's the verdict?"

"I believe that Flynn's trial can be attacked on Sixth Amendment grounds."

Staring at her over his half-glasses, Baylor took a puff from his pipe and nodded. "That seems to be in the right direction. Just remember, Michelle, like one of my law school professors told a young law student in the throes of a Socratic exchange, 'a little knowledge is a dangerous thing.'"

"Did that law student happen to be you?"

"Indeed, it was!" Baylor said, leaning forward to check the legal opinions she had copied. She watched on anxiously as Baylor perused them. He recognized most of the cases by name and the importance that each represented, and personally had a hand in two of them. Mickey then explained her theory that much of the evidence used at trial, including Flynn's statements upon his arrest, were improperly admitted into evidence. She directed Baylor to highlighted passages from the cases that she felt supported her position, and the more she discussed them, the more exercised she became, until Baylor held up his hand to stop her.

"Michelle, is it your position that Judge Sullivan should have excluded Flynn's statements and all this other evidence Hill let in?" She nodded vigorously. "And an order suppressing that evidence should have been granted?"

"Precisely."

"Was a motion to suppress filed?"

"No, but the court should have—"

"Excuse me, but don't you think that any error in admitting this evidence was waived by Hill and can't be attacked on appeal?" Baylor inquired, and Mickey flopped into a chair and stared silently at the stacks of papers. "These evidentiary issues had to be preserved by raising each on the record, to allow Judge Sullivan to hear arguments and make a ruling."

"Mr. B, aren't these fundamental errors? I mean, as the gate keeper, Judge Sullivan should have intervened."

"Michelle, your approach seizes on the court's errors, but the court did nothing wrong here. The advocates determine the evidence they want in versus that which they wish to object to. Here the court, for lack of a better term, is innocent."

"But there's so much bad evidence in here!" she argued, pointing to the volumes of transcript.

"I'm sure there is, but this is an appeal, and all the appellate court has is a record of unchallenged—thus unpreserved—error."

"But Flynn's not going to understand that distinction. After all, I'm not trying to spring the guy. I simply want to scare the hell out of him."

"Don't you think that Hill's going to see right through this, though? He's a fine lawyer, and I know for a fact he's handled many appeals. He'll realize the attack, as you've outlined it, is not a threat to the conviction at all."

"You're right … of course. So what do you suggest?"

"I think you need to go ahead and make those arguments. Your research is solid. But as I see it, the only way the brief being can appear effective is to make the primary charge that Hill, not the court, failed to properly handle these issues."

"Tell the appeals court that Hill's the one at fault?"

"Yes, and after all, isn't that the case? You see, this is the only angle to take for this brief to have the appearance of success. The theory is known as ineffective assistance of counsel. Look it up, and you'll see oodles of cases on it. It's essentially that the lawyer messed up, *and* the wrong result occurred because of that."

"I see—but Flynn instructed Hill to do it that way."

"It doesn't matter. Remember, the justices will only have the record you have on this table, and there's nothing in it about their little—shall we say—arrangement."

"I see, but to publicly accuse Hill of what's tantamount to malpractice?"

"Whoa, Michelle! Remember, this won't be filed, thus it will never be public."

"You're right," she agreed, perking up. "I'll just shift gears and point to Hill's mistakes."

"Do that, but don't forget the second element. It's not just his failures but also that the wrong result occurred because of them. I've seen appellate courts absolve many a lawyer screw-ups by finding there was enough good evidence to support the result. There's actually a published case where evidence showed a defendant's lawyer slept through significant portions of the trial. Despite that fact, the justices found no 'ineffective assistance'."

"How can that be?" Mickey asked in disbelief.

"I personally disagree with the ruling, but they found the evidence so incontrovertible that the snoozing lawyer didn't influence the outcome. As an aside, I knew this defense lawyer personally, and the defendant was probably better off when he *was* sleeping."

"Pretty bad, huh?" Mickey asked with a snicker.

"Oh, you don't know the half of it, Michelle," Baylor said, shaking his head. "So the essence of your brief has to be that Flynn was deprived of his Sixth Amendment right to counsel by Hill's poor performance. That argument is lodged in almost every death penalty appeal, and that's why I'm surprised that Hill's still on the case. Usually, another lawyer handles the appeal, so that claim can be effectively lodged."

"You know Hill, and he knows you. Are you okay with me doing this?"

"I honestly don't know what to think. On one hand, the trial's over, and this scourge has been adjudicated and sits on death row, and my gut says leave well enough alone. But that's easy enough for me to say since I'm not in your shoes. You don't reach my age without experiencing some fair share of tragedy, but the loss of a child …" Baylor stopped and turned away.

"It's okay," Mickey said as she patted his shoulder. "Mr. B, my respect for you is unquestionable. If you tell me not to do this, I'll walk away in a heartbeat and never look back."

"I appreciate that," Baylor said, removing his glasses and using a handkerchief to dab his eyes. "I know you've invested a lot to make this last attempt for your own peace of mind. Hill's a big boy, and I actually sense he'll immediately know why you are doing this and won't take it personally."

Mickey continued her research over the weekend and began to outline content for her amicus brief in accord with Baylor's instructions. She wanted an airtight brief that left no question about its accuracy, potency, and legal foundation and labored through several versions. By Monday, she felt comfortable presenting a draft to Baylor. He agreed to read it that evening, and when he walked into Mickey's office the next morning, brief in hand, her tension spiked. Mickey was drawn to several pencil marks on the front page, including scratch outs, notes and interlineations. He handed her the draft, and she shuffled through the other pages, finding more of the same.

"Don't worry about my edits, Michelle. They're mostly stylistic changes. The court of appeals is persnickety when it comes to how things are arranged and how certain points are addressed. I found the substance of your brief to be spot-on."

"Really?" Mickey said with relief.

"Really! I couldn't have done better myself."

Relishing in the high praise, she thanked him and wasted no time making the changes and having a copy hand-delivered to Hill, with a cover letter:

Dear Mr. Hill:

I'm providing you a courtesy copy of an amicus brief I intend to file in the Willie Flynn appeal. Recognizing how the success of this brief could affect your client, I assume you will fulfill your duty him by providing a copy to him and explaining its importance.

Yours Truly,
Michelle Grant

After a day at the courthouse, Hill arrived at his office that evening and found Mickey's letter and brief among other papers on his desk. He read it, and though he sensed it was a ploy spawned by their meeting, he was nevertheless impressed by Mickey's arguments, so much so that he express mailed a copy to Flynn the following day. With the slow nature of mail filtering through the prison system, Flynn did not receive Mickey's brief for several days, but when it arrived, Flynn read it and was confounded. He immediately commenced the bureaucratic process to arrange a call with Hill. The following afternoon, guards took Flynn to an administrative holding cell, and Hill's number was dialed. When Hill answered, Flynn jumped to the point. "Listen, man, I got a package of stuff from you. What does all of this mean?"

"Sometimes these briefs are submitted by outsiders to advise judges to do one thing or another."

"I just scanned through the main part of it, and it's a bunch of legal gobbledygook, but it seems to be attacking you?"

"I know, but I think I know where she's coming from with this."

"She? Who did this?"

"It's Michelle Grant, and she's—"

"That crazy bitch did this!"

"Yes. If you'll look, her name's on the last page of the brief. Willie, I think this is all just an idle threat. She seizing on the fact that I let things into evidence that I shouldn't have, and she's asserting that you weren't properly represented and didn't get a fair trial."

"Whoa, whoa, whoa! Let me get this straight. That nut's trying get *me* another trial!"

"That's what she's threatening. If the appeals court believes you didn't get a fair shake, they could send it back to the trial court."

"Shit. Why would she do this?"

"You know she's really obsessed with getting information about those missing girls and believes it can only come from you. She feels thwarted and desperate, and I'm sure she sees the threat of a new trial as a form of leverage."

"Oh, I get it. She came all the way here to meet with me, and since I didn't tell her nothin', she comes up with this shit!"

"Willie, I need you to know something. After her visit there, she came to meet with me too. I told her very little other than you didn't mind being confined on death row and why, and she's seizing on that. In hindsight, I shouldn't have told her anything, but I did, and for that I'm very sorry."

"What's done is done, but where do we go from here?"

"I'm not issuing any guarantees, but I don't think she'll go through with this," Hill said.

"So this thing ain't been sent to the court?"

"No, I checked with the court. She's only threatening it at this point, and frankly I don't think she means it at all."

"Thank God, man. What if I don't cooperate?"

"I believe she'll go away. I don't want to give you false hope, but I sense this is her Hail Mary. She's got nothing else left. I'll monitor the court to see if she files it, but I wouldn't worry too much about that if I were you."

"Please do that checking, man. Look, I know you ain't getting paid much, and—"

"You're still my client, Willie. I'll handle it," Hill said. "How are you doing otherwise?"

"I'm getting good books to read, and the food's tolerable."

"What about you're ALS?"

"Problem is I don't get much time to move around, you know, but they actually got a decent doc here. He's given me some stuff that helps the pain in my muscles and joints."

"That's good, Willie. Let me know if you need anything."

"You know, Counselor, this brief has a point," Flynn said.

"Oh?"

"Yeah, you did do a shitty job on the trial."

Hill laughed. "Thanks, Willie. The next envelope you get from me will be my bill!"

Though reassured by Hill's comments, Flynn found himself spending a large portion of his abundant time focusing on the threat that could return him to the Taylor County jail. Mickey on the other hand grew tired of waiting. Over two weeks elapsed from the day she delivered the brief to Hill, and with no response, she decided to call him at his office, and he took it.

"Mr. Hill, I provided you a courtesy copy of the amicus brief for a reason and really expected a response before now. Did you send it to Flynn?"

"I did, and I'm sorry, Mrs. Grant. I don't think he's going to respond."

"Well, that's too bad, but it's his call, I guess," she said, masking her disappointment. "Tell him I'll see him back here real soon."

"Come on now. You're not really thinking of filing that thing, are you?"

"Believe me when I say I don't want to, but that's why I'm calling. But, if Flynn doesn't cooperate, I'm damn sure gonna file it."

"I really think that's a can of worms that you won't open."

"You think I'm bluffing."

"Yes, as a matter of fact."

"If that's what you're telling Flynn, you're doing him a disservice. The bottom line is I'm willing to sit tight for a while longer, but I don't want this appeal decided while I wait. So if he doesn't come around *very* soon, I'm filing it."

"Well, my client and I will leave that up to you," Hill said, concluding the call.

Mickey hung up. *Baylor was right, Hill saw right through it, damn it! He knows what's at stake and that I can't follow through, and that's exactly what he told Flynn.*

Over the next couple of days, Mickey was haunted by Flynn's rebuke and saw it as nothing short of a dare for her to escalate. Mickey found herself confronted with the realization that she was down to two choices: concede defeat and walk away or up the ante and file the brief. She knew that if she did the latter, she would have to find a way to conceal it from everyone except Hill. Once done, and if Flynn did not cooperate, she considered that she could simply withdraw her brief, and no one would need to know. *It's just one last step, that's all. I've come too far to turn back, right? But it's a big step—a very big step—a risky step. But how can that risk be any worse than feeling the way I do now for the rest of my life?*

Surrendering to her frustration, Mickey made up her mind, and drove to the court of appeals, with brief in hand. She sensed that if she waited any longer, she might relent and not muster that level of resolve again. She proceeded directly to the law library on the first floor of the same building. Knowing that she needed six copies of the brief for the court, she paid a nominal fee for the copies and walked up the stairs to the third-floor clerk's office. She paused at the door, finding beads of sweat forming on her forehead. Whether by exertion on the stairs or the tension of the moment, Mickey's breathing had accelerated, and she consciously inhaled deeper than normal to compensate. She took one very deep breath and walked in the clerk's office and placed her papers on the counter.

"Can I help you, ma'am?" a well-dressed female clerk asked.

"I want to file these, please," Mickey said sliding the documents toward her.

The clerk glanced at them, assured that the required number of copies were included and began writing an entry in the book used for cataloging newly filed documents. "Is the extra copy for you?"

Mickey nodded, and the clerk completed the log. She then took the papers to a machine used to file stamp all incoming documents, by sliding the top right corner of the front page of each copy. This act triggered the machine to imprint each with a seal bearing the name of the court and the date and time of filing. The clerk prepared the copies for stamping when Mickey blurted out, "Wait! I can withdraw this brief if I decide to, right?"

"I'm sorry, ma'am" the woman replied, pointing to a sign near the counter that read: *Court clerks are not allowed to render legal advice.*

"I see," Mickey said with a troubled expression.

"Do you want to speak with a law clerk?" the clerk asked.

"Yes, ma'am, and please don't stamp those until I do."

The clerk walked to the back and returned with a young man in a suit, who asked, "You need to speak with me?"

"I do. Are you a lawyer?"

"Yes but not official yet. I'm waiting on bar results."

"Oh, you just took the July bar?" Mickey empathized.

"Yes, and lived to tell about it too. Are you a lawyer?"

"Yes, but I don't do a lot of appellate work."

"I see. So what can I help with?"

"I'm filing an amicus brief in one of your appeals and wanted to confirm that I can withdraw if I decide to."

"Yes, with a notice under appellate Rule 48. You have to withdraw your brief in writing, not verbally, but you don't have to file a motion and an order, it's just the notice."

"If I do that, it will be as if it had never been filed."

"Correct."

"And it can't be considered by the court?"

"Right," the clerk said and then leaned close to Mickey and whispered, "Between me and you, the justices don't pay much attention to amicus briefs anyway."

"I see. So it's a rule 48, huh?" The clerk nodded. "Thanks and good luck on the bar results. I remember waiting for mine."

"Yeah, I'm not getting much sleep these days, and I don't get the results until November."

Mickey gave the nod to the woman, who stuck the front page of the first copy of the brief into the machine. The apparatus made a characteristic slamming sound, one Mickey had heard many times in the past. This time, however, it rang out like a gunshot that echoed through her mind. After stamping each document, the clerk handed Mickey her extra copy. "I know this case is a big deal, ma'am. Are you one of the lawyers in it?"

"I am now," Mickey quipped. "Thanks for the help."

"Take that, you bastard!" Mickey muttered under her breath as she walked down the stairs and out of the building and into the sweltering summer heat. A sense of domination had replaced the fear and trepidation gnawing at her moments earlier, but she knew time was now her enemy. She wanted to assure that Flynn received word of the filing right away, and she did not want to involve any firm personnel in doing so. Once at her office, she went directly to the mailroom on the upper floor. She opted to fax rather than to scan and e-mail the file-stamped copy so nothing would remain on the firm's network server. She filled out a fax cover page, marked it urgent, and dialed Hill's fax number. She watched hopefully as her file-stamped brief transmitted one page at a time.

CHAPTER 14

NULLUM SECRETUM EST

(There Are No Secrets)

Tyler accepted Mickey's invitation to spend Friday night with her, and when he arrived, he pulled their old charcoal grill from her garage, cleaned it, and prepped it to cook steaks. They shared a pleasant dinner, which including copious amounts of wine, and stayed up much too late watching old black-and-white movies. The sun was rising the next morning as they lay in her bed asleep, until her phone rang.

"Who could that be?" Mickey whispered and answered it on the fourth ring.

"Is this Michelle Grant?"

"Yes, and who's this?" Mickey asked in a raspy voice.

"This is Evelyn Howard, dear. Sorry to call so early, but I just couldn't wait. Have you seen the paper this morning?"

"No, I haven't."

"There's an article in it that says you filed some sort of paperwork with the court in the Flynn case. Is that true?" she asked.

Grogginess and mild hang over aside, Mickey shot straight up in her bed, inadvertently pulling the covers and drawing Tyler's attention. He whispered, "Who is it?"

"Mrs. Howard," she mouthed, and then she said, "Yes, ma'am, I filed a brief in the appeal."

"I realize from experience how the newspapers can get these legal type things wrong, and this is going to sound crazy, but this article says you're trying to get Flynn a new trial."

"Not a chance, Mrs. Howard."

"That's good, but you should know that the article says that you're pointing out all of Mr. Hill's mistakes from the trial and how it wasn't fair to Flynn."

Mickey panicked. "The brief does say that, but believe me, I—"

"Oh, dear! I don't understand."

"Don't be alarmed," Mickey urged, trying to conjure the right words. "I filed this document only to put pressure on Flynn. It's simply a ploy to get information about the missing girls."

"Forgive my ignorance on these legal things, but how is trying to get Flynn a new trial pressuring him?"

"I'm not trying to get him a new trial, at least not really. I mean I only … This is complicated, Mrs. Howard, but I assure you that—"

"But it says right here that's what you're going for," Mrs. Howard pressed

"I'm sure that's what it says, but just know it's only a threat, and a new trial is the last thing that Flynn would want," Mickey said, willing confidence into her voice. "It's simply a tactic, and if I don't have any luck, I'm going to withdraw the brief, and that'll be the end of it."

"You know that I have the utmost trust in your judgment, Michelle, but this is so *very* disconcerting to read. I know that I'm going to get calls on this and just want to be prepared."

Desperate to allay this fount of information's concerns, Mickey explained the details and mechanics for her actions. She emphasized Flynn's fear of returning to the county jail for another trial and her right to withdraw the brief and render it a nullity, and slowly, Mrs. Howard seemed at ease with Mickey's explanation.

Having gone to the kitchen to start a pot of coffee, Tyler returned and whispered, "What does she want?"

"Excuse me, Mrs. Howard," Mickey said, covering the phone receiver. "I'll tell you when I'm done. Would you please go get the paper out of the yard?" He nodded, and Mickey returned to the call. "So you see, Mrs. Howard, this is all planned out and under control."

"I think I understand it now. Forgive me for being so hysterical."

"You weren't. But please understand that this can't get out that I'm bluffing. If Hill learns of my intention to withdraw it, we're all gonna lose."

"But people are going to ask me about this, so what do I tell them?"

"Hmm, I see the point," Mickey said. "Here's what I suggest. If you get an inquiry from a group member, explain the real reason for filing the brief and the withdrawal part, but make sure they too know to keep the strategy secret. If the press, the police, or some other official contacts you, just refer them to me. Does that sound fair?"

"Yes, I think I can handle this."

"Thank you *very* much, Mrs. Howard. I'm so sorry that you were alarmed and are now in the middle of all of this. But this will all work out fine, I promise." Hanging up the phone, she looked at Tyler, who was standing next to her.

"You filed that brief?" Tyler asked, handing her the paper.

"Yes, and shit! Shit! Shit! Somehow it's in the damn morning paper!"

"Mick, this is going to be all over town, and my clients are going to think we're crazy."

"I've got a handle on this. God knows I'm going to feel the heat, but trust me that one way or another this will be over soon." Mickey removed the paper from its plastic wrapper and began perusing the pages. She was gratified to see the story was not on the front page but located it on page one of the local news section and the headline read: "Local Mother of Suspected Victim Files Brief to Spring Condemned Killer."

"Oh, goddamn!" she gasped.

"Is it bad?" Tyler asked.

"Very, and it even mentions Triple-B"

"How'd this get in the paper anyway?" Tyler asked.

"Who knows? It could have been the court, or, hell, Hill could have leaked it out just to sabotage me. Either way, this is gonna cause a real shit storm."

The rest of the day, Mickey fielded calls, including from support-group members, two old classmates, and even her hair stylist, and she grew weary with the endless explanations. But the call she most dreaded came that evening from Ford Becker.

"So what took *you* so long?"

"Been a long day, has it?" Becker said.

"Oh Jesus, you don't know the half of it, Ford."

"Mickey, I know you've been through the wringer, but this will draw a lot of negative publicity to the firm."

"I hate like hell that the paper mentioned y'all."

"Me too. Now, I'm going to get an earful about this from the partners, so I need to know the scoop. I was generally aware of the brief and at some point spoke to Harrison about it, but it was my understanding that it was never to be used."

"Everything you just said is true. But I was so outraged at Flynn's continued recalcitrance that I betrayed Mr. Baylor's trust and I filed it. I confirmed, though, that I can file a withdrawal it under rule … let's see … it's …"

"Rule 48?"

"Yes, thank you. I can file a Rule 48 withdrawal, and it will be as if it never was filed. Ford, I only did this because Hill told Flynn the brief was just an idle threat."

"But it was only to be an idle threat," Ford said.

"Believe me, I know that. I also realize there'll be consequences to this, and I'll accept any and all of them, and I'm very sorry. I stupidly believed that I could keep this under wraps and just withdraw it before it leaked out, and I'll be damned if it didn't hit the papers within hours."

"When do you plan to file the Rule 48? I'm sure Harrison will want to know."

"That's a fair question, but look—since the harm's done and the whole world now knows, I'd like to have a little grace period to see if it works. This should really frighten the hell out of Flynn, and he may just come around and work with me and the other families. Can you explain that to Mr. Baylor?"

"That doesn't sound unreasonable to me, but I'm not sure what he'll think. What exactly do you mean by a grace period?"

"I'd like five business days and would pledge to withdraw the brief on or before next Friday."

"You may have at least a couple of days, since some of the partners, including Harrison and me, are supposed to head out to a continuing legal education conference in Phoenix tomorrow."

"You said 'supposed to'?"

"Yeah, there's real bad weather predicted between here and Arizona, and we're scheduled to take a nine o'clock flight tomorrow night. If it cancels, we're canceling the CLE conference and scrapping the whole trip."

"I'm very sorry for all of this, Ford. I mean it when I say I stand to accept any punishment, including dismissal."

"Fire you? Don't be silly. Harrison's going to be taken aback by this, but he's a fair man, and I don't think this will inflict any lasting harm."

"God, I hope you're right," Mickey said.

"I know it seems bad right now, but I'm sure it'll work it all out when we're back from the trip."

"So CLE in Arizona, huh? Is that Continuing Legal Education or Constantly on the Links Every Day?" Mickey asked.

Ford chuckled. "Mostly the former, but we are bringing our clubs."

The following evening, Becker was late leaving for the airport, and once he arrived and cleared security, he walked briskly toward the gate, stopping only to check the flight arrival-departure board. He noted their flight was still scheduled but delayed forty minutes, and when he reached the gate, he saw Baylor and two other partners sitting in the check-in area. Baylor was reading a book, and when he noticed Ford approaching, he said, "You're lucky the flight's delayed, or you'd have been cuttin' it mighty close."

"I know. I got a late start to begin with, and then ..."

"Did the Texas Rangers' extra innings have a role in that?"

"Yes, and then the state had 84 shut down for construction," Ford explained.

"I hope they'll have the highway open by morning. Half of our staff comes in on it."

"The sign said it was closed until 4:00 a.m.," Becker informed.

"That's good. So have you spoken to Michelle?"

"Yes. I guess you read about the amicus brief in the paper?"

"No, I actually didn't get around to reading yesterday's paper, but I sure heard about it this morning."

"Oh?"

"Yeah, after the early church service, the bride and I decided to go to brunch. We were enjoying perfectly cooked crepes when Detective Adams walked over and asked if he could speak to me. He looked really exercised, so I walked with him to the veranda, and he explained the whole situation."

"Was Adams hacked off?"

"He was diplomatic, but there are flares going off throughout the city government. So what did Michelle have to say?"

"She's beside herself. She thought that she could file the brief and send a file-stamped copy to Hill and try to break the log jam with Flynn. Then one way or the other, she would file a Rule 48 and get everything back status quo. For what it's worth, she owned up to everything and was very apologetic and is worried about how you'll react. She's even concerned that she might get fired."

"Really?" Baylor asked as Ford nodded. "Don't get me wrong. I'm *real* disappointed but nowhere near that level."

"I told her that, but she's worried that you feel betrayed."

"I do, but I also accept some of the blame," Baylor said as Becker raised his eyebrows. "I didn't think any of this tampering was wise or even healthy for her. I helped her with this out of sheer sympathy, but I knew she was vulnerable and not thinking clearly. I should've known better than to arm her with this when she lacked the capacity to deal with it objectively."

Becker sighed. "But she's dedicated to making this go away."

"Fine, but she can't make the story go away."

"What a mess."

"Yes, and I think it's going to get worse before it gets better. I'm going to have a barrage of calls starting in the morning. You know how I hate flying, but I can't recall being this happy to get on an airplane since I detached from the army and they flew me back home from Germany."

Mickey awoke Monday morning, having slept little and suffering from cold symptoms. Her predicament and the scratchy throat and watery eyes had kept her stirring most of the night. She rarely allowed aches, pains, or sniffles to keep her from her work, and even with looming controversy, she elected to face head-on whatever the day would bring. She stripped from her night clothes and placed the shower handle at full heat. She stood bare in front of the bathroom mirror until the steam vapors crept from the shower, across the ceiling, and halfway down the mirror. She entered the shower and let the stinging drops pelt her back and shoulders. She expected that the steamy shower would relieve her symptoms and angst, but it did little for either. She drove to the office, and her dread escalated as she activated the sliding gate and pulled into the parking garage. The partners' slots were empty, and when elevator doors opened, and Mickey walked reception area Wanda confirmed that each had indeed made their flight.

When Mickey reached her office, she greeted Marlene and said, "I'm hoping to hear from Chester Hill or Flynn. Please do whatever it takes to track me down if either calls."

"I will," Marlene replied, while taking note of Mickey's haggard appearance. "I saw the article in the paper. Are you doing okay?"

"I'm making it. Thanks for asking," Mickey said as she walked to her desk. She looked to her left and saw out her window an ominous red glow on the horizon. "Come look, Marlene—it's a sandstorm. That's probably one of the reasons I feel so awful."

"Yeah, no telling what that thing's stirring up," Marlene said as she stared out at the menacing sky. "Crap, I think I left the windows cracked on my car."

"Who knows if it'll come this way or not, but either way you ought to go roll 'em up."

"I'll do that right now, if you don't mind?" Marlene asked.

"By all means, go!"

"Thanks. I've had a car full of sand before, and it's a real pain."

"Me too. That sand gets into spaces you'd never dream of," Mickey said.

"Yeah, like sunbathing on the beach!"

Mickey chuckled and said, "Thanks Marlene, I needed a laugh."

That afternoon, Marlene buzzed Mickey's office, informing that Chester Hill was on the line. Her heart thumped, and she eagerly accepted the call.

"Mrs. Grant, I'll get right to it. Rumor has it that you filed the brief as just a ploy and that you intend on withdrawing it. Is that true?"

"Not at all," Mickey lied. "I have to tell people that because I'm taking a lot of heat over filing it."

"Surely you're not serious about going forward with this?"

"You can bet your ass I'm serious! Nothing against you, but as long as your client's sittin' in Huntsville with the information I need, I'm going to try to make his life as miserable as I can."

"Ms. Grant, I've said before that I empathize with you, but if this is some sort of game, it's imperative I know it right now."

"A game? Is that what you call it? This is the most important thing in my life, and I'm going to either get the information I want or see to it Flynn comes back here to Brinkman."

"Okay … fine … I just needed clarity. Since you've appeared in the case, I'll need to serve you with paperwork going forward, so I need to know what address you want me to use."

"The office is fine."

"I have that, and we'll add you to the service list."

Not wanting to end the call, she asked, "So what did your client think of me filing it?"

"Well, first of all, he's now my ex-client. I'll be removing myself from the case."

"What?" Mickey asked.

"You heard me. Because of your allegations of my ineffective assistance, I'm officially off the case, and if it was your goal to piss off Flynn, consider your effort a resounding success."

"Mr. Hill, I hope you recognize that the brief was not intended as a true reflection on you. I understand that you had marching orders, and you followed them."

"Forgive me for saying so, but I think you've gone way over the line here, Ms. Grant. I truly don't take any of this personally, but what you've done is very dangerous, and I don't sense you have a healthy appreciation of that."

"I'm simply trying to get him to come clean, Mr. Hill. He must help me and these others families. Can't you do something about that?" Mickey pleaded. "I can make all of this go away in an instant, and you can stay on the case. No one really wants a retrial!"

"You'll have to deal with his new counsel about all of that."

"That's it? You're just gonna walk away? You've got a relationship with him, and I know he trusts you."

"Trusts me? He knows that I'm to blame for you knowing his disease and the fear of being in gen-pop. You decided to use that, and I bear responsibility for it."

"I'm sorry for that. Do you know who the new lawyer's going be?"

"It's not confirmed, but it looks like Gerald Campbell will agree to step in."

They hung up, and Mickey jotted down the name of Flynn's new lawyer, and was spooked that her plans were beginning to fray and unwind. She decided to draft her Rule 48 withdrawal so she could file it at a moment's notice. She took the stairs to the library and saw Woodrow updating a reference books.

"You faxed a document on your own," Woody stated as she entered.

"Excuse me?"

"You sent a fax last Friday."

"Nothing gets past you, Woody," she responded as she walked toward the bookshelves.

"What about the log?"

"Log? What log, Woody?"

"The fax log. You didn't fill it out. Everyone has to fill out the fax log, including the partners. It's firm policy per my memo of 12 October 2006."

"Sorry, Woody, I forgot. I'll take care of that right away."

"I did it for you—and since it's your first violation, I let it slide."

Though she didn't know the penalty for any such violation, she accepted the reprieve and with conjured contrition, "Thanks. It won't happen again."

"Good, but since it wasn't related to a firm case, it will be charged back to you."

"Fair enough."

"So what brings you up here?"

"I need the Texas Rules of Appellate Procedure."

"Case three, third shelf," he fired back, pointing to the row of book cases to her right.

Mickey looked up Rule 48, made a copy, and returned to her office. She typed up the withdrawal notice, made the requisite copies, and called it a day.

When Mickey arrived at the office Tuesday morning, she was surprised to see two particular cars in the parking lot, Becker's jeep and Baylor's Cadillac. Neither were due back until the following day, and apprehension gripped her as she sat in her car. Dodging fire was not a plan, so she locked her car and made her way to the reception area.

"What are the partners doing back so soon?" she whispered to Wanda.

"One of Mr. Baylor's schoolmates died, so they decided to come back for the funeral. There's already been a couple of closed-door meetings."

Mickey managed to reach her office without seeing any of the partners. She shut her door and worked at her desk, cringing each time she heard footsteps. Midmorning, Marlene buzzed in and said, "Mr. Baylor wants to see you."

Mickey didn't tarry and proceeded directly toward his office and tapped on his closed door and eased it open. She saw Ford Becker across the desk from Baylor. Their conversation ended abruptly as she entered, and she could feel blood rushing to her head and was incapable of managing even a word of greeting. She took her seat on the couch and alternated glances between the two men.

"So, Michelle, what have you been up to lately?" Baylor asked facetiously, trying to ease her palpable tension.

She exhaled and said, "I know you're aware of everything, Mr. B."

"Yes, and I've spoken to Ford about his conversation with you too."

"I want you to know that I'm very embarrassed about all of this. It was a huge error in judgment. I let my desperation get the best of me, and all I can say is I'm really, really sorry."

"Your apology is accepted, but Ford and I are most interested in what you're going to do now."

"I need to make this right and will withdraw the brief. I've already drafted the Rule 48 notice and can file it any time."

"I'm very disappointed about this, and as I'm sure you know, I would've never helped you with this if I thought for a minute you'd actually file it. You broke a promise to me and, in the process, created a dangerous situation for the firm."

"Dangerous? To the firm?" Mickey asked.

"Yes, Mickey," Becker said. "All of this reflects very poorly on us, and getting Chester Hill disqualified is an affront to the justice system."

"You know about that too, huh?"

"Yes. Chester left me a message as a courtesy. He knew the firm might get calls on this and didn't want me to be blindsided," Baylor explained.

"Has the firm gotten calls about this?"

"Yes," Ford confirmed. "I've spoken to the police, including and Chief Buchanan, and Harrison has had a long conversation with Garland Adams, Lyndon Tucker, and had to talk the mayor off the ceiling a half hour ago."

"Goodness, this is all so awful. I promise that I'll take care of this," Mickey advised, her voice now trembling.

"This is why barbers shouldn't cut their own hair and lawyers should never represent themselves," Baylor counseled. "A lawyer, just like a barber, needs to be able to step back and see all the angles."

Becker added, "It's like that old saying that 'a lawyer who represents himself has a fool for a client and an ass for a lawyer'."

"Well I'm both of those, all right," she said, dabbing tears.

"Mickey, if you could have just separated the grieving mom from the tenacious attorney, this would have never happened. You, as a lawyer, would have told the grieving mom that this was ill advised and stopped her."

"You're absolutely right, Ford. I did consult with my lawyer side, but the grieving mom fired her. Look, guys, like I said—this is all going away this week, but since Hill says I've got Flynn's attention, I'd truly like to give it a chance until the end of the week."

Becker glanced to Baylor and, sensing his discomfort, intervened with a compromise. "How about first thing Thursday morning? That gives you essentially forty-eight hours."

They each looked to Baylor, who nodded. "I can live with that."

"Thank you, Mr. B, and please accept my condolences for your friend."

"Friend?" Baylor asked.

"Yes, Wanda said one of your classmates died."

"Oh, that. Thanks, but Red Garfield wasn't a close personal friend.

We did go to law school together, but I hadn't seen him since he left the bench twelve or so years ago. But when a former Taylor County District judge dies, the partners are expected to be represented at the services. Now, would you two excuse me for a moment? I have to sign some papers."

"Want us to leave?" Becker offered.

"No, you two make yourselves at home. This shouldn't take but a couple of minutes, and I have something else to discuss."

With Baylor out of the office, Mickey said, "He doesn't seem too pissed."

"He's not happy, but I spent the better part of two long flights mollifying him. He really does sympathize with you a great deal but wants to get this behind us quickly."

"I do too. Thanks for brokering me a couple of days," she said.

"I think it's a long shot, but I hope he somehow helps you and the others."

"Me too."

"By the way, we also have a separate complaint about you."

"That's all I need," she sighed "Who from?"

"Woody," Ford responded with a smile.

Mickey laughed. "So much for my reprieve."

"Your what?"

"Oh, never mind. Is this about the fax log thing?" she asked as Ford nodded. "Oh, hell. Marlene does all of my faxing, but I did one on my own and just forgot all about the log thing. I apologized to him, and then he has the gall to squeal on me. He's so damn meticulous!"

"Yeah, he runs the upstairs the way Ahab ran the *Pequod*," Ford said.

"I have a Melville-related description of him, but since it involves the whale's last name, I think I'll keep it to myself."

Becker was chortling as Baylor reentered and asked "What's this about?"

"We were just discussing Woody," Becker said.

"Well that explains the laughter."

"Harrison, you said you had something else on the appeal thing?" Ford asked.

"Yes. Michelle, are you aware that Gerry Campbell's been appointed to replace Hill?" Baylor said as Becker pivoted his head rapidly to Baylor.

"Hill told me that, but I've never heard of him."

"You may know him better by 'Cannibal' Campbell."

Mickey knew that name, and though she did not know Campbell personally, she had heard stories of the flamboyant lawyer from her dad. "He's pretty good, huh?"

"Good? He's one of the best," Baylor said.

"I've always wondered how he got the Cannibal moniker. Do you know?" Becker asked.

"I'm sure that if you ask him, he'll say it's for the way he chews up prosecutors," Baylor said. "The truth is, as a pup lawyer, Campbell represented a man accused of a series of murders. His client captured random victims and held them as prisoners on his cotton farm. The guy tortured each until they died, but he was also accused of eating some of his victims. During his closing argument, Campbell told the jury that his client was no more a cannibal than he was. After his client was convicted, people started calling him Cannibal Campbell," Baylor explained. "But that loss proved to be rare, as he's lost sparingly few cases since."

"Why in the world would he take a case like this?" Mickey wondered.

"Well, first of all, I'm sure that Judge Sullivan asked him to do it as a favor. You don't usually turn that down. In addition, he's always been a publicity hound and probably sees this as a chance to get his name back in the news."

"But the state pays very little on these court-appointed cases."

"The money's not the issue for him, Michelle. He has plenty of that. You see, he gets something by taking a case like this case that money can't buy, and that's notoriety. It gets him case referrals, speaking engagements, and assures he's invited to the good cocktail parties."

When Mickey returned to her office, Becker closed the door and looked to Baylor. "If there's a new trial, Campbell's not going to take a dive, is he?"

"Nope. Hill told me that as we speak, Campbell's on his jet heading to Huntsville for a meeting with Flynn."

Campbell's plane landed at the Huntsville Regional Airport, and a driver met him and took him directly to the prison. Two guards escorted Flynn from his small, narrow cell to the larger conference room to meet his new counsel. As one guard unlocked the door, the other escorted Flynn into the room and toward the stainless-steel table. The room as a whole was dim, illuminated only by a single light bulb suspended by a black cord from the high ceiling. Campbell was sitting at the opposite end of the table, clad in a western-style suit, with brown blazer, tan slacks, and a shiny pair of eel-skin cowboy boots. Chewing on a larger than normal cigar, Campbell leaned back on the rear legs of the metal chair and peered across the table at his new client. Then the two guards shackled Flynn to the bolted down table leg and then stood within a few feet to observe.

Campbell turned from Flynn to the guards, saying, "What the hell do y'all think you're doing?"

"This is a maximum-security zone, and we're required to be here," One of the guards responded.

"Wrong! You're *allowed* to be in *here*," Campbell said using the hand holding the cigar to point toward the four walls of the room. "But you ain't allowed to be *there*!" he said, pointing at the spot where the two stood.

"Perhaps you aren't acquainted with protocol, but we get to monitor this visit," the guard responded.

"Son, I've been coming down to this shithole you call a prison since you were in diapers."

"I understand, sir, but—"

"Now, I do recognize your right to be in this room, okay? But you two don't have the right to listen to my conversation with my client. So I don't want you or your buddy anywhere near this table. Got it?"

"The rule says that—"

"I know the rules, and the state ain't gonna be a part of my goddamn client consultation!"

The other guard interjected, "Sir, we have instructions to—"

"Do I have to get old friend and warden, Hal Harding on the phone?" Campbell threatened raising his cell phone from his jacket pocket. "I have him on speed dial."

The guards looked at each other, and one said, "That's not necessary. How about we sit on those chairs over there in the corner?"

"Fine, fine. Y'all sit right there in the corner and don't strain to listen, okay?" Campbell said grinning.

The guards nodded and took their seats twenty-five feet away as Campbell moved his chair closer to Flynn.

"Is it a requirement for lawyers in Texas to dress like this?" Flynn asked, surveying Campbell's attire.

"Well, hello to you too," Campbell retorted. "Do you not approve of my apparel?"

"Oh, it's great," Flynn said facetiously. "I was just wondering if it was mandatory, that's all."

"Is it mandatory for you all in here to dress like that?" Campbell said, pointing at Flynn's standard-issue prison garb.

Flynn grinned and nodded. "I know about that brief being filed. So my main question is can I be placed in isolation during the next trial?"

"Whoa, son! Let's not get ahead of ourselves. What makes you think there will be a retrial?"

"Well, isn't that what you were hired to do?" Flynn asked.

"No. My immediate responsibility is to represent you in the appeal, from this point forward, since—shall we say—the *quality* of your prior representation was called into question."

"Fine, but I want to know right now what's going on with that brief and what you intend to do about it!"

"You're a demanding son of a bitch! Hill warned me about you, but I—"

"Sorry ... I'm just a little agitated about this, that's all."

"Fair enough, but look—the court of appeals can do a variety of things with this, and reversing your conviction and ordering a new trial is just one very unlikely possible outcome. They're far more apt to affirm your conviction as to overturn it, with or without that brief."

"What do you mean by 'with or without it'?"

"First off, they don't have to consider amicus briefs at all. I've known many a justice who sees those that file them as nothing more than 'meddling interlopers' and that's a direct quote from one of 'em. Secondly, rumor has it that the goofy-assed lady who filed it will withdraw it, and if she does, they can't consider it even if they wanted to."

"She can really withdraw it?"

"She can, and I expect she will. Based on my intel, she's taken quite a ration of shit over this."

"Good. She deserves that and a lot more."

"Now, there's something we both can agree on," Campbell said. "But, Willie, with Hill out of the way, I should be making those same arguments, you know."

"No way. I want that brief withdrawn and for *you* to leave well enough alone!"

"Calm down, now," Campbell said pointing back to the guards. "You should know, Willie, that brief raises some very salient points."

"You've read it and think it's good?"

"Good? No, it's excellent. I detect Harrison Baylor's fingerprints all over it."

"Who's that?"

"Only one of the best damn trial lawyers to ever hail from the great state of Texas, that's who. He also happens to be the senior partner in that crazy lady's law firm."

"If he's so great, why does he hire nuts like her?"

"She may be nuts, but her legal arguments aren't. Hill told me a little about her and this crusade for information. What's up with that?"

"She wants information about her daughter and those other missing girls. She actually came here to try to get it from me."

"She came here? To Huntsville?"

"Yes, and we met, but in a different area."

"Damn, she *is* nuts!"

"Yeah, and she just filed this thing just to screw with me because she knows I don't want no retrial!"

"Well she doesn't either. That would be disastrous for her, and that's why she'll make it go away"

"I don't know man. Hill said she wouldn't file it, and she did. Hell, I'm thinking about talking to her to get her off my ass."

"I guess you're free to do what you want, but I advise against it. Truthfully, I'd rather get the new trial and kick Lyndon Tucker's ass," Campbell said testing Flynn's resolve.

Flynn shook his head vigorously. "I'm the client here, and I want no such thing!"

"So you're against a retrial, even with a chance to win it?" Campbell asked.

"Yes. I'm perfectly content with things right here."

"Oh, I can understand that. After all, this is such a charming place," Campbell said facetiously, waving his arm around the room. "Come on, son. What could be so great about being in here, huh?"

"A cell to myself, for one. I get plenty of books to read, decent food, and good medical care."

"Well shit, man! You make this place sound like a resort. Hell, I think me and the bride just might vacation here next summer!" Campbell joked, drawing belly laugh from Flynn. "Look, Willie—let me go on the record and say I do think we can win the case if it's retried, you need to think long and hard about that."

"I don't want no retrial!" Flynn yelled and pounded his shackled hand on the table, stirring the guards to their feet.

"I got this!" Campbell said, extending the palm of his right hand toward the guards. When they stood down, he turned back to his client and whispered, "Keep it down, damn it! Now, look. Let's be realistic about this. Hill took a dive on your trial and another one on your appeal. His briefing stinks, and we may well be stuck with it, and as such the verdict is very likely to be affirmed, so I—"

"Good," Flynn said, and Campbell shook his head.

"Hill wasn't lying about you. You're a zealot," Campbell said, leaning back in his chair and looking up to the dim light bulb. "Have you considered that you could be acquitted and go free?"

"Sure, but if I win this one, they'll just pin one of those other crimes on me."

Campbell again leaned forward. "They don't have enough on those other cases to even go to the grand jury."

"Fine, but I'm on parole and can't sneeze without creating a reason to revoke it," Flynn insisted as Campbell shook his head and opened his manila folder.

"I know you think I'm dense, but I—"

"Willie, you're as dense as a goddamned anvil," Campbell said as he slipped on glasses and struggled to read materials from his file. Frustrated, he looked at the guards and said, "Next time you see my friend, the esteemed Hal Harding, tell him Gerry Campbell asked if there are enough funds in the Correction Department's budget for a goddamned 100-watt light bulb for in here!"

The guards nodded, and Campbell turned back to Flynn. "Look—you're a young man, and you're gonna let them warehouse you in here until the day comes to haul you out of your cell on a gurney? I know about your illness and all, but I looked it up. You've got potentially many years to live. You need to think about what you're doing and stop being so damn intent on pissin' your life away."

"You don't understand, man. I don't mind it in here. I know it don't make no sense to you, but as I see it, you work for me, and this is the way I want it."

"Well, that's what Chester warned me I'd hear. This is the damnedest thing I've seen since the three-headed dog at the state fair in Dallas," Campbell said and closed his file. "Now, you say you're gettin' good medical care in here, but I noticed you limping when you came in."

"Yeah. It comes and goes, but the doc's managing it pretty well."

"Good," he said, patting Flynn on the shoulder. Campbell rose to leave, and looking at the nearest guard, he said, "Okay, Colombo, I'm ready to get my ass out of this cavern."

CHAPTER 15

⚖

MANUS MANUM LAVAT

(One Hand Washes the Other)

July 25

Tuesday came and went without contact from Flynn, and as Mickey dressed for work Wednesday morning, she felt the pressure of the ticking clock and feared Flynn would not give in by the Ford-Becker-brokered Thursday deadline. But as she was walking out of the door, her phone rang. She reversed course answered it, and heard an operator informing that she had a collect call from the Texas Department of Corrections.

Mickey eagerly accepted the call, and when she heard a click, she said, "Michelle Grant here."

"This is Willie Flynn. The guards looked up your number and let me call, and I ain't got much time, so let's get to it. You had the balls to file that brief thing. I didn't think you would, but you did, and I have to deal with that."

"Yes you do," Mickey said, straining to conceal her anxiety.

"I'm told you can withdraw it, and when I get confirmation you have, I will tell you what you want to know."

"Oh, right! I'm just supposed to trust your word."

"It's a two-way street, smart ass. You know that I have to trust you to withdraw it and not refile it, right?"

"Let's be clear. Are you willing to tell me the truth about *all* of the girls?"

"That's why I'm on the phone, but you have to perform first. That's the only way that this'll work."

"I'll do my part. You have my word," She said. "Here's what I'll do. I'll go to the court and withdraw it right now. The paperwork's done, and it'll only take me a half hour to do it. Will they let you make more calls today?"

"I doubt it. There's a limit to 'em. Once this is over, I have to make another request and get back in line. At best, it would be a day or so—at worst a week."

"Can you make a call to your lawyer quicker?"

"That's a lot easier."

"All right, I'll fax the file-stamped withdrawal to Campbell's office. You'll have to call there to confirm it."

"Then what?"

"Then once you know I've kept my end of the bargain, I want you to call and tell me everything. You have until 5:00 p.m. tomorrow to call me back or I refile it. Understand?"

"Tomorrow? That's three calls in two days," Flynn said. "I can only promise to call as soon as they let me."

"Look, Willie—I can't leave this hanging. I need a commitment, now!"

"I get that, but unless you've forgotten, I'm on death row. I don't exactly have a lot of control over phone privileges."

"Fine. I'll move it to Friday at four o'clock, but that's it. If you haven't called by then, I still have an hour to refile the brief before the court closes for the weekend."

"Friday, huh? What day is this?"

"Wednesday."

"I'll do everything I can, that's all I can say," Flynn said.

"Okay, and when we next speak, I want the *whole* truth, in detail, about my daughter and all the others. No bullshittin' around like you did when we spoke in Huntsville."

"Fine."

"And there are no unfair questions, right?"

"Sure, but I have a limit on how long a call can last, so we'll have to go quickly."

"We'll just have to deal with that. But I want all the truth, you hear?"

"Lay off, damn it! I said I'd help," Flynn urged, and Mickey sensed desperation in his voice.

"All right then. We have a deal."

Mickey drove straight to the court of appeals, heartened that with a single act she could fulfill her promise to Baylor, early, and could redeem herself by delivering closure to her and the grieving parents. With copies of the withdrawal in hand, she marched into the court clerk's office.

"How can I help you, ma'am?" asked the young man behind the counter.

Having not seen him previously, Mickey asked, "Are you the clerk?"

"No, ma'am, I'm a law clerk. The intake clerk had to pick up her sick kid from school."

"I thought I met the law clerk last week."

"You probably did, but there's two of us, and we each manage our own docket."

"I see. Listen, I really need to file these rule 48 withdrawals. Can you do it?" Mickey asked, handing him the notices.

"Sure," he said, punching the case number in the computer. "Oh, I see the amicus brief on here. Is that what you're withdrawing?" Mickey nodded "Fine, I'll get these file stamped and entered for you."

"Thanks," Mickey said as the clerk started stamping each document.

Once done, he said, "Here's your file-stamped copy, ma'am, and it's entered in the system."

"Perfect. I appreciate it very much."

"You're very welcome, but I'm not sure what good it does."

"What do you mean?" she asked.

"Well, I didn't notice the case caption until I was stamping them, but this is on the Flynn case."

"Yes. Is it one of yours?"

"No, it's on my friend's docket, but I know that the court's already ruled on this one."

"Ruled? Are you sure?" she asked.

"Positive. It caused quite a stir around here on Monday," he confirmed.

"How'd they rule?"

"They reversed and remanded it to the district court."

Mickey grabbed the counter with her right hand, and her index finger began tapping the top of it. "Are you certain? I mean, being that this isn't one of your cases."

"Yes, and I confirmed it again on the computer when I entered your withdrawal. Though it's not one of my cases, I've been following it," he said as Mickey's tapping finger accelerated. "We thought the justices had a decision last week, but the three of them met most of Saturday and half a day Sunday and then issued the ruling late on Monday."

"Why hasn't anyone heard the news?" Mickey asked, struggling to breathe normally.

"We've been asked by the DA's office not to disclose this decision until the victim's family has been notified."

"Are you sure they reversed and remanded?"

"Positive. This baby's going back for a new trial."

"Do the lawyers on the case know?"

"I don't know for sure, but I doubt it since nobody here's supposed to—" the clerk halted, and concern washing over his face. "Hey, ma'am, I—"

"Don't worry. I'm certainly not letting *this* cat out of the bag," Mickey assured.

"Thank you," he said exhaling. "They'd skin ma alive if this leaked out because of me."

"How do you know so much about it if it's not one of your cases?"

"Goodness, ma'am, this was the biggest appeal we've had since I've been here. I wasn't directly involved, but my friend worked his butt off on it, and that's why he asked to start his vacation starting yesterday."

"I see," Mickey said, placing her file-stamped copy in her purse. "Are they close to having the opinion?"

"It may be done. I know they've been working hard on it."

"Can you check?"

"Sure, just hang on a minute," he said, returning to the computer screen. "Oh, here it is. It was posted within the hour."

"Can I get a copy?" Mickey asked.

"Oh, I don't know. I just …"

"*Please*, I really need to see it and swear I won't share it with a soul."

"All right then," he said. He printed her a copy, and Mickey thanked the young man, then walked out of the clerk's office with the opinion in hand. When she reached the hall, she placed her free hand on the cold marble wall to brace herself and tried to catch her breath. She felt blood pulsing into her head and felt hot, almost feverous, and then out of necessity took a seat on the hallway bench. She raised the opinion and looked at page one, and the first thing she noticed, just below the case caption, in bold letters was *Reversed and Remanded*. She began to peruse the substance of the court's decision and noted three references to her amicus brief in the first two paragraphs alone. She then folded it and placed it in her purse and headed for her car. *I can't worry about this right now. If Flynn's not aware of this, then there's no reason for the exchange of information not to take place. All I have to do is speak with him before Campbell finds out. Once I know what he knows, he can't take that back. And after all, getting the details about Reagan and the others will vindicate me—right?*

Mickey drove straight to the law firm, and with her stamped withdrawal in hand, she hurried through the lobby and up the staircase and walked briskly toward the mail room. She wrote out her message on the fax cover page, including in large letters, "Urgent!" and faxed the papers to Campbell's office. She signed the fax log and received confirmation of its successful transmission.

As she started back to the stairs, Woody saw her and asked, "Another fax?"

Without looking back, she said, "I signed the damn log, Woody!"

Then came the waiting game. She remained holed up in her office well into the afternoon, then decided to wait for contact from Flynn at home. She packed her things to leave, and gave instructions to Marlene. She walked down the hall toward the reception area, and when she neared Baylor's office, the door opened abruptly and two partners exited and passed her without acknowledging When she neared the door, she heard voices, and as she eased by the discussions stopped, and Becker motioned her inside.

"Hey fellas," she said as she entered.

"Have a seat, Michelle," Baylor said.

She took a chair and looked at Ford and then back to Baylor. "You know, don't you?"

"Yes," Ford confirmed. "Chester Hill called an hour or so ago and shared the ruling with us."

"You're not a popular figure right now," Baylor said sternly. "As we discussed, I've already had many calls about this, and with this ruling, it's only going to get worse. This will soon be public, and many in the community are going to turn their eyes toward us."

"Mickey, we've all been very empathetic and patient, but this is a real mess you've created," Becker added.

"I'm terribly sorry that y'all have gotten dragged into this. I never intended for this to become such a problem for the firm."

"Mickey, that's just it. No one questions your intentions, but we all know what the road to hell is paved with, right?" Becker said.

"You're right," she conceded.

"I wanted you to hear this from me," Ford said. "There's been a meeting since learning this news, and the partners have voted to place you on an administrative leave."

"What exactly does that mean?"

"You're relieved of all of duties for—"

"Am I fired?"

"No!" Becker said emphatically. "It's a temporary hiatus, that's all."

"Michelle, it's a paid leave of absence," Baylor explained. "You see, we feel the need to react to this. The community will expect it, and when those eyes do turn to us, we want to demonstrate that action has already been taken."

Becker added, "It's like you've seen in the news when a cop's accused of some misconduct and the officer's relieved of duty pending an investigation. Now, between us, the leave is only for sixty days, though our press release will read 'indefinite.'"

"Press release?" Mickey asked.

"Yes," Becker said. "I'm sorry, but this has to be public to start getting the monkey off our back."

"When does it start?"

"It's effective immediately, but we won't release this until Friday to coincide with when we're told the news will pick up on the story."

"I see." Mickey sighed.

"This will hopefully allow all of this attention on the reversal and new trial to run its course and fade," Baylor explained. "In the meantime, Ford has agreed to work with Marlene to keep an eye on your cases."

"So she knows about the suspension?"

"Yes," Ford confirmed.

"That's fair. I deserve it and worse, and I consider myself fortunate to still have a job. But I have one request."

"What's that?" Ford asked.

"I refuse to get paid for not working. This should be an unpaid leave."

"Michelle, that's admirable but not necessary," Baylor said.

"I insist. After all, I've had plenty of paid leave already, right? Plus, the public gets hacked off when the bad cop gets paid during a misconduct investigation. This way you can tell the media that I am out—and out without pay."

"We both thought you'd say that," Ford said.

"So it's sixty days without pay," Mickey said.

Baylor nodded and Becker said, "Yes."

Mickey awoke the next morning at 5:15 a.m., restless and weak. She showered, dressed, and sat in her living room, maintaining a vigil with her phone within arm's length. For hours, her phone remained silent, but at 10:40 it rang, and she picked it up immediately and was enthused that it was another collect call, and accepted the charges.

"It's Willie."

"Okay, let's get to it," Mickey said.

"Campbell told me that you filed your document with the court."

"That's right. I've lived up to my end. Now the ball's in your court," she said, trying to contain her excitement.

Flynn paused. "I guess you expect me to tell you about the girls, right?"

"Yes, that's our deal, Willie."

"You stupid bitch! How goddamned dumb can you be?"

"What do you mean?" Mickey asked, rising to her feet.

"Oh, please. When I called Campbell's office to check on this, they told me what you done. You had to play your little chicken-shit game, and now I have to go through this hell again. I want to tell you one thing, and you need to remember it: I will *never* forget what you've done to me, and will—" The guards disconnected the call and Mickey set the phone down and placed her head in her hands and sobbed. *What else in the world could go wrong?* Though dreading it, she was desperate to reach out to Tyler. She had no illusions of how he would view this latest turn of events but was nevertheless placed the call.

"What's up, Mick," Tyler answered.

"You're not going to believe what's happened!" she blurted.

"Let's see ... Flynn hasn't given you any information, he's getting a new trial, and you've been fired by the firm," he said facetiously.

"Well, you got two out of three, but the third is not out of the question."

"What? I don't understand!"

"The court reversed Flynn's conviction, and there will be a new trial," She sobbed.

"God almighty, Mickey! Is it because of you?" he asked.

"It doesn't matter. It's going to be all on me in everyone's eyes," she cried. "Tyler, I need you desperately. I'm going to lose a lot because of this, perhaps even my career, and I don't want to add losing you to that list."

"You're not going to lose me. I know you must feel awful. I'll come over."

"Thank you, Tyler. I simply can't be alone right now."

As predicted, Friday morning the news of the ruling went public. Mickey opened her paper and saw the bold letters across the top of the front page:

Retrial of Flynn Granted
Victim's mother was primary advocate

I wish I could say this is unfair, Mickey thought as she opened a kitchen drawer in search of a cigarette. She had foolishly hoped the paper might report the court's decision without mentioning her and her involvement, but the article chronicled her influence on the process, its impact on the appeal, and her resulting suspension from the firm.

"Are you smoking a cigarette?" Tyler asked from the bedroom.

"Yes, and I'm about to have another!"

Tyler emerged in his boxer shorts, using a towel to dry his hair, and said, "I know you're under stress, but stress isn't an excuse for smoking."

"I beg to differ. I think stress is the primary justification for it."

"I think drinking is primary for stress," he replied.

"I got that covered too," Mickey said, pointing at an open bottle of champagne and a carton of orange juice. "Mimosa?"

"Why not."

News of the reversal of Flynn's conviction spread like a wild fire throughout the community. Mickey was tempted to simply withdraw and isolate herself, but instead she consulted her calendar and gathered the strength to attend the support group's next meeting at Evelyn Howard's house. She wanted to test the waters to see if the group was yet another burning bridge she had left in her path. Mickey arrived at the meeting ten minutes early, and Mrs. Howard welcomed her in. They whispered to each other for a moment before entering the living room. There she found several couples already seated, and upon seeing her, all conversation halted. Mickey quietly sat quietly on a love seat and awaited the arrival of the others, and as more members arrived, the tension rose. None present engaged in the customary social exchanges, resulting in an uncomfortable silence. Mickey saw a variety of expressions, from penetrating glares to tearful, strained stares, and others simply diverted their eyes altogether. At the top of the hour, Mrs. Howard looked to Mickey, and nodded.

Mickey composed herself, cleared her throat, and said, "If you'll pardon me, I think I have some explaining to do. You all have surely heard by now that Flynn's conviction has been overturned and the fact that I played a big part in that. The newspaper got this right, and it is my fault. I felt like I needed to talk to you all and—"

A knock at the front door interrupted Mickey, and the attention turned to Mrs. Howard as she walked to the front door and opened it. Through it walked Bess and Ted Abram.

"Sorry we're late," Bess Abram said in a hoarse voice as the couple followed Mrs. Howard into the living room. Mickey swallowed hard as the couple somberly greeted some of the others, oblivious to her presence. But when Bess turned and saw Mickey, she instinctively recoiled as one might react if a snake had slithered across their path.

Ted pulled her close to him, and realizing that Mickey had the floor, they took seats and listened.

"As I was saying, I fully realize the controversial nature of my actions and the bad result that I have contributed to. I know many of you are upset and disillusioned by this outcome, and you should be. But nobody's more disappointed than me, and I—"

"Excuse me, but I beg to differ!" Ted Abram said, rising to his feet red-faced and trembling. "We endured the torture of a trial to get to get Taylor's murderer on death row, and now you've given him a second chance! Now we have to relive that hell all over again. No, I don't think you're more disappointed than we are."

"I understand, Mr. Abram," Mickey said calmly. "I can't put myself in your place, and you have every right to be angry with me. But just know I never wanted this to happen. All I was trying for was peace of mind for me and for you, and for you, and you," Mickey said as she pointed to the parents of three other missing teens. "For as much pain as the Abrams have gone suffered, I know I've added to it immensely, and for that I am profoundly sorry. All I can do is beg for forgiveness. But for those of you who don't have a missing child because of this animal, you can't put yourselves in our place, either. It's a relentless, endless nightmare, wondering if my Reagan's alive somewhere, and if she's dead, where he put her body. Is she buried somewhere? Where are her clothes? Are animals gnawing on …?" Tears streamed down Mickey's cheeks, and she put her head in her hands and sobbed uncontrollably as the Abrams clung to each other and others wiped tears of their own.

A weepy Mrs. Hayes spoke up. "I'm haunted by those same thoughts and have recurring nightmares that my Christine was buried alive. Mickey, I don't know what's right or wrong here, but you did more than even the police to try to end my nightmares, and I'm thankful for it."

Mickey, looked up, sniffling, and said, "I had learned that the threat of my brief was the biggest fear in Flynn's life, literally greater than death itself. He refused to level with me, and in a moment of desperation, I filed it. Had it not been for some unfortunate timing, I would be standing before you tonight with the truth about our daughters. But despite my best intentions, I failed. I failed myself, my law firm, Reagan's father, and all of you."

Bess Abram rose to her feet. "I obviously don't agree with what you did, Ms. Grant. But by the same token, I don't believe you intended to cause harm to anyone. I believe your heart was in the right place, and I know it was tough to come here tonight. I just hope Flynn will be found guilty and return to death row."

"I have every confidence in that," Mickey said firmly.

"Good ... but God help us all if you're wrong."

CHAPTER 16

⚖

TRIAL DE NOVO

(New Trial)

With no objection from Campbell, Lyndon Tucker wasted no time in getting Flynn's second trial on the court's docket for August. Upon learning of the reversal of the conviction, prison officials extracted Flynn from death row and moved him to an isolation cell in a medium-security section of the Walls Unit. Flynn knew that he would soon return to Brinkman and consequently risked the loss of his treasured isolation, and he anguished over it. On the day of his transfer, guards escorted Flynn into the oppressive Texas heat and onto a poorly air-conditioned white Texas Department of Corrections bus. He was guided to a seat in the rear and, and like his trip to Huntsville, was cuffed to the metal leg of the seat. As they crossed the West Texas plains, Flynn had ample time to reflect on his previous confinement in Brinkman and the person most responsible for his return to it.

When they neared the Taylor County jail, dusk was giving way to night, and a light mist descended from the sky. As the bus rounded the corner and eased to the rear of the jail, Flynn peered through the metal-mesh-covered window and saw a figure that he believed to be Campbell. Also present was a gathering of newspaper and television reporters separated from Campbell by a chain-link fence. As the bus rolled to a stop, Flynn flinched when the poorly lit area burst into intense brightness from the TV-camera lights. Guards unshackled Flynn from the bench seat and helped him to his feet, then down the aisle and toward the front exit of the bus. Flynn struggled greatly taking the steps down to the pavement, but when he reached it, several Taylor County detention officers assumed custody of him. It was then that he confirmed that the figure he saw was indeed Campbell, and he was standing stoically in a waterproof overcoat and a short-brimmed Stetson hat that was protected from the elements by a fitted, clear plastic, elastic cover. They escorted Flynn past the fenced area containing the media, and as he neared Campbell, they paused to let them speak.

"How was the trip?" Campbell asked as the camera flashes escalated.

"Oh, it was terrific. You should try this bus when you take the bride to Huntsville."

"I'm sure she'd like that," Campbell said, grinning from a mouth that had an unlit cigar that was wet from the rain except for the portion protected under the brim of his hat.

"Did you cause all of this?" Flynn asked, nodding toward the media.

"Maybe. Listen, I arranged for a meeting with you inside while they do all of the paperwork. I'll see you in the conference room once they've performed all of their niceties on you and given you your new duds." Flynn nodded, and was taken to a holding cell where he was strip-searched and traded in his white and blues for orange. Then the guards led him to the conference room where Campbell sat waiting.

"I saw you limping pretty bad out there. Are you all right?" Campbell asked.

"I'm just a little stove up from the trip, that's all."

"I pulled some strings with a higher-up in here and secured you an isolated cell for the time being," Campbell said, and Flynn's body went limp with relief. "I don't know how long he'll be able to do this, but it's good to go for now."

"Thanks, man."

"If this gets out, there's some concern that the administration will start catchin' shit for it, and if that happens they'll have to put you in the jail population. Understand?" Flynn nodded. "Now let's talk about the trial. I've got some ideas on how to—"

"I know what you're about to say, but I haven't changed my mind on this. Let's just get this thing over with as soon as possible and get me back to Huntsville."

"So, Nathan Hale, it's still give you death but no liberty?" Campbell joked.

"I guess you can put it that way. Listen, when I'm convicted this time, can that moron screw with that appeal shit again?"

"Sure she can, although it's unlikely. From what I hear, this little stunt's made her persona non grata around here."

"Translation please?"

"It's Latin and means that she's like the bastard child at the family reunion," Campbell said.

"So you speak Latin?"

"No, but all lawyers know a little—very little. It's mostly used to impress people at dinner parties and to weave into legal documents to justify exorbitant hourly rates," Campbell said as he rose to leave. "Take care, and I'll schedule a meeting soon."

Following his dramatic contribution to Flynn's first trial, career mall employee Robert Jackson had returned to the comfort of obscurity. Though he had found testifying at the first trial unnerving, he was pleased with his contribution to Flynn's conviction. But following the recent turn of events, Jackson had dreaded, but was nevertheless prepared, for another courtroom appearance.

Two Sundays before the trial, Jackson rose at sunup, and as was his custom, he donned his maroon, terry-cloth bath robe before retrieving his newspaper from the front yard. He quietly opened the front door, cautious not to wake his slumbering wife, stepped outside, and walked down their driveway. After stooping to grab the paper, he started back toward the house when a sudden burning sensation returned to his chest. He had experienced such episodes in the preceding days, and each time, antacids had successfully combatted them. Once back inside, he put two antacid tablets in his mouth and chewed as he took the wrapper off of the paper. He took a seat at the dining room table, and the burning sensation subsided. He spread out the sports section and sipped coffee while he read the box scores. As he perused each column, a sound emerged from the kitchen, interrupting his concentration. He walked in that direction and stared as another drop slowly emerged and fell from the sink faucet.

"Damn faucet seat," he said under his breath as he twisted the hot-water handle, trying to cease the nuisance. When he did, the formation of the next drop abated. He stared closely at the spout and, after a few seconds, deemed the problem remedied—for the time being. But, as he turned to walk back to the dining room but heard another drop fall. He again examined the faucet and saw another drop already forming.

Ever the handyman, Jackson decided to make this his project of the day. Often on his day off, he searched for chores that gave him cause to visit the nearby hardware store. He had frequented this store for years and had spent countless hours perusing the aisles, looking at the latest gadgets and tools. Jackson left a note for his wife, walked back outside, and climbed into his fully restored, candy-apple-red 1963 Chevrolet pickup that he used just for this type of short weekend trip. He drove out of his neighborhood he took his time in the light, weekend morning traffic. When he turned onto the multilane road that would take him toward the hardware store and accelerated to open all four barrels on the carburetor to tax the vintage engine. When he did, the burning discomfort flared in his chest, and this time it was even stronger. His chest felt tight, similar to a foot or leg cramp, and he noticed a menacing ache in his jaw and around his shoulder blades. Jackson fumbled with his antacids as he drove and began chewing two more tablets, but instead of relief, the pain escalated, and Jackson started struggling to breathe. Short breaths became gasps, and although he was trying to breathe deeper and more slowly, he couldn't manage to get enough air into his lungs, and panic set in.

Consumed by his circumstance, he failed to notice the traffic light just ahead had turned red, until the last instant. Jackson slammed his foot on the middle pedal, depressing it to the floorboard. Despite the inefficiency of the truck's old manual brakes, he managed to stop, after skidding partially into the busy intersection. Cars and trucks from his left were now proceeding through the intersection on their green light, and several honked and used gestures to express their displeasure for having to navigate around the protruding front end of Jackson's antique truck. Jackson's pain and anxiety only grew, as he waited for the light to change, and had to wipe beads of sweat from his forehead. He was becoming dizzy and nauseous and placed his hand on his chest, trying to massage the now constant, intense pain. Cognizant of the seriousness of his symptoms, he checked in both directions and decided to floor it through the red light and across the intersection, speeding toward a nearby hospital. With one hand on the steering wheel and the other on his chest, he slumped his head close to the wheel, fighting to stay conscious. As he neared the hospital emergency entrance, the pain forced him to lean on his right side toward the middle of the cab of the truck.

He managed to turn into the driveway closest to the emergency room entrance, but his treasured truck careened off of a concrete pillar supporting the portico over the entrance, bringing it to a stop. He was breathing heavily and did not notice that he was now leaning on the truck's horn. Jackson managed to open the driver's side door, and as he tried to exit, the horn honking ceased. He managed to place his left foot down to the pavement followed by his right, before tumbling face-first into a mulched flowerbed.

A nurse in the emergency room, having heard the honking, rushed outside in time to see Jackson collapse. As she ran to Jackson, she turned back toward the entrance, and seeing another nurse, she yelled, "Code blue!"

Monday morning, Mickey was sewing a button on one of her business suits when the phone rang. She saw it was from the police department and answered it.

"Ms. Grant, this is Bud Buchanan."

"Good morning."

"Since you're home on a weekday, I guess it's true what I read in the paper?"

"Excuse me?"

"I'm referring to the article that said you lost your job at Triple B?"

"I haven't been fired. I'm just on a leave."

"Leave, huh?" he said in a skeptical tone that riled Mickey.

"With all due respect, is there a point to this call?"

"There damn sure is. Robert Jackson suffered a heart attack and died yesterday. I just thought you'd want to know."

It took her a moment to place the name, but she quickly recalled his importance to Flynn's conviction and realized this was not a courtesy call. "I didn't see anything in the news about it."

"There'll be plenty in tomorrow's edition."

"Gosh, that's really awful, but why are you calling me?"

"He was our main witness. Don't you understand?"

"I've been blamed for a lot of things lately, but I didn't kill the man."

"But you're killing our case! Can't you step back for a moment and grasp what you've done to the community?"

"I grasp what *Flynn's* done to the community!" Mickey said. "There are seven unsolved cases in your—"

"That's another thing, little missy. You need to quit commenting on things you have no knowledge of. I've heard about some of the lies you've been spreading around out there, and it's gonna stop."

"I have a right to do—"

"This isn't about your rights, it's about police business and your interference with it. Now I want a commitment from you that you'll stop!"

"I'll stand down," Mickey conceded. "But I don't appreciate you talking to me that way."

"See it from my stand point. We had our man! My officers worked hard and placed themselves in harm's way to get Flynn's ass off the street and on death row. You single handedly cut him loose, and now he's back in our jail!"

"Yes and I hope he's being tormented there worse than the last time!"

"Oh, you haven't heard that either, have you?"

"Heard what?"

"Flynn's being confined in isolation."

"You're kidding, right?"

"Nope. You can call the jail yourself if you like. But for now, we have an understanding, and I expect you to live up to it!" Buchanan said, ending the call.

The community reeled from the news of Jackson's death, but Campbell felt invigorated. Until now, he thought he had only a modest chance of getting Flynn acquitted. But with the demise of the state's key eyewitness, he quickly recognized a viable road to victory, and consequently, scheduled a follow up visit with Flynn. Campbell arrived at the jail, checked in with McKinley.

"Hey Gerry, long time no see."

"Good morning, Mac. How's the family?"

"Fine, just fine," McKinley said. "Who are you here to see?"

"Willie Flynn."

"Oh? Stealing Chester Hill's clients are you?"

"Didn't you hear?"

"What?"

"The court decided Flynn needed a *real* lawyer."

McKinley laughed, and reviewed Campbell's credentials and assigned Millard to take him to the fifth floor. As they entered the elevator Campbell silently stared forward until, Millard asked, "So have you ever visited an inmate here before?"

Campbell slowly turned his head to Millard and said, "Are you shittin' me?"

"What?"

"Do you know who I am?"

"No. Should I?"

"No ... Of course not. I think I'm perfectly fine with that," Campbell smirked.

They reached the top floor, and Conference Room 1 was assigned. Campbell thumbed through his file at the table until the guards emerged with Flynn, secured him and then took their spot behind the Plexiglas.

"How are you, Willie?" Campbell greeted.

"Much better than last time, thanks to you."

"Good. You're walking better too," Campbell observed.

"I'm in a good stretch right now, but I'd just as soon be back in Huntsville."

"That's what I want to talk to you about."

"Here we go again," Flynn lamented, hanging his head.

"Hear me out now—things have changed. I know that you have this strange notion that a death sentence is the only acceptable way to go here, and I'm worn out from wracking my brain to understand that. But I'll tell you that you now have an *excellent* chance to win this thing."

"Excellent?" Flynn asked.

"Yes. Do you remember that mall janitor that testified against you at the first trial?" Flynn nodded. "Well, he keeled over with a heart attack. I can't promise anything, but my experience tells me you could walk out of that courthouse a free man!"

"That black dude died?"

"Yep, he's deader than Elvis, and the prosecution's gonna miss him too."

"That's too bad, but I don't see how that's such a big deal. They got all of that other stuff on me, and the jury already heard that man testify."

"The same jury ain't gonna hear your case, son! This is trial de novo; it starts all over, as if the first one never happened. Now I expect the prosecutors will try to read in Jackson's testimony from the first trial, but I'm going to fight that hard. You see, Willie, they've got a real uphill climb now."

"What about the fingerprints and DNA stuff?"

"They can prove you touched the girl's shoe. Who gives a shit?"

"What about my arrest statements?"

"First off, I got a shot of getting the judge to throw it out. I'm gonna set a hearing on my motion to suppress before the trial. But either way, I read what Buchanan said in the transcript, and even if the judge won't exclude it, I frankly don't think it constitutes a confession. So what about it, son?"

"Listen, man, I appreciate what you're saying, but this still ain't of no interest to me."

Exasperated, Campbell said sternly, "Look, buddy—you aren't going to get a better opportunity than what you have right now. I suggest that you reconsider your weird view on things because, I plan on winning this case."

"What else is new? You've planned on winning this case since the day you took it."

"You are a perceptive man, Willie."

"But, as the client, aren't you supposed to follow *my* wishes?"

Campbell smiled and whispered, "This is pretty simple from my standpoint. If I lose the case and you get the death penalty, you're tickled pink. And if I win, try filing a malpractice suit or even grievance over that and see how far that gets you. Willie, I've looked at the main parts of the trial transcript, and his case is as thin as the toilet paper in this jail, and I wanna fight for your freedom!"

"Freedom ain't always pretty! Things are more complicated out there than you will ever know!" Flynn said, pointing out the bulletproof window with a view of downtown Brinkman.

"I'm going to tell you something, and I'll call you a goddamn liar if you ever say I did," Campbell said, leaning close to Flynn's ear. "If I were you and I got out of this jail, I'd get my ass as far out of this country as I could and never look back."

"Don't forget I'm on parole. Wouldn't I need a passport or something to do that?"

"Yeah, if you go to a travel agent and book a goddamned Mediterranean cruise. But hell, man, there's ways out of the country without doing all of that shit."

"I do have a good friend in Mexico," Flynn said.

"Well, there you have it!" Campbell said, slapping his hands together.

"But how am I supposed to get across the border without documents?"

"Haven't you seen the news? The border's a sieve, son. Plus every flea market in Texas has a booth that can create phony passports."

"What do you think the chances of winning are?"

"They're fifty-fifty right now, but if I get your statements thrown out and the jury can't hear Jackson's testimony, I don't think they have a case at all."

"When will we know about all of that?"

"I'm waitin' for a call back from the judge's office. Tucker says he's got a motion he wants heard too, so I'm sure Sullivan will give us a hearing."

"What motion does he have?"

"The little prick wouldn't tell me, but I'm sure it's about Jackson's testimony."

The next day, Judge Sullivan's clerk notified both sides that the judge would hear their respective motions the following morning at 8:00 a.m. Word of the hearing reached the support group, and Mrs. Howard, Mickey, and three other members joined other spectators and members of the press in the courtroom. Campbell had two legal assistants accompanying him that morning, one of which, a buxom blonde, and she handed the judge and the prosecution a copy of a recent legal opinion.

"Okay, I've read this case," Sullivan said after a few minutes. "Now we have two motions on the docket, one for each side. The defendant's motion to exclude was filed first, so let's hear that one. Mr. Campbell?"

"Are we on the record, Maggie?" Campbell asked.

"Yes, sir."

"Good. Gerald Campbell here for the defendant. Judge, you may recall from the first trial that the state used statements allegedly made by my client at the time of his arrest. I think they took the statements out of context, but that's another argument for another time, but we—"

Tucker interjected, "Wait a second, Judge! The state takes umbrage at—"

"Umbrage, my ass!" Campbell retorted. "I take umbrage at you letting—"

"Hey now, guys!" Sullivan intervened. "I was worried about this battle of egos. Listen to me carefully, fellas. This hearing and, more importantly, this trial ain't gonna turn into a pissin' match between you two. Excuse me, Maggie," Sullivan said, nodding toward his reporter.

"I'm fine," Maggie said, smiling.

"I don't like that Campbell," Mrs. Howard whispered to Mickey, who nodded her agreement.

"Let's get back to it, Gerry."

"Thanks, Judge. The trial transcript makes it clear that Chief Buchanan egged my client on with questions, and, yes, they were questions," Campbell said, glancing at Tucker. "This recent court of appeals opinion we provided validates a long line of similar cases, ruling the admission of such statements as unconstitutional. Judge, there's no question that Mr. Flynn was detained at the time of the statements, and none other than Chief Buchanan himself commenced an interrogation of him. These cases, from the Miranda decision all the way to the one in your hand, prohibits using *any* interrogation done before the accused is first advised of his rights, including the right to remain silent and the right to have counsel present."

"Yes, Gerry, I've heard something about that," the judge said sarcastically.

"Thought so," Campbell said, grinning. "Mr. Flynn was not the beneficiary of such an admonition until after this questioning and alleged responding statements. Now, they eventually got around to reading him his rights, but all the pre-Miranda statements must be stricken!"

"Mr. Tucker?"

"We concede that the defendant was in custody at the time, but the state strongly denies there was any interrogation. Mr. Flynn blurted out these damning statements extemporaneously and was—"

"That's just it, Judge!" Campbell interrupted. "These weren't damning at all, and they—"

"Stop!" Sullivan said, silencing Campbell. "Gerry, I listened to you, and it's their turn."

"Thank you, Your Honor," Tucker said. "You see, Flynn blurted out his comments, and that's not our fault. The law's clear that if the detainee volunteers information, it's admissible even without the Miranda warning."

"Response?" Sullivan said, turning to Campbell.

"Judge, I thought they'd say that, but it's just plain horse hockey," Campbell said, placing a foam-backed board on an aluminum easel. "Here's the excerpt from the trial transcript. This is Buchanan, himself, telling the jury exactly what *he* thought happened during the exchange. As you can plainly see, Flynn was just responding to him." Campbell paused to allow the judge to read the question and answer exchange. "You see, Judge, the chief's initial question asking about Taylor Abram started it all off," Campbell said, pointing at the board. "This was the original sin, so to speak. All statements made by Mr. Flynn from then to the time he was given the Miranda warning is what the line of cases refers to as 'fruit of the poisonous tree' and the law dictates that it stays out!" Campbell declared in a loud flourish.

"Lyndon?"

"Well, Your Honor, to quote the great Yogi Berra, 'This is déjà vu all over again.' We've been through all of this in the first trial, and these statements were allowed in then, and that result here should be replicated here. You see, the inquiry by Buchanan was innocuous and rhetorical, and the fact that Flynn commenced to spill his guts on matters *not* inquired about means it should be admitted."

"Gerry, they say the statements weren't responsive," Sullivan said.

"Look at the exchange, Judge. These aren't my words. They're the chief's. And, I maintain that 'You won't find her here' is not confessing anything, and 'I took them all, right?' is a question not a statement of fact.

"I understand your position on that, but address the responsiveness of the comments," the judge said.

"Each were directly responsive. They would have a point if Buchanan had asked, 'What's the weather like?' and Mr. Flynn responded, 'I kidnapped the Lindberg baby!' But that ain't the case here, and the fruits of that unlawful interrogation should not be used as evidence of guilt. And might I add, Judge that I for one am citing the court to rock-solid, appellate jurisprudence to support my position," Campbell said, waving the court opinion in his hand, "and they're citing a goddamn baseball player!"

As the laughter subsided, the judge shook his head and said, "Gerry, I know you're passionate about this, but curb the vulgarities."

"Sorry, Judge, and pardon me, Maggie. I'll type that part for you if you'd like."

"I've transcribed worse, Mr. Campbell," Maggie advised.

"Oh?" Campbell said with mock surprise.

"Yes, remember your Coolidge case?" Maggie said.

"Indeed I do."

"Me too," Sullivan said.

"Thought you might," Campbell added.

"Anything further, fellas?" the judge asked, the lawyers shook their heads. "Guys—we all agree that once in custody, the accused should be Mirandized before questioning, and I mean *any* questioning," Sullivan emphasized to Tucker. "Of course, no one can help it if the suspect just blurts out a statement, but that's simply not the case here, Lyndon. Buchanan asked about the other victims, and that led to the statements. Though the statements aren't a direct confession, the only relevance to this case would be to use it as such. I rule the statements are inadmissible and excluded. Gerry, give me an order." Many in the courtroom mumbled in response to the ruling while Sullivan received and signed the order.

"Lyndon, let's do your motion," Sullivan said.

Tucker put his on glasses and looked at his notes. "Judge, this is a motion to use prior sworn testimony from the transcript of the first trial. As you may recall, we presented a witness who worked at the mall where the Abram girl went missing."

"Mr. Jackson, right?"

"Correct. He was the white-haired gentleman, and he had—"

"I recall him well," Sullivan said.

"Then you know Mr. Jackson's testimony places the defendant in his van, speaking with Taylor Abram the morning she disappeared. Rule 804 of the Texas Rules of Evidence allows, as an exception to the hearsay rule, prior sworn testimony of a witness who is 'unavailable.'"

"Why's Jackson unavailable?" the judge asked.

"Mr. Jackson died suddenly from a massive heart attack, Your Honor."

"I'd say that's unavailable," Campbell said.

"That's enough, Gerry!" Sullivan warned.

"Another requirement in 804 is that the statements were under oath—and we obviously have that. Finally, the rule requires that someone to have been present with the same motivation to cross-examine the witness. Mr. Hill was present and did, indeed, cross-examine Jackson, with the same motivation Mr. Campbell would have had. We move to read the entirety of Mr. Jackson's testimony from the first trial into the record for this one."

"Gerry?"

"Judge, this is truly a noxious affront. As I'll remind the court, this case is being retried due to ineffective assistance of counsel. Now, due to an unfortunate turn of events, the state wants to go back and use the evidence from a flawed trial—the result of which has been reversed by the court of appeals. I think this is more than just an 804 issue; this is a due process matter, and to grant this motion would surely be an abuse of discretion."

The judge turned to Tucker, who said, "Like I say, Judge, the defendant was represented, and Jackson was cross-examined. We've not heard anything from Mr. Campbell, either in his written response or on this record, as to what he would have done anything differently. So there's no prejudice here, and I think the motion should be granted."

"Your Honor, I don't think the law requires me to tell the court what I would have objected to, and on what grounds, and what I would have asked the dearly departed. But I don't think there's any credible debate, that I would have done it much differently and, may I say, more effectively. After all, we're all gathered here on the eve of a second trial because of the poor performance of my predecessor. So I—"

"Excuse me, Gerry," the judge interrupted and looked over at Tucker. "Lyndon, do you have any other witnesses?"

"Non-experts?"

"Right. Fact witnesses?"

"There's a Timothy Pierce that we listed, but I don't think we'll be using him."

Mickey, who had been watching Flynn off and on, saw him bolt straight up in his chair at the mention of the name. She took a pen from her purse and jotted it down on one of her business cards.

After confirming neither side had anything further, Sullivan said, "I'm going to deny the prosecution's motion."

"What does this mean?" Mrs. Howard whispered to Mickey.

"The state's case is in deep trouble," Mickey said candidly.

Tucker leaned over the bench toward the judge and whispered, "That guts our case!"

"I fully understand that, Lyndon," Sullivan said with his hand over the microphone. "But the law's the law, and I think with a trial set next week, you two need to find a way to work something out on this. Why don't y'all go to the jury room and see if you can come up with some sort of resolution?"

"Can we have a minute?" Tucker asked.

"Sure," Sullivan said, and Tucker huddled with his team at their table, and they whispered amongst themselves for several minutes.

"What are they doing?" Evelyn Howard asked Mickey.

"I'm not sure, but I don't think it's in any way good."

The huddle broke, and Tucker motioned to Campbell to follow him to the jury room. After shutting the door, Campbell stood at the head of the table and said, "Looks like you've got your ass in a crack on this one."

"We still have a case," Tucker insisted.

"Oh bullshit, Lyndon! It was tenuous coming in, and now it's gone."

"What about the shoes and the fingerprint and—"

"Who cares? You're not gonna risk your streak on a goddamned pair of shoes, are you?"

Tucker stared down at the table and said, "What if you plead him to murder."

"You've lost your ever-loving mind if you think—"

"Manslaughter?"

Campbell shook his head. "Not no, but hell no!"

"Then what do you want!" Tucker yelled, loud enough for those in the courtroom to hear.

"I want to leave this courthouse with my client, that's what!" Campbell insisted.

Tucker shook his head. "What are you willing to plead him to?"

"You don't get it, do you? I wouldn't recommend the client to take jaywalking charges at this point," Campbell said as Tucker continued shaking his head. "Come on, Lyndon. Things didn't go your way on this one. Cut Flynn loose and get him on the next one. Do that and your record's still intact, and you can tell the voters the judge screwed you."

"It's not about the election."

"Fine. Then dismiss the goddamn charges if that's the case."

"Doesn't dismissing this end my streak?"

"Hell, no! You didn't lose this. It was taken away from you before the trial even started. But if you start this trial, I guaran-damn-tee your streak ends."

Tucker rose and walked back into the courtroom, with his expression grim. He nodded to Carl to retrieve the judge from his chambers. As they waited, Tucker conferred with his assistants, while Campbell sat silently and confidently at the defense table. As the judge entered and took the bench, and Maggie had them on the record, Tucker said, "Your Honor, in light of the court's rulings today, the state dismisses all charges against the defendant."

The stunned attendees in the gallery didn't make a sound, but Campbell slapped his hands together, turned to Flynn, and shook his hand. Mickey put her hands over her face as Mrs. Howard patted her back. The judge retired to his chambers, and Campbell walked to the bar and faced the onlookers "For you members of the fourth estate, it is Gerry with a G and Campbell, C-a-m-p-b-e-l-l."

Though on suspension, Mickey felt compelled to go directly to the law firm with the news. Her career hung in the balance, and she refused to dodge the fallout from the catastrophic results of her actions. As she drove to the office, she caught a red light, stopped, and then lifted a pint of bourbon from her car console. She broke the seal, unscrewed the top, and took a quick drink. Then she waited until the light changed to take another swig and proceeded on to the office. As she pulled up to the entry gate, as fate would have it, she noticed both Becker and Baylor walking across the parking garage. She popped a couple of mints in her mouth, and as the gate slowly slid open, she drove forward.

The men noticed her car approaching, and Mickey motioned for them to wait as she pulled into her assigned space. Mickey laid her purse on the back of her car and leaned against the trunk, and asked said, "I know I'm on leave, but is it all right to park in my spot?"

"Certainly, Michelle," Baylor said.

Mickey nodded, but the strain had her on the verge of becoming physically ill. "I wanted to speak with you two about …" she started until overcome by her emotions.

"What's wrong, Mickey?" Becker interjected as he noticed her quivering lower lip and ashen complexion.

"Oh God! It's just so awful!"

"Is it about Reagan?" Becker asked as he glanced awkwardly toward Baylor, but Mickey shook her head.

"Is this about the Flynn trial?" Baylor asked.

"Yes, sir, and there won't be one," she uttered as she struggled to compose herself. "Campbell gutted the state's case on a couple of favorable rulings, and the prosecution dismissed the charges." She put her hands over her mouth and wept.

"It's going to be okay," Becker said as he put his arms around her shoulder to console her.

"Oh, I wish that were true, but how could it be? It's all my fault!"

"Michelle, what's done is done," Baylor said.

"Harrison's right, and we're a family here, and things happen in families. We'll just have to deal with this as best as we can," Becker said.

"You guys are too kind, but if you need to go ahead and fire me, I understand. It may be the best way for the firm to fade the heat and for you all to move on."

"Nonsense!" Baylor said. "Ford's right you're part of our team."

"This is certainly more loyalty than I deserve, guys," she said, and she dabbed her tears.

"Make today a new beginning, Michelle," Baylor advised. "As bad as this outcome is, it's time for *all* of us to move on and let the process take care of itself. And I think that with the Flynn case over, your suspension should end too." Becker's head swiveled rapidly toward Baylor.

"Really?" Mickey asked as Baylor smiled and nodded. "Gosh, I came up here with this disastrous news and expected to get my butt fired, and you guys do something like this."

"I said we're moving on, and we can't do that with our protégé on suspension. So, welcome back!" Baylor said.

"I appreciate that, but what about the DA, the police, and the media and all?"

"I'll handle all of that," Baylor declared. "Just lay low and don't make a big deal about your return, all right?"

"Yes, sir, and if it's all right with y'all, I'd like to get back right away."

Baylor smiled and said, "Fine with us."

"Thanks, fellas. I'll be in first thing in the morning. With this dismissal, what'll happen to Flynn?"

"He'll be in kept in the holding cell for a number of hours as the paperwork's processed, and then he will be freed," Baylor said.

"Freed?" she said with alarm. "They won't hold him while the state appeals the judge's rulings?"

"No Michelle. According to you, the district attorney dismissed the case, and there's nothing to appeal," Becker explained.

Until that moment, Mickey had failed to grasp the full implications of the dismissal. "So he gets to just walk out of the courthouse and roam the streets like nothing's happened?"

"Just as much as you and I can," Becker said.

"Then the cops need to immediately arrest him for one of the other cases," Mickey said.

"I'm sure they'll work on that, and if sufficient evidence surfaces, he will be arrested and indicted again," Baylor replied. "But until then, he's a free man."

"Well, surely the court can make him live somewhere else or issue a restraining order to make him stay away from the victims' families."

"Mickey, I really don't think you get it," Becker said. "This isn't a situation like a convict being paroled with a list of restrictions. As of today, Flynn's innocent and I don't mean to alarm you, but he could literally come right up to your door tonight and knock, and you'd have little recourse."

"Thanks for not alarming me," she said with a sigh.

"Perhaps you should seek some police protection," Becker advised.

"Oh, fat chance of that," Mickey said. "I think it's a toss-up as to who I should fear more, Flynn or the police."

"I doubt Flynn will do anything," Baylor added. "But for now, just to be on the safe side, maybe you ought to get away for a few days."

"I appreciate that, but I can take care of myself," she said, patting her purse. "Besides, since I'm back on the job, I want to dive right back into my work, and spend all of my time trying to earn back your trust."

"Good," Baylor said.

As Mickey drove out of the garage, Ford noticed the strained expression on Baylor's face and asked, "What do you think, Harrison?"

"I think we're in deep doo-doo. Ford, one of our lawyers has freed a condemned killer back into the community, and we, as her employer, own this situation."

"Not legally, though."

"No, not in a legal sense, but in a defacto way, we do. Like it or not, the community and the authorities see her and her as *our* problem."

"I know, and that's why I'm surprised you lifted her suspension. Why'd you do it?"

"First of all, I figured we did it long enough to display to the officials that we took it seriously."

"Is that it?" Ford asked.

"No. I received a call from Chief Buchanan. It seems that Michelle's been raising a stink about the inactivity of police about the other abductions. She's been very vocal about that and spreading the word to that group she's a member of."

"Really?"

"Yes, and according to him, she's obsessed with it and has been whipping them up in a frenzy about it and proclaiming the need for her to investigate on her own. The department's real ticked about it, and I assured him that we'd keep tabs on her until this all blows over. We can't do that with her at home with all of that time on her hands."

"But lifting the suspension on the day of the dismissal sends a—"

"I'm not going to do a press release announcing her return," Baylor said. "We just need to lay low and try to move on until this runs its course."

"What about the long term?" Ford asked.

"For Michelle?" Ford nodded. "I know you two are close, but the other partners are justifiably irate, and I'm afraid the partnership bridge is burned. They may acquiesce to her staying on as an associate if she wants, but even that's in doubt."

"Did you smell the liquor on her breath?" Ford asked.

"I did, and on top of everything else, I hope she's not self-medicating."

CHAPTER 17

CLARA ET PRAESENTIS PERICULI

(Clear and Present Danger)

Mickey earnestly intended to reestablish her place in the firm but, likewise felt she had caused a problem that she had an obligation to rectify. She was well aware of the cost of her interventions and the expectation by all that it would stop. But she recognized that one loose end remained, and it involved the name Timothy Pierce. She used her lunch break to walk down the street to the district clerk's office, thinking a good start would be reviewing the prosecution's case filings. When she arrived, Mickey requested access to the file, though she thought it might still be in the court room. The clerk searched and found the bulk of the file was on a metal transfer cart.

"You know this case is over, right?" the clerk asked as she pushed the cart toward her.

"Yes, ma'am, I'm aware of that."

"Are you a lawyer involved in the case?"

"Yes, ma'am," Mickey responded, reconciling in her mind that in a sense she was.

"What exactly are you looking for?" the clerk asked as Mickey looked at the tabs on some of the folders.

"The state's witness designation for starters."

"Oh, I think I can pull that up on the computer," the woman informed, and she walked over to a terminal and punched the keyboard. "Yes, here it is," she said as she pushed a button and the printer next to her ejected three pages, and he handed them to Mickey.

The first page was titled: *State of Texas Fact and Expert Witness Designation*, and Mickey reviewed it and asked, "What do I owe you?"

"Three dollars unless you want them certified." Mickey handed her a five. "Thank you. Let me get your change and a receipt," the clerk said, walking to her desk.

Mickey waited by the transfer cart and took the opportunity to thumb through some of the file folders on it. She found one manila folder marked "Photographs," flipped it open, and gasped as she stared at a black-and-white picture of Taylor Abram's nude body at the coroner's office. She quickly shut the file and took three rapid breaths. With her change and a receipt in her purse, Mickey left the clerk's office and leafed through the list of witnesses and found the listing for Timothy Wayne Pierce and noted that it included an address.

Sunday morning, Mickey left her house, intending to put in a half day at the office. She found the solitude of the office on weekends more conducive for her to work. But her curiosity about Pierce influenced her to detour toward his address. Using the GPS function on her phone, she soon found herself in a part of Brinkman she was unfamiliar with. As Mickey entered the neighborhood, she was drawn first to the squalor. Passing the series of dilapidated houses, she proceeded slowly from block to block, noting the remarkable lack of activity. She sensed an unusual calm and was so engrossed by it that she ignored the phone's instructions and nearly passed the address. She braked and backed up slowly to a stop in front of the home. She confirmed the address by two of what once were three metal numbers and the outline of the missing third on the fascia board above the front porch. She surveyed the ramshackle structure and noticed someone walking along the side of the house toward the front yard. When the young man saw Mickey's car, he conspicuously pivoted and headed back in the direction of the side of the house.

Mickey rolled her passenger-side window down and yelled, "Excuse me, sir!" but the man continued to slink away with his head down. Mickey quickly exited her car and trotted after the young man. "Excuse me, sir. I just have a question for you," she said, in as nonthreatening of a tone as she could.

The man slowed and then came to a stop, and Mickey eased to casual gait, and he turned toward her and stared down at his old and worn-out sneakers. Slight in stature, he looked to be in his early twenties, with thick, curly, rust-colored hair. He wore a ripped and threadbare black AC/DC concert T-shirt and faded blue jeans. Freckles stood out on each check of his thin face, and he was scared and seemed incapable of making eye contact.

"Sorry to bother you, but I'm looking for information on Timothy Pierce. Do you know him?"

"Why do you want to know?" he said nervously.

"Look—I'm not here to cause any trouble. I just want to know if you know him."

"I'm him."

She smiled. "You're Timothy Pierce?"

"Yes, it's me," he said in a way that alerted Mickey that the boy might suffer from some mental disability.

"It's nice to meet you. Do you know Willie Lee Flynn?" His eyes darted about, and his agitation grew. "Clearly, you do. So let me just ask you some questions, and I'll be out of here. Does Willie live around here?"

"This is our house," Pierce said, nodding at the old structure.

"Flynn lives here?" Mickey asked, glancing in all directions and Pierce nodded. "He's not around now, is he?"

"No, he's gone," Pierce said. "This is really our mom's house, but she's real sick and don't live here right now."

"I'm sorry to hear that, Tim. So you're Willie's brother?"

"Yes," he confirmed and began to walk away.

"Hold on now," Mickey pleaded.

He turned around again and asked, "Are you a cop?"

"Heavens no."

"Are you from the newspaper?"

"No, no, nothing like that," Mickey said.

He seemed to relax, and for the first time, he looked directly into her face. "You're very pretty."

"Why thank you, Tim. Is it okay if I call you Tim?"

"You can, but I go by Wayne," he said, keeping his hands in his jean pockets and returned to staring downward.

"Did you give a statement to the police about your brother?" Mickey asked.

"Yeah, I talked to them the night they took Bubba to jail. They took me down there too for a couple of days."

"Two days? At the jail?" she asked as he nodded. "That doesn't seem fair. Were you charged with something?"

He shrugged. "They never said. So who are you anyway?"

"I'm sorry, Wayne. My name's Michelle Grant, but my friends call me Mickey."

"Like the mouse?" he asked, smiling.

"Yes, just like the mouse. I want to ask you something about Willie. Okay?"

"I don't think I ought to talk to you no more," he said and again turned to walk away.

"Please, Wayne. I just want to ask a couple of things, and I'm done."

"All right, but only two more questions."

"What all did you tell the police during your interview?"

"I told 'em that Bubba couldn't have done all those things. You know, with all that stuff in the news. He was with me on some of those days."

"Are you talking about the abductions?"

Pierce grimaced. "I don't really like to think about all of that."

"Are you tending to the house for your mother?" Mickey asked as he nodded and began walking to the back of the house, with Mickey in tow. "What happened to your fence?" she asked pointing to the pile of boards from the collapsed fence."

Pierce looked at and said, "I think the police did that."

"Why do you have a different last name, Wayne?"

He stopped and turned back toward her. "My mother remarried for a while when I was little. I got my stepfather's name, and Bubba didn't."

"Why didn't you testify at the trial, Wayne?"

Pierce shrugged again and hopped up the back steps into the house. Mickey felt she had pressed him enough for that day. She walked back across the front yard, and when she reached her car, she looked back and saw Wayne staring at her through a gap in the sheets covering the front window.

Mickey drove to the office, put in a substantial day at work, and when she arrived home that afternoon, she poured herself a bourbon. She added an ice cube, took a sip, and looked to see her phone's message light was blinking and played it. *Mrs. Grant, this is Chief Bud Buchanan. You need to call me right away. This is Sunday, and I'll be here most of the day. It's important that I talk to you.*

He included a direct number, and Mickey knew she should call him immediately. But she finished the first drink and poured a second before dialing his number. Buchanan answered on the first ring, and Mickey said, "This is Michelle Grant. I just got your message."

"I gotta tell you, ma'am, I'm getting more than a little pissed off about your interference with police business."

"What do you mean?"

"Well, let's start with you continuing to bad mouth my department on the open cases. Then there's you going to look at our file on the Flynn case, and on top of that, you went down to Flynn's neighborhood nosing around. This is dangerous stuff, even for the police, and I am concerned that you're meddling in an area that you aren't equipped to handle, little missy!"

"The name's Michelle, and even if what you said is true, what's the big deal? I mean, don't I have a right to go where I want to and review public records in a court file?"

"This isn't about your rights, and the police file's not public record," Buchanan charged. "You misled the clerk, telling her you were on the Flynn case. I ought to have your law license for that alone!"

"Wait just a moment, Chief. You know as well as I do that I *was* involved in the Flynn case."

"Yes, and because of that, there's a freed serial killer walking our streets. I thought we had an understanding when we talked after Jackson's death, but you broke it. Just so that there's no further misunderstanding, all of this is going to stop right now! Do you understand?"

"I just—"

"Do you understand?" Buchanan pressed.

"Yes, I understand," Mickey relented.

"Don't you think getting Flynn turned loose demonstrates how jackin' around with the process is dangerous?"

"You're right, and I'll back off," she agreed.

"Now, that's more like it. We have a *real* agreement now, and you better live up to it—or things are going to get, let's say, a little uncomfortable for you."

"Is that a threat, Chief?" Mickey said.

"No, it's a goddamned promise if you want to know!" The line went dead.

Mickey set her phone down, sipped her drink, and thought, *how in the world did he know about me looking at the file and learn so quickly, on a weekend, that I went to Flynn's neighborhood? Shit, are the police tailing me?*

Mickey return to her work routine, but notwithstanding her conversation with Buchanan, she continued to make occasional passes through Flynn's neighborhood, but only very early or late in the day. One Friday evening, she was putting the finishing touches on a set of interrogatory responses and lost track of time. When she looked up, the sun had set, and the lawyers and staff had long since departed for the weekend. This left her and Truman Betts, the office custodian, as the only ones left in the building. In the years before Reagan's disappearance, Mickey frequently worked late into the evening. This day felt like old times, and it pleased her. She sat back in her chair, took a deep breath, and thought about her upcoming weekend and the security and companionship she enjoyed when she was with Tyler.

She walked down the hall to the firm's break room and retrieved a club soda from the refrigerator and returned to her desk. She pulled a bottle of bourbon from her bottom drawer, mixed a drink, and took a sip. The effervescence of the club soda married with the warmth of the whiskey pleased her throat and tongue. Betts, through with his tasks for the week, dropped by to bid Mickey farewell. He was a soft-spoken man who for decades had handled cleaning duties and performed odd jobs for the firm. He had a tall, thin frame, a gray stubble beard on gaunt, light-brown cheeks, and a snow-white head of hair.

"Miss Mickey, I'm about to head to the house. Will you remember to set the alarm before you leave?"

"Yes, Truman. I'm about done here myself. We're the last two, right?"

"Yes, ma'am, that's right. You still know how to set the alarm, don't you?"

"Why, Truman Betts! How many times have you and I closed this place up together?"

"Sorry, but I ain't seen you here late in a while, and if it don't get set right, I get called on the carpet." Mickey nodded and smiled. "You know, ma'am. Uh … I don't read too good. But I read some of those stories in the paper about you. There's words in there I don't know, but from what I can tell, you was in a pickle."

Mickey smiled and put down her drink. "Yes, Truman, I guess you could say that."

"I've been worried about you, and so are some of the others around here. I don't mean to pry, you know, but I hear things around here, and I'm praying for you, Miss Mickey."

"Thank you, Truman. I need it." Betts nodded and turned to leave. "You take care of that sweet wife of yours, you hear?"

"Yes, Miss Mickey," he said cheerfully as he walked away.

She finished her drink, and with the clock nearing eight thirty, she decided that it was time to close up and head home. But before she set the alarm, she needed to make sure no one remained in the two-story building who might inadvertently set off the alarm once activated. Firm protocol required a building-wide intercom call as the last step before departing. Accordingly, she picked up her receiver, pushed the intercom button on her phone, and said, "If there's anyone in the building, please call extension 221."

Not expecting a response, she picked up her purse and started out of her office, until her phone rang. Puzzled, she walked back to her desk and pushed the speaker button. "Who is this? I thought I was alone."

A voice whispered, "You're definitely not alone. I'm here!"

"What?" Mickey asked as she heard a click and the dial tone. The caller had hung up before she noted the extension from which the call was placed. She tried to imagine who would make such a statement, and her thoughts naturally turned to Flynn, and she considered calling the police. She peeked out her office door and looked both ways down the hallway. The only lighting in the hall emanated from several small, dimly lit sconces spaced every few feet and only on one side. Seeing no other lights or movement, she eased down the hallway experiencing nervous twinges with each open office door she passed.

She reached the reception area, which was illuminated now only by the outside lights beaming through the louvered blinds of one large window. It was then she realized the call could have come from the phone at the entrance gate to the parking garage. To avoid unwanted visitors, the firm had installed a phone and key pad at its gated entrance. Employees could dial a security code to activate the gate, and visitors could call any of the listed extensions inside the building. Since her page would have reached all parts of the office complex, including the parking garage, she considered that the return call was likely placed from the outside and could have come from anyone passing by.

She passed it off as a prank, but nevertheless, she reached in her purse then remembered that she left her pistol at home in the purse she used the day prior. She opted for her can of pepper spray and with it in hand, she went down the elevator and headed for the exit to the parking garage. She walked slowly, watching for any movement—both inside the building and from the garage. Mickey looked toward her car through the window of the metal exit door. She scanned as much of the parking area afforded from the window before deciding to open the door and leave the safety of the building. She punched in the code to set the alarm and crept into the garage, then she turned to lock the door. She felt a hand on her shoulder, and her heart leapt as she wheeled around. The abrupt movement caused her to drop her pepper spray canister, which bounced and then rolled on the pavement. Instinctively, she dropped to her knees, reaching for it, while screaming desperately for help.

"It's me, Miss Mickey! It's me!" yelled a frantic voice behind her.

Gasping for air, she recognized Truman's voice. "Damn it, Truman!"

"I'm sorry, ma'am!" he wailed as he reached to help her up from the pavement. Once on her feet, Mickey realized that he was as frightened as she was.

"I apologize for yelling at you and cussin'," she said, brushing the specks from the pavement off the knees. "I thought you'd left."

"I'm sorry, ma'am, but I got a few blocks toward the bus stop and realized I left my readin' glasses here. Ain't no way I can read anything this weekend without my glasses."

"Did you hear me page for anyone in the building?"

"No, ma'am. I just got back here a second or two ago."

"So you didn't dial my office extension?"

"No, ma'am."

"Truman, this is important. Did you see anything or anyone around the building when you were walking back?"

"Come to think of it, there was a vehicle around the front entrance when I walked onto Brazos Street."

"Was it a car, or a truck, or perhaps a brown van?"

"It was too small to be a van or a truck. It looked to me like it was a small car."

"Could you tell the make or model?"

"Oh no, ma'am. When I first saw it, I was still a ways away, you know."

"What did it do?"

"I saw him back out and go the other way."

"You said him. Was a man driving?"

"I just said it that way, like I always do. I don't know for sure if it was a man or woman."

"Thanks, Truman," Mickey said. "Why don't you go get your glasses, and I'll drive you to the bus stop?"

"That's all right, Miss Mickey. I like to walk there, especially on nights like this."

"I'm not sure it's safe," she warned.

"Oh, I can take care of myself. You don't need to worry about me."

"Suit yourself, but you be careful, you hear!"

"Yes, ma'am, you know I will. I'm just going to go on back in and get my glasses, and I'll lock up."

"Do you know how to set the alarm?" she asked, grinning.

Truman smiled, nodded, and entered the building. Mickey got in her car, locked the doors, and headed toward the exit. As the garage gate slid open, she looked in both directions for activity. Seeing nothing, she turned right onto Brazos and headed toward Tyler's house. Checking her rearview mirror, Mickey saw the lights of a car enter the street immediately after she moved beyond the front of Triple B's building. It continued behind her, and Mickey strained to get a good look at the car from her mirror but could not discern the make of the car or the size or gender of the driver. It was a small vehicle though, and its left headlight was markedly dimmer than the right. This car had maintained a distance behind her, but when Mickey made her turns, each time the car reappeared.

"Shit!" she said as the traffic light in front of her turned red, and she slowed to a stop. The mystery car had caught up to her and idled behind her until the light showed green. She accelerated through the intersection and soon found herself at a speed greater than she was comfortable with. She made two random turns, but each time the odd headlight pattern reemerged in her rearview mirror. Mickey then turned a corner with very little braking and was not fully stopping at stop signs, and the pursuit persisted.

Convinced now that she had a stalker, she weighed her options. Though only a couple miles from Tyler's house, she decided she should not endanger him or disclose his location, so she accelerated past the cutoff to his house, opting to head back toward town and to the police department. When she took a left on a road that she knew would take her in that direction, she could see the pursuer had accelerated and was approaching rapidly. She turned on a side street, hoping the stalker's speed was too great to execute the turn. But the car skidded and joined her on that road, which was a dark, poorly maintained two-lane road with drainage ditches running parallel to it on each side. The deteriorated pavement featured loose dirt and gravel, adding greater danger to her speed.

The car followed on the gravelly surface but was now maintaining a distance. So focused on her rearview mirror was she, Mickey failed to notice that she was nearing a sharp curve to the left. She shrieked and struggled for control, using a combination of the steering wheel and her brakes to execute the turn. The speed, the curve, and the gravel took dominance, and her car fishtailed—hard to the right, then sharply back left, then right again—and stopped only when she slid partway into the soggy ditch on the right side of the road. The motion was so abrupt that her purse and its contents tumbled into the passenger-side floorboard. Looking in all directions, Mickey jumped on the accelerator, with her rear tires spinning fruitlessly and slinging mud. Though she saw no headlights approaching, she knew she remained vulnerable and continued on the gas pedal.

Mickey looked to her left and now saw a set headlights approaching with extreme velocity. She braced for a collision, but the approaching vehicle screeched to stop just feet from the side of her car. Blinded by the vehicle's lights and the bellowing dirt and debris, she considered running on foot into the darkness but saw nearby houses and had no idea where she would flee to if she tried. Now trapped, she made sure her doors were locked and pushed on her horn with her left hand while feeling for her phone and pepper spray with her right. She watched helplessly as a figure appeared from her left. Continuing to spin her wheels and honking her horn, she looked straight ahead until the apparition stooped and stared at Mickey through the driver's side glass. She eased off the horn and her accelerator and saw the figure was a teenage boy who himself looked quite alarmed. Mickey used her hands to block the glare of the headlights and saw that the teen had arrived in an older-model Dodge pickup with fully intact headlights.

She lowered her window, and the large boy, wearing blue jeans the legs of which were now mud spattered, a cowboy hat, and red jacket said cautiously, "Are you all right, ma'am?"

"I'm fine. You just scared the hell out of me the way you came up on me so fast."

"Sorry, ma'am. Me and my buddy was just out fooling around."

"I understand," Mickey said as her tension flowed from her. "I'm sorry I got you muddy."

"I pretty much stay muddy. Listen, if you want, we can help you out of the ditch."

"Oh God, that would be great, but I want to see your buddy before I get out."

He motioned to his friend, and from the passenger seat of the truck emerged a tall, thin, young man who walked over to her. The pair seemed harmless enough, so Mickey got out of the car and watched as the young men went to work. The driver backed the truck to the front of her car while the other boy retrieved a thick, heavy chain from the bed of the truck and hooked it to both vehicles.

The boy in the cowboy hat asked Mickey to get back in her car, and when she did, he explained, "We're going to pull forward slowly until the chain gets tight. When I give the signal, you may need to give it some gas to get you all the way out." Mickey nodded her understanding. "You're in there pretty deep, so when you're gunning it, you need to be ready to brake quickly when your wheels hit the pavement, or you're gonna shoot forward and might go slammin' into my truck. Also, my truck's gonna sling some gravel toward *your* car, okay?"

"I understand," Mickey replied and raised her window. Moments later, with the wheels on both vehicles spinning, they managed to successfully free Mickey's car from the ditch and safely back to the poor road surface. The teenagers checked her car and found nothing amiss, except for the mud spatter and a chip on her windshield, that she did not know was new or old. Mickey produced her wallet and offered the two money for their rescue, but they politely declined. Thanking them profusely, Mickey started toward her car and then stopped and walked back to the truck.

"Yes, ma'am?" the driver asked.

"When y'all turned to come down this road, did you happen to see another car?"

"No, ma'am," the driver said.

"Wait a second! There was a car in front of us," the other boy said. "You was fiddlin' with the radio and missed it, but there was a small car that hung a right on a side road and took off like a scalded dog when we made our turn."

"Did you see the make of the car or who was driving?" Mickey asked.

"No, ma'am, only that it was a little car."

"Is everything okay?" the driver asked.

"Everything is fine now," she said, smiling. "Thanks again, fellas."

She watched as her two Good Samaritans drove away and shook her head when she heard tires squealing and saw the truck fishtail as it headed recklessly around the next curve. She drove her car back toward the main highway, thinking since she had broken the pursuit that she would now proceed to Tyler's house and report the incident to the police from there. But as she drove, she gasped when the car with the bad left headlight situated in her rearview mirror, and she aggressively hit her accelerator. Despite her speed, the pursuer was moving faster than her, and within seconds the front of her attacker's car contacted her bumper—twice—threatening to send Mickey's car spinning off the road again, before backing off.

Now speeding down a two-lane, well-maintained, asphalt county road, Mickey glanced forward and noticed the reflective white X signs of a railroad crossing. She was familiar with the elevated crossing and knew the roadbed rose several feet up to the tracks; and if she hit that incline at anywhere near her current speed, her car would go airborne. Complicating matters further, she spied the unmistakable gyrating front light of a fast-approaching freight train, and the locomotive's horn was already employed in anticipation of the crossing. The rural crossing had no protective crossing arms, and she assessed her strategies. *If I stop on this side of the tracks, I'm stuck with him behind me for God knows how long. He could simply walk up to my car and do to me whatever he wants. But if I can get past the crossing and he can't, I'll be home free.*

Her eyes darted from the raised crossing to the approaching engine, but with the angle and the darkness, she had trouble gauging the train's speed. "I have to go for it, right?" she said aloud as she neared the point of no return. Then, with a final look, she could clearly see "Southern Pacific Railroad" in white letters on the side of the lumbering locomotive as it bore down on the crossing. Glancing in her mirror, she sensed the pursuer was now lagging behind as if awaiting her decision. In that moment, she realized that she could not risk it and slammed on her brakes, and her tires locked and squealed. Pressing the brake pedal as hard as she could, she calculated it wasn't enough and she was going to slam into the side of the passing train. As she slid, Mickey leaned to her right with her left arm locked around the steering wheel and braced herself. She closed her eyes—and suddenly heard nothing beyond the sound of the passing train. Aided by the brakes and rise in the roadbed, she managed to stop short of the train. She smelled burnt rubber from her tires and looked up to see the front of her car was within a few feet from the squealing wheels of boxcars. Her stalker sat directly behind her, and she strained to see the driver's face in her mirror. But her tinted back windshield, the other car's headlights, and the ambient darkness combined to obscure her view.

Suddenly she felt her car start forward and realized her stalker's bumper was on hers and was pushing her car toward the train. "Oh shit!" she yelled and pressed the brakes as hard as she could, but despite the effort, her car crept closer. She snatched upward on the handle of the emergency brake with all her strength, halting the forward movement. The dust from the passing box cars rose up and over the hood of her car as she glanced to her rearview mirror and saw the attack car backing up. For a moment, she dared to think that the pursuer was relenting, and in those few seconds of separation, Mickey's taillights shined down the grade toward the car, allowing her to ascertain that her attacker was driving a light blue Accel Sportiva. Then she heard the driver rev the engine.

"He's gonna ram me!" she yelled as she struggled to see the end of the train and then looked back to the car. In a flash, the car accelerated up the incline and rammed her bumper. Though it was only advancing at ten to fifteen miles an hour at impact, it succeeded in bringing Mickey's car within a foot of the passing train cars. She knew that another similar ramming would send the front of her entangling in the large, rotating metal wheels. Mickey was hyperventilating and sweating profusely as the pursuer again backed up. Seeing no end to the train, she prepared to take her chances by jumping from her car, until inspiration sprung from her many hours spent with the Accel mechanical engineers during the preparation for the Monroe case.

As her pursuer again revved the engine for the next assault, Mickey released her emergency brake, threw the gear into reverse, and stomped the gas pedal just as the pursuer advanced. Her car backed down the incline and slammed the pursuer's front bumper as it approached, rewarding Mickey with a flash as the driver-side airbag in the Sportiva deployed. As Mickey heard the last of the train rumble by, she raced over the tracks and away from that fateful crossing. Seeing no headlights behind her and locating her phone, she dialed 911, while making a beeline for Tyler's house. The 911 operator agreed to have an officer meet her at Tyler's address, and then she called Tyler and informed him of the chase.

"Are you okay?"

"Yes," she confirmed.

"Thank God. What do you think this was all about?"

"It was Flynn!"

"Jesus! Where are you now?"

"I'm on County Road 5," she gasped. "I'm coming straight to your house."

"You're closer to your house. I'll just meet you there."

"No! I already gave the police your address, and they're sending an officer."

"Is he still chasing you? I mean maybe you should …"

"No, I ditched him. I'll see you in a few minutes."

When Mickey pulled into Tyler's driveway, she was relieved to see him rush off of his porch in her direction. They embraced in the middle of his front yard as he looked up and down the street for approaching cars. Then Tyler examined the damage to the back of her car. "Your bumper's a little mucked up, but it's hard to tell how much with the darkness and mud."

"Thanks. Let's wait for the police inside," she said as they walked, arm in arm, through his front door. Once inside, he handed her a cup of hot tea he had made for her. Mickey began to recount the evening in detail as she sipped the tea, until they heard a loud knock at the door. Mickey jumped, spilling some tea on her pants as Tyler dashed toward the door.

"It's the policeman," Tyler said, peering through the peephole. He unlocked the door and led him into the living room. The officer introduced himself and looked down at Mickey's pants.

"It's not what you think. I just spilled some tea."

"Are you okay?" Tyler asked, handing Mickey the paper towel her cup was sitting on to dry her pants.

"I'm fine. Thankfully, it wasn't too hot."

Mickey described the events of the evening as she blotted her pants, and the young patrol officer took notes. She started with the threatening call at the office, then took him through the entire chase and concluded with the episode at the railroad crossing, "It was Willie Flynn! I know it was and if you'll get over to his house, you should find a small light blue Sportiva with a damaged front end and deployed airbag!" she said.

"It was who?" the officer asked.

"Flynn—you know, Willie Lee Flynn."

"Is he your ex-husband or something?"

"*He's* my ex-husband, goddamn it!" Mickey shouted, pointing to Tyler. "Did you just join the force this week?"

Tyler put his arm around her, trying to calm her, and explained, "The guy in the news on that capital murder case."

"Oh, that guy. I thought he was in prison."

Sensing Mickey might erupt again, Tyler interjected, "He got out."

"And you think he's the one that followed you?" the officer asked dubiously.

"First of all, forgive me for yelling and cussing at you. You're the second person I've had to say that to just tonight," Mickey confessed. "But yes, it was Flynn. Every time I turned, he turned, and if I slowed down, he slowed down. If I sped up, he did too, and he got close enough to hit my bumper, more than once, at over sixty-five miles per hour!"

"You said he had a wreck with you at the tracks, so tell me exactly what happened."

"We had collision at the railroad crossing on County Road 5. He tried to push me into a passing train!"

"On the dispatcher's notes, there's mention of a deployed airbag?"

"Right, I collided with him and made it deploy."

"But the notes say he rear-ended you, so how did you—"

"He did, but he didn't hit me hard enough to deploy it. So when he tried again, I rammed into him going backwards to stun him with the airbag."

"Did you see him, Ms. Grant?"

"I saw him, but only an outline."

"You didn't see the face?" the officer said as he stopped writing, and Mickey shook her head. "Did you write down a license number?"

"No! I apologize, but I was kinda busy trying to stay alive!"

"Ma'am, I'm sorry, but if you didn't see the license plate or the person driving the car, I don't see that there's much that we can act on. I'll submit a report though, and if you get any other information, just call us and use the case number on this," he said, handing a card to Mickey.

"If I get more information? Aren't y'all going to investigate?"

"I'll drive out to the railroad crossing to see what's out there before I go back to the station."

"Please do," Mickey said. "But you *really* should go by Flynn's house to check for that car. I have his address."

"Good. Write it on here, and I'll do that. Do you think his car was drivable?"

"I'm not sure. I left as quick as the train passed, but he didn't follow."

"I'll talk to my sergeant and see if we can assign a patrol officer to make regular checks on this street."

"We'd appreciate that," Tyler said.

They thanked the officer, and when he drove away, Mickey handed Tyler the tea cup. "Here, I need a real drink."

"That's another thing, Mick. I'm worried about …"

"I know … my drinking," she said, exasperated. "Let's postpone the intervention to tomorrow. Right now I need a drink and not a lecture."

"Sorry to nag, Mick. Is scotch okay?"

"I'd drink rubbing alcohol if that's all you have."

He poured her a scotch with two ice cubes.

CHAPTER 18

FIAT JUSTITIA RUAT CAELUM
(Let Justice Be Done Should the Sky Fall)

On Monday morning, Mickey rose as Tyler was dressing to go to a doctor's appointment. As he headed for the door, she gave him a hug and thanked him for the weekend. She grabbed his Sunday newspaper from the dining room table, removed the wrapper. She was surprised that they ran a story on her Friday night encounter, which included the chase and the collision with the light blue Sportiva. It was a small piece buried in the local section, but it nevertheless irritated her that she again made the papers, and bristled at the fact that there was no mention of Flynn or any investigation by the police. *Damn it. All I need is a reminder about me and Flynn in the paper. I win the Monroe case, and they print nary a word. Now every time I sneeze, they print an article. I bet that officer didn't lift a finger when he left here. Shit, this is a chance to arrest Flynn, and they won't do a damn thing about it.*

She showered and dressed to go to the office, but during her drive she could not resist easing back to Flynn's neighborhood to check for a damaged Sportiva. To assure she was not being tailed, she took a convoluted path on lightly traveled roads, increasing the chance she would spot a tail by the police if one emerged. Once confident that she was not being followed, she doubled back toward Flynn's neighborhood, but when she arrived, she did not turn onto his street right away. Considering the likelihood that the police were maintaining regular vigils in that area, she wanted to check to see if there was any sign of law enforcement before moving further.

She sat idling on a side street three blocks away, but from there, she could see Flynn's front yard and driveway and saw no cars or activity. Staying vigilant, she turned her car slowly onto his quiet street, and reaching the front of his home, she saw no signs of Flynn or Pierce. She stopped a block away and waited several minutes. She considered taking a peek inside Flynn's garage for the Sportiva, but she noticed that there were no windows on it and presumed its door to be locked. Then she noticed a person walking down the sidewalk toward her. The sun's glare proved her enemy but she saw enough to know that it was a man, but appeared too small to be Flynn. As he drew closer, Mickey recognized that it was Pierce. He ambled aimlessly, with head down and oblivious to Mickey's presence, until she got out and walked toward him. Pierce glanced up and then turned and walked in the opposite direction.

"Wayne! Please stop. Come on, now, it's me. You know, Mickey like the mouse," she pleaded, but he walked even faster. "Fine! I'll just wait in front of your house till you come back." With that, he stopped, and stood with his hands in his pockets, until she caught up.

"How's your mom, Wayne?" she asked, trying to break his palpable tension.

"What?" he asked, glancing to her face.

"Your mom. You said she was ill, and I just wanted to—"

"She died."

"Oh, no," Mickey said flashing a compassionate expression. "Wayne, I'm really sorry to hear that."

"She was she sick, you know. They had her in a hosp–hospi–"

"Hospital?"

"No. I know that word."

"Hospice?" Mickey said, and he nodded, teary-eyed. "That's terrible."

"Yes. Terrible."

"Wayne, have you seen Willie?"

"He comes and goes, but I ain't seen him today. Why are you back here?"

"I just wanted to ask you something, Wayne."

"What?"

"Does Willie have access to a small car?"

"No," he responded nervously and turned to walk away.

Walking behind him, she failed consider the growing distance her pursuit was creating between her car and the purse with her pistol. Finally, Mickey grabbed his arm, and wheeled him around to face her. With her hands on his shoulders, she said, "Listen to me, Wayne. I'm not your enemy, understand? I've just got a question or two to ask you, and then I'll be out of here, okay?"

"You said that the last time."

"C'mon, Wayne, I just—"

"Why are you doing this?"

"Wayne, it's about my daughter, Reagan. She's one of the missing girls."

"Willie didn't do that!" he shot back.

"I'm not saying he did. I just need a little help for my little girl, that's all," she explained. Wayne's expression changed from anxious to one of genuine fear, and Mickey realized he was reacting not to her, but rather from something seen over her left shoulder. She turned in that direction, and to her horror, she saw an old, blue Ford LTD approaching.

"Wayne! Is that Willie?"

"Yes! He's using my mom's car 'cause his van broke down."

She froze, and her throat tightened. She released Tim's shoulders and instinctively began to backpedal. Tim walked rapidly away from her and toward the front door of their house, and the brakes of the Ford squealed as it rolled to stop. Flynn got out of the car, and staring toward Mickey, began walking unsteadily but deliberately down the sidewalk toward her. Mickey weighed her options, but since Flynn was now between her and her car, she stood petrified. Continuing toward her, and sensing no other options, she turned and ran in the opposite direction from him and her car.

"Stop!" Flynn yelled. "We need to talk!"

Mickey ignored the plea and ran faster as Flynn mustered all of his strength and ability to pursue. Though urging her to stop, Mickey's fear dominated, and she kept running as fast as her legs would allow. The sidewalk was riddled with uneven spots and cracks, many of which had weeds emerging from them, and she paid careful attention to them, daring not to trip. As she crossed driveway after driveway, she alternated screams between, "Help me!" and "Call the police!" But no one seemed present to hear the pleas. Not seeing any obvious refuge, she glanced back and, despite wearing low-heeled dress shoes, she found that she had put considerable distance between her and Flynn, who was limping slowly. She continued down the sidewalk but slowed her pace to catch her breath while continuing the pleas for help between gasps. She turned again and saw that Flynn had relented and was now walking back toward his house. She placed her hands on her knees, slumped over, and continued the effort to regain her breath.

She looked two houses down and noticed a home with a freshly mowed lawn and a late-model car parked in the driveway. She trotted to its front porch, rang the doorbell, and knocked forcefully. She put her ear to the door but heard nothing, so she banged on the door harder and yelled for help. She next heard a revving engine behind her and turned to see Flynn in the LTD, stopping across the yard from her.

"Hey, let's just talk!" Flynn yelled through his open window. Mickey, having none of that, bolted off the porch. Flynn eased out of the car and started up the driveway while Mickey ran around the side of the house and toward the rear of the house that once had the protection of a cedar-slat fence. Now, however, the rotting fence lacked a gate, and there were entire sections missing on each perimeter. Mickey darted into the backyard, which unlike the front, appeared to have not been mowed in months. She ran to the rear property line and beyond it through one of the huge gaps in the fence that led her into an expansive, overgrown field. She slowed when she found getting through the tall grass and shrubs proved its own struggle. Hoping Flynn would find the obstacles insurmountable, she kicked off her shoes and continued barefooted.

To her right she heard a guttural growl and turned her head in that direction. "Shit!" was her reaction as she stared at a large, muscular, fully grown and agitated bull mastiff. The dog apparently guarded an old mobile home in the field, and she tried to appear nonthreatening. Nevertheless, the massive canine lurched toward her with bared, slobbery fangs. She changed her direction, hoping the dog would abandon its pursuit and turn its attention to Flynn who was now entering the field and watching her dilemma. Undeterred, the mastiff kept raging toward her, and knowing she couldn't outrun the animal, she turned and knelt, trying to make herself small. Next, the dog yelped, and opening her eyes,

Mickey saw that it had reached the end of a very long chain. She rose and started running again, hearing the dog's ferocious barking fade as she did.

Going further into the field, Mickey glanced back, and watched as Flynn was easing around the dog, until she tripped and fell on the broken wooden pallet. A large piece of the pallet with an exposed nail tore her pants and cut the shin of her left leg. She picked herself up and labored on through the seemingly endless grass, which was taller and thicker the deeper she went. Mickey scanned in front of her, spotting only a freshly plowed cotton field a hundred yards ahead, but suddenly happened upon a deep ditch and instinctively jumped to try to cross it. Losing her footing at the muddy edge she toppled against the mucky incline on the other side. She attempted to rise, but her hands and feet were mired, and though trying hard to rise, each attempt had her slipping back to her original spot. She knew exhaustion was overtaking her but continued her struggles as she heard the sounds of Flynn gasping for air from behind. Mickey managed to get up on her knees, but without warning, Flynn leapt and landed on the same slope as her and wrapped his arms around her feet.

Mickey thrashed her legs violently, desperate to escape, but Flynn only tightened his grip and yelled, "Stop it! Stop, Stop!"

"Help! Somebody help me!" Mickey screamed in desperation as one of her kicks connected with Flynn's face, bloodying his lip and nose.

"Listen to me for a second, goddamn it! I ain't gonna hurt you!"

Mickey heard his plea and continued to fight, but Flynn's arms were superior in strength to his legs, and fatigue and weakness were taking their toll on her. She rolled over on her back, cupped her muddy hands around her mouth, and screamed again, "Someone help me, please!"

"I mean it—stop!" Flynn pleaded through gritted teeth as he continued to grip her lower body and her thrashing began to ease. "Listen, I'm letting go now, so no more kicking."

As he released her legs, Mickey sat up facing him, but before Flynn could utter another word, she rose to flee again. Flynn lunged and grabbed her right pant leg with his outstretched arm, and as Mickey struggled to run, her pants slipped down to her thighs, and she fell back to the side of the ditch. Mickey again appealed, "Help me, God! Someone help!" But by then, even her voice was weak and hoarse.

"Please, give me a chance!" Flynn said. "Just listen for a minute, and you can go!" Whether by persuasion or exhaustion, he felt her fully relent and released her pant leg. "Listen, all I want to do is talk to you. You sit right there," he said, pointing up to the edge of the ditch, "and I'll sit on that stump over there. Just hear me out, and if you still wanna leave after that, I won't stop you, okay?"

"Okay, but you don't make a move, you hear?" Mickey said as she struggled to rise to her feet.

"Fine, and pull your pants up. I ain't lookin'," he said, turning his head. Mickey looked down, and tugged her pants by the waistband over her muddy panties and hips. She took a seat on the grassy edge of the ditch, still breathing deeply, readying herself to flee again if necessary. Flynn assumed the stump while using the sleeve of his T-shirt to staunch his bleeding nose and mouth.

"You kick like a mule, you know," Flynn said, shaking his head. Mickey did not respond and carefully watched his every move. When he reached into his pocket, she prepared to run, until she saw that he produced a red mechanic's rag. "Here, you're bleeding too," he said, tossing her the rag. She looked at him puzzled, until he pointed to her torn pant leg and bleeding shin. She took the rag and dabbed the blood, not taking her eyes off of him.

"I know what you think, but I didn't kill your daughter. In fact, I believe she's still alive."

"Don't screw with me, you son of a—"

"Stop it! Just hear me out," he demanded. "I mean it, your daughter probably ain't dead, and neither are any of the others except, of course, for the Abram girl. And by the way, I didn't kill her neither!" He waited for Mickey's reaction, but she sat frowning. "It's Buchanan, you see. He's the person behind all of this."

"Wait, wait, wait!" she said, incredulous. "You want me to believe that the chief of police is responsible for all of the missing girls—and *not* you?" When he nodded, she said, "Look—if you're going to kill me, do it! But don't fill me full of this shit before you do!"

"I told you I ain't gonna hurt you," he said firmly and rose to walk toward her.

"What are you doing?" she said with alarm.

"Helping you over the ditch. We need to get out of this field before we get snake bit."

"You stay back! I can get up over on my own," Mickey insisted, and struggled awkwardly to the other side. Without another word, Flynn slogged back across the ditch and started in the direction of his car. As he trudged through the field, Mickey followed, lagging eight to ten steps behind to keep watch on Flynn. Looking back at her, Flynn continued, "I know that all of this is hard for you to believe, but it's the truth, and I just want you to hear me out. Let's get your shoes, and you come on back to the house and let me get you something for your cut."

"I'm not getting anywhere near your house with you!"

"You don't get it. We can't just stand in the middle of the street or even my front yard. If the police see us together, we're both in deep shit."

"What are you suggesting?"

"The back of the house would be best," Flynn said as they walked past the barking dog still struggling at the end of its chain.

"No way!" Mickey said. "You're not going to lure me to the backyard to—"

"Look—if I was going to hurt you, I'd a done it by the ditch, right?" he said as Mickey stopped to pick up her shoes

"You need a weapon, and that's why you want me to come to the house."

He stopped and turned and lifted his shirt, revealing a leather sheath and the handle of a knife with a six-inch blade.

"Fine, we'll talk in the backyard, but I want to go to my car first."

"That's okay. I'll move my car back to the house, and you can walk to yours. But when you get to it, move it to a side street, and I'll wait for you behind the house."

They made their way through the backyard and out to the street, and Flynn got in his car and turned it around. He drove past Mickey as she walked down the sidewalk, carrying her muddy shoes. Flynn pulled into his driveway, and when Mickey reached her car, she opened the door and placed the muddy shoes on her floorboard and considered driving away. But instead she relocated her car and parked. Mickey grabbed her .38 pistol from her purse, then walked barefooted up Flynn's driveway, then stepped over the fallen fence. With the gun at her side, she saw Flynn was sitting on the railing of the back porch, trying to scrape mud from his old sneakers, while Wayne stood nervously by the backdoor.

"I'm willing to listen to what you have to say, but let's keep it honest," she said, brandishing the gun and pointing it in Flynn's direction.

"Hey! Hey! What the hell are you doing?" Flynn exclaimed as Wayne retreated into the house.

"I'm just leveling the home-field advantage."

"Fine, but don't point the damn thing at me!"

"Yeah, don't shoot my brother!" Wayne yelled through a rip in the screen door.

"Sorry, Wayne. I'm not shootin' anyone," she said, lowering her voice and the gun.

"Wayne, get her a clean, towel and a couple of Band-Aids," Flynn instructed as he rose from the porch and took a seat on a nearby rusty metal chair. Still apprehensive, Mickey stood near the porch, not taking her eyes off of Flynn. Wayne emerged from the house with a yellow towel and bandages and handed them to Mickey. She took a seat on the steps and then multitasked by lifting the musty-smelling towel and wiping the worst of the dried blood and mud with one hand while maintaining her grip the gun with the other, all the while maintaining an eyeful watch on Flynn. Wayne took a seat on a chair inside the kitchen and situated it where he could watch through the ripped screen.

"This is going to ruin your towel, you know," she observed.

Flynn shrugged. "You've got a gun. The towel's the least of my concerns."

"Well, get on with it," Mickey said, continuing to clean herself.

"First off, I don't blame you for not believing me after what I done to you," he conceded. "I'm sorry for all of that, but once you know the whole truth, you'll understand the position I was in. It all starts with the chief. I know it sounds nutty to you now, but Buchanan's been involved in organized crime for a *real* long time. He's the one behind the disappearance of every one of the missing girls."

"You're saying Buchanan abducted my daughter?" She asked skeptically.

"No, of course not, but he arranged for it. He uses people like me to do the dirty work."

"What do you mean by 'people like you'?"

"Misfits. Those he can lean on and trust not to squeal on him, and if they did talk, no one would believe them."

"How can you *possibly* expect me to believe any of this?" Mickey asked.

"I don't, at least not just by my words. But I can prove all of these things to you, and when I do, I'm gonna need some help from you."

"Help from me?" Mickey asked incredulous.

"Yes, and you're gonna do it too. You see, I need your help getting down to Mexico."

"You should have gone with the insanity defense, Willie. You're certifiable!"

"Maybe, but aren't we both at that point?" he said with a grin.

She placed the towel on the steps and stood to leave. "Thanks but no thanks, Willie. I believe I've heard quite enough."

"I'm not through" Flynn pleaded.

"Well, I am," she said, not looking back and turning toward the fence debris.

"I think your daughter's still alive!"

"I don't believe a word of It," Mickey dismissed.

"Your life's in danger, you know."

"Yes, from you!" she said stepping back over the fence.

"I don't own a small, light blue Accel sports car!" he said.

Mickey stopped on a dime and turned. "How do you know about that?"

"Believe it or not, I read the newspaper. The Indian guy that owns the convenience store around the corner lets me have unsold ones from the day before."

"Open your garage door," she demanded.

Flynn walked to the two-car detached garage and reached down to the handle of the poorly painted and partially rotted door. He lifted the door, revealing the interior, which housed his old, brown van, and was otherwise so stuffed with junk that there wasn't room for a bicycle, much less another car.

"Give me your phone number," Mickey said. "I want to think this through."

"I don't have a phone, at least one that's connected, and even if I did, it would be tapped."

"What do you want to do?"

"I'd like to explain all of this to you," Flynn said.

"I'm not comfortable doing that right now, and certainly won't do it here."

"Fine, but no one, and I mean no one, needs to know we're talking! Understand?"

"Why?"

"You really don't get it, do you? This is deadly shit, lady!"

"Come on. You think Buchanan's really worried about me talking to you?" she asked then considered the chief's insistent admonitions.

"Worried? He's deathly afraid. They're going to be watching, so don't come here anymore. Things are unraveling, and we need to act fast. I have your number, and will call you later from a phone at that same store around the corner. They'll let me use it, and it'll be safe."

Mickey agreed, and when she reached her house, she headed straight for the shower. Once clean and dry, and her wound dressed, she put on a robe, and sat in the kitchen, sifting through a sizable stack of mail. She came across a flyer with Buchanan's photograph reminding the community that his hat was in the ring for reelection in November. *Big news, right? I wonder if anyone alive remembers who he succeeded. Is Flynn gaming me? I mean, can any of this possibly be true? Could Reagan really be alive?*

She stared at Buchanan's photo, reflected on their two conversations, and walked to her desk and boot computer. She searched for a home address for the chief and was pleased at how readily she located it. She jotted it down, quickly dressed, and hurried to her car. Within minutes, she was cruising an affluent area of Brinkman where she had seldom been. She turned from a tree-lined esplanade onto Buchanan's street and drove slowly, scanning house numbers. She found Buchanan's two-story, colonial, brick home with a detached two-car garage in the rear. The empty driveway made Mickey wonder what might be inside the garage, and surveying the garage from the street she spotted a window on the side.

She parked across the street from the house next door to Buchanan's and carefully looked for anyone one who could witness her presence. She calculated that she could ease up the driveway, grab a glance through the garage window, and return to her car with minimal risk. She looked again at the surrounding manicured lawns of the stately homes, and seeing no one stirring, she exited her car. She walked across the street and up the driveway, toward the garage with a deliberate but non-suspicious gait.

The garage had a brick façade on the front, with two, large wooden, windowless garage doors. She slipped around two plastic garbage cans on the right side of the garage and into a narrow pathway between the garage and an adjacent redwood slatted fence that separated Buchanan's yard from that of his neighbor. She peered into the garage through a gap in a set of curtains and saw two cars. Parked nearest the window was a white Lincoln town car, and next to it sat a much smaller car, the features of which could not be ascertained from that vantage point, but from there she saw that a window existed on the rear wall of the garage.

She slipped further down the path and around back for a better angle. After cleaning the grimy window with some spit and her shirt sleeve, she squinted inside and gasped. The smaller car had a Sportiva emblem, the front end was damaged, and its driver-side airbag hung crumpled and limp from the steering wheel. Then came a noise from the other side of the redwood fence. Considering her height and the fence was only five feet tall, Mickey instantly squatted and crabbed from the rear of the garage back around to the side. She peered through a small gap in the vertical slats, and saw the back of a shirtless man in plaid Bermuda shorts, whistling and watering plants in his backyard. *Shit! I can't walk away without risking him seeing me, and if I crawl or duck walk anyone seeing me will be suspicious. No, I can't leave until he's back inside.*

She maintained her crouch and waited for several minutes, astonished at how much watering Buchanan's neighbor deemed necessary. The squatting began to burn her thighs, so she sat with legs crossed on the dirt. The whistling grew louder, and Mickey peeked between the slats and saw the man had made his way to her side of the yard. Praying she wouldn't cough or sneeze, she heard water spattering the fence and was moving closer to her position, and when they came, she was prepared to accept the drops splattering from between the slats. She then heard the unmistakable sound of a diesel engine arriving. She craned her neck toward Buchanan's driveway and watched as a white, four-wheel-drive Ford pickup roared toward her, stopping abruptly just short of the garage doors.

The man next door shut off the water and looked over the fence. "Hey, Chief! Working banker's hours?"

"I wish," replied Buchanan's unmistakable course voice. "I'm actually up to my ass in alligators, but I left a file here."

"Say, what happened to your face?" the neighbor asked.

"Oh that. I uh … I just—I got up in the middle of the night to take a leak and ran squarely into a partially open door."

"Ouch! Sorry to hear that. Get better and give my best to the missus."

"I will, Millhouse," Buchanan said and walked toward the backdoor of his house.

Mickey looked back through the fence slats and saw that the neighbor was now winding up the hose and once done he put it in a storage shed before disappearing into his house. Mickey eased to the front of the garage. Seeing nothing of Buchanan or anyone else, she trotted quickly down his driveway to her car and sped out of the neighborhood as she tried to dial her office with her trembling hand.

"Wanda, Michelle here. Please get me Marlene," she said tapping her finger on the console until Marlene picked up. "Marlene, it's me. Listen carefully. I'm not coming in today, and don't mention this to anyone, but I'm expecting a call from Flynn and—"

"Willie Flynn?"

"I know it sounds crazy, but yes. If he calls, tell him I'm at home. I think he has them, but offer both my home and cell numbers, okay?"

"Sure thing. Are you okay?"

"Yes … I'm fine."

Heeding Flynn's advice, Mickey refrained from calling anyone, even Tyler, and drove straight home and waited. Midafternoon, she was sitting on her porch, sipping iced tea and thumbing through a deposition transcript, when her cell phone rang.

"Hello?" she said anxiously.

"It's me, Willie. I was calling to—"

"Listen to me, Willie. We have to meet as soon as possible but in a public place."

"What do you mean by public place? We're being watched, and I don't think we should meet anywhere we can be easily seen."

"I get that," Mickey conceded. "But I just can't meet you in a secluded place … I'm not there yet. I'm starting to—you know—see some issues here, but I'm just not comfortable."

"Where then?"

"Do you know the Dixie cafe in old downtown?"

"Sure."

"It'll be safe there. Meet me in thirty minutes."

"Whoa!" he interjected. "That's still a place where we can be seen. Plus it's only a few blocks from the police station."

"Willie, do you know any better place? Look—no one really goes there anymore, especially this time of day."

"What time do they close?"

"At four, but I know the people who work there, and we can stay as long as we need while they clean up."

"I might be followed."

"Do your best, Willie. That's all I can say. If you sense you're being followed, stop somewhere and call this number, and we'll go to plan B."

Flynn hung up and then packed a paper grocery sack with some clothes and toiletries and had Wayne drive him to the old part of Brinkman. "Here's your bus ticket," Flynn said, setting it on the dashboard as his little brother started to cry. "Come on, Wayne. Don't be like that."

"But I'm worried about you and scared that this is the last time I'm ever gonna see you."

Flynn patted his brother on the shoulder. "I've told you five times that I'm coming back."

"I hope so. What do I do with the car?"

"Don't drive it to the bus station, you hear? Go home, lock up the house, and leave the car in the driveway. Do you remember how I told you to get to the big bus station?"

Wayne thought for a moment as he drove. "I take the city bus downtown and get off at Caldron."

"Calder Street," Flynn corrected.

"Calder, and the station's right there."

"Good job, Wayne. Just in case, I wrote that on the back of the ticket, and there are two twenties clipped to it too."

"When you get back to Texas, you're gonna let me know so I can come back, right?"

"Sure, if you wanna come back. Hell, you might like it on the farm, Wayne."

They pulled to the back of café, but before getting out, Flynn leaned over and hugged his brother. "Good bye, Wayne. I'll see you soon, I promise."

"So long, Bubba," Wayne replied as he dried his nose and eyes on his shirt sleeve. Flynn waved to Wayne as he drove away, then lit a cigarette and looked around for signs of the police. He paced behind the diner until he saw Mickey pull up. He walked to the front of the diner and entered, leaving the afternoon sun for the comparably dimly lit interior.

As Mickey entered and removed her sunglasses, she was unable to see much of anything until her eyes adjusted. She then saw Flynn taking a seat in a booth in the rear and the bulging paper sack resting at his feet. As she made her way through the diner, she greeting several employees by name, assuring that Flynn knew she was in familiar territory, just in case.

"What's that?" she said, pointing at the paper sack.

"It's what I packed for the trip."

"You don't own a suitcase?"

"Yes, an old one. I just didn't think it would be a good idea for me to be walking around downtown Brinkman with one."

"Good point. Where are you going?"

"I told you. Mexico."

The waitress asked if either wanted a menu. They declined, but Mickey ordered a coffee, and he a Coke. The waitress wore a calf-length, yellow print dress and a blue apron that took every inch of the strip of fabric to tie it in back. She jotted down the order and walked over to a stainless-steel table in the corner that served as a drink station.

"I want to tell you right now that I hate a lot of what you've done to me," Mickey said severely. "You have no idea how—"

"Look. If you came here to—"

"No! You need to hear me out. You have no idea what pain you—"
Mickey stopped as the waitress returned and sat their drinks on coasters.

"I already confessed my sins in mistreating you, so can we please just get down to business?"

Mickey exhaled. "I'm sorry, but I guess I'm a little wound up."

"You should be. When you understand this whole deal, it ain't gonna make a damn how we got to where we are. The only thing that really matters now is the truth and where we go from here. To understand all of this, you have to know a little about my background. It was a slippery slope, you see. I got on dope in my teens and stole stuff to fuel the habit. Once you're caught a time or two, things get all tangled up. I ignored the early slaps on the wrist and then ended up servin' almost three full years in two stints, but in the process, I whipped the habit and got clean."

"You quit altogether?" mickey asked.

"I had a couple of slipups early on, but I ain't used in years. So once I got straight and we moved down here to Texas, I tried to work. But no one would touch me with my prison record. Since my parole status moved with me to Texas I reported to a parole officer down here, and had to really fly right, you know? They kept tabs on me, and that included drug and alcohol testing—and it all went fine. I did deal drugs for a few months but with my parole, I wouldn't touch the stuff myself. When I quit all of that, I just did odd jobs, mostly off the books, including doing roofing and workin' on a landscape crew. Later, I got a GED and even started looking at vocational schools."

"This is all interesting, Willie, but what's this got to do with anything?"

"Please hear me out. This all connects. So I got a job doing air-conditioning. I worked for a fella who had four crews with three guys each, and mine had a couple of dudes I liked. They was clean too, though they did like to drink beer and *a lot* of it. Soon, I learned how to do the A/C work, and though it sucked climbing around attics in Texas summers, but it paid well. But a year and a half ago, things changed on a dime. Buchanan himself picked me up one night and put me in his squad car. I was familiar with Buchanan, and his power was well known on the street, so when he put me in his cruiser, I figured I was going to jail for something. But when I realized we wasn't going back to the police station, I got *really* scared."

"Where'd he take you?" Mickey asked, taking a sip from the coffee cup.

"We went about five miles out of Brinkman toward the old drive-in-theater. He stopped the car and killed the engine and headlights. It was pitch dark except for the dashboard lights, and he told me he had enough information on me to put me away for a real long time. He knew I'd been goin' to what he called a 'beer joint' after work with those guys on the crew. I did play pool with 'em at an ice house, and though I never drank a single drop of beer there, Buchanan knew just being inside it was a violation of my parole. Then he handed me some photographs and turned on his dome light. I flipped through 'em, and I'll never forget him saying, 'Willie, you've been a naughty boy.'"

"What were the pictures of?"

"Mostly of me coming in and out of the ice house, and not from just one night either. He had me there several times with dates on each picture. I was concerned since any violation of my parole could land me back in prison for years. On top of that, I could have been sent back to Ohio, separating me from my mom and Wayne. Also included were photos of me and my brother at home. When I got to the last of the pictures, he even had shots of my mother sitting on the porch and workin' in her flowerbed, and that really scared me."

"Why?"

"He was letting me know that they were at risk. He didn't say nothin' outright, but I got the message just the same."

"Why was he picking on you?"

"I didn't ask, but I guessed it was just my turn. He said I wouldn't have to go to jail if I did what I was told. At first, he wanted me to use my van to deliver drugs for him. For years, I'd heard that Buchanan was involved in the drug trade, and this just confirmed it. I found out he started by selling drugs that the police confiscated from dealers on busts. He'd wait till the legal cases were over, and instead of destroying the drugs, he'd sell 'em. It made him a lot of money, and it only got bigger from there. I kept doing my air-conditioning work but spent a lot of my off time making pickups and deliveries around town."

"Are others in the department involved in all of this?"

"It's hard to say. On one hand, it's hard to believe that some of 'em didn't know something was going on, but on the other hand, Buchanan is real good at concealing things and not getting too close to it. But, once he got confident in me, he started sending me on the bigger jobs like picking up drugs coming in from Mexico. Buchanan arranged for ex-cons like me to pick up large bundles about halfway between here and the Mexican border, some marijuana but a lot of cocaine."

"So y'all met up with people coming up from Mexico?"

"Yes, they used smugglers they called *la mulas*."

"Mules?"

"Yeah. They'd get the bundles on this side of the Rio Grande, using cartel-controlled Mexican drivers. They would take it from there to meet guys like me in the middle of nowhere between here and there for the exchange. Guys like me would get it from there to here."

"You said exchange. Did you handle the money for the drugs?"

"Lord, no! We're talking hundreds of thousands and maybe millions of dollars per transaction. That was all handled between Buchanan and the cartels."

"Did you get paid for doing this?"

"He gave us cash for gas and meals and a little extra, but that's it. Depending on how far we traveled, we got a $125 to $175 in cash, in envelopes like these," Flynn said, pulling from his paper sack two crumpled empty envelopes in a clear plastic bag. "Both of these have my first name written on them, likely in his handwriting. You take these, but keep them in the bag, as they may have Buchanan's prints on them too."

"Okay," Mickey agreed, placing the bag into her purse.

"This went on for many months with no major problems, until one day last November when I got word from one of the guys that Buchanan wanted to see me ASAP. I was told to go to that abandoned cotton mill, out on the old highway, and this is when I was scared the most. But I drove my van there, and after I got to the parking lot, I saw headlights coming from a car."

"The Sportiva?" Mickey asked.

"No, not this time. Buchanan was in a police SUV. He pulled up next to me, unlocked the backdoor, and motioned for me to get in the backseat. As I sat down, I wondered if something was wrong, but he actually told me I had done a good job and that he was very happy with me. We drove around some deserted back roads, and he told me he had one last job for me, and then I'd be done. He said he wanted me to pick up a girl for him, and I remember him staring at me in the rearview mirror for a few seconds, trying to see how I reacted."

"How did you react?"

"I didn't, since I had no idea what he meant. He said he didn't have anybody available and said he needed it done 'pronto.' He told me I had to go to a mall and just lure this girl into my van. He explained that this was a young girl with rich parents who had what he called 'family problems'. He said she was out of control he said and needed to be reined in. He made it sound like it was for her own good, and the family needed to be kept out of the news, so there could be no warrants or a public arrest by the police. She was supposedly going to walk to the mall that morning, and I needed to intercept her."

"Was she having trouble, like drugs or something?"

"I didn't know it then, but that was all a lie, and there was no specific girl to be picked up. So he told me to park way out on the mall parking lot over in Delano. He said there would be a small sports car in the area, and I was supposed to park where I could see it but not too close.

"The Sportiva?"

"Yes, and Buchanan was in it. He said the car lights would flash if the rich people's girl showed up, but I know now it was not a particular girl but just one of a certain profile. She had to be young, grown enough to have … you know …"

"Matured?"

"Yes. They also had to be white, thin, pretty, and alone."

"Why didn't Buchanan just do it?" Mickey questioned.

"Unlike me, Buchanan didn't let his fingerprints get on anything. It all went through channels. So I went out there where I was told, and I saw the little blue car. I backed into a parking spot and just waited. Buchanan didn't make a move, and I had almost dozed off when the headlights from his car flashed. I looked up and sure enough, there was a girl walking near my van."

"Taylor Abram?"

"Yes, and she was chasing a couple of bills that had blown from her change purse. So with another flash of the lights, I knew she was the target, and when I nodded, Buchanan hauled ass out of there. So I rolled down the window and called her over and cooked up a story about looking for my lost dog. It took some pleading, but unfortunately she agreed to help and got in the van. I swear I thought that in some way I was helping her," Flynn said as his lip quivered and he turned away.

"Where'd you take her?" Mickey asked

"Buchanan gave me this map," Flynn said, as he handed her a photocopied page from a key map tucked in a plastic sleeve, with the route highlighted in yellow. "He assured me that no one was going to accuse me of nothin' and she would be safely tended to when I got her there. But what took place next wasn't supposed to happen. I left the mall, and she stayed kinda calm at first, but when she saw I wasn't headed in the direction of where my made-up dog was supposed to be, she began to cry out loud and yelling that I was going the wrong way. It was all I could do to focus on driving, and when I stopped at a red light, she tried to open the door. I managed to stop her and keep on her on the seat as I tore through the intersection. She knew she was in trouble, and she began yelling and kicking. I tried to block out her screaming, but I *still* hear it in my head."

"How'd you keep her from getting out of the van?"

"It was tough. I had to drive too fast for her to risk jumping out while holding her with my right hand and driving with the left. When I stopped at the warehouse on the map, she started really kicking and yelling, but two men wearing rubber gloves came running out to help. I didn't recognize the first guy, but the other one I knew from the drug-dealing days. They seemed to know what to do, but she was really pitchin' a fit. When they tried to take her out by her shoulders, her feet were pointed toward me, and that's when she landed a foot to my face and busted my lip. I guess that's when my blood got on the shoe. I grabbed her by her shoes and pushed them around in the direction of the two guys."

"Thus your fingerprint."

"Right, and sometime during all of this, the one shoe came off and ended up under my seat. I knew this was not the way it was supposed to go, but I didn't know what the hell to do about it. The one guy I knew got one of her feet and pulled, but she was now hangin' onto the head rest on her seat with the right hand. Then the other guy got ahold of her other leg and yanked her. She lost her grip and fell to the concrete, hitting head-first on the pavement." Flynn hung his head and ran his fingers through his hair as the waitress refilled Mickey's coffee cup.

"She was knocked out and lay there without moving, and the one guy lifted her up, and blood was getting on everything, including her hair and clothes, and when he threw her over his shoulder, it was dripping down the back of his shirt as he walked away with her. I yelled at the guy I did know and asked where the girl's parents were. He leaned through my window and explained that there were no parents involved and all the girls that had been snatched had all been taken to a man down in Mexico who ran one of the drug cartels."

"For what?" Mickey asked.

"Don't kill the messenger, but they were taken across the border for prostitution."

"Dear God, do you mean Reagan's ..."

"That's very likely. Apparently, these young American white girls are in real demand down there, and Buchanan had added that to his operation last fall."

"Fourteen- and fifteen-year-olds?" Mickey asked tearfully.

"It's sick, isn't it? So, when Taylor died in that warehouse, Buchanan was more than pissed, but luckily he didn't blame me. But, he had to do something, so when the Jackson guy came forward, Buchanan realized they had a scapegoat for everything—yours truly."

"Wait a second. Wouldn't that be too risky for Buchanan? I mean, you knew everything at that point."

"He didn't care. After all, I had no proof of anything, and who was going to believe me anyhow?"

"Plus there was the threat to your mom and brother," Mickey added.

"Now you're getting it, and that's why I was stuck. You see, I was going to jail one way or another. Whether for the kidnapping felony or the parole violations, I couldn't avoid doing time and a lot of it. So I chose the way that would be the least risky."

"Isolation on death row."

"Yes. I was the perfect fall guy. I had a rap sheet, and they had an eyewitness. And when they found the shoe with my blood and fingerprints. They had a golden opportunity to lay all of this mess off on me and take the heat off of Buchanan. But God as my witness, I never had anything to do with those other girls, including your daughter."

"Why didn't you tell me this when I met you in Huntsville?"

"First off, I still had to worry about Mom and Wayne, and secondly I hated your guts!"

Mickey laughed with him, saying, "Well, at least you used past tense."

"Plus, if I had told you any of this in Huntsville, would you have believed a single word of it?"

"Of course not. What were you going to tell me on the phone if you hadn't learned of the court of appeals ruling?"

"I was going to admit to everything and cook up the details. It wouldn't have affected me none, and I hoped it would get you off of my back. But the death of my mom was a big game changer. Buchanan lost some of his leverage, and he knew it, and with that and you snooping around, he began cranking up the heat. That's why we need to act fast."

"What do you propose?"

"Like I said, we're going down to Mexico to try to find those girls."

Mickey shook her head. "I can't do that, Willie."

He leaned toward her and said, "Everything I've told you is the absolute truth, and you know it's the truth, and we're going to do this."

"Why don't *you* go on down there? Why do you need me?"

"Several reasons. My van is broke down and I don't think the LTD will make it down there. Secondly, I think traveling as a couple is safer, and lastly, we're really going to try to get one or more of the girls home."

"What if you're just luring me down there to help you cross the border and you intend to slit my throat the moment we do?"

"What could I possibly say to convince you that I won't?"

Mickey thought for a moment and admitted, "Nothing."

"Right. I truly believe that your daughter and the others are alive, and you're going down there to help."

"What about Wayne? Aren't you worried about him?"

"He'll be fine. In an hour, he'll be on a bus back up to Ohio to stay with our uncle. He has a dairy farm there, and he's going to put Wayne to work on it. Now, I have a question for you. Why did you agree to meet me?"

Mickey blushed. "I went to Buchanan's house."

"You did what?"

"You heard me. I drove to his house, and I peeked in his garage, and it was there."

"The car?"

"Yes, the blue Sportiva with front-end damage and all."

"What if Buchanan would've come home while you were there?" he asked.

Mickey laughed and said, "He did, but he didn't see me."

"Holy shit! You're crazy," Flynn said, shaking his head. "Listen, we need to get on the road. Do you have a passport?"

"Yes, but, Willie, I can't just leave like that," she said, snapping her fingers for emphasis. "I have a job and bills on the kitchen table to pay and I'm—"

"We're talking about your daughter! Go home, pack some things, get your passport, and let's go."

"Speaking of that, how are *you* going to cross? Do you even have a passport?"

"Sure," Flynn said as he tossed his counterfeit version on the table.

Mickey lifted it, opened it, and looked at the photo. "Nice smile. Where'd you get it?"

"I took a tip from Campbell and got it at a flea market," he said, grinning. "Check out the name."

She looked back down, read it, and placed her hand over her mouth as she mumbled, "Cary Grant?"

He laughed and said, "Since we'll be traveling as husband and wife, I just thought, what the hell."

"I guess it's better than Ulysses S.," Mickey joked.

"So are we on?"

Mickey closed her eyes to think and wondered how she could possibly get herself this entangled with Flynn, especially in a foreign country. With every ounce of her training to critically think and assess logically, she pondered and then said, "I'll go. I need an hour to arrange things, and since this place is closing, I'll meet you behind the drugstore down the block."

Mickey drove home to pack some belongings, and in a moment

of optimism, she went to Reagan's room to retrieve a couple of outfits for her. Realizing that if found, Reagan would have grown some, she grabbed the largest sizes she could find. She left an innocuous phone message for Tyler, simply saying she was leaving town for a few days, offering no details. But in case things went badly, she left a lengthy note on her bar, explaining the whole turn of events and the planned rescue mission to Mexico with the most unlikely of cohorts.

CHAPTER 19

⚖

PERICLITATURUS OMNIA

(Risking It All)

September 3

Mickey arrived at the drugstore and found Flynn pacing the alley behind it. As she pulled up, he stomped out a cigarette and looked in all directions before jumping in the passenger seat with paper sack in hand.

"Are you ready?" he asked as he removed a folded laminated state map from his sack.

"I guess, but I can't tell you how nervous I am," Mickey said with the downtown area of Brinkman in her rearview mirror.

When they had reached the main highway, her phone rang, causing them both to jump. She saw it was Tyler calling and urged Flynn to remain quiet before answering via Bluetooth.

"I got your message. So where are you heading, Mick?" Tyler asked with enthusiasm.

"I'm on my way down to Mexico."

"Mexico? Oh, Mickey, that's great! Where to? Cancun? Cozumel?"

She glanced to Flynn, smiling. "Yeah, something like that."

"When will you be back?"

"In a few days. I just, uh ... need some time to, you know—unwind."

"Long overdue, dear. Enjoy it!"

"Thanks, Tyler. I'll be in touch," she said as she ended the call. Flynn was studying a Texas road map as she turned south out of Brinkman.

"Getting it figured out?" Mickey asked.

"I think. The fella at the warehouse said the mules alternated between a couple of border entry points, and they're near each other and close to where we need to go. They told me names, but stupid me didn't write them down."

"We're on the right highway, right?"

"Yes, at least for now. This is the route I used to take down there, but it's the mid-point and beyond that's tricky. I know we need to cross near an area called near Piedras Negras, around a town called Fuentes. I just have to find that on the map and figure the best way down there and across."

"Does that map show portions of land across the border?"

"Yes, the first few miles, and that's all we should need. This operation's supposed to be very close to the border. I think I'm gettin' ... wait, here it is."

"What?" Mickey asked glancing to Flynn.

"I found Piedras Negras. Let's see ... you stay on 163 until we're through Ozona, and that will get us to close to the border. Then we'll go southeast along the border and pick a crossing. Traveling through the night, we should be in Mexico by sunup," Flynn advised, returning the map in her glove compartment.

"Man, there's nothing out here," Mickey observed, looking at the pitch blackness on all sides.

"It's not a place where you want to break down. That's for sure."

"Oh God, don't even mention that," Mickey chastised.

"How are you on gas?"

"Still more than half a tank, but I need to pull in here for a potty break," she said, turning into a truck stop to use the bathroom, get coffee, and top off the tank.

Flynn drove the next leg as Mickey dozed, and then four hours later, they stopped again to switch off. Mickey resumed the wheel four and a half hours into the trip. She was cruising along fighting fatigue when flashing lights of a patrol car penetrated the darkness. The lights moved up from behind her, and she slowed and eased her car over on the shoulder. Gripping the wheel tightly, she braked to a stop. She had been traveling slightly over eighty miles per hour, and she prayed that the officer had only speeding, and not their connections to Brinkman in mind.

"We've got company," she said, stirring Flynn, who sat up, rubbed his eyes, and saw the approaching blue and red lights in his side mirror. The squad car stopped a short distance behind Mickey's car, and the siren fell to silence. Through her mirror, Mickey saw a uniformed man get out of his car and position his spotlight squarely on Mickey's side-view mirror, throwing a blinding glare in her eyes. She could tell by the silhouette he was a large man and he approached with one hand on a holstered gun and the other with a flashlight as he walked cautiously toward them. Standing closer to the rear driver's side door, the man reached forward and rapped on Mickey's window with the flashlight. Mickey turned to him, and he motioned for her to lower her window. She complied, and though it was in the dead of night, the arid air rushed in and she was relieved to see that the uniform belonged to a Texas state trooper.

After scanning the car's interior with the flashlight, the trooper asked, "Where y'all headed?"

"Uh … El Paso," Mickey said, blurting out the first Texas border town she could conjure.

"What for?"

Mickey stared up to him. "We're going to visit relatives, sir."

The officer nodded and asked for her driver's license and proof of insurance, which Mickey had on hand. "You were going a little fast back there," the officer charged while reviewing her information. "I clocked you going over eighty. I know people think that they're out in the middle of the nowhere here, but it's dark, and there's still a speed limit."

"Yes, sir." Mickey said.

"You're also in open-range territory."

"Open range?" Mickey asked.

"Yeah. No fences are required out here, so livestock can cross the road. If you hit a cow, not only will it ruin your car and risk your life, but you also owe the rancher for the cow."

"Ouch! Point taken," she said as the trooper returned to his car to run a check.

"El Paso?" Flynn questioned.

"I couldn't think of anything else! Are we not going in that direction?"

Flynn shook his head. "No, not even close."

"So just where are we crossing?"

"Near Eagle Pass," Flynn explained.

"That's the first I've heard of that, Mr. Navigator!" she accused.

Only four or five minutes elapsed before the officer returned. Mickey took a deep breath, rolled the window down, and accepted her license and insurance card. "You do know that this isn't a highway to El Paso, right?"

She leaned toward Flynn's seat and backhanded him across his chest, saying, "Damn it! I told you we were on the wrong road." She turned back to the officer, shaking her head. "And they say wives can't read road maps! Sir, since he apparently can't navigate, can you tell us how to get to the right road?"

The officer nodded and gave them directions, then added, "I've issued you a citation for the speeding, ma'am."

Flynn broke his silence. "And they say husbands have the lead foot!"

The trooper smiled as he handed Mickey the clipboard with the citation. She signed it, took her copy, and the officer wished them a safe trip before returning to his car. Mickey waited for the officer to pull around her and enter the highway and only relaxed after seeing the trooper cross the median and head back north.

"You want me to take another shift?" Flynn offered.

"Yes, but I saw a sign back there saying Juno is only thirty-three miles. I'll stop there for another break."

At the truck stop, they bought more coffee and some donuts and filled the gas tank, and Flynn drove the next shift.

"Mind if I smoke?" Flynn asked from behind the wheel.

"No, as long as I get one."

"So you smoke?"

"Not really. I only smoke when I'm stressed."

He stared over at Mickey and said, "Hell, you should be a two-handed chain smoker."

Flynn drove the next three and a half hours while Mickey slept, until they drew close to the Mexican border. She stirred, yawned, sat up, and opened her eyes noticing a slight orange glow on the horizon to her left. "Where are we?"

"Close to Eagle Pass, and I believe I know a way across at Adwano. I think that'll be safer than a larger international bridge."

"So how in the world are we going to find Reagan in the middle of all this?" Mickey asked, looking at the vast dry wasteland around them.

"I'll tell you about my homework," Flynn responded. "You see, when my mom died and I was out of jail, I started thinking about what I could do to help with the missing girls. I needed information and had the idea that I could find it from my old friend from the warehouse in what we call crack alley."

"Crack alley? In Brinkman?" Mickey asked.

"Yeah, it's near the old Palace Theater, in the park across the street."

"I know where you're talking about. The city swimming pool was there, and it was a nice park."

"Not anymore. Now it's a home for bums and addicts, and since this guy was always looking for crack, I figured I might find him there. It took three trips, but sure enough I ran into him, and when he saw me, he was scared shitless. He was sure Buchanan was going to get back at him for Taylor Abram's death and the stupid way he and the other guy handled her body. So the last thing he wanted to see was a face from Buchanan's operation. He tried to walk away, but I stopped him. Crack addicts are naturally edgy, but he was really spooked. Hell, I even bought him a ten-dollar rock as a sign of good faith."

"You bought him some crack?"

Flynn chuckled. "Yeah, and *man*, I now had a friend for life, and he was more than happy to talk. He told me a man named Carlos Galleon used to call the warehouse and discuss the drug deals and what he called *putas*, which is Spanish for whores."

"Can you use prostitutes?" Mickey requested.

Flynn nodded. "Back when I worked on that Mexican landscape crew, I learned quite a bit of Spanish, starting with all the cuss words of course. I knew that this guy spoke Spanish well, and had been going to down there for years, and talked to the mules a lot more than I did. Turns out that Galleon is a big-time drug lord that runs a big operation down there. Hell, one mula even offered for my friend to go down there."

"To the brothel?" Mickey asked.

"Yeah, and that's when they discussed Piedras Negras."

"Did he go to the brothel?"

"He really wanted to, but he had warrants and was worried about getting' arrested at the border. But he told me a little about where to find the place. He also confirmed that Buchanan had shut down his operation at the warehouse, but he was real close to cranking it back up, until I got the new trial. But, I needed to know more, so I went to the warehouse, and when I got there, everything and everyone was long gone. The place was locked up tight as a drum, so I broke the padlock. When I got inside, it was mostly cleaned out—except an old rolodex in one of the desk drawers. I looked at the G cards and didn't see Galleon, so I just flipped through it from the beginning and finally found it under C, for Carlos." Flynn reached in his pocket and pulled out the rolodex card in a plastic sleeve. It had a handwritten name, address, and phone number. "This too is probably Buchanan's writing, so I also want you to keep it. Also, know that the full rolodex is at my house, and it could be helpful."

"Buying crack. Breaking into buildings. Why take all of this risk?" Mickey probed.

"I owed it to all those parents and to my mom's memory to do something."

"You really did love her, didn't you?"

"Yes. My mom did the best she could with me, and she made me know right from wrong. I truly did understand it, but I always picked wrong, and it hurt her a lot. But she never gave up on me, even during all of this mess, and I wanted to do something right. You know—something good."

"How are you going to get along in Mexico?"

"You mean money-wise?" Mickey nodded. "My mom left us some money, and she actually had a decent life-insurance policy from her job, and when it's funded my half will be wired to a bank down there. I have a friend who lives just over the border in Acuna, and it's actually not too far from where we're going. I'm going to stay with him and his wife for a while. He set up the account for me down there, and I'll have plenty to live on until it's safe to go back to Brinkman."

"What do you mean by 'safe'?"

"When that scumbag Buchanan's behind bars, and that's where

you come in. Whatever happens here, you got to get in touch with the authorities and give them all of the stuff I've given you."

Mickey nodded. "What about your medical care?"

"My friend found me an osteopath who can treat the ALS. I'm told the cost of medical care is reasonable there, and this doc's supposed to know what he's doing."

"You're dying, aren't you?"

"Aren't we all?" he said, pulling the car to the side of the road. "Look—we're getting close to the border crossing. I think it's best if you get us across, and once we're there, I'll tell you where to go."

"Do you think you're flea-market credentials will hold up?" she asked.

"It should. Word is that they really don't care too much down here, and the more remote the crossing the less they care, and this one's very remote. And besides, the flea-market vendor said if it didn't work, I'd get my $16.95 back."

"Oh, that makes me feel better."

The rising sun was now casting a larger, diffuse orange glow to the east as they switched seats. Soon they reached the crossing and filed into a short line with six cars ahead of them. They inched along, and when they reached the checkpoint, Mickey rolled down her window, and the uniformed official asked for their papers while another officer led a drug-sniffing dog around her car. Mickey handed the two passports to the man. The man studied them and then looked inside the car and back at the two of them. Mickey was relieved when he handed the passports back to her and motioned for them to proceed across a narrow bridge over the Rio Grande River and into Old Mexico. Flynn knew the town of Fuentes would be only a few miles inside the border and watched the road signs closely.

"Are we near it?" Mickey asked.

"Yeah, we are, but pull over for a second. I'm not sure which way to turn off of this main road. We're supposed to take this one," he said, pointing to a white sign with a shield outlined in black with "Mexico" written at the top and "183" below it. "I just don't know if we go left or right. It makes sense to go south, but I'm just not sure." Glancing right and left, Mickey saw nothing but abject poverty, and while she desperately hoped Flynn was right about the missing girls, she shivered to imagine what Reagan and the others would have endured while there. "I'd better make a call before we go any farther, and here's a phone booth over there," Flynn said, pointing. Mickey pulled her car into the parking lot of an old strip center, and Flynn asked for the rolodex page back.

Mickey handed him the plastic sleeve from her purse to him and offered, "Hey, you can use my cell phone if you want."

"Thanks, but check it. It won't work down here," Flynn replied, and Mickey saw the screen of her phone was blank. "How are you going to use the pay phone?"

"I got some pesos from the bank," he said as he walked to the booth, inserted the coins, and turned the dial on the old rotary phone. Mickey rolled her window down and heard Flynn speaking Spanish and nodding his head. "Gracias. Voy a sen pronto," Flynn said, hanging up and walking back to the car.

"I called the number, and it's Carlos's place all right," Flynn confirmed, handing the rolodex card back to her. "I explained to this raspy-voiced lady that I wanted a whor—uh prostitute, but Carlos must own two places, because I believe she was trying to ask me which location. I think she was saying they were near each other and tried to give directions. I'm not positive about what she was saying, except we *do* have to go south on 183."

He got back into the car, and as Mickey turned south on the highway, she said, "Let's say we find this place. How are we going to know which one to go to?"

"We'll pick one and check it out."

"All right. Then how do we know if Reagan or any of the others are there?"

"I'm not exactly sure."

"And if she or any of the others are there, then what?"

"Look—don't take this the wrong way, but there's no way to plan all this out."

"Fine, but if this goes wrong, we can get killed!" Mickey said anxiously.

"Yes. We could die down here. Jesus, do you wanna head back?"

"No, of course not, but I just thought this would be—you know—a little more planned out. That's all."

"I'm sorry, but I'm an ex-con, not a commando!"

Highway 183 narrowed to a poorly maintained dirt road barely wide enough for two cars to pass each other. Though she drove slowly, they suffered the jolts and jars of the bumps from pot holes and soon found themselves approaching a collection of small, dilapidated, one- and two-story buildings.

"Slow down. I think this is one of them," Flynn said, and Mickey took her foot off the pedal and coasted to a stop.

Mickey was repulsed by the sight. "People come here for a 'good time'?"

"It ain't Vegas, is it? But as long as you pay and don't cause trouble, it's a safe and cheap place to … you know …"

"Lovely."

"Do you have a picture of Reagan with you?" Flynn asked.

Mickey nodded gave him a couple of school photos from her wallet. He studied each, then put one in his pocket and returned the other.

"Are you ready for this?"

"Yes," she said firmly, then guided her car to the back of one of the buildings.

"This is a good spot," Flynn said. "Now I'm going to poke around and see if I can get some information. Stay behind the wheel, leave the car running, and be ready for anything."

"Be careful—and good luck," Mickey said.

Sitting in the car for hours had stiffened Flynn's bad legs, and Mickey watched nervously as Flynn struggled to walk. As he rounded the building toward the common area where the fronts of all the buildings faced, Mickey recited the rosary to pass the time and lit another of Flynn's cigarettes to ease her nerves.

Studying each of the crudely constructed, wooden structures, Flynn spied two Mexican women standing in a doorway of one of the two-story buildings with a blue sign above the covered porch. He noticed by their attire that they were on duty and walked toward them saying, "Buenos dias. Yo necesito info … inform," he stammered.

"Informacion?" one said.

"Si, informacion," he responded as each noticed the picture in hand. "Solve esta chica," he asked, displaying Reagan's photograph.

The one woman that appeared much younger than the other, seemed disinterested. The older glanced at the photo and back to him, then said, "Por que busca la chica?"

Flynn did not fully understand the question but responded, "La chica es aqui, no?"

The younger woman gave him a suspicious stare and walked inside while the other stared skeptically, but Flynn pulled a twenty-dollar bill from his wallet and handed it and the photo to her.

She looked at Flynn and said, "diez mas."

Flynn nodded, and handed her a ten. She stepped off the porch into the light and took a closer look at the photo. The woman was shapely, but had a large nose, sunbaked brown skin, and deep inset lines on her forehead and cheeks and around her mouth and eyes. She looked at Flynn and handed the photo back to him.

"Very pretty," she said.

"Oh, you speak English."

She nodded. "Your daughter?"

"No, but do you know her?" Flynn asked, as the woman moved back into the shade of the porch, and darted her eyes nervously in all directions. "Please help me."

She whispered, "You no hear from me, but I seen her working at Carlos's," the woman said, providing a discrete nod in the direction of one of the larger one-story buildings. It was a wooden structure with peeling white paint situated about fifty yards away. Flynn thanked her, and as he turned toward that direction, she warned, "Listen, amigo, Carlos ain't someone to mess with, *comprende*?"

Flynn nodded, and turned to walk toward the white building, and as he neared, he paused and looked at the open double doors of the front entry. He then scanned the area again, and seeing no one stirring, he opted to ease around the side of the building to assess doors, windows, and other potential means of escape. The serenity of the morning seemed the best opportunity for action, so Flynn returned to the front of the building and entered.

He walked into an area that he assumed served as a waiting room for the brothel. The floors were made of wood-slat boards that bowed slightly under each step he took, and the boards were spaced enough to see beyond each down to the dark crawl space below. The walls and ceiling were likewise constructed of wood slats, and in the rear of the room sat a long wooden counter lit only by a small, low-watt light bulb set in a cheap, plastic lamp with no shade. Though dim, Flynn could nevertheless see the dust and dirt in the room, which had an underlying stench that competed with the smell of patchouli oil and burning incense. He stood waiting for someone to appear, and after a couple of minutes, he walked to the wooden counter and cleared his throat loudly. Behind the counter, an older Mexican woman emerged from a back room by pushing aside a green terry-cloth towel hanging in the doorway. She was a large woman and wore a loose-fitting, floor-length, dark blue dress printed with large, bright yellow sunflowers.

"Hola, amigo, que quiere?"

"Quiero una chica … pero anglo solo."

Frowning, she stared at him for a few seconds. "Why white puta? You prejudice?"

"No, but … I like what I like … that's all."

Shrugging her shoulders, she reached for a clipboard hanging on a nail in the wall and held it under the lamp light. She was squinting at a sheet of paper baring a list of names, and the same light revealed the woman's thick makeup on her puffy face. Her skin was oily and featured thick, black painted-on lines serving as eyebrows.

"It cost more, you know"

"Fine, but I want to see her first," Flynn said as the irritated madam disappeared beyond the towel. Moments later, she emerged from the back with a girl, looking as if she just awoke, who followed the madam to the space behind the counter. She seemed groggy, and her hair was messy and matted, and the madam was applying bright red lipstick to her lips. Though Caucasian, she was clearly not Reagan, but on cue, the girl forced a smile, winked at Flynn, and awkwardly licked her freshly tented lips. Flynn informed the madam that she was not the type he wanted, which aggravated her further. "Senor, it's the morning. I have only one other, so don't be—how do you say?—so picky!"

Flynn nodded, as the madam and the girl disappeared into the back room. The madam was gone longer this time, and Flynn started to get anxious. Then the towel moved aside, and the madam reemerged, but no one followed. She turned, reached back around the towel, and pulled a reluctant girl by the arm to the threshold of the doorway. Patently shy, the girl stared at the floor, and the madam prodded her to raise her head and move out of the darkness. When the girl was moved nearer to the lamp, Flynn, knowing Reagan was a brunette, was disappointed to see this girl had long blonde hair that was parted down the middle. But when the madam shoved her closer to the light, Flynn could see dark strands near the part of her hair.

"Look up," the madam commanded, but the girl shook her head and maintained her gaze at the floor. The madam stood in front of her, grabbed her chin, and pushed the girl's face upward.

"She will do," Flynn said.

"Good, that will be fifty dollars," the madam explained. "Plus three for the room."

Flynn threw three twenties on the counter and the madam walked to a cabinet and put the three bills in a metal lockbox. As she started to count the change, Flynn told her to keep it. "Gracias, mucho big spender," she said disingenuously and plunged the five and two ones into her oversized orange bra.

"De nada."

"Muy de nada!" the woman said, smirking. "Follow me," she said escorting the two through a door on the right-hand side of the waiting area and into a hallway. Flynn noticed doors on each side of the hall and a set of shelves for bed linens on the left. The hall reached about thirty feet and turned sharply to the left, which he knew would take it in the direction of the rear of the building. "You have thirty minutes, macho gringo," the woman said, opening one of the doors on the right side of the hall. The madam followed the two in, made sure the bed had a sheet, and walked out and turned left back toward the waiting area.

Flynn closed the door, and the girl walked to the low, single-mattress bed. She sat stiffly on the side, with head down, anticipating his next move. Flynn knelt in front of her, and she cringed slightly, and her eyes closed tightly as he touched her face. Tilting her head up, he looked at her and whispered softly, "Reagan?" Her eyes flew open. "Listen to me carefully and don't make any noise. I'm here to help you. Your mother, Michelle Grant, is outside. We're going to get you home. Understand?"

She nodded but still looked distrustful. Flynn pulled out her school photo from his pocket, handed it to her, and she collapsed into his arms, crying. "Shhh," he pleaded while wiping her tears.

"What're we going to do?" she whimpered.

"We've got to get out of here, very quietly, but you're going to have to help me understand this place."

"I'll try," she said.

The room offered only a small rectangular window to the outside, which was closer to the ceiling than the floor. Flynn doubted Reagan, much less himself, could squeeze through. Nonetheless, he reached high and tried to open it and realized it was nailed shut. "Reagan, is there door at the end of this hall that exits outside?"

"I think so."

"Okay. Do you know if it can be opened from the inside?"

Tears welled in her eyes. "Maybe, but … I just don't know."

"That's all right. Don't worry. Listen, I saw that there are several doors in the hall. Do you think any of those lead outside, or are they all rooms like this?"

"I think they're mostly like this."

"Okay. We'll figure this out." Flynn felt that the rear of the building offered the most advantageous means of escape, but getting from their room to the correct door without detection was the key. "Stay here, okay? I'm gonna check things out."

Flynn opened the door to their room, looked each way, and eased left down the hallway's creaking floors to the door leading back to the waiting area. He cracked the ajar door about an inch and could see the counter and the flabby upper arm of the madam folding sheets. With her there, he thought that presented an opportunity to get out at the end of the hallway. He eased back to their room, opened the door, and motioned for Reagan to follow. Without hesitation, she rose and took Flynn's hand, following him slowly out of the room and to their right and quietly down the hall. The sharp left turn revealed a hall of more closed doors on each side and one at the end, and hoped that the latter led to the outside, but nothing designated it as an exit. He decided to take a chance on the door, but froze, when he footsteps from back down the hallway. Flynn instinctively shoved Reagan toward the end of the hall and began walking in the direction of the steps. Rounding the corner, he nearly collided with the madam, who held a stack of the folded sheets in her arms.

She jumped back. "What are you doing?"

"Yeah, uh … I was trying to find you. Look—I need a condom. I just figured you'd have them in the room," he stammered, watching her face for a reaction.

"They're in the top drawer of nightstand, amigo. Are you a virgin or somethin'?" She rolled her eyes and roared with laughter while placing the sheets on the hallway shelf.

Flynn grinned sheepishly at her and began to walk back toward the room. But when he glanced back and realized the madam was not returning to the lobby, but rather was walking farther down the hall toward Reagan, he pursued. He grabbed her arm, blurting, "I forgot! I did check the drawer and didn't see any."

"I'll bring you one in a minute! This is coming off your time, you know!" she said, jerking her arm free and continuing toward the bend of the hall. Flynn followed stealthily, preparing to seize her if necessary, but when they rounded the corner, there was no Reagan. Flynn watched as the madam entered the last room on the left and the door closed behind her.

Flynn stood befuddled—until a door to his right eased open, and Reagan peeked out. She had overheard Flynn's encounter with the madam and took refuge in a room, which fortunately was not occupied. With the madam for the moment beyond the two of them, Flynn reassessed his strategy, opting for an escape through the front. He grabbed Reagan's arm and walked as quickly as he could, without elevating the sound of the squeaking floorboards. They neared the door to the waiting area and Flynn signaled Reagan to wait in the hall as he moved cautiously into the lobby. Seeing no one, inside or out, he motioned for Reagan to follow, but she moved tentatively and then froze. Flynn signaled furiously with his hand for her to hurry, but she still stood as if her feet were bolted to the lobby floorboards.

He walked to her, took her arm and led her toward the door, "Reagan, we need to go now. I can't run fast, but I'll do my best to keep up. If you can get ahead of me, don't look back and go behind that building with the blue sign," he instructed, pointing in the direction of Mickey's car. "Your mom's behind there, so *please*, let's go!" Reagan complied, and Flynn pulled her out the front door, across the porch, and down to the dirt and as they started to run, a primal scream emerged from behind them. Flynn kept going, but Reagan instinctively hesitated, and the angry madam was barreling toward Reagan and proved much faster than Flynn would have imagined. The madam grabbed Reagan by her shirt, and her momentum sent both of them tumbling to the dirt. The madam quickly wrapped her arms around Reagan's lower body, and began screaming for help as Reagan commenced flailing her legs.

Flynn ran back to the two and repeatedly and painfully kicked the madam's arms until she wailed in pain and released the frightened Reagan. With the madam writhing in the dirt, Reagan jumped to her feet and ran with Flynn toward Mickey. They were about thirty yards from Mickey's car when someone yelled in an angry male voice, "Alto … Alto, ahorita!" Adrenalin and fear spurred Flynn into a labored trot, but Reagan quickly got ahead of him. More angry voices emerged from behind as Flynn yelled, "Don't look back, Reagan. Just keep goin' to your mom!"

The yelling voices from behind increased in number and volume, as Flynn limped toward the building. To Mickey's astonishment, she saw Reagan rounding the back corner of the building, and threw it in drive and accelerated toward her. She unlocked all the doors and slammed on the brakes stopping dangerously close to Reagan, who jumped from the billowing dust into the passenger seat. Mickey spotted Flynn—and five irate men in aggressive pursuit, one of which was loading a pistol as he ran.

"Go!" Flynn yelled to Mickey as he motioned her toward the highway.

"Mom, we gotta save him!" Reagan demanded. Mickey again floored it and then turned the wheel sharply while hitting her brakes. The car spun around in a way that allowed Flynn to jerk the rear car door open and dive into the backseat. She stomped the gas pedal, and her spinning tires spit a cloud of gravel and dirt toward the approaching men. Then the tires gripped the packed dirt on the road surface, and the car roared away. Then a shot rang out, followed by another, and then a third.

"Ignore it, Michelle—and, Reagan, you get on the floor!" Flynn yelled from the back as another shot rang out. Mickey had to slow some to navigate the road and avoid the potholes, as Flynn turned to see puffs of dirt now pluming in the air behind them and knew the chase was on. Flynn sensed that the only way to evade the pursuit was to beat them to the main road to the international bridge and urged, "Keep your speed up! They're after us!"

"I'm trying, but this road is just awful!" she said giving it more gas.

"I know," Flynn said. "We can't risk breaking down here, but you're at a good speed now."

Mickey trained her eyes on the road ahead, not daring to look in her rearview mirror. Soon she was at the part of the road that was wider but still laden with potholes, dirt, and gravel. She took a sharp curve fast, fishtailed, and accelerated again as the car straightened out, but the bumps and jars were intense, and she desperately wanted an end to this godforsaken road.

"You're doin' fine. Just don't miss the right turn that'll take us toward the border," Flynn urged.

"I see it up ahead," Mickey said, and when she turned onto the firmer and smoother pavement of that road, Flynn could no longer see the dust up from behind.

"I think they've given up," Flynn said.

"Are you sure?" Mickey asked, staring back at him in the rearview mirror.

"Yes," Flynn replied as he massaged his aching legs and hips. "This road's too risky for 'em."

"Thank God! But I'm not taking it for granted," Mickey said, continuing to push her car to the limit.

"Really, I think you can slow down now, before you have a wreck," Flynn advised. Reagan got up in her seat, buckled her seatbelt, and laid her head on her mom's lap and sobbed. Mickey checked her speed and stroked her daughter's head, and when they spotted houses and businesses, they knew they were a couple of miles from the border crossing. Flynn asked her to pull into a public parking lot near a phone booth.

"Are you sure it's safe to stop here?" Mickey asked.

"Yes, but I'll keep an eye on the road and you keep the car running, while I make a call." She nodded as he exited and pulled more pesos from his pocket. Leaning against the phone booth, he looked in all directions before inserting some coins and dialing. Mickey and Reagan embraced and cried, and both seemed determined to hold on forever. Mickey then took her by the shoulders and stared at her face noticing a couple of lines around her eyes and that her teeth were yellowed. She only reacted by smiling and kissing her forehead and embraced her again. She knew she was not holding the same innocent girl that disappeared on that fateful December day, but neither said a word as they just rocked back and forth, sobbing softly.

Mickey asked with a tearful chuckle, "What did they do to your hair?"

"Oh, Mom, it's what they wanted me to—"

"Don't worry, honey. We'll fix that first thing," Mickey said.

Then Reagan sniffed twice. "Have you been smoking?" Mickey nodded sheepishly. "Mom!"

They both laughed tearfully and hugged. "I'm so glad to have you back to nag me. I promise that I'm done with them forever!"

Flynn hung up the phone and pulled a piece of paper from his pocket. Wanting to give them space for their reunion, he stayed by the phone booth and made glances down the highway while drawing on the blank sheet. Reagan got out of the car and, without saying a word, walked toward Flynn. He had not noticed her approaching and jumped when Reagan wrapped her arms around his waist and put the side of her head on his chest. In a soulful voice, she said, "I don't know who you are, but you saved my life. I couldn't have stayed there any longer, I just couldn't … Thank you." Speechless, Flynn apprehensively placed one hand on her shoulder and patted it in an awkward effort to acknowledge her. Wiping her tears, Reagan walked back to the car.

Flynn wandered to the driver's side window, saying, "Well, I guess this is where we part company—at least for now."

"Did you reach your friend?" Mickey asked.

"Yeah, I did."

"Want us to drive you to Acuna?"

"No, they're gonna come get me. You need to get Reagan on back to Texas."

"Do you think they'll ask for an ID for Regan?"

"They might, but you're a citizen, and she's your daughter. The main thing is to get to the highest level of US authority you can find when you get to the checkpoint and explain everything." Mickey nodded. "Hopefully they'll get you to the FBI. There may be enough for them to nail Buchanan, and hopefully they can get a plan for finding the other girls."

"Did you see any others?"

"There was one, but I don't know if she's one of the girls from Texas or if she was even there against her will. When you contact them, you must tell them all the details about the operations down here," Flynn said, handing her the sheet of paper. "Show this to them too. It's a rough map showing our entry point and where we went to get Reagan. Let them know Galleon likely has more than one location in the area," he instructed, and Mickey nodded. "Do all of this from a distance. As long as Buchanan's walking the streets, you ain't safe anywhere near Brinkman."

"I can do this."

"I know you can! Would you hand me my bag?" Mickey reached in the back and hauled out his paper sack and handed it to him. Flynn's expression turned serious as he leaned into the window, and whispered, "I ain't made much of my life, but I hope this gives you two a chance for a great one."

"You've changed our lives forever, Willie 'Cary Grant' Flynn, and we'll always be indebted to you for as long as we live. You're a remarkable man, and I can only imagine what you could have become if you just had a better chance in life."

He smiled as Mickey grasped his hand and squeezed it hard. Then, trying for confidence, she said, "I'll polish off Buchanan, and I won't rest until we get every one of those girls back."

"I know you will. After all, you are *very* persistent."

Mickey smiled, checked her side mirror, and pulled onto the road toward the border.

CHAPTER 20

⚖

UNITAS STAMUS

(United We Stand)

When Mickey and Reagan reached the check point and US officials approached, she provided her passport. Once cleared for entry back across the border, Mickey asked to speak with someone in charge. She was questioned briefly, and when border officers learned of the general nature of their circumstances, both Mickey and Reagan were taken to a nearby corrugated metal building. Mickey relayed to the chief customs agent details of their situation, and they were asked to follow a marked Homeland Security van to a building located a few miles inside the Texas border. Once there, they were taken to an office where they waited until agents from the FBI arrived from San Angelo.

Mickey and Reagan were debriefed at length and chronicled the whole depth and breadth of corruption tied to Brinkman. It was during those hours, she learned that the FBI had been investigating Buchanan for months. The agents pledged to use the information they provided to build the case against the chief and to expedite efforts to rescue the other girls and reunite them with their families. They then recommended that they each return with them to a San Angelo hotel, explaining that it would be safer there, and they could arrange to get medical care for Reagan. Mickey welcomed the chance to have Reagan assessed—physically and psychologically. Special Agent Garrett Nixon was assigned to drive them to San Angelo, as a field agent followed in her Mickey's car. While driving to a hotel that would be their home for the time being, Reagan repeatedly asked Mickey when she could talk to her dad. Seeing she had a weak but serviceable phone signal, Mickey asked Nixon, "Can I make phone calls?"

"To whom?" he asked as he glanced at her in the rearview mirror.

"First and foremost to her father."

"Sure, but we're getting close to San Angelo, so why don't you wait until we get to the hotel. When you do call, please don't discuss your daughter, Buchanan, or the investigation."

Reagan whimpered, and Mickey implored him, "But telling him about our daughter is the primary reason we want to call. He needs to know that she's alive and with me."

"I certainly understand, but it's just not safe, and his phone may well be tapped."

"I'll call his cell phone."

"That's better, but I don't fully trust that either," Nixon said.

"Why?"

"Your cell transmission can be intercepted," he said staring back to the two in the rearview mirror. But sensing the disappointment and being sympathetic to their circumstances, he offered, "Listen—y'all can call him on my phone. It's very protected," he said handing it to Mickey.

Mickey dialed, and when he answered, she said, "Tyler, it's me."

"Hey, Mick, I didn't recognize the number. How's Mexico?"

"Tyler, I'm headed to San Angelo, and this is an FBI agent's phone."

"Have you been arrested?"

"No, nothing like that. In fact—"

"Are you okay?"

"Yes, we're just fine!"

"We're fine? You and who?"

"Tyler, someone wants to say something to you," Mickey said, handing off to Reagan.

"Daddy! It's me!" Reagan cried, her voice trembling.

"Who is this?"

"Me, Daddy. Reagan!"

"Reagan … I don't understand …"

"Daddy, it's *really* me!"

"Reagan … darling, it is you! Oh thank God in heaven! But how?"

"Mommy and this man rescued me from Mexico."

"Mexico?"

"Yes, Dad … it was awful there," Reagan said as her hand began trembling, and she broke down in tears.

Mickey took the phone. "Oh, Tyler, do we have a lot to tell you!"

"Is it really her?"

"Yes Tyler, it is."

"Is she okay?"

"I think so. She's been through a lot, so only time will tell," Mickey whispered, with her hand cupped over the phone. "But we have her back, and that's the main thing!" They talked for a half hour as they drove, and Tyler ended the call by pledging to pack his things and leave right away for San Angelo.

They checked into the hotel and the next morning, Mickey heard a knock at the door, and peeking out of the window, she saw Nixon with another man and a woman. She opened the door, and the agent asked her to step outside.

"Ms. Grant, this is Nina Arthur, an FBI psychiatrist. She's very good with children and young adults, and we thought Reagan could benefit from talking to her."

Mickey smiled and shook her hand. "I think that's a great idea."

"How's she doing?" the psychiatrist asked.

"As well as can be expected, I guess. She's spontaneously cried a couple of times and woke up in the night with a yelp of sorts, but then she dozed back off. Her dad will be here soon, and I'm sure that will help a lot."

"That's good. When will he be here?"

"Weather permitting, late afternoon."

"Have you noticed any physical changes?"

"Her teeth have yellowed and there's some rash on her arms, but that's about it," Mickey said.

"I want to try to size up her mental state, but with your permission I'd like to do a cursory physical exam."

"Nothing intrusive?" Mickey asked.

"No."

"I think that would be helpful. Thank you."

Nixon turned to the tall, distinguished man in a black suit. "And I want you to meet Henry Stone, head of the Southwest Region for the bureau. He's been spearheading the Buchanan investigation since its inception."

"It's nice to meet you, sir," Mickey said, shaking his hand.

"The pleasure's mine, Ms. Grant. We were wondering if Garrett and I could meet with you while Ms. Arthur talks to Reagan."

"Sure. Let me introduce her to Reagan and make sure she's up for it."

Mickey walked back in the room and posed the question. Reagan agreed to talk to the doctor, and they stayed in the hotel room while the two men escorted Mickey to the main part of the hotel. Nixon opened the door to a hotel conference room, and Mickey saw a large computer server on the floor, multiple computers atop the conference room table, and a host of electronic communications equipment. "For now, this is the base of our operations," Stone explained. "The State Department's dealing with the Mexican government about the other girls, and we're here to augment that, while developing evidence on Buchanan. We already know that some of them girls are alive down there."

"That's fantastic! But how were y'all able to learn that so quickly?"

"We can't discuss details, but suffice it to say the CIA has resources down there. But it's a sticky diplomatic mess, as you might expect. This is delicate, and none of this can get public, or it all may crater."

"I understand. I sure hope y'all can do something for the families and nail the chief."

"We truly believe we can do both. As you know, we've been on this Buchanan thing for a while. He's eely, and we just haven't been able to make much stick. But with testimony from you, help from Mr. Flynn, and the other physical evidence, we're optimistic."

"So you all have reached out to Flynn?"

"Yes, and we think he'll be helpful, and we have an outside chance of getting a federal indictment on Buchanan."

"Only an outside chance?" she asked.

"It takes a lot of evidence, and he's been very shrewd in separating himself from direct involvement," Nixon informed.

"When the time comes, you are willing to testify before the grand jury, right?" Stone asked.

"Absolutely!" Mickey pledged without hesitation.

"Good. I know that you'd like to go home, but until we get this done, you're safer down here."

Mickey nodded and said, "Whatever it takes, guys."

They spent another half hour with Mickey fleshing out the details of her experience in Brinkman and the rescue in Mexico and her explanations for the evidence given to her by Flynn. "Thank you for all you've done," Stone said when they concluded, and Mickey nodded. "I need to speak with Garrett, so would you mind showing yourself back to the room?"

"Not at all. Let me know if you need anything else" Mickey said as she left the conference room and headed her room to check on Reagan.

"Garrett, did you hear her say that her husband's coming here from Brinkman?" Stone asked.

"Yes. I should have anticipated that," he admitted.

"Shouldn't be a big deal, but to be on the safe side, let's add another detail to patrol this area."

As Mickey returned to her room, she saw Dr. Arthur and Reagan sitting at the small table in the hotel room, talking and laughing.

"Well, that's a good sign," Mickey said as she entered and sat on the side of the bed.

"Reagan and I have had a *very* nice initial visit, and she's agreed to talk some more," Arthur said cheerfully as she rose to leave.

"Look—if y'all want to continue I can …"

"No, I think we've done plenty for now," Arthur said. "It was nice speaking with you, Reagan."

"Thank you Nina."

"Ms. Arthur," Mickey corrected.

"Oh, I hope you don't mind, but told her it was okay to use my first name," she said

Mickey smiled and said, "I think that's fine."

Mickey then showed the doctor out the door, and once beyond earshot of Reagan, she asked, "So what do you think?"

"We hit it off really well and she's one tough girl, but she's been through an awful lot, and will need extensive therapy. But, from a psychological standpoint, my over-all thought is she's coping as well as could be expected."

"Good. What's the biggest issue?"

The doctor chuckled. "On an immediate level, it's that terrible blonde hair!"

"Oh, I promised her we'd get that fixed. Any problem getting her hair done in the morning?"

"I don't see why not. That represents a constant reminder of that place at this point. The sooner she can look in the mirror without seeing that bad dye job the better."

"Did you detect any physical harm?"

"Some, but I only looked at what I could see without moving clothing around. She has some old scarring near her ankles and—"

"Really. I didn't notice that."

It's right around her sock line and it's minor, but she was likely restrained at some point."

"Oh God," Mickey said shaking her head.

"Also, I'm afraid that's not a rash on her arms—they're needle marks."

"Oh, no. Are you sure?"

"Yes, but she shows no signs of addiction, so I don't believe it was narcotics. She was likely just sedated on occasions."

"I hope you're right. Anything else?"

"That's all I found, but I've been trying to find a lead on a good pediatric gynecology specialist down here. She needs to be examined and get extensive blood work."

"For STDs?"

"Yes, but that's not as big a threat as you might think. Believe it or not, those God-awful places control that pretty well. I also doubt she got good nutrition down there. How much weight has she lost?"

"I'd say some, because her face looks thinner, but she's grown some too," Mickey explained. "What about her mind-set?"

Tyler arrived that evening, and they shared a glorious and tear-filled reunion. Like Mickey, Tyler could see Reagan had changed but he remained hopeful for the long term. The three discussed many topics that evening, but Mexico was not among them.

The following morning, Reagan ate a good breakfast in the lobby, and seeing Mickey and Tyler comporting as a couple did more to boost her mood than any other single fact. Mickey explained their planned trip to a nearby beauty salon, and Tyler said he would wait for them at the hotel pool. Mickey located a hair salon from the phone book, called for an appointment, and with directions in hand, they drove straight to it.

Once at the salon, a friendly debate arose between Reagan, Mickey, and the two hairstylists on duty over the proper shade for Reagan's hair. In the end, all three enthusiastically endorsed the restoration of her natural raven hair. After dying, drying and styling, Reagan looked and felt much better.

At the hotel, Tyler had secured himself a lounge chair next to the pool and was relaxing with a club soda and a book when Nixon passed by. "Now you've got the right idea."

"It's not bad," Tyler agreed, removing his sunglasses. "You ought to try it."

"Don't rub it in. I've cancelled two vacations messin' with this investigation."

"That's too bad," Tyler said.

"It comes with the territory. So how's your wife and daughter?"

"All things being considered, pretty well."

"Good, I was actually on my way to talk to your wife, but I guess I can tell you instead. Our contacts in Brinkman believe Chief Buchanan left the Brinkman area and may well be heading in this direction. So it's more important than ever that all three of you stick around the hotel."

"That's a problem. My wife and daughter went to a hair salon!"

"They left the property?"

"Yes. The psychiatrist said it would be good for Reagan to get her hair colored."

"Damn it! Do you know the name of the salon?"

"No, she didn't say."

Driving back from the salon, Reagan stared at herself in the visor mirror while turning her head in different directions.

"I love your hair, don't you?"

"Yes, but with it fixed it makes my teeth look even worse."

"That's just your imagination," Mickey said diplomatically.

"You don't think they're ugly?"

"No! They just need to be brightened up some. After a couple of treatments they'll be good as new," Mickey encouraged. "Hey, it's a bit early, but do you want to do lunch?"

"Sure! A big fat pizza sounds good to me," Reagan said.

"I'm doubtful that San Angelo is known for its pizza, but I bet we can find something. I need to get gas anyway, so I'm going to pull into this store, and I'll ask for a recommendation." Mickey swung into a convenience store that had a set of gas pumps on the side of the building. She pulled a credit card from her purse and got the gas pump started. She then opened the driver's side door and said, "Watch my purse while I go inside."

Reagan nodded and said, "Mom, will you leave the keys so I can listen to the radio?"

"Sure, dear." Mickey pitched her the keys and then entered the store. She grabbed two bottled waters from the cooler, and went to check out. She glanced at the rack of cigarette packs, repented, and paid only for the waters. She asked the clerk for a restaurant recommendation, and the friendly teenager heartily endorsed an Italian buffet less than two miles away.

Mickey left the store and walked around the building toward the pumps, until she heard the clattering sound of a diesel engine and turned to see a large white truck roaring to a stop in the parking lot. Her first thought was of the driver's recklessness—until Buchanan jumped from the truck and faced Mickey, holding his pistol at his side. She was trapped between the driver's side of his truck and the windowless brick wall of the store.

"So you got tired of doing your meddling bullshit in Brinkman and moved it to Mexico, huh?" Buchanan said with an eerie and wild-eyed expression.

"How'd you find me down here?" Mickey asked, dropping the two bottled waters to the pavement in order to free up her hands.

"Easy," he laughed. "I can't believe the feds let your ex-husband just drive straight down here."

"What's the gun for?" she asked.

"What do you think it's for, dumb ass?"

Mickey glanced toward her car and saw that the pump had stopped and Reagan was in the passenger seat, mouthing the words to a song on the radio. "You won't shoot me here in broad daylight," Mickey challenged as she started walking away from his truck.

He chambered a round, and she hesitated. "Look—this is just between you and me, little missy! You get in my truck, and I'll let your daughter over there live."

"I'm not getting in your truck. You're going to kill me!" Mickey said.

"That's a fact," he said, grabbing her by the arm with one hand and holding the pistol at the small of her back with the other. "The only question is, are we having a single or double homicide today?"

Mickey tried to delay him. "Getting rid of me doesn't solve anything. Flynn's in Mexico just waiting to drop the bomb on you."

"I'll deal with that crippled, drug-addict son-of-a-bitch next," he said in a voice that sounded subhuman. "So save your daughter and get your goddamn meddling ass in the truck!"

Wanting to protect Reagan, Mickey didn't resist and let him lead her around the front of his truck and toward the passenger side door. Seeing no one to yell to and no way out that would not endanger Reagan, she struggled to climb up and onto the truck's passenger seat with the pistol still pressed against her. Once she was seated, Buchanan instructed, "Now, listen carefully. I'm going to walk back to the driver's side, and if you pull anything, I swear I'll drop you and the girl right here in this parking lot!"

Committed to getting Buchanan and his gun as far away from Reagan as possible, Mickey planned no resistance and confirmed, "I'm not going to do anything."

"Good." Buchanan smirked as he took a step back and reached to close the passenger side door. As he did, Mickey looked over his left shoulder to get her last glance at her beloved Reagan. Mickey's eyes instinctively grew larger, and she nodded her head rapidly. Buchanan, realizing something was happening behind him, turned just as a gun exploded. Buchanan gasped and collapsed to the pavement, from a round from Mickey's .38 lodged in his gut. Reagan sat still in the car holding the gun with both hands as smoke rose from the passenger side window.

CHAPTER 21

☫

FAMILIA SUPRA OMNIA

(Family over Everything)

Office of Harrison Baylor
Saturday, September 23

"Welcome, Michelle!" Harrison Baylor said cheerfully as he and Becker rose to greet Mickey.

"Good morning, guys. It's great to see you," she said excitedly, taking a seat on the couch and dropping a rolled-up, rubber-banded poster on the floor next to her.

"It's great to have you back in town!" Becker said.

"Thank you. It was awfully nice of you guys to meet me on a Saturday, especially during football season."

"Well the game I'm interested in is not on until this afternoon," Ford said, pointing to his Sam Houston State University cap.

"Oh that's right, your alma mater's playing on TV."

"Yeah, but national coverage means playing a ranked team, and I believe they're in for a blood bath."

"You have to have hope, Ford," Mickey urged.

"I do, after all you've proved that miracles do happen."

"So, Michelle, how's your Reagan doing?" Baylor asked.

"She's doing pretty well, Mr. B. She's in therapy, and they're making progress. She's also repeating ninth grade and is doing well there too."

"And how about that marksmanship?" Becker asked.

"Indeed," Baylor added. "Had you ever taken her to the shooting range?"

"Oh, sure, but luckily for Buchanan not too many times, or he'd be a dead man."

"Oh, I don't know. A gut shot from over twenty feet is still pretty good," Baylor observed.

"I don't mean to diminish a shot made under that pressure, but that belly was a pretty big target," Mickey remarked, and they all laughed.

"How are they coming with the missing girls?" Baylor asked. "I read in the paper that two more are on their way home as we speak."

"Yes, that makes four returned, including Reagan, and they have solid leads on two others. They're really ramping up the investigation and putting the heat on the Mexican government to clean up this mess and get *all* the girls back to their parents."

"Those families owe you a tremendous debt of gratitude, Mickey," Ford said.

"I appreciate that, but oddly enough, the true hero's still in Mexico."

"Flynn?" Becker asked.

"Absolutely!"

"Is he coming back?"

"I think so, Ford. He cooperated fully with the investigation, and they're working out the details for his return. The government gave him full immunity in exchange for his cooperation, and that along with the physical evidence he provided was a big factor in forcing Buchanan to plead guilty to everything, including the attempted kidnapping of me."

"The paper says he's being sentenced Monday afternoon," Becker said.

"That's right. He dodged the death penalty by pleading out, but he's getting forty-five years in the federal pen and will likely die behind bars."

"Is it true he'll serve his time with a colostomy bag?" Baylor asked.

"Yes and because of that ..." Mickey paused, placing her hand over her mouth and laughing.

"What?" Becker asked.

"It's a bad joke. I can't say it," Mickey responded, nodding toward Baylor.

Ford turned to Baylor and said, "Put your fingers in your ears, Harrison. I want to hear this."

"Oh, go ahead, I can take it," Baylor said.

"I'll clean it up a little," Mickey said, clearing her throat. "With the colostomy bag, he won't be the only thing in his cell that's full of crap."

"You've got that right, Mickey," Baylor said as the two men chuckled. Baylor then peered over his desk at Mickey's poster and asked, "Does that have something to do with the sentencing?"

"How'd you guess?" Mickey said smiling.

"We have to see it," Becker said.

"I thought you'd want to, and that's why I brought it." Mickey picked up the poster, slid the rubber band off, and unrolled it to display it:

So long, Chief
/s/ Little Missy

Both men guffawed as Mickey rolled it up. "Look—I know you two have better things to do, so I'll get down to business. I want to talk to you about my position here at the firm."

"We thought so, Michelle," Baylor said as he and Ford smiled. "I want to make this perfectly clear. All the turmoil of the last several months is behind us. If there's any lingering sentiment from all of this, it's the fact that you're a woman with great fortitude and vision, and these are just the characteristics we want in a partner in the firm."

"That's right, Mickey," Ford added. "Our next partners' meeting takes place at the end of the month, and you're a shoo-in."

"That's very generous, and I'm truly honored to be considered for it. But I must respectfully decline."

Becker's expression belied his dismay. "I don't understand. This was what you've worked toward and hoped for all these years."

"I know, and I owe you two and this firm a huge debt of gratitude that I can never repay. I can't tell you how your loyalty and understanding bolstered me during all of this craziness."

"Michelle, we weren't always so charitable to you," Baylor said.

"Nonsense. You guys were very understanding, even when I pushed things well beyond the limits and broke solemn promises along the way."

"So you want to stay here as an associate?" Becker asked.

"No. I am actually resigning from the firm, effective immediately." This time, both men sat stunned and speechless. "Now, with that said, I'll devote my time, as an unpaid volunteer, to have a good transition and make sure nothing slips through the cracks around here. I would also be happy to do some contract work for the firm down the road, on an as-needed basis, if you'll allow me, of course."

"We're very disappointed to hear this, but we certainly respect your decision," Baylor said.

Tears formed in Mickey's eyes as she rose to leave and said, "I truly love you guys. You've been so good to me, and I owe you so much."

"Just know that the feeling's mutual," Becker said. "But forgive me for asking, but you're not taking a position with another firm, are you?"

"Heavens no," Mickey said, dabbing her tears.

"Another non-legal job?" Baylor asked.

"I guess you could say that. You see, from this very moment until Reagan leaves for college, I am now employed as a low-paid, full-time mom."

Becker exhaled with relief and smiled. "I know I speak for Harrison when I say that you've made a very wonderful decision, Mickey,"

Baylor rose to shake her hand. "It's certainly a career move that we as a firm fully endorse. We'd be happy with any time you can give to the firm around your new and, I'd say, more important, duties."

"Thanks, guys, but it'll be awhile before I can even do that. You see, Tyler, Reagan, and I are going on a honeymoon."

"You have to have a marriage to have a honeymoon," Ford observed.

"You're right," Mickey said, displaying her original wedding ring back on her ring finger.

"That's wonderful, Mickey! When's the ceremony?" Ford asked.

"It was last Saturday. It was a private affair in the elegance of the office of the justice of the peace."

The men nodded and smiled, and as Mickey turned to leave, Baylor said, "Bis vincit qui se vincit!"

Mickey paused. "I have to know what that means."

Baylor smiled and said, "One who prevails over oneself is twice victorious."

Printed in the United States
By Bookmasters